Books by D.C. Shaftoe

*Imperfect*
(Winner – Next Generation Indie Book Awards)

Also published as *Lethal Intentions*
(Finalist – Word Awards)

*Reckless Association*

*Enemy by Association*

*Forged in the Jungles of Burma*
(Finalist – Canadian Christian Writing Awards)

*Assassin's Trap*
(Winner – Word Awards)

# COFFEE, KAMLOOPS, AND A COPPER MINE

## D. C. SHAFTOE

Cornerstone Research & Publishing
2016

Cornerstone Research & Publishing books are available through online booksellers or by contacting the author through www.dcshaftoe.com.

http://www.latimes.com/local/great-reads/la-me-c1-blind-clicking-20150713-story.html

ISBN: 0993717640

ISBN: 9780993717642 (sc)
ISBN: 978-0-9937176-5-9 (e)
www.dcshaftoe.com.

*To my husband, Crispin, and my children, Nate and Jared.*
*To my grandmother, Lillian Fidler, who read her Bible every day and loved the Lord.*
*To Marjorie Shaftoe.*

*"I will lead the blind by ways they have not known, along unfamiliar paths I will guide them; I will turn the darkness into light before them and make the rough places smooth. These are the things I will do; I will not forsake them."*

*Isaiah 42:16*

# Tell Me the Story of Jesus

Frances J. Crosby, pub.1880
Copyright: Public Domain
Scripture: 1 Timothy 2:5-6

Tell me the story of Jesus,
Write on my heart every word;
Tell me the story most precious,
Sweetest that ever was heard.
Tell how the angels in chorus,
Sang as they welcomed His birth,
"Glory to God in the highest!
Peace and good tidings to earth."

Refrain:
Tell me the story of Jesus,
Write on my heart every word;
Tell me the story most precious,
Sweetest that ever was heard.

Fasting alone in the desert,
Tell of the days that are past,
How for our sins He was tempted,
Yet was triumphant at last.
Tell of the years of His labor,
Tell of the sorrow He bore;
He was despised and afflicted,
Homeless, rejected and poor.

Tell of the cross where they nailed Him,
Writhing in anguish and pain;
Tell of the grave where they laid Him,
Tell how He liveth again.

Love in that story so tender,
Clearer than ever I see;
Stay, let me weep while you whisper,
"Love paid the ransom for me."

Tell how He's gone back to heaven,
Up to the right hand of God:
How He is there interceding
While on this earth we must trod.
Tell of the sweet Holy Spirit
He has poured out from above;
Tell how He's coming in glory
For all the saints of His love.

# ACKNOWLEDGMENTS

My first thought is always to thank my husband and children for their continual support. In addition, I want to thank the following for lending me their expertise: Mary Harrison for her advice on augmentative and alternative communication solutions to Grady's silence; Tara McInerney and Micheline Barrest Martel for their help with French language pizza. I hope I got it right. I want to thank my brother, Wes Fidler, who took time away from writing his own book to help me with research with respect to Noah's injury and the medical professionals assigned his case. Any mistakes left in the manuscript are mine, not his. I want to thank my sister, Diane Fidler-Gray, for reading the manuscript, and my nephew, Tyrone Gray, for computer tech advice. As always, I want to thank all those who encourage me. Thank you.

# Prologue

<u>Ten Years Ago</u>

Chenche Hernandez-Guerra preferred his coffee bitter and dark, his lovers compliant, and his business partners silent. Unlike his uncle, he would not spend his life in the shadows, too weak to stride into the light and take what he wanted. He, *El Miedo,* The Fighter, the man every man feared, would make the northwest know his name. He would make all of North America remember *El Cartel Pandilla* and quake in terror.

While Guerra reclined in his leather chair in the second-storey office at the False Creek Harbour Authority building in Vancouver, British Columbia, he pondered the legend of his fame, the legend of the man who had killed with one punch, his uncle, the former head of *El Cartel*. In truth, Guerra had arrived with six loyal men who had subdued and murdered the man while he watched. *El Miedo's* renowned bruised knuckles had resulted from the beating he had given his aunt when questioning her as to his uncle's whereabouts. But the facts didn't matter, only the power of the myth. This power, bought and paid for by the trafficking of *drogos* and *humanos,* he would one day hand over to his son and heir, Maximiano.

This deep into the night, the building was dark and the wharf largely deserted. A light breeze riffled the water in the bay, the scents of fish and brine wafting in through the warped wooden slats of the shuttered window at his back.

The phone on his desk rang. Testing the words on his tongue, he used the front name of the company for which he had signed the final papers only six hours ago, "Foncé-côte Imports." He thought the French was a nice touch to distract Canadian law enforcement from its Mexican connection.

"One down. One to go." That was Macken Roy. He and his two older brothers, Monroe and Mason, had established a local west coast gang through a series of brutal home invasions and selected murders. Macken was in talks with *El Cartel* to develop an on-demand delivery system for cocaine which Guerra planned to supply through his import/export company. Monroe as the eldest and de facto leader of the gang had refused to deal with Guerra. Mason followed his older brother's lead. Hence the need to exclude them and develop a channel through Macken, the brother Guerra considered the most violent and capricious of the three.

"Somehow he got caught with a sample of the goods," Macken said. Though his message was cryptic to foil the surveillance of the *policía*, his sarcasm was unambiguous. Macken had planted a hefty quantity of cocaine in his brother's home and then tipped-off local law enforcement. With his record, Mason Roy would serve considerable time for this.

"*Su hermano*?" Guerra asked.

"Monroe? That's coming."

"*Bueno*." Guerra disconnected, returning the handset to its cradle. He suspected that Macken planned to kill his eldest brother. There was a deep-seated hatred between the Roy siblings that made Guerra glad he had only one son.

The room was silent once more, no sound but the creaks and groans of wooden hulls as the wind kicked up light swells against the wharf. But still, something, a darker shadow, a whisper of breeze, alerted Guerra that something was wrong. Coming upright, he dropped his feet to the floor. His left hand reached for the phone as his right delved beneath the desk to palm his handgun.

The breeze outside sent a cloud skittering. Moonlight filtered through the window behind Guerra, illuminating for an instant a figure cloaked in black.

Filled with wrath at the impudent intrusion, Guerra swept the papers off his desk as a distraction and came up with the secreted handgun. "You dare disturb me? *Fuera!*"

Taking aim, Guerra felt the twin impacts in his chest before he heard the muted explosions. Shocked, he watched the gun fall from his nerveless fingers. Lungs locked in spasm, he struggled to breathe. Black rushed in from the edges of his vision, chased by the screams of a hideous fear.

"Hell," Guerra said. He was dead before he hit the floor.

"You got the right address," the figure in black muttered. He skirted the desk to check Guerra's pulse. *Nada.* Then he snatched up the handgun, pocketing it.

*"Nice work, Capital K!" "Quiet!"*

The black-cloaked figure clapped his gloved hand over his ear to capture the chatter in his earpiece. He removed it and slipped it into a zippered pocket on his lightweight armoured vest.

"Papa?" Quiet words emerged from the shadows.

The figure spun, gun up and ready. With the back-light from the hallway, it was difficult to perceive the identity of the silhouette though its size indicated a child.

The figure backed to the window, fumbling with the shutters before he stepped through onto the tin roof covering the first floor docking bay. At the edge, he dropped to a stack of crates, and then the ground. He imagined the eyes of his little witness tracing his progress across the wharf.

His weapon holstered, he fastened the Velcro strap to keep it in place. The itch between his shoulder blades stayed with him as he hurdled the low wrought-iron fence and dove into the bay. His arms dug deep, propelling him ever closer to the waiting launch. As soon as he boarded, the launch was away.

"You," he hissed as he drew his first full breath. He shoved two men aside to get his fists on the one behind them. "You provided intelligence on the family?"

"Yeah. Get off, K." The man shrunk back, his retreat halted by the gunwale.

"The kid. The son. You said he was in Mexico City with his mother."

"He was, last I checked."

K jerked him closer. "When was that?"

"Yesterday morning."

Incredulous at the bare stupidity of the man, K pointed out his obvious error. "That's over twenty-four hours ago."

The Team Commander pressed a hand to each man's chest, quelling the rising violence. "What happened?"

"The boy was there. Maximiano," K replied in disgust.

"Did he see you?" the Team Commander asked.

"I don't know."

"What did you do?"

K glared at the surrounding men. "He's eight years old, TC. What do you think I did?"

"Eliminated witnesses."

K turned on the man. "No. I did not. He's a child."

Grim silence met his reply.

Present Day

Chenche Hernandez-Guerra was dead, had been dead for a decade. Maximiano Perez-Guerra poured a bottle of his favourite tequila on the headstone of his father's grave in tribute. Buried in the northern ground so distant from his ancestors, his father's spirit could not rest. His gelid bones cried out to his son for vengeance.

Now that he had come of age and proven himself by an act of terrifying violence—he shuddered at the memory—Maximiano would broker his father's alliance. He would make the northwest fear the name of *El Cartel,* as his father intended. One other thing Maximiano vowed, he would not rest until his father's killer lay in the earth.

# PART 1

# CHAPTER 1

Noah Kristofer stretched his legs out beneath the rectangular table in the Blenz coffee shop on West Broadway Avenue in Vancouver, British Columbia. From the corner of the rear booth, he could see every customer coming and going from the front door, side door, and the bathrooms.

While his laptop powered up, he inserted ear buds, an act which created a zone of privacy around him. The ear buds were a wireless device which connected remotely to the security system of the coffee shop. This allowed him to monitor the conversations of the customers and staff. A program running in the background allowed him to view the feeds from the cameras located around the café and in the kitchen.

Noah sipped his caramel macchiato. This was a sweet assignment. Tasked to spend two hours a day in a coffee shop, monitoring the niece of a criminal who also happened to be the wife of a man on the national security watch list. After a dozen years as a police officer with the Royal Canadian Mounted Police, this was a pie assignment, as in easy as.

The problem was, he couldn't keep his focus. He was tired. *Fatigué.* Three years of regular policing followed by another nine of undercover work with the Terrorist and Criminal Extremist Project had worn him down; observing and infiltrating criminal and terrorist organizations; spending time in the company of the wicked and perverse. He was thirty-five years old, and he'd never had a relationship that lasted longer than a mission, never considered any place home. Oh, he kept an apartment in

Montreal where he stored his clothes and a few mementoes from his childhood. None of his neighbours knew his name nor did they miss him during his frequent absences.

During his last hiatus, two days of leave between the end of the Rutgers operation in Regina and this mission in Vancouver, Noah found an invitation to his brother Sammy's wedding stuck to the back of a flyer for New York style pizza and crammed in his mailbox with accumulated junk mail. He'd never met his sister-in-law, only knew her name from reading the cream-coloured invitation; missed the ceremony and had to use Canada-411 to find an address to send a gift.

His job had become his life, with no end in sight. Enough. *Fini*. He intended to complete this assignment and then find a way out of his undercover life. Perhaps then he would have his chance at a normal life like his little brother, a normal life with Ella Hanover. She was unremarkable. He hadn't even noticed her until she'd smiled. That smile had taken over her face. It had transformed her medium features into bright beauty. And he couldn't get her off his mind.

⅄

Ella Hanover advanced as the line at the coffee bar shortened by one: "half-sweet, half-caff, maple-vanilla latte macchiato with skim milk and extra foam."

People revealed so much by what they ordered at a coffee shop. Ella made the Broadway Blenz her daily stop more for the slice of psychology it provided than the actual caffeine. Although, to be honest, she enjoyed coffee. More, even, than banana-pecan muffins, her favourite breakfast.

As Ella moved a step closer to the counter, she scanned the surrounding space. Even though the individual players changed from day to day, the composition of the crowd rarely did. The four soft chairs in the windowed alcove—which were about as soft and comfortable as an inquisition chair—were occupied by three university students who were either trying to hold an informal seminar, or look busy enough that the baristas didn't send them packing. At the two-customer tables scattered around the small open space sat a familiar assortment of business-people. Men in corduroy suit jackets and scruffy beards. Women in pencil-skirts and heels. Each trying to turn a coffee break into a business opportunity.

The three tiny booths at the back of the coffee shop were empty except for the last in line. For the past month or so, it had been occupied by The Loner when she arrived every morning. A real treat to watch, he was taller than any of her six brothers, the tallest of which, Perry, was six feet. The Loner's broad shoulders dwarfed even her brother, Andras', who bore the approximate dimensions of a Mack truck.

The Loner had coffee-brown eyes, brown hair which looped in a chaos of curls, and a coiffed goatee. His swarthy complexion made her think of heat and horses, sand and shimmering moons. The open top buttons of his cerulean blue dress shirt offered a tantalizing glimpse of chest, and his black slacks hugged his long, muscular legs. In contrast to his otherwise semi-formal wear, he wore rugged-looking, black, canvas, closed-toe sandals on his bare feet.

Ella had tried to get his attention one day, choosing the booth next to his rather than a table at the front. She had allowed her conversation to grow louder than usual and shared her funniest stories. To no avail. Ella couldn't suppress her self-deprecating smile at the memory. Her attempt to turn The Loner's attention from his computer had been a worthy endeavour. But the fact remained, gorgeous guys like him simply weren't attracted to women like her. Oh, she could hold her own in an academic debate, throw and catch a football, and beat everyone at Scrabble—except her grandmother who excelled at the game—but none of these attributes drew a man's emotions to romance.

Ella was twenty-nine years old and plain, with her medium brown hair and medium brown eyes. She was unremarkable, and short to boot. At only five-foot-five, simply too short for her weight. Height-challenged, not plump. She chuckled. She was definitely not the sort of person who drew the attention of a man like The Loner.

It was just as well. Fantasizing about a handsome man was one thing. The reality of dating was far more complicated: finding common ideals and beliefs; creating common dreams; and a future. *Oh, well.* It never hurt to fantasize a little as long as you kept your feet anchored in reality.

"Caramel Cappachillo, please, and a banana-pecan muffin," Ella ordered and joined her friends at the table.

⋏

Noah had never known anyone happy enough to smile when they were alone. Ella did. When she smiled, her entire face transformed; when she smiled, her mocha-brown eyes sparkled with joy. The fluorescent lights in the coffee shop glinted off the hints of gold in her chestnut brown hair. Her softened curves were voluptuous. Soft. Sweet. *Parfait.*

An icon appeared in the bottom corner of Noah's screen. He clicked on it to read: Reports you requested are ready. L.

Noah hit reply: Got it.

L stood for Detective Constable Henry "Hank" Longford of the Criminal Intelligence Unit of the Vancouver Police Department, Noah's contact with local law enforcement for this assignment. Noah didn't like Longford, didn't trust him. Wouldn't have chosen him. But it wasn't his call.

A flurry of chatter and fuss at the doorway drew Noah's attention. Althea Treherne was in the house. She and her flank of gossips flounced in to take their place in line, loudly tittering and indelicately pointing. Men stared openly. Women frowned and looked away.

Noah's mission was to determine whether Alex Treherne, head of the Treherne crime family, was using his niece, Althea, to funnel money to terrorist organizations. Althea was married to Zaki Zidane, a former Algerian with tentative ties to the *Groupe Islamique Armé,* also-known-as the Armed Islamic Group or GIA. The GIA was born out of the war in Afghanistan in the early 1990's. Collecting veterans of that war, it quickly took its place as one of the most extreme and violent terrorist groups in Algeria, particularly noted for targeting intellectuals. No one wanted to see them gain ground in North America.

Noah had monitored Althea for the past four weeks. By piggy-backing on the coffee shop's Wi-Fi, he'd uploaded a virus to her phone which she had then downloaded, thinking it was merely a coupon for a free cappuccino. Now he could read and listen in on everything Althea sent and received via her cell phone. The app came with tracking software which allowed Noah to follow Althea to her husband and her husband to a meeting of an Islamic group which had recently branched north from Seattle. Its name could be roughly translated as The Brotherhood of Men. Thus far, no violence was attributed to its members.

Noah had run a background check on each man in the group as well as the individuals in Althea's klatch and found nothing, no threat from either Althea or her husband. He'd requested one final check from Longford then he'd be finished. But then he'd have to submit his final report to his handler, the team commander for this operation, Staff Sergeant Mike Rainer. And Noah wasn't ready to leave West Vancouver yet.

Once Althea exited the Blenz, Noah headed back to the RCMP safe house temporarily serving as his "home" to read the police checks from Longford. He'd snuck in a request on Ella, simply to feed his fantasy. *Fou.* Crazy.

A few hours later, Noah received an email. "Six. LF." Mike's patience was spent.

Noah arrived at the meeting place early, wandering around the Literature and Fiction section of the Broadway and Granville Indigo Books. Ten minutes later, Mike entered the store and rode the escalator to the third floor. Noah waited another minute then followed. All very cloak-and-dagger, reminding Noah of the long-ago days before his mother died, when he and his younger brother had snuck around whatever embassy was their temporary home, pretending to be spies.

When Mike was nowhere to be seen amongst the bookshelves, Noah entered the bathroom. One man occupied the space.

"What's taking so long, K?" Mike asked from his position at the furthest urinal.

"Complications."

"Serious?" Mike shook and zipped up.

What did Noah say to that? He didn't want Mike calling in the big guns. He simply wanted more time to be near Ella, an opportunity to strike up a conversation, perhaps invite her to dinner. She was something pure in the midst of the crime and terror in which he'd spent his career. So, "no," he said.

Mike leaned toward the mirror, inspecting the new shocks of grey in his afro. "I've got a new assignment on hold, waiting for you. The DCW are up to something. We think it may be linked to Treherne."

"What if I'm not ready to take a new assignment?" Noah asked, watching Mike's reaction.

Mike frowned, tilting his head to meet Noah's reflected gaze in the mirror. "What do you mean?"

Noah laid it out. Well, not the whole story, the impetus. "I'm tired, Mike. I need a break."

"You had a break." Mike walked to the end sink, turning on the faucet.

"Two days. That's hardly a vacation. For most people that's simply a weekend."

Mike squirted soap into his hands. "Is that what we're talking about, K? A vacation? A few weeks to kick back on the beach and drink Mai Tai?"

Noah leaned back against the counter. "That what you're offering?" He crossed his arms over his chest. A couple of weeks wouldn't be enough. He needed more, enough time to get to know Ella and see if there could be anything between them. "How about a years' worth of weeks?"

"A—" Eyes wide, Mike shook his head in disbelief. "Not a chance, K." Mike shook the excess water from his hands. "You're too valuable. Your training alone cost the tax payers a small fortune."

"I'm tired." Noah turned his head to meet Mike's gaze. "Give me six months."

Mike rubbed his hands over the coarse brown paper that passed for a towel, calculating something from Noah's expression. "I'll try," he replied slowly. "No promises." He crumpled the paper and, skirting Noah's feet, deposited it in the garbage pail. "Now wrap up Treherne and Zidane. One more assignment and I'll see if we can get you a few weeks leave."

"Months, Mike, not weeks. Six months, commencing the moment I close this op." Though Noah kept his posture relaxed, he was resolute. Regardless of whether Ella was a possibility, Noah needed a rest from police work. There had to be more to life than duty and diligence. Sammy had found something. Maybe he could, too.

"I'll try. That's the best I can do for you, K." Expression mild, Mike gave little away.

Was that a good sign? Probably not. Noah nodded, accepting Mike's statement at face value. If Mike was playing him, Noah would deal with that later. "I'll have it wrapped by the end of the week."

Mike paused at the door. "So long?"

Noah shrugged off the question.

"Fine." Mike sighed. "By Friday."

# CHAPTER 2

Ella Hanover was missing. Noah couldn't find her. He'd checked the Blenz coffee shop. Scoured the Safeway where she bought her groceries, the hospital where she worked as a psychologist, and St. John's, the Anglican Church she attended on Sundays for services and Tuesdays for "small groups", whatever that was.

Noah pulled his faded blue Ford Taurus, his nondescript undercover vehicle, to the curb on West 12th. After lowering his window to allow an unimpeded view of Ella's apartment building, Noah rested his elbow on the door. His head dropped into his hand, his fingers digging into his scalp. *Why am I driving around the city like a madman instead of finishing up my report on Treherne and getting out of Vancouver? Idiot!* All this effort and angst for a woman he'd never spoken to, a woman who paid him no heed. How long did he feed this fantasy of a happily-ever-after?

One day in the coffee shop, Ella had taken the booth next to his. He still remembered the thump in his chest that her proximity had caused. *Fou.* He'd focussed every camera in the place on her, capturing the sparkle of life in her joyful smile. He'd wanted to preserve the moment. No, that wasn't right. He'd wanted to remove the man in the knitted vest and take his place.

Noah was definitely losing his edge. Perhaps he needed to capitalize on this convenient exit of Ella from his life. Move on. Except that, Noah had a hunch Ella's disappearance had something to do with his interest in her.

And if true, then Noah needed to act. He needed to find her. And when she was safe, he'd move on with his life.

*Or not.*

An elderly woman wearing a long blue coat and dragging a shopping cart approached the front entrance to Ella's building. Noah slipped out of his car and jogged over, holding the door while he lifted her cart the few steps to the lobby. He responded with a "no problem" to her rheumy gratitude and then slipped away, past the elevators and up the stairs to the fourth floor. First scanning the empty corridor, he approached apartment 418. Ella's home.

Once he knocked on this door, he would become a part of her life. There would be no more fantasy. And reality could be a slam of the door or slap to the face, neither of which he craved; both of which could curtail his chance of a relationship with her. But he needed to know if she was okay. So Noah knocked. When no one answered, he disengaged the locking mechanism with his lock-picks. *Too easy.* She hadn't engaged the deadbolt. *Careless.*

"Miss Hanover?" Noah called, not too loud. He didn't want the neighbours to hear him and then report back to her about her *prowler.*

He ensured the door shut behind him before inspecting the space. There was a galley-style kitchen, tiny dining area off that, a small living room, bedroom, and bathroom. Noah resisted the urge to rifle her cupboards, already feeling a little too much like a stalker for comfort.

In spite of the underwhelming beige of each room, Ella had placed her stamp on the place. Photographs of people, paintings that spoke of aspiring artists rather than fine art, and childish doodles that spoke of love, covered the walls.

Noah stopped in front of a large photograph centred above the television. Ella stood front and centre surrounded by a United Nations of men. The oldest in the group stood behind her, hands resting on her shoulders. They shared no features in common. On her left and right, Noah counted six males in total. Again, aside from the occasional hair colour or face shape, few shared any characteristics that would speak of common parentage. Yet, this was her "family".

That was the problem with police reports and background checks, they told you nothing of the person behind the name and social insurance number. They gave facts and details but no essence. Noah knew the name of Ella's birth mother but nowhere was her father's name listed. And nowhere did there exist an explanation of why she'd moved to Langley, B.C. when she was seven. Or why she'd remained when her mother had not.

*Zut!* This accomplished nothing. Ella was not home.

Noah cursed the advent of cell phones and voicemail. There was no answering machine to check for clues. There were no scraps of paper lying around with hastily jotted notes, something like, "gone on vacation, please feed the cat". Just as well. There was no cat.

Once the corridor was quiet, Noah exited, locking the door behind him. The feeling of unease grew into a sense of impending disaster. *What if Alex Treherne somehow found a link between Ella and my investigation? What would Treherne do to her?*

Noah jogged down the stairs and back out to the Ford Taurus. He would follow Ella's usual route to work.

From 12th Street, he took the left on Arbutus, driving north between rows of four-storey buildings filled with an assortment of surviving and defunct businesses including organic coffee shops, nail salons, and a natural living health food store. Left on West Broadway took him past their Blenz coffee shop. Slowing, he glanced to the right, down Maple Street where Ella usually parked, and then slowed enough to look through the large first-storey windows of the coffee shop. Nothing. He passed two organic markets, three Sushi restaurants, two computer stores, and a Money Mart before turning right onto Granville. A left onto Connaught brought him to Oak Street and the B.C. Children's Hospital. It was a large complex of right-angled, glass-and-brick structures with a grossly inadequate parking zone. Her SUV, a 2003 metallic green Honda Element, was nowhere visible along the way.

Ella often commented to her friends that parking at the hospital was a nightmare. Noah could see her point. He pulled to the curb to download a map of possible parking locations. It took half an hour to check each one only to find that Ella's Element was not in any of them.

Maybe she'd had car trouble. Noah drove back toward Ella's apartment via the side streets, all named after trees, Cypress, Maple, Pine, anywhere she might have taken a shortcut. If a visual search didn't reveal her location, he would hack into the British Columbia Automobile Association's database to see if she'd made a distress call.

Parking along the curb on Maple Avenue near 12th, Noah called Vancouver General to see if she'd been admitted to the hospital. Perhaps she'd been in an accident. Or had a heart attack. Or something.

When that gained nothing, Noah booted up his laptop and hacked into the security system in Ella's building. Without a warrant or probable cause, the act was illegal. But he did it, anyway. Starting yesterday morning at six, he scrolled through the digital images, until there, at 9:35 am, he spotted her exiting between two uniformed police officers. They'd handcuffed her. *Huh?*

Noah rewound and played the video at normal speed. At 8:55 am, Detective Hank Longford arrived with two officers, a tall woman and a shorter, rounder, balder man. Longford was wearing a wrinkled brown suit with a dark grey tie. The officers wore the traditional dark blue uniforms and red-banded caps of the city police. Longford and the officers took the elevator to the fourth floor then exited and headed straight to Ella's apartment. At 9:25 am, Longford re-entered the corridor wearing an expression of triumph on his face. In her wool jacket, long skirt, and low-heeled suede boots, Ella strode through the building, back straight, eyes forward; eyes that shimmered with unshed tears.

*Zut!* What did Longford know that he didn't?

# CHAPTER 3

Ella Hanover traced Detective Hank Longford's movements as he paced the perimeter of the interrogation room within the Vancouver Police Department. She tried to convey poise and innocence from her seat in a butt-numbing, green plastic chair. But she was afraid, and the laminate-topped table seemed a feeble barrier between her and the angry detective spewing threats.

Longford reminded her of Pig Pen from the children's cartoon, her imagination filling the air around his head with a cloud of garlic-laced filth. Even that comical image, though, could not lessen the dread in the pit of her stomach. *Why am I here? What have I done?*

"Excuse me, Detective. I would like to call a lawyer," Ella said. She imbued her words with strength, trying to sound like a woman confident in her rights rather than a frightened twelve-year-old caught stealing ten dollars from Blaine Hanover's wallet so she could sneak out to the movies with Tiffany and Kelsie. If only this situation was as easily handled as that had been. But Detective Longford bore little resemblance to her kindly indulgent step-father.

Longford ignored her request like he had every other time she'd made it. He leaned forward on his hands, invading her personal space. His proximity heightened her fear.

"Capital K's had an eye on you," Longford said. "Things will go easier if you tell me what you know, now. You will tell me everything, eventually."

*What is a Capital K?*

Another man entered the room. Detective Chessey, Longford's partner in the Criminal Intelligence Unit of the Vancouver Police Department. Ella had met him earlier. He'd been subdued, and she wondered if he was the good cop to Longford's bad. Chessey was definitely the better-looking man, tall and lean, with jet black hair combed back from his face. But his eyes didn't seem good. Truth be told, Ella didn't like his eyes at all.

Chessey gave Longford a note, stepped back to the wall, and folded his arms across his chest. His pale brown eyes should have softened the lean lines of his face, but they watched her with a sharpness that belied his easy posture.

"Capital K," Longford breathed the words as though he hated them.

Longford had come to her home yesterday morning, greeting her with accusations of terrorism. *Me? A terrorist?* In spite of her denials, he'd handcuffed her and transported her here.

She was a Christian by faith and a Child Psychologist by profession. Not a terrorist. Not a criminal. Yes, she worked with any children who came to her, regardless of their parents' proclivities. Yes, she had worked with the children of criminals. Terrorists? She didn't know. She didn't ask. Not that they would tell her, anyway. It was a stupid question.

What a relief it would be to move away from Vancouver. Kamloops was a smaller centre, far enough away from Vancouver she should be able to forget this whole incident. Once she got out of here.

*This is crazy.*

Longford was linking her to some organization she knew nothing about.

"I don't know what that is," Ella said, hating the tremor in her voice that broadcast her fear. "Capital K? The letter?"

His attention refocussed, Longford kicked the leg of the table. Ella braced her arms to keep it from slamming into her.

"There's no need to keep up the innocent act," Longford snapped at her. He leaned in close, his body odour wafting up her nose. "It insults my intuition."

Ella swallowed the despair rising within her and replied, "I don't know what you're talking about."

# CHAPTER 4

Noah dialled the Vancouver Police Department, asking for Longford. That was it. He simply said, "Longford" when prompted. He didn't use any of the adjectives from the variety of languages he spoke to clarify his reference to the pathetic, conniving, filthy, wretched blowhard who called himself a peace officer. Okay, so he also needed to keep shtum over those adjectives.

After a buzz and a click and five minutes on hold, Longford came on the line. "Yeah?"

"This is Sergeant Kristofer speaking—"

Longford cut him off with a chuckle of glee. "I figured you'd be in touch. Took you longer than I thought to miss your target."

"My target? Why do you sound so pleased with yourself?" Noah asked.

"You undercover guys think you're all that, above the wall, outside the boundaries. But you're not getting credit for this one. She's mine. And I'm not letting her go until I squeeze every ounce of information from her sweet little mind."

And there was that premonition of doom. *Zut.* "What are you talking about?"

"Don't try to pull the wool over a kidder. Hanover is mine. This case will boost my reputation."

How did you trust a guy who couldn't get his idioms right? "You've arrested Ella Hanover? On what charge?" Noah asked.

"Suspicion of terrorism." Longford produced the phrase with satisfaction.

"Terror..." Noah's belly clenched. With the new laws enacted since 9/11, terrorism had become permission to ignore an individual's civil rights with impunity. "She's not a terror suspect."

"I'm not stupid, Capital K." Longford used the stupid nickname with a sneer.

Noah had earned it in Ottawa during his first year with the Terrorist and Criminal Extremist Project. He'd participated in an operation to uncover a terror plot within Parliament Hill. An eavesdropping journalist had heard him giving his report to the Sergeant-at-arms: "Kristofer with a capital K". The reporter had created the nickname for his papers the next day and Capital K had been dubbed the hero of the hour. The nickname was remembered by only a few and fewer still knew of its connection to Noah. Unfortunately, because of a common mission a decade ago, Longford was counted among the few.

"You asked me to trace her," Longford replied. "Well, this time I'm not passing you information that helps you bust a case wider open."

*Zut.* "What did you find?" Noah asked, caution beating at his temple. It could be that Longford knew something he didn't.

"Nothing. Of course. She'd be no use to any terrorist organization if she had a record or known affiliations. She's good. Appears clean as a penny flute."

"Because she is." *A penny flute?*

Longford snorted.

The beating he'd threatened Longford with a decade ago had been unwise. But the idiot had provided inferior intelligence that had altered the life of a child. The official complaint that Noah had made to the team commander had resulted in Longford being removed from the Terrorist and Criminal Extremist Project while Noah remained. Longford had done all right though, advancing to detective within the Criminal Intelligence Unit of Vancouver's city police.

"She's not a terror suspect," Noah insisted.

"Oh, right," Longford replied, sarcasm lacing his voice. "I'm supposed to accept your word?"

He was tenacious, Noah had to give him that. *Zut.* "She's not a suspect, Longford." How was Noah supposed to explain? He'd violated the privacy rights of a woman to feed the fantasy of a normal life.

"So she's an informant. Works equally well for me. I could tell her innocent act was all a bluff."

"It's not a bluff, Longford." Noah's frustration altered the tenor of his voice, making it strident. "She's not a part of this case." Silence greeted him. "Have you let her contact her attorney?"

"Not required to under the anti-terrorism laws."

Noah could hear exultation in the man's voice. "Are you going to release her?" He spoke through gritted teeth.

"Not a chance. This resolution is mine." Longford disconnected.

"Argh!" Noah slammed the phone against the dashboard until the screen cracked. Noah dialled again. "Mike. I need a favour. Meet me at Stanley in twenty."

"Right."

Mike was standing at the penguin enclosure in Stanley Park when Noah arrived.

"We need a new meeting place," Mike complained. "Penguin guano stinks."

The odour was the reason they'd chosen the penguins. People didn't linger.

"I need you to arrange to transfer a suspect into my custody." Noah's throat tightened as his apprehension ratcheted up a notch. He needed to keep the conversation focussed on the transfer so that Mike didn't suspect the extent of Noah's stupidity.

"You picked up Treherne?" Mike asked, hope lifting the tenor of his voice.

"Not Treherne." Noah lowered his voice. "Ella Hanover."

"Hanover? Who is that?"

"Surveillance. Longford picked her up thinking he was scooping her out of my hands."

"If she's a suspect—"

"She's not," Noah insisted.

Mike shot him an oblique look. "Then why the surveillance? An informant?"

"No," Noah responded wearily. "She has nothing to do with the case. Nothing at all."

"Follow me," Mike ordered, leading Noah to a private corner in the forested centre of the park. Western Red Cedars towered over them. The smell of grass and earth was heavy in the air, a nice change from guano. "Explain."

Noah sighed, capitulating. "She's a civilian, an innocent bystander."

Mike zeroed in on his face.

Noah sighed again in resignation. Time to admit it. "I like her."

"You like her?" Mike gaped at him.

"I like her." *Sacre bleu.* "She's sweet and intelligent and fiercely loyal and I've watched her for weeks. I thought—I wanted something better. Pure. A normal life." Noah's voice faded. "Somehow Longford got hold of the wrong end of the rifle and he's arrested her on suspicion of terrorist activities."

"Because of a fantasy," Mike repeated, derision in his voice. "You don't get a normal life, K. None of us do."

"You're married," Noah protested.

"Barely. My wife spends her time with a series of young men. My son won't see me. I didn't earn these grey hairs living happily ever after." He passed a hand over his head, skimming the blend of grey and black curls.

"Still, it has to be possible."

Mike's frown deepened. "And you thought this woman would give you this magical 'normal' life?"

"I hoped." Noah shifted a quarter-turn as he dug his fingers into the mass of loose curls on his head. "I hoped, when this case concluded, I could ask her out."

"But instead Longford arrested her," Mike repeated dead-pan.

Noah wasn't certain if the man wanted to laugh out loud or beat him to death.

"Yeah." Noah paused a moment, considering what information might alleviate Mike's irritation. There was one useful piece of intel. "Althea is clean. No connections to her uncle's business. Alex Treherne, on the other hand, is gathering resources to open a new pipeline for drugs up the west coast from Mexico. Wants to set up competition for the Japanese."

"Confirmed?"

Noah scanned the evidence in his mind then nodded once. "Looks like. I'm meeting with an informant today. He's been reliable in the past."

Mike studied him for a long moment. "I'll arrange the transfer. Then you'll move on Alex Treherne and you'll involve Longford in the operation."

"Yeah. Okay." Noah's chest squeezed, but whether from relief, guilt, or apprehension, he couldn't tell.

# CHAPTER 5

Ella's head was pounding so relentlessly she almost missed the knock on the interrogation room door. Chessey had departed though Longford remained, continuing his relentless pursuit of a truth that Ella didn't own.

"You should have told me you were Capital K's informant," Longford said, only glancing at the door. "It would have gone much easier for you."

*Who the heck is Capital K?*

A uniformed officer entered with a note. Not good news for Longford given his deep scowl. But was it good news for Ella?

"He can't do this," Longford protested, aiming his wrath at Ella. She didn't bother to respond.

"Watch her." This order Longford barked at the uniformed officer who'd delivered the message. He seemed to take it in stride, even when Longford slammed out of the room. The officer, Wright by the name on his uniform, took up a position beneath the video camera in the corner of the room. He was not the same man who'd accompanied Longford to Ella's apartment. That man had been shorter. Rounder.

Ella rubbed her throbbing temples. She was wrecked and probably looked worse than she felt. But did it matter what she looked like confined as she was in this cramped and smelly room? *Oh, when will this nightmare end?*

Yelling sounded in the corridor. It was loud enough that even the languid Officer Wright turned toward it. Ella clenched her fists to camouflage her shuddering. Her heart rate accelerated and her armpits dampened.

After a few minutes, Longford re-entered the room with an unfamiliar man. He looked to be of African descent, in his late fifties with shocks of grey in his close-cut afro. His dark suit looked expensive and custom-fit to complement his medium build. He greeted her with a nod, an unreadable expression on his face.

"My name is Smith." The man drawled, as though he had all the time in the world. "It has come to my attention, Miss Hanover, that you have been detained in error." Smith reached out to shake Ella's hand. She relaxed her fists so she could return the gesture. Smith continued, "The department apologizes for any inconvenience you've experienced. If you will accompany me, I will take you home."

Ella gripped Smith's hand harder, a little desperately. She was afraid he'd disappear if she released her hold. "Thank you, Mr. Smith. I don't understand how this happened." Her knees felt rubbery as she stood.

Smith used his other hand to remove Ella's, gently but firmly. "Detective Longford was following up on leads," Smith replied, his face giving nothing away. "I'm sure you understand the importance of investigating to the extent of the law in order to keep our country safe."

Ella didn't respond because she kind of agreed, but not completely. Was it ethical to arrest someone with no evidence of wrongdoing? Was that really what being Canadian was all about?

Whatever she thought, though, Ella wanted out.

"We have determined without doubt," Smith pinned Longford with a glare, "that you are is not involved in anything illegal." Smith's gaze swung back to Ella. "You will be released at once. Thank you for your assistance in this matter, Miss Hanover."

Smith left, taking the now apoplectic Longford with him. Wright led Ella to the booking area where he returned her winter coat, purse and the few items of jewellery she wore. She clipped the faux-sapphire necklace her brother Perry had given her on her sixteenth birthday around her neck and donned the silver Columbia watch that Blaine had given her when she'd completed her Master's Degree. She asked to use the bathroom and then was delivered to Smith in the lobby.

"If you'll permit me." Smith gestured for her to precede him through the front doors of the police station. He followed her to a Chestnut Bronze Infiniti Q70 parked at the curb, a sleek, sporty sedan. Then held the front passenger-side door for her. He paced around the hood to take his place in the driver's seat. Pushed the ignition button, shifted into drive, and pulled into traffic.

Ella skimmed the sleek contours of the sedan with her fingertips. The wooden accents looked rich without seeming ostentatious.

Smith's phone beeped once and then again within a minute. As he scanned the messages, he looked askance at Ella.

*What is that all about?*

Continuing down Cambie Street, Smith crossed 12th Avenue. He simply drove on past.

"Um, Mr. Smith?" Ella's gaze followed the path home. *So close.*

Then, to her surprise, he turned left onto West 6th Avenue and pulled to a stop in Charleson Park.

"Mr. Smith," she began again, but he held up a hand, cutting her off before she could ask her question: *why are we here?*

"I need to make a phone call, Miss Hanover. Sit and enjoy the scenery for a few minutes. Enjoy the end of your adventure." Smith slipped out of the car.

Was he kidding? *Enjoy?* After the past two days, she wasn't sure she would "enjoy" ever again; not the green lawns, mini-waterfall, or the view of the downtown shoreline. She simply wanted to go home. Without shedding tears in public. She'd kept her tears to herself at the police station. She didn't want to lose her composure now, not when she was so close to freedom. But not very near any answers. Like, why was she suspected of terrorism? She wasn't a terrorist. Had someone set her up? Who hated her enough to do such a dreadful thing?

Ella scanned the interior of the vehicle. Smith had left the keys in the ignition, that at least meant he trusted her not to run him over, didn't it? Or was she stupid to trust him, to sit here and wait while he sat talking on the hood of the car? And if she drove away? Exactly where would she go that the police couldn't apprehend her?

Ella opened the door on her side to give her a semblance of freedom and then fished her cell phone out of her purse. Though the early December air was brisk, the fresh air felt nice after the dankness of the interrogation room. She considered checking her voicemail but decided, instead, to do as Mr. Smith had suggested. Relax. After she tucked her phone in her boot, she closed her eyes and leaned her head against the soft leather head rest.

# CHAPTER 6

"**S**peak," Alex Treherne said.

He was not at all concerned about treating the city-pigs as pets rather than men and women dedicated to protecting the public. His only interest in the public was the wealth and power they provided when they indulged in unhealthy past-times. His only concern for his little pet pigs was their service to him which he forced upon them when he uncovered their dirty little secrets.

"Ella Hanover." The pig spelled the surname.

"Who did it?" Alex asked.

"Smith."

*Unlikely.* "It's a pseudonym, idiot."

"Agreed."

"Find out who it is. This Hanover, she know anything?" Alex asked.

"Why intervene otherwise?"

"Find out." Alex gave the order, trusting that he would be obeyed.

"You know anything about someone called Capital K?"

Alex stilled a moment. Three months ago, word went out that the Dark Coast Warriors were seeking information on something called Capital K. He'd assumed it was a new drug, a new form of Ketamine or something. That assumption may have been premature. "Tell me."

"Not sure."

"Find out." Alex disconnected the call and dialled through to one of his fixers. "Hanover. Find her. Find out what she knows. Everything she knows."

"Yes, boss."

∧

Macken Roy didn't recognize the number appearing on the screen of his Smartphone. He let it ring through to voicemail, then listened to the message.

"I got a hit on Capital K. Call me."

Treherne's voice. Alex Treherne wanted a bite of the Dark Coast Warriors' drugs trade. He offered police protection in exchange, claiming he had a detective, and a couple patrolmen on his payroll. Not enough, had been Macken's response. This was Treherne's additional offering.

Capital K was rumoured to have killed *El Miedo* ten years ago. With the identity of Capital K, Macken could barter an old deal anew with the heir of *El Cartel Pandilla;* with that one name, he could earn the trust of Maximiano Guerra.

Macken had updated his obsolete cocaine delivery model. *El Cartel Pandilla* was set to move into Canada, providing a new source for Blow, among other things. With Capital K within reach, everything was falling into place.

# CHAPTER 7

"**I've got her,**" Mike said when Noah answered his cell phone. "She's in my car as we speak. She's confused and upset. Brave little thing. Trying hard not to cry."

Noah's tension released in a whoosh of air. "Thanks, Mike. I owe you one."

"One? Right," Mike quipped. "Where do you want me to take her?"

"Where are you?"

"Charleson Park off West 6th."

Noah was at the University of British Columbia's main campus where he'd met with an informant, a chemistry major who'd been approached by Treherne's scouts to develop a new, more addictive formula for Meth. Ella's apartment was about halfway between here and Charleson Park. "Take her home."

"Am I explaining something to her?" Mike asked.

"I will." Noah was already moving, pulling out his keys as he exited the Chemistry Building. He jogged down to his vehicle parked on Main Mall Road. The divided road ran straight through the main campus. "I'll meet you there."

Mike's voice chilled. "Think for a moment, K. This woman knows you only as a frequenter of coffee shops. What would a coffee-drinker have to do with a woman accused of terrorism? And if Zidane learns that a novitiate in his non-militant Islamic men's group is involved with a woman accused of terrorism? You'll jeopardize your cover."

"Maybe it's time I retired. There's nothing here, anyway, Mike. Treherne and Zidane are crazy as a bag of cats, but harmless. They're not terrorists. Zidane doesn't have the brains or ambition. See if Vice can flip Treherne against her uncle." Noah keyed the ignition on the Taurus and pushed the gearshift into drive.

Mike seemed to ruminate on the possibilities. "Does Zidane realize he's married to the niece of a mob boss?"

"Doesn't seem to. Thinks her uncle's a businessman."

Noah pulled into traffic, heading east, toward Ella's apartment building. He switched his phone to hands-free. The last thing he wanted was to be pulled over for distracted driving. He wanted to get to Ella. Maybe, just maybe, he could explain everything and still have a shot with her. In spite of the fact that she didn't know him. And when she did meet him, she'd learn that his illegal surveillance had led to her arrest, and—who was he kidding? He had no shot with this lady, no chance of a real life at all.

But, maybe. *Mon Dieu, I'd like a chance.*

"How long have you known about Althea and Zidane?" Mike asked.

Though his voice was quiet and even, Noah heard the accusation. "Not long," he prevaricated.

Mike continued, "You been dragging this out, K? For this girl?"

Mike's tone changed in tandem with sounds of a car engine. "Hey, guys, what's up?" A pause. "Put those guns away, guys. That's not necessary."

Noah accelerated to catch up with the beating of his heart. He took a sharp right onto Macdonald to avoid a van turning left. His heart pounded in his chest. His palms slicked with perspiration. Something was going down. If he didn't get there in time, Ella would be caught up in another disaster *a lá* Noah.

"Get the girl!"

Noah snagged his spare phone from the glove compartment, a burner he kept for anonymous moments.

*Sacre bleu!* Noah dialled 911, said, "Charleson Park" when it connected, then disengaged. Gripping the steering wheel with both hands, Noah floored-it. He prayed that all the traffic cops were otherwise occupied and not at all interested in catching a weaving, speeding Taurus roaring along West 4th to the park. He'd gladly buy a river of coffee and a truckload of doughnuts to make it so.

# CHAPTER 8

Noah stepped out of his Taurus as soon as it stopped in Charleson Park. Mike leaned against the passenger-side door of his Infiniti, bent at the waist. Ella was nowhere to be seen.

Noah's angry strides ate up the distance between them, bringing the two men face to face. "Where is she? What happened?"

When Mike didn't immediately respond, Noah shoved him back. "How did they get her away from you?" Noah's voice rose with every word.

"Watch it." Mike raised his arms to fend off Noah. His voice was slow and thick as were his movements. "They tased me. Not much I could do about that." Mike wavered on his feet.

"You could have shot them," Noah insisted. He tapped Mike's holstered handgun through his suit jacket.

Bending, Noah glanced around the interior of the Infiniti. Empty. Of course it was empty. Ella was gone. Taken.

"For what?" Mike protested, his voice breathy and strained. He jerked his jacket together, fastening the button. "Reckless driving? How was I to know they were going to snatch the girl?"

"Who were they? Who took her?"

Mike drew a few deep breaths as he screwed up his eyes. He blinked rapidly to clear his vision. "What difference does it make?"

"It matters. It informs what they'll do with her, where they'll take her." Noah grabbed Mike by the lapels, shaking him once.

"Hands off." Mike shoved him away, staggering back until the bulk of the Infiniti stopped him. He lost his balance, his expensive slacks picking up a layer of dust as they slid along the chassis. He slapped a hand on the trunk to halt his progress before he ran out of car and landed on his butt in the parking lot. "It was Treherne's doing. I recognized a couple of the goons."

"Treherne? Althea?" Was she paying better attention than he'd thought?

"Alex," Mike replied.

*Alex Treherne.* Noah paused, searching the blank canvas of the clear blue sky to help his thoughts settle. *Why would Treherne snatch Ella? How did he even know her name?* Ideas formed, bit by bit, into a pattern he hadn't expected. "Our assignment," Noah began, "was to discover a connection between the Treherne crime family and terrorism. Althea and Zaki are not connected. Ella is connected to nothing. How did Treherne learn of Ella Hanover?"

Mike shrugged, wobbling a bit before he regained his balance. He glanced at the sky and then the ground. Everywhere except Noah's face. Why the evasion? The very lack of eye contact spoke volumes about Mike's culpability.

"Mike." Noah insisted on an answer.

Mike's gaze finally landed on Noah's face, hard and unapologetic. "Your assignment was Zidane and Treherne. My assignment was to find the leak in the Criminal Intelligence Section of the Vancouver Police Department."

"A leak? What leak?" Noah slumped to sit on the front fender of his Taurus.

"Chief Constable Aldrich realized that Treherne's operation was moving west into Vancouver, much sooner than you realized, I might add," Mike snarled at Noah. "But they haven't been able to tie him to anything in the past six months. Aldrich suspected that someone, probably one of his officers, was informing for Treherne, warning him of the movements of the department. He thought it was one of his detectives, possibly the ill-mannered Longford."

Noah's fists clenched of their own accord. "Ella's arrest had nothing to do with my request for a background check. You leaked Ella's name to Longford, didn't you? Why?"

"You were checking up on her, spent an inordinate amount of time in that coffee shop. How was I to know you'd flipped your lid and fallen for a civilian?" Mike's voice rose on every syllable.

Noah dropped his head into his hands. "She's an innocent, Mike."

"How was I to know?" Mike replied, clearly exasperated, but not in the least bit repentant.

"So Longford was the leak." That at least was something. Noah had never liked the man, not once, not even for a moment, in the ten years of their acquaintance.

"Nope." Mike shook his head then stopped abruptly, pressing his fingertips to his temples. An expression of pain flitted across his features.

*Good.* Noah wished him a lingering headache, a small punishment for betraying Ella.

Mike continued, "Longford presumed Hanover was connected to you. He really hates you."

"Well, I hate him, too." Noah gritted his teeth. "So you sold her down the river."

"We now know who the leak is. Not Longford. He's clean."

*Clean? The smelly Longford, clean?* "Pah," Noah spat on the ground. *Zut!*

"It was his partner, Chessey," Mike said. "We've had them both under surveillance. After your call to Longford, Chessey called Treherne."

Noah had forgotten the full extent of Mike's expertise in subterfuge and deceit. Generally, Mike used his skills to trap and contain criminals and terrorists. Or so Noah had always assumed.

"You used me, Mike. You used Ella, an innocent civilian." Noah's anger, his betrayal, rose within him, turning his body hot then cold. He'd given his life to law enforcement and this was how his employers rewarded him?

"I assumed you would do your job and make the connection," Mike replied. "But you got yourself distracted by a piece of tail."

In a rush, Noah crossed the distance to Mike. He fisted his jacket and jerked him up off his feet. "Don't talk about her like that."

Mike returned Noah's glare, his unrelenting accusation making little impact on the man's conviction.

Noah released him with a hard shove. "They'll hurt her, Mike. If they think she's an informant, they'll torture her for everything she knows."

"Which is nothing."

"Nothing." *Nothing* was worse. *Nothing* left you with nothing to bargain for your life.

Leaning into the vehicle, Noah searched the rear seats of the Infiniti. "Did she have her phone?" he asked.

"What? I don't know."

Noah searched beneath the front seats. There it was, beneath the passenger seat, the small brown leather purse Ella usually carried to work. Removing it, he dumped the contents on the passenger seat.

Noah straightened, facing Mike across the roof of the Infiniti. "Phone. Did she have her phone?"

"She had a purse."

Noah lifted the empty bag, shaking it at Mike. "Phone. Did you see it?"

Mike straightened, awareness dawning on his features. "You installed tracking software. What is wrong with you?"

"Did she use it?"

"Could be. Yeah. She pulled it out while I was talking to you."

Mike frowned as Noah retrieved his phone and started pressing and swiping. He could almost hear the gears in Mike's brain processing this new information.

"Why didn't they find the software in her phone at the police station?" Mike asked. "If she was arrested for suspected terrorist involvement, they would have checked."

"Should have." Noah kept his gaze averted to hide his guilt.

"You used the Deepware. Why?" Mike grabbed Noah's arm. "Why?"

"She's got a dozen freaking brothers. How was I to know if one of them was a computer genius?"

"You're disturbed, man." Mike dropped his chin to his chest.

Sirens sounded in the distance. His head jerked up.

"Come." Noah glanced up at the sound and then grabbed Mike's coat sleeve, hauling him toward the Taurus. "Get in. We need to get out of here before the police arrive."

Mike pulled back. "You called the regular cops? Why?"

"It seemed like a good idea at the time," Noah muttered. He jerked his head at Mike in a *come-on* gesture.

"I can't. I can't leave my car here for the cops to trace." Mike pulled out of Noah's grasp. "I'll follow you."

Noah nodded once, hard, then slipped into the Taurus. He checked his rear-view mirror to see that Mike was also getting into his Infiniti, though a little unsteadily.

Wheeling out of the parking lot, Noah took the left onto West 6th away from the approaching lights and sirens. He followed where the flashing blue dot on his phone led him. North on Cambie, heading into downtown Vancouver.

Calling Mike on his burner, Noah filled him in on speakerphone. "Downtown. Past BC Place toward Canada Place." He placed the phone in the cup holder.

Noah concentrated on navigating around traffic, trying not to kill anyone, on his way to save the woman he needed to save. He didn't review or analyze the reason the life of this virtual stranger meant so much to him. For now, he simply accepted it.

The blue dot stopped short of Canada Place and turned onto West Hastings on the tiny virtual map, moving toward Gastown. Treherne had several investments in the Waterfront and Warehouse Operations. Maybe he was taking her there. *Nope.* At Main Street, the dot shifted right, away from the waterfront. *Zut. Why travel into downtown only to travel back out again?* Then the dot disappeared. Noah cursed aloud. One minute it was there, pointing the way to Ella, and then it was gone.

Noah swiped the screen, manipulating the map as he drove. He glanced up from time to time to maneuver around traffic. The locator program might have glitched. Noah exited the program and entered again using the code he'd assigned Ella. Nothing. He resisted the urge to panic. *Think. Think.*

"You don't actually think that Treherne's goons will let her keep her phone," Mike pointed out, his voice sounding tinny through the inexpensive speaker of the burner phone.

"But they might keep it with them."

"Unlikely," came Mike's response.

What did it matter, anyway, if it wasn't transmitting her position? They could get the phone company to ping her cell, but that would take time. One thing Ella didn't have.

Noah continued down Main Street until it joined with Kingsway. If Treherne's men had merged onto Kingsway, they could be anywhere now. The major road cut diagonally through the city.

"They're gone," Mike said. His voice was gaining strength as the effects of the taser faded. "Meet me at Robson Park. We'll try this another way."

Mike was waiting beside his car in the parking lot next to the community gardens when Noah arrived. He propped his arms on the open door, calling across to the older man, "Treherne have any other holdings down here?"

Mike reached inside his car and pulled out a tablet computer, tapping and swiping before he responded. "There's a motel near here, owned by one of Treherne's shell corporations. Mountain View Motor Inn on East Hastings. Could it be that easy?"

"I hope so." Noting the address, Noah reversed out of the parking lot.

Crowded between two equally dilapidated buildings, the Mountain View Motor Inn was a four-storey brown brick structure, more reminiscent of an abandoned prison than a place of recreation and rest. The dirty white trim framed several broken windows which made the building look like an oversized game board; as if the drug dealers had challenged the gang-bangers to a gigantic game of Tic Tac Toe.

Noah drove for a block past the Mountain View, then parked at the curb. He pocketed a handful of plastic restraints from his glove box. Removed his Glock from beneath his seat, tucking it in the back of his charcoal grey dress slacks. Then untucked his forest green dress shirt to cover it. After he removed his tie, he unfastened the top two buttons of his shirt. That would lend to the casual look of an untucked shirt. Either way, a sloppy executive was less out-of-place than a gun-wielding one—though perhaps not on these streets. His SIG was in the holster on his left ankle as usual. Mike would be carrying his Smith & Wesson.

Mike was parked at the Burger King half a block down from the Mountain View. Noah's gut told him to rush inside the Motor Inn and get Ella out. But enough caution beat at his brow to mediate his brashness. Instead, he entered the BK to find Mike settled at a booth that afforded him a clear view of the Mountain View's rear parking lot.

Mike passed a coffee across the table to Noah while he popped a French fry into his mouth. Noah removed the lid on the steaming beverage, sniffed once, and passed the coffee back to Mike.

"Get the room number from the clerk," Noah said.

"No." Mike emptied a packet of ketchup onto his fries. "If I do that, he'll warn Treherne and we'll be dealing with a truck-load of goons instead of a few."

"Wait," Mike said. "Look." He nodded toward a lone figure weaving between the assortment of pickup trucks, cargo vans, and last generation SUVs behind the Motor Inn. "He was there."

The man Mike indicated was slender, but wiry rather than thin. He was wearing jeans and a black leather vest over a dark T-shirt. His right ear glittered with so much metal it was a wonder he could hold his head straight. A silver chain dangled from his ear to disappear into the collar of his shirt.

"Looks like Freddie Urich," Mike murmured. "One of Treherne's fixers."

Freddie leaned into the cargo space of a faded SUV that might once have been black, and pulled out a set of tools. He placed each one in a faded red canvas bag. There were pliers, a hammer, and a few items that looked more surgical than mechanical. Noah gulped down his fear for Ella. This was a torturer's kit bag.

"We have to get her out of there, now, Mike." Noah's voice was husky and he cleared it to sound more normal. Treherne's goons were going to start right away. They were going to hurt Ella. Because they thought she worked for him. Noah's interest had landed her in a mess.

Noah sprang from the booth at the Burger King and slammed through the exit, not concerned about the picture he was leaving in people's minds. Jogging across the patchy browned lawn separating the two structures, he stopped at the edge of the building. Peering around the corner, he noted Treherne's man punching buttons on a keypad beside the rear fire door. Mike pressed against Noah's shoulder as he glanced around the corner, making his own observation of the situation. The rough, brown brick pulled on the fine fabric of his suit jacket.

Freddie glanced around him before stepping through the door. Noah took off at a sprint to grab the security door before it closed. He slipped through, Mike right behind him.

Noah drew his Glock, keeping the safety on and his finger beside the trigger as he leapt up the stairs. The clanking of metal tools sounded above followed by the groan of hinges on a tired fire door. Noah turned the corner on the third flight in time to see Freddie exit the stairwell.

"Wait." Mike's whisper reached Noah a moment before he stepped through after Freddie. In the time it took to decide whether to heed the order, Mike caught up. He lingered a moment, propping himself against the wall by the door while he settled his breathing. Then nodded. "Okay."

Noah pushed the door open a crack so he could peer down the corridor. It was empty with no clue to where Freddie had gone. Curse Mike for slowing him down.

Noah walked on the left side of the corridor with his weapon pressed against his leg to camouflage it. He paused to listen at each door. Mike moved to the right to do the same.

"Wake her up, dickhead." A voice boomed from room 318.

*Her who?* Noah pressed his ear to the door.

"Shaddup…" The dickhead's vocabulary disintegrated into profanity. "Need to wait for the boss."

More profanity, f-this and f-that, falling and rising in loudness. "Boss didn't say…couldn't enjoy her…Wake the…up."

*Has to be the room. Just need to wait for the right moment.*

"Why bother. Asleep is just as good."

Noah's skin chilled. *No time to wait.*

Mike appeared at his side. When Noah reached for the door to burst in, Mike intercepted his arm with a "wait" gesture. Raising his fist, Mike knocked and called in, "Pizza."

"Didn't order nothin'," the dickhead replied.

Mike knocked again. "Pizza delivery. For Mr. Urich."

"Freddie? Watcha' doin'? You sh…" The voices faded in and out. A thump sounded, followed by the sounds of a tussle.

"Not me," Freddie protested. At least Noah assumed the squeaky denial came from Freddie.

With much cursing, the door opened and Freddie poked his head out. His upper body followed. "Yeah?"

Noah grasped Freddie's vest and yanked him the rest of the way into the hall, letting the door close behind him. Freddie yelped as the silver chain tore from his ear lobe, blood sliding down the side of his neck. Mike took him down from behind. While Noah searched Freddie's pockets, pocketing the keys to the SUV and the room key-card, Mike removed Freddie's shoes, gagging him with his own socks. Mike took possession of Freddie's gun and switchblade while Noah zip-tied Freddie's wrists behind his back. They deposited Freddie at the end of the corridor behind a potted plant. Mike rapped him on the head to still his muffled protests.

Mike returned to the room, knocking on the door again, and then muttering loudly enough to be heard but not understood.

"Use the key!"

Mike shrugged, muttering, "Invitation." Technically, it could be considered the correct vocabulary for permission to enter. No one, however, would believe that a member of Treherne's crew willingly opened his door to a cop of any sort or description. Except maybe *crooked.*

Using Freddie's key-card, Noah cracked the door a hairs-breadth. Crouching, he pushed with his fingertips, creating a gap big enough to provide a glimpse of the players in the room. It was a large room with one queen-sized bed in the middle bracketed by nightstands, and a bathroom off to the left. The wallpaper was faded and peeling, the carpet a bright orange pile decorated in an irregular pattern of brown diamonds.

There were three occupants, two thugs, and a body on the bed. One of the men Noah recognized by the barbed wire tattoo which snaked from his bicep up the side of neck as Terry Davidge, a shot-caller for Alex Treherne. Of the other goon, he could only perceive size; thickset and menacing, as he bent over the bed, pawing at the covers.

Suppressing his rising rage, Noah blanked the thought of where the goon's hands were on the body in the same way he blanked the knowledge that the body was Ella's. Rescue now. No more waiting.

Mike tapped Noah on the shoulder. When Noah glanced up, Mike pointed toward the goon to indicate his aim. Then he counted to three before he shoved the door wide, shooting at the bull-necked figure hunched over the bed. The goon spun to the side, clutching his left shoulder as he cursed Mike and all his female relatives.

Noah rolled beneath the trajectory of the bullet then sprang at Davidge, hitting him midsection. Even as Davidge grunted, he drove his fists down onto Noah's back. Grabbing the man's ankles, Noah thrust his shoulder deeper into Davidge's abdomen. Davidge fell back, cracking his head on the bedside table. His head lolled to the side.

Noah checked for a pulse, finding one. "You were lucky," he muttered. He shoved Davidge over and confined his wrists with a disposable double restraint.

"You got any more zip ties," Mike asked, breathing unevenly in his struggle with the downed shoulder-shot goon. One rap on the head with the butt of Mike's Smith & Wesson silenced his blistering threats and stilled his furious movements.

Noah tossed another restraint to Mike. "Call for backup."

"Better check your girl. She hasn't moved." Mike pulled out his phone, sending in codes to get another unit, most likely some local security personnel he'd hired on retainer. He wouldn't want a trail from this leading to the RCMP.

Balancing with one knee beside Ella on the bed, Noah checked that she was breathing then pulled the coarse brown blanket down to her ankles. He breathed a sigh of relief. She was still fully clothed, her ankles bound with more duct tape. She lay on her left side, face pale, eyes closed, her head tilted awkwardly, positioned as it was on a thick pillow with the properties of a cement block. Her bound wrists were tucked beneath the edge of the pillow. A long piece of duct tape looped between the bindings, tethering her to the cheap plywood headboard.

Noah held his fingers below her nose to feel her breath escape. He slid his fingertips down across the obscene silver tape covering her lips, over her chin, and down her throat to measure the pulse beating there. Rapid, but steady. Stroking his palm along her hair, he pushed it back from her face to reveal a bruise and a small tear in her pretty skin. Blood oozed from the wound. *Zut!* Someone had hit her. He moved the lamp on the nightstand closer so he could check her pupils. Equal and reactive. No concussion.

"Help me get them out of here."

Noah jerked to awareness at Mike's words. He'd forgotten the man was still here.

Mike stepped over the goon's body to lift his tree-trunk legs.

They'd hurt her. Sweet Ella. Noah struggled with the urge to pop the guy's shoulder out and leave him to wake in agony.

"K!" Mike spoke his name sharply.

Resigned, Noah released the vengeful thoughts and helped Mike, grasping the goon under the shoulders.

"You got a plan for what to tell her, how to explain?" They moved toward the door to the corridor.

"Only what she needs to know." *The truth.*

Mike paused, meeting Noah's gaze across the body. "Risky. Could blow your cover." Mike's expression gave nothing away.

Noah held his gaze, giving nothing back. *You have no idea.* "I'll deal with it." *This may be my one chance at something good and real, a normal life.*

Mike dragged the goon far enough into the corridor to use his torso as a doorstop. He stepped back into the room across the goon's head to collect Davidge while he muttered. "You do need a vacation."

Goon was rousing by the time they stepped back over him into the corridor with Davidge's still-inert form.

"That's what I've been trying to tell you," Noah replied.

It was interesting to note that not one single person had come out of their room to see what was going on. Assaults and arrests were clearly same-old, same-old on East Hastings. The clientele who frequented this place were not at all eager to get involved.

Once Davidge was lying on the faded hallway carpet, Mike bent over the goon and rapped him on the head again, stilling his agitation. Mike straightened, grunting as he stretched out his back. "Six months. Finish up this case, complete all your reports, and I'll arrange for you to have six months leave. Without pay. I'm not paying you to chase tail."

Noah bristled. "I have at least that much coming to me in unclaimed leave."

Mike grunted. "Fine. Six months."

"Thank you," Noah gritted out.

Mike didn't respond, he simply dragged the goon out of the doorway and closed Noah in the room with Ella. A short time later, Noah heard Mike's backup arrive in the corridor and Mike's voice respond. And then Noah ignored it all.

Now, before he tackled what to tell Ella, he had to clean the blood from his hands.

# Chapter 9

Noah reclined against the wall near the bathroom in room 318 in the Mountain View Motor Inn, his right arm draped over his bent knee and his left leg extended. *How am I going to explain all of this to Ella?* She'd been arrested. Kidnapped. Because he'd conducted surveillance on her. *Zut.* He waited for her to wake, hoping each moment for inspiration. Because if he started sawing at the duct tape on her wrists and ankles, or pulled the tape from across her mouth, she would regain consciousness. With him standing over her and holding a knife. *Très mal.*

Ella groaned, a muffled sound of pain and confusion. Her breathing accelerated as her gaze darted around the room. When her eyes landed on him, they widened in fear. She whimpered, the sound muffled by the tape.

"You're safe," he told her, rising, but keeping his posture open and unthreatening.

She raised her bound hands to her mouth, pulling on the tape.

"Wait," Noah ordered.

He moistened a facecloth then used it to coax the sticky tape from her skin. She hauled in a lungful of air, and coughed. Noah set the facecloth aside and retrieved the plastic cup he'd previously unwrapped and filled, anticipating her need for water. He offered it to her. "Your mouth must be dry from the tape."

Her brows furrowed, either from wariness at his offering or a headache from the knock on the head she'd received from Treherne's goons.

When she didn't reach for the cup, he took a sip to show her it was untainted. He extended it once more.

Her mouth twisted in disgust. "Why did you do that? I have no idea what kind of germs you have."

*Huh?* "I did it so you'd know it wasn't drugged."

Her mouth twisted as she considered what he'd said. "What if it's like Iocaine Powder?"

"What?" *What is she on about? Did they hit her harder than I thought?*

"From The Princess Bride," she explained. "He puts the poison in both cups because he's built up a resistance." She paused, watching him like she was waiting for him to understand the meaning of her incomprehensible words.

He had nothing to offer her. "There's no poison either?" he finally said, breaking the odd silence.

She rolled her eyes at him as though he'd missed something important. Well, not so much important as obvious. And he'd obviously missed it.

Noah placed the cup on the table beside her. She eyed it enviously but didn't touch it. Instead she asked, "Where am I?"

"Mountain View Motor Inn, room 318. In Vancouver. Canada." Noah's voice trailed off. He withdrew his knife and opened it.

Her eyes widened. "Wait. What?" She used her heels to scoot back against the headboard.

*Maybe they did molest her. She is behaving oddly, not panicked but not calm and collected.* "Did they hurt you?" he asked.

"Yes." She coughed then licked her lips.

"Your clothes. They're intact," he noted.

She frowned. All at once, understanding dawned in her eyes. "No. Not that." She frowned again. "You asked if they hurt me, not if they—you know."

"So they didn't?"

Her faced instantly flushed. "No. I mean, you asked—it's not what you asked—I don't—no. What are you—"

Noah waited as she sputtered to a stop. This conversation had become very confusing.

Ella shook her head as if to dismiss the conversation but winced as though the movement hurt. She lifted her hands to her head, the movement foreshortened by the length of duct tape. When her fingertips pressed a particularly tender spot on her scalp, she flinched. "They hit me on the head twice."

"I'm sorry," he said, nodding toward her head, "but glad." He traced his eyes down her body.

"Why?" she asked, pausing her exploration of her skull to look at him. *Why? What?*

"I mean, who are you? Why do you care?" she asked. Her voice was hoarse. She coughed to clear it.

*That will take some explaining.* Noah lifted the knife. "If you give me your hands, I'll cut you free."

Ella studied him for a long moment, making his scalp prickle at the intensity of her perusal. "I've seen you at the Blenz coffee shop on West Broadway. The one beside the organic market."

"Yes. I've seen you there as well." He waited patiently for her to decide whether she wanted his help to be free of the tape. He kept his body still, the knife held in a nonthreatening position; if that was possible when holding a knife on a bound victim.

Finally, slowly, she extended her wrists toward him. He sliced the tape then cut the loop attaching it to the headboard.

"My feet?" she asked.

Once he sat on the edge of the bed, he motioned her to put her feet on his lap. She braced her body on her hands and complied. Her eyes tracked his every move and twitch as he cut the tape then gathered all the pieces, tossing them into the room's garbage pail. He would take the bag and everything in it with him when he sanitized the scene. He wouldn't leave any trail to either himself or Ella.

As Noah returned his knife to his pocket, Ella scooted against the headboard, drawing her knees up and linking her hands around them. She clenched her fingers and toes several times to restore the circulation as she gazed longingly at the cup of water and asked, "Who are you? Why are you here? Are you one of the jerks who kidnapped me?"

"Ella. If I wanted to harm you, I've had plenty of opportunity. You can drink the water." He rose. "I'll even open a new cup and fill it. All right?"

She chewed the inside of her cheek, clearly considering all the evil he could do with a flimsy cup of lukewarm water. Finally, she nodded in agreement.

Under her scrutiny, Noah unwrapped the second cup, filled it, and brought it to her. She gulped the water down thirstily then placed the cup on the nightstand. "Thanks," she murmured. "Why does everyone think I know something I don't?"

*How best to answer that?* "What do you remember?"

She rubbed her forehead, clearly plagued by a headache. "Beefy chests and swearing. Mr. Smith. The smelly cop in the ugly, brown suit." She straightened as more details returned. "It all started when he arrested me. Why would someone arrest me? He kept saying I knew something called Capital K. I have no idea what that is. Mr. Smith came and picked me up. That made the smelly cop, Longjohn ... Longstone ..."

"Hank Longford."

"Yeah." Her eyes widened then narrowed. "How did you know?"

"I've, uh, dealt with Longford in the past. And you're right, he does smell. Garlic and cheap deodorant."

Her lips tilted. "Why did Detective Longford think I was a terrorist?"

*Detective. How Longford attained any rank rather than finding himself unemployed, I will never understand.* Noah measured his words. "I have a story to tell you that you're going to find hard to accept."

"I'll bet," she murmured. "Am I free to leave?"

He traced her line of sight from his chest to the door then sighed. "It would be best if you listened to me first. Your life may depend on it."

She stiffened and, rather than fear as he'd expected, he saw anger rise within her. Her responses never ceased to surprise him.

"Is that a threat?" she asked.

"I am no threat to you. Those other guys are." *Sacre bleu. What a mess.*

"If I listen to this *story* then will you let me leave?" She made an attempt at sarcasm that fell flat when her voice wobbled.

"Of course." Though, in this neighbourhood, he'd have to drive her somewhere. She'd never be safe on East Hastings after dark. And she was definitely biding her time until she was free to call the police. Which would lead Chessey right back to her and Chessey would inform Treherne. And the cycle would begin again.

"I'm listening," Ella prompted. "Wait. I need to pee."

Noah reached over to help her off the bed. Ella avoided touching him, scooting to the edge of the bed. Her knees buckled when she tried to stand but she shook him off when he tried to help, instead, bracing herself on the wall. She stumbled into the bathroom, turning on the light which also activated a fan.

He followed her. "Leave the door open," he said, stopping it as she went to shut it.

"Seriously?" Her expression bathed him in scorn.

"Seriously. If you try something foolish, I'll have to stop you. And after all I've gone through to keep you safe, I really don't want to hurt you."

Her face paled.

"By accident," he added.

She didn't respond, but she did pull the shower curtain out and around her to relieve herself in private. *Well, a sort of privacy*, he thought. The cheap, plastic curtain hid little, but the noise of the fan partially camouflaged the sounds of liquid impacting liquid.

"So what's this story?" she asked from behind the barrier.

He watched as her silhouette searched for her cell phone. The phone, however, was gutted and lying inside one of her boots beside the bed. Why they'd chosen that location to dispose of it, Noah couldn't imagine. But he guessed the moment she realized that her phone wasn't on her. She produced the cleanest tirade, full of words like "darn" and "blast" and "crappolla".

"I'd rather explain face to face," Noah replied.

After a moment Ella stood, righted her clothing, and flushed the toilet. She released the curtain and walked to the sink where she washed her hands. She scooped water into her mouth, drinking from her hands until she seemed satisfied. Only when she'd completed her ablutions, did she glance at him. Then she kept her eyes on him as she approached the doorway of the bathroom, stopping just out of reach.

"Excuse me," she said, stiffly but politely.

Noah stepped back to let her exit the bathroom, keeping his body between her and the door to the hotel room.

She headed toward the bed then seemed to change her mind, scanning the room for furniture. There was the bed and two nightstands. Nowhere else to sit but the bed, the toilet, or the edge of the rust-stained bathtub.

"I won't hurt you," Noah said. "I guarantee you're safe with me."

Ella hesitated then seemed to give in. She resumed her position sitting against the headboard. Taking the cup from the nightstand, she sipped the water he'd originally given her. That spoke of some progress in their relationship, right?

Noah resumed his seat near the foot of the bed. *Where to begin?* "I'm not sure how to start."

"Who are you?" Ella asked.

"Noah Kristofer." He extended his arm to the mattress, propping himself on it.

"I've never heard of you. Why were you at the coffee shop?"

*Why indeed? Treherne? Zidane? What information will help her trust me?* "Look, the specifics of the case won't mean anything to you. Suffice it to say that I'm a police officer and I was there because of that."

"Oh." She looked disappointed. *Interesting.* "What kind of mission happens at a coffee shop? Was it a drugs bust or something?"

"It's a bit more complicated than that." A lot more complicated. He drew in a breath, held it a moment, then blew it out forcefully. *All in. Skip the story. Go for truth.* "The first time I saw you, you were meeting some friends for coffee. I listened to your conversation, your laugh, saw your smile." He swallowed noisily. "I came back the next day and the next for another glimpse. I saw you with your brother, your nephews—"

She surged forward, her hands fisted. "You leave them out of this. If you—"

Frustration surged through him and in a lightning-quick but poorly thought-out move, he grasped her wrists, tugging her closer. Her knees slid along the blanket until they impacted his thigh. "What? What will you do?" He pulled her closer. "If I wanted to hurt you or your nephews, it'd be done. Understand?"

When he released her, she scrambled away, resuming the distance between them.

"I told you that I wouldn't hurt you. I keep my word." Noah wanted to wail in consternation. What did he know of normal relationships?

Ella rubbed her wrists, examining them for injury.

"Quit the drama." Noah scowled in reply. "I'm not the one who kidnapped you. But I am the man who released you."

She scowled right back at him, making some sort of "tch" sound. "You won't hurt Gil or Jack?"

"The kids?" he clarified. "I said I wouldn't."

She glowered at him for a few more moments and then seemed to resolve something in her mind. "Okay. So you're a cop, just like Longford—"

*Like Longford?* Noah scowled. "Not like Longford. Nothing like him."

Ella frowned. "What does that mean? You're not an investigator? Or you simply smell better?"

Surprised out of his anger, Noah chuckled. He couldn't help it. She was priceless. "Longford is a detective here in Vancouver. My assignments take me across Canada."

"Okay." She drew her knees to her chest and linked her arms around them. This time, though, she seemed more intrigued than afraid. "Are you a spy or something?"

"Undercover officer."

"All right. I'd like to see some identification," she said.

She'd surprised him again. "I don't carry ID when I'm on a job."

"Then how do I know you're telling the truth?"

*Sacre bleu.* There was no way to win with this woman.

Ella scrambled across the bed and scooped up her boots. She paused a moment, fishing the gutted remnants of her cell phone out before slipping them on. "It doesn't matter, anyway. I'm free and I'll be away from here in a few days."

*Leaving? She was moving away?*

Ella skirted the room, keeping her distance from him, on her way to the door.

"Don't go to the police," Noah warned.

"Why not?" She stood, back to the door, hands on her hips, and faced him defiantly.

"There's a leak in the police department. You call them, they call Treherne, the owner of the goons who grabbed you." Noah exhaled. "Look, Ella. I'm sorry, sorry you were arrested, sorry Treherne's guys grabbed you, sorry I put your life in danger."

Ella scanned his body from toes to forehead. "Officer Kristofer—"

"Sergeant."

"Noah. None of this makes any sense. What do you mean you put my life in danger?"

*Zut.* Miscalculation. That was a question he probably shouldn't answer straight out. But he could still offer her the truth. Just not the truth she was looking for. "You intrigue me. I wanted to get to know you. My personal interest in you was mistaken for professional interest. Longford got it wrong. Treherne got it wrong."

"Intrigue? That's it?" She crossed her arms over her chest, looking annoyed, and, if he was honest, radiant. "Are you some kind of weird stalker, like a psychopath?" she said then added in a murmur. "I guess any psychopath would be weird."

That made him chuckle. "No. I am quite sane." He sighed. "I like you. I like how you see the world. I like how your eyes sparkle with utter joy at times."

They weren't sparkling now, though. Her eyes bugged in disbelief. "You cannot be serious."

Change of tactic. "Let me ask you a question."

"Then I can leave?" she asked.

Noah nodded. Though he had no intention of setting her loose on East Hastings after dark. And it was cold tonight, too cold to wander without a winter coat.

"Okay," she replied.

"If you met a guy in a coffee shop, a guy who thought you were special, a guy you liked, what would you do?"

She chewed the inside of her cheek, a thoughtful expression on her face. "You answer first." She uncrossed her arms. "How would you approach this woman you think is so special? I mean, in some way that didn't involve kidnapping or arrest. If you were a so-called normal guy, what would you do?"

Noah felt a grin pull at his mouth. She had the capacity to make him smile even though he'd so rarely smiled in the past two decades. Grief, duty and diligence left little time for humour.

Yet he had an answer for her. I mean, how many times had he imagined that scenario? "I'd buy the last banana-pecan muffin and offer it to you when you arrived to order coffee. I'd ask to sit with you. We'd chat about the weather and anything else that came to mind. Then, after we'd had coffee together a few times, I'd ask you to dinner. At Bridges. Or the Pink Peppercorn. Have you ever had their salmon wellington?"

Noah wanted to join her at the door, to take her hand, force her to listen until she believed. But she suddenly looked haunted, pursued. Afraid. Instead, he turned the conversation back to her. "Now answer my question."

Ella palmed the door handle. "I-I guess I would invite him to church." Then she opened the door.

"Ella?" She paused, watching him through her peripheral vision. "It's late. I'll drive you home."

She turned, surprise printed on her face. "You know where I live?"

Noah chuckled. "I'm a cop. It wasn't difficult to find out."

Her eyes glimmered. Was she going to cry? Now? Because he knew her address?

"This is all very confusing." That was all she said for a moment. Then she swallowed and added, "I don't want to get into a car with you."

That sobered him. "All right. I'll call you a taxi. Okay?"

"If you give me my battery, I can call," she said, taking out her phone and wiggling it at him.

"I didn't take the battery. Treherne's crew must have." He pulled out his own cell phone. "Here. Use mine."

Slowly, she approached and took the phone, darting away. She called a company and then returned the phone to him. "Noah?"

"Yes."

"Why did you ask me about the dating thing?"

"Someday, when life is a little less about kidnapping and arrest, I'd like to get to know you. I'd like you to get to know me," he said then added in a murmur, "and find out that I'm not a crazy stalker."

She nodded sagely. "The taxi said he'd be here in ten minutes."

"Okay. I'll walk you down." When she hesitated, he raised his arms in a nonthreatening gesture. "Simply to make sure you're safe."

"All right."

"So you'd really invite a guy to church, would you?"

"Yes. It tells you a lot about a fellow."

Noah inclined his head. *Church, eh?*

# PART 2

# CHAPTER 10

Noah Kristofer awoke to the chime on his cell phone, anticipating the day. It had taken longer than he'd expected to finish up with Treherne in Vancouver and hand over his case files. That had been difficult, handing over evidence and trusting another officer to follow up and follow through. But he'd had no choice. If he wanted a chance at a family of his own, a little slice of *normal*, then he had to leave his job behind and follow Ella.

For that reason, Noah had flown from Vancouver to Montreal to retrieve his White Pearl Honda CR-Z Premium model and make the drive back across Canada. The CR-Z was Noah's one indulgence. With its newly minted winter tires, paddle shifters and 360-watt stereo system, it was a pleasure to drive, making the miles of granite, gorse and snow disappear behind him. Noah experienced the Canadian Shield of northern Ontario, the Red River Valley of Manitoba, the rolling hills of Saskatchewan, and the foothills of Alberta, as a tourist. He'd never done that, explored his own country as a pleasure destination rather than a hotbed of crime or a training ground for terrorists.

Noah swung his feet to the floor. In spite of the cramped size and uninspired cushioning of the double bed in the Howard Johnson's, he'd managed a solid seven hours of sleep last night. Not bad considering all the hours he'd spent languishing on his behind in the soft leather seats of his CR-Z; five days of driving the Trans-Canada Highway from Montreal to arrive at the astonishingly tranquil Kamloops, British Columbia. The tiny city was a northern desert partially built on an ancient river delta and wedged between the Coastal Mountains and the Rockies. The city sprawl and outlying areas encompassed copper mines, extinct volcanoes, glaciers, and the Thompson River. The semi-arid climate allowed for fog and damp to co-exist with cacti and Ponderosa pines. Eighty thousand people called this blip on the map home. Including Ella Hanover.

Noah pushed off the bed, heading to the shower. As the steamy spray enveloped him, calming his body, his mind spun. News of his younger brother's wedding three months ago had stopped him short. Noah had been undercover when the invitation arrived. Back on assignment during the wedding. He'd never met the bride, rarely even saw his brother.

In the early days of his career, the intrigue and adventure of undercover work had filled Noah with excitement and a sense of purpose. It had connected him by duty and diligence to others serving as he did, working to root out criminals and terrorists bent on destroying peace. Somewhere along the way, that connection had become a cocoon, isolating him from the opportunity to form lasting relationships. Well, he wanted his chance; he wanted something permanent and pure, something that was his.

Ella Hanover might be that chance. She was full of joy. Kind. Intelligent. And quirky. She made him laugh.

Noah shaved, trimmed his goatee, and dressed for church. Today he'd wear his black Canali herringbone, the suit he'd bought for the casino job. He'd been tasked to win the confidence of a Syrian businessman with a penchant for gambling and terrorism.

Noah shook out his blue silk dress shirt, smoothing out the few wrinkles it had acquired crossing the country. He complemented it with a cross-hatched red and blue silk tie. Adjusting his shirt cuffs, he scanned his body in the bathroom mirror before donning his black wool topcoat. He was freshly groomed and dressed to impress. Ready to pursue Ella Hanover.

Retrieving his CR-Z from the motel parking lot, Noah drove east on Columbia Drive past rows of single-family dwellings before turning south on Highland Road. He continued on, trusting his GPS even though the road took him away from civilization into a shallow valley between rugged hills. Scrubby bushes and hydro poles lined the road. There were no dwellings visible and only one building, an oddly round siding-clad structure with no visible signage.

Long after he felt he'd left the city he came to Qu'Appelle Boulevard. It took him past a soccer field limned by mountains, and rows of two-storey, cookie cutter houses. At Nechako Drive, he turned east. A couple of kilometres more brought him to the end of a tree-lined circle and the smallest house on the street.

Two months ago when she'd moved from Vancouver to Kamloops, Ella had bought this little bungalow with brown-painted wooden siding and white trim. The exterior looked well-kept but Noah suspected that the inside was not, given the price for which the property had sold. A layer of snow covered the lawn which fronted the yard. A clump of scraggly shrubs struggled to survive beneath the bow window. More green shrubberies stood sentinel along the brick path that led from the front door to the detached garage. From the aerial views he'd studied, Noah remembered that the grassy backyard sloped down toward a gulley that meandered between subdivisions to the foot of a mountain. From her rear-facing windows, he imagined that Ella was afforded a view of the timbered mountain range beyond.

From the back seat, Noah retrieved the white sweetheart rose he'd bought on the way here. He smoothed his tie and brushed a stray piece of lint from his trousers. He'd done all he could to impress Ella with his appearance. He'd even had his hair cut by a stylist, taming the curly mop into a controlled style with short sides and a little length on top.

Noah crossed the lawn to ascend the three concrete steps to the narrow stoop at the front door. He rang the doorbell, then retreated a step to make sure he wasn't looming when she opened the door. Considering he was six-two to her five-five. He didn't want to intimidate her.

Footsteps sounded. The door opened. And, *voila*. His heart gave a little trill. She looked fresh and free from fear. Her hair was shorter, cut to brush her shoulders. She wore a long flowered dress of midnight blue. The deep red and bright yellow of the fabricked flora lent brightness to the midwinter gloom. He was fairly certain they were tulips.

Her brows dropped in lack of recognition and then her eyes widened in surprise. Shock, really.

"Good morning," he said with a broad smile on his face and hope in his chest.

"What are you doing here?" she asked.

Nope, definitely not a welcome anywhere in her posture or expression.

"You invited me to church," he replied while presenting the white rose he'd bought for her. "For you."

She glanced between the rose and his face. "How did you find me?"

He shrugged. "I looked. It wasn't difficult."

"But it's not like I put out an ad," she retorted.

"I'm an investigator." Her frown deepened so he extended the rose toward her again, tickling her cheek with the soft petals. "For you."

Ella yanked it from his grip and he was glad he'd had the thorns removed. Otherwise, he'd be bleeding all over her front stoop.

She didn't bother to smell the flower and there was still no smile anywhere in her demeanour. "Look, Norm—"

He cut her off. "*Oui, Édith?*" She remembered his name, he was sure of it.

Her visage brightened minutely, he thought, though he wasn't certain, because she dipped her head. Probably to hide her face so he wouldn't see the hint of a smile lurking behind her eyes. He wanted to see that smile.

"You will be late if you don't leave soon," he said.

Ella frowned into his eyes.

*Zut.* This was not going well.

"Go where?" she asked.

So she wanted to play at evasion. He was the master of this game, so she stood little chance of beating him at it. "Church."

"What makes you think I'm going to church?" she asked, crossing her arms over her chest like a shield.

*Shield of irritation or fear?* "You're dressed up." He crossed his own arms in a more relaxed posture, nodding toward her. "You look very pretty, by the way. *Belle.*"

A blush crept across her cheeks.

He continued, "It's Sunday. And you told me you go to church." *Add something personal, something that will keep her from slamming the door in my face.* "The last time I went to church I was fourteen. It was the week after I moved to Montreal to live with my aunt and uncle. My cousin's First Communion, if I remember correctly."

"Really?" she asked. For a moment she looked intrigued. And then she remembered that she didn't want to be interested in him and closed down her expression.

He wanted to sigh but resisted the urge. "If we don't get going," he prompted her, "We'll be late for church."

Ella jerked to attention. "Oh, yeah. Coat."

She disappeared into the house. There had been no invitation to follow her—the closed door had been a big clue that his presence in her home was unwelcome. When she reappeared in a red compressed-down jacket, she flinched. Had she expected him to vanish? Her hands were filled with her small leather purse and three books. Indecision gripped her.

"Okay. Okay," Noah said, stepping up to push the door open.

"What are you doing?" Ella shrank from his suddenly looming pose.

"Holding the door open so you can step outside." He gestured for her to move.

Her gaze crawled up the length of his body. "Right. Church," she repeated, licking her lips.

Clearly, she resorted to cheek-chewing and lip-licking when nervous. Noah quashed the images that thought provoked in his mind, the gestures so innocently erotic. *Get a grip, Noah,* he admonished himself.

"El-là." He dropped his left arm to his side. He considered retreating down the steps but decided against it. He needed every advantage he could manufacture. "I told you I would come."

"Two months ago." She dropped her gaze. "I, uh, guess I didn't think you really would. Noah."

His heart skipped a beat. She remembered. Of course she did. It had only been two months since he'd last seen her. "Church, okay?"

"Right." She still hadn't moved. "I put the rose in water."

"Cool," he replied. "I'll carry your books." He held out his hand.

Still eyeing him, Ella gave them over. Carefully avoiding him, she closed and locked the door. *Finally.*

Turning, she gestured toward the white CR-Z as if she'd only noticed. "Is that your car?"

"*Oui.* If you tell me where we are going, I can drive," he replied. He gestured for her to precede him across the lawn. But she still didn't move.

"I'm not going in your car."

"Why not?"

"I don't even know you. You could be some weird-o."

"Okay. Fine," he replied, pulling out his key chain to press the locks closed and activate the alarm. He started toward her garage.

"What are you doing?"

Noah kept walking until he was standing in front of the silver garage door. It looked like a manual door. Switching the books to his left hand, he twisted it and lifted with his right.

"Noah," she reprimanded him. "What do you think you're doing?"

He turned back to find her standing exactly where he'd left her. "Did you want me to drive?" he asked.

"No."

"Okay. Fine. You drive."

When she didn't move, he continued, "Ella, if you want to drive, you'll have to be closer to the car." He smiled in what he hoped was a humorous yet not mocking manner. "You'll never reach the pedals from there."

Noah walked into the garage, giving his eyes a few seconds to adjust to the low light. A scan of the interior told him she was living here on her own. He'd yet to meet a man who didn't pack his garage with useless crap immediately upon taking possession. The only thing inside this garage was a metallic green SUV.

"Honda Element. Super fine." He yanked on the door, anticipating what would come next.

The car alarm sounded and Ella came running. "What did you do?" Along the way, she'd pulled her keys out of her purse and now pressed the button to quiet the bleating sound.

As soon as the alarm quieted, Noah slipped into the passenger seat. He watched her in the side mirror. She was ticked-off. But out of her depth. He counted down the seconds until she gave in and sat in the driver's seat.

"Put on your seatbelt," she grumbled at him.

"Of course." Setting the books on the floor at his feet, he clipped his seatbelt. He was feeling pretty good about his skills. He hadn't gotten inside her house, but he was sitting in her vehicle.

But she didn't turn on the car. Instead, she asked, "How did you get here?" while her eyes bored into the blank wall of the garage.

"In the biological sense?" he asked.

She looked askance at him. "Don't be a twit."

He chuckled. She had no difficulty calling *blarney* on him. "I drove," he replied.

"You were in the middle of an investigation the last time I saw you."

"I wrapped it up."

"Why aren't you working on another one?"

"I took a leave of absence."

"Why?" She sounded flummoxed, so completely out of her depth.

"So I could go to church with you."

She turned in her seat. He rotated toward her so they were roughly face-to-face, mirroring her movements and expression. His eyes were adjusting to the dimness and he could see her features fairly well. Her face was heart-shaped, her cheeks round and soft, and her forehead broad. She had high cheekbones and a perfect mouth.

"Why is it so important to go to church with me?" she asked. "There are plenty of churches in Vancouver."

"You invited me."

"That was a hypothetical discussion. You kidnapped me."

Irritation flashed across his mind, charging his expression. *Is that what she thinks?* He quickly neutralized it. "I did not kidnap you. I rescued you."

"But you told me the reason those goons took me is that their boss thought I was working with you."

"True. When I realized you'd been taken—"

"After I was arrested because of you."

"Yes." He blessed the dim light in the garage which hid a growing ruddiness in his cheeks. "Well, I came and got you. Before they hurt you, I might add. And then you invited me to church."

"That is *not* how I remember things."

"You don't remember me cutting the tape?"

"Yes, of course. How could I forget that?" She rolled her eyes at him. "But I did not invite you to church."

"If you don't leave soon, you'll be late. Unless we're going to the church at the bottom of Qu'Appelle."

"No. I go to the Alliance church across the city."

Noah slapped his knees. "I'm ready. Let's go."

*Finally,* she keyed the ignition and reversed out of the driveway.

# CHAPTER 11

After a silent, angst-filled journey across downtown and west beyond the university, Noah followed Ella into the Kamloops Alliance Church. Every two steps she responded to a greeting, a hug or a handshake, sometimes just a wave. Noah felt an almost irresistible urge to insinuate himself into each "greeting", to protect her from people who meant no harm. Or maybe he wanted her to smile at him like she smiled at the frisky octogenarian with the shock of iron-grey hair and mahogany cane.

The auditorium had two sections with rows of soft chairs, and a central aisle. At the front there was a platform with a drum set, several microphones, guitars on stands, and a keyboard of some sort. Two large screens occupied the walls on either side of a simple wooden cross.

When Ella finished chatting with everyone and their granny, she sat about halfway down on the left. Noah sat beside her and laid his arm across the back of her seat. He removed it when she gave him the sideways skunk-eye. Too much, too soon. He resigned himself to linking his hands across his lap.

A group of men and women of varying ages filed onto the stage and took up positions around it. Noah was surprised to see a grey-haired woman take up her position at the drum set. Equal rights, he supposed.

Everyone stood to sing. The screens displayed the lyrics. Then a woman stood up and talked about upcoming events. A guy prayed and then there was more singing. About forty minutes into the service, a fifty-something man stood up and spoke. He was short, slim and dark-haired, reminding Noah of Praveen, the boy who'd lived in the white, wattle-and-daub house near the embassy in Delhi. He had the same round face, bright eyes, and even a similar cow-lick at his part that Noah's mother had ceaselessly tried to bring under her control. Noah and Praveen had spent hours together getting into any kind of mischief a diplomat's son and his friend could engineer.

Noah hadn't thought about Praveen in years. A grin tugged at the corner of his mouth and he realized there were reasons to smile when alone.

The priest interrupted Noah's thoughts as he introduced himself as Enoch Nagi and told everyone how happy he was to be here today. The name, Nagi, reminded Noah of *nag* from the story *Rikki Tikki Tavi* by Rudyard Kipling. His mother had read the story to him and Sammy their first week in India. She'd always wanted them to embrace the culture of whichever country they'd found themselves. There was another consideration. The English meaning of "nag", a fitting name for a priest. Noah caught himself before he chuckled aloud. Given that the self-same Nagi was ramping to preach about God, Noah supposed that laughter was not the correct response.

When Nagi stood at the pulpit, Ella reached across Noah for her Bible. She'd passed the other two books off to a young blonde in the congregation. Noah tried to capture her hand on the return journey across his lap but she slipped away. The blush that appeared on her cheeks heartened him. She was clearly aware of him as a man.

Once she'd found the passage, she slid the Bible over so he could read along. He took the opportunity to skooch close enough to touch shoulder to shoulder. The blush bloomed afresh on her cheeks.

After twenty minutes of God, Jesus, and redemption, the priest who referred to himself as "pastor", wrapped it up and everyone rose for a final song and prayer. The woman who gave the final prayer invited everyone to stay for coffee. *Groan.* Noah hoped Ella wasn't planning on staying. He wanted to spend time alone with her. Somehow he had to convince her to give him a chance.

Ella chatted with a few more people before exiting the building.

"What did you think?" she asked him. They walked abreast across the lawn to the parking lot with her hugging her Bible to her chest like a shield.

He shrugged. "Good. Fine."

Noah joined her in the Element for the return journey to her house.

"You got your hair cut. And you sound different than when I first met you," Ella said, navigating away from the heavier traffic around Thompson Rivers University. He knew that the office she worked from for the Thompson Rivers Counselling Association was somewhere on the university's campus.

"What do you mean by that?" Noah asked, shifting in his seat to better see her face.

"Your speech patterns. Before, you sounded more normal. Now you have this lilt to your voice. It's familiar, but not quite."

"When I'm working I keep my accent neutral," Noah replied. "Anonymous."

"I guess that makes sense. You say 'okay' and 'cool' a lot. And it's 'cool' with a rounded and high 'oo'. Very French-Canadian. And you say my name with an emphasis on the second syllable, like El-là." She demonstrated for him. "But when you say your own name, you put the emphasis on the correct syllable."

"You're saying my dialect is wrong?" he asked, bemused by her comment.

Ella turned to him, astonishment and an expression almost of shame printed on her face. "Of course not. Wow." She seemed to realize something, paling. "You're right. That was ignorant of me. Your dialect is your own. How many languages do you speak?"

Noah shrugged one shoulder. "French, English, Hindi, a little Marathi, some Spanish." As a child, he'd learned the most common swear words in five or six other languages.

"So this is your own personal dialect of English. It's musical."

"Okay. Cool." He put his best Quebeçois into the two words. He detected the hint of a smile on her face.

Ella parked in her driveway, locking the doors of her Element as soon as he'd stepped out.

"Well, goodbye," she said as she walked away.

Disappointment was a sharp pang in his chest. She wasn't going to invite him into her new little bungalow. He wanted her to understand, though, that he was coming back. He intended to get to know her and let her get to know him.

"See you next week," he said, catching up to her.

Ella paused, the halting of her gait causing her to trip over the lawn. "Next week?"

He caught her with a hand to her elbow, helped her regain her balance. "Next week," he replied. "I'm here for the duration, Miss Hanover."

She walked backwards, slipping out of his grasp. "I didn't realize— you're going to—what?"

"Ella, I want a relationship with you."

"I don't even know you." She crushed her Bible to her chest. "I mean I've seen you at the coffee shop. You kidnapped me."

"I did not," he insisted. "I rescued you."

Ella paused at the bottom of her front steps. "So you say."

"So I say because it's true." Noah waited. He refused to leave until they reached a resolution. The drone of traffic layered over the *swoosh* and *whomp* of shovels shifting piles of the three centimetres of snow that had fallen in the early morning.

"None of this makes sense," she said. "Why are you here? Are you a weird stalker?"

Noah gritted his teeth to hold in his exasperation. He knew everything about her, what coffee she drank, her favourite muffin, where she went to school, even what grades she'd received. He'd had weeks and the resources of the Royal Canadian Mounted Police to learn everything there was to know about her. Except how to make her trust him.

"You're asking me to just believe you, Noah. With no proof," she said.

"What do you want to know, eh?" he asked, taking one step closer to her. He had to find a way to convince her to give him a chance.

"That I'm not making a huge mistake," she said. "Why did you come to Kamloops?"

"To be near you." He took a few steps closer, stopping when her eyes narrowed.

"For what purpose?"

"Ella, you've enchanted me."

She frowned but then her eyebrows lifted and he thought she'd smile, maybe blush. Instead, she burst out laughing. "Seriously?"

She clearly wasn't enchanted by him, but neither was she angry. *That's something.* Noah pursed his lips in thought. "Wrong vocabulary?"

She shook her head in exasperation at him.

"Ella," he shoved his hands in his pockets. "Get to know me. I'm a nice guy."

She studied him for a long moment.

He levelled a gaze at her, guessed the moment she gave in.

"All right. Next week."

*Yes!*

# Chapter 12

Noah greeted Ella with a bouquet of tulips. The flowered dress she'd worn on his first Sunday in Kamloops had been adorned with tulips. Surely that meant she liked them, would appreciate them, would possibly favour a gentleman who offered them. Because the roses he'd brought hadn't thawed her attitude toward him, that was for sure. Not the white sweetheart, the dozen pinks, or the half-dozen reds with baby's-breath.

Ella left him outside on the stoop while she put the tulips in a vase. He sighed. Four weeks and he'd still not gotten past the front stoop.

She returned with her Bible and a black shawl-sweater thing which matched the little black rosebuds woven into the material of her dusky green, long-sleeved dress. The material hugged her curves.

"You look lovely," Noah said. "Super fine."

A light blush highlighted her cheeks. "Thank you." She reached back in to snag her spring jacket, a lined blue Marmot, before locking the house. There was a chance of rain this afternoon.

As she approached her Element in the driveway, Ella unlocked the doors remotely. Noah scooted around to hold the driver-side door for her.

"Thanks." She scooped the skirt portion of her dress beneath her before she sat. "What did you do this week?"

He shrugged. "Looked for a job. Found an apartment."

She paused with the key in the ignition, glancing up at him. "You're staying?"

*Still asking the same questions. Still expecting me to give up and go away.* "Problème with that?"

"Uh. Yeh. If what you told me is a lie, then there's a huge problem."

Noah unlocked his jaw before his teeth clenched. "I didn't lie." He was unaccustomed to distrust from law-abiding citizens. He was a good guy, for cripes' sake.

Once he closed her door, Noah rounded the SUV and sat in the passenger seat.

Crimson was creeping up her neck. "Noah…I just don't know. This is all so weird." Her voice faded away.

He covered her hand with his, maintaining his hold when she tugged. "I am no danger to you."

When he released her, she keyed the ignition.

"We can take this at your pace, as slow as you like until you trust me," he said. *Though I don't know how much slower we could go.*

Ella chewed her lower lip. She clutched the steering wheel. "I must be crazy," she murmured.

"Crazy's not a bad neighbourhood," he replied.

Startled, she frowned. Her gaze traced his features as if scanning his brain for the meaning of his words. He grinned and the intensity of her mood broke. "Yeah. Well, I guess we'll see." She added just enough wry humour to her voice to encourage him.

Progress. Slow, but definitely progress. But so slow. Noah asked, "So what pace are we talking about here, eh?"

Her mouth quirked. "Let's keep on with church and go from there."

"Okay. Cool. I can live with that." At least it kept her in his world and he in hers. "Is lunch included this week? I didn't have breakfast. Got busy and didn't buy groceries."

"If you behave in church."

He frowned.

She laughed at his petulant expression. "Gotcha. I rarely eat out on Sundays, but, okay. There's a diner we can go to."

"I'll find a place to make us a picnic for another time."

Her eyebrows rose in astonishment. "I guess we'll see."

Church was much the same as usual. Ella was forced to introduce him to more and more of the congregation as the weeks passed and their curiosity grew. She introduced him as "Noah". That was it.

After the service, Ella drove out of the church parking lot toward her home. When he realized where she was headed, he protested, "Whoa. Wait. Lunch. You promised me lunch."

"I didn't promise you anything." She glanced at him. "But lunch is fine. There's a diner not too far from here."

*Right.* She'd said that before. Had she forgotten? Or was she hoping that he'd forget? "I'll pay."

Ella didn't respond until she was parked at the curb in front of Monty's Deli and Diner. "Buying lunch doesn't buy you anything else." She gave him the skunk-eye. "Maybe we should split the tab."

Noah's gaze hardened. "I will pay. I don't expect anything except the opportunity to eat with you. What kind of guy do you think I am, eh?"

"I don't know." She flung her arms as wide as she could in the confines of the vehicle. "That would be the point I've been trying to make."

"Lunch?" Noah asked.

Ella grunted. "Come on."

Noah grinned. *Victory.* Small, but not to be discounted. If he could keep her from running in the other direction, he might just have a chance at happily-ever-after.

# Chapter 13

Noah greeted Ella with a picnic basket. She left him outside on the front stoop while she placed it in the fridge. At least that's what she told him she was doing. Likely, she was rooting through it looking for listening devices or poison. This relationship was an uphill adventure.

She returned to the front door with an iPad, a heavy sweater to wear over her slacks and blouse, and a question. "Where did you get the picnic?"

"I bought it at a bakery downtown, took me a while," *three weeks,* "to find a place in this *petite ville* that would make one up for me. You'd think no one had ever picnicked in March before."

"It is especially warm today." Her face dipped into a scowl. "There are eighty thousand people living here, you know. It's definitely a city, not a tiny village. Why do you hold it in such disdain?"

"I don't hold it in disdain. I simply don't understand why you moved from Vancouver to this deserted area of the country."

"There are smaller places. Monte Creek."

"Monte Creek?" he repeated, incredulous. "You couldn't move there. There is only one house, a renovated school. It doesn't even have census data!"

"Well. Fine. I don't live there." She pulled the front door shut, hard enough to slam, and locked it.

"No, you live in this small and insignificant city," he added a tone of sarcasm to the word, "hours from anywhere."

"It's not insignificant." She looked hurt. *Hurt?* "I live here. I work here. I have a lovely little house that's all my own, nestled between the South Thompson River and a mountain. I work in a well-funded clinic that offers cutting-edge programs through the local university."

"Vancouver has mountains. Not to mention ski resorts, restaurants, shopping centres—"

"But in Vancouver," emotion crowded her words, "I am just another psychologist serving the children of those who can afford it. Here, I'm able to serve children from a variety of backgrounds, including those whose parents can't pay for intervention. We are linked into Thompson Rivers U, providing us with access to the newest research and government grants. We have a pro-bono program as well as privately funded and government funded programs. I can make a difference here. In Vancouver, there are plenty of counsellors to take my place. Few professionals relocate to Kamloops."

"Cool. I get it," Noah replied. His voice even sounded gooey. He understood the desire to make a difference in people's lives, to have your life count for something.

"You do?" She sounded surprised.

"I do." He walked across her lawn toward his own car. "Let's go to church. Where's your Bible?"

She followed him. "I downloaded a Bible app and thought I'd try that."

She didn't even hesitate before getting into his car. Once he'd keyed the ignition and pulled onto Nechako, Noah said, "Your preacher visited me last week."

"Really?"

"I'm not even sure how he found me. I've only been there a couple weeks, only put my name on the mailbox on Thursday."

"I guess he's as good an investigator as you are," she said smugly. "What did he want?"

Noah returned her smile. "He welcomed me to the community and the church, hoped I was enjoying the services."

Looking startled, she asked, "You didn't tell him you're here to chase me, did you?"

Noah huffed a humourless laugh. "Was I not supposed to admit to that? You embarrassed by me, Ella?"

She hunched her shoulders, her gaze shifting out the window. "It's sort of a weird situation, that's all."

"You use that word a lot," he replied, turning onto Highland Road. "Weird."

"If the word fits." She kept her face turned away from him but he was sure she'd smiled again.

"Where do you want to go for a picnic, eh?"

"Let's get through church first, all right?"

"Sure," he replied, refusing to sigh.

Noah pulled into the parking lot of the Alliance church, turned off the car, and rounded the hood of his CR-Z to hold the passenger door for Ella.

She thanked him, leaning back in to retrieve her iPad.

"Mr. Kristofer."

Noah swivelled from his view of Ella's fine posterior to see the preacher heading his way. Nagging. Nope. Nagi, Enoch Nagi.

The preacher shook Noah's hand firmly. "I'm glad to see you here. How was your week? Any luck on the job search?"

Ella stiffened and frowned. So, Ella wasn't too pleased to hear that he was building a spot in the community.

"Still looking."

"We're a small community, but there are a few opportunities, if you're not fussy. Bob Thornton is looking for an assistant for the landscaping part of his business. Mavis Smythe needs someone to take the evening shift at her pottery store."

Noah nodded thoughtfully. "Cool. I'll look into it."

"Great." Enoch seemed pleased. Maybe he was hoping to fill out his quota of good deeds by getting Noah a job.

Someone called the pastor away and Noah offered Ella his arm. Her gaze shifted to him in one of her sidelong glances as her body shifted away. He caught up to her at the door.

During the sermon this week Enoch spoke about forgiveness. Noah was still considering the man's words as he rose from the pew, stepped aside to let Ella out, and followed her down the aisle toward the exit.

When they reached Enoch and his wife at the back door, Noah was surprised when the man pulled him aside. "There is someone I'd like to introduce you to, Noah." Enoch led him across the rear of the sanctuary to an older gentleman with iron-grey hair and a wooden cane.

"Roderick Blanchard I'd like you to meet Noah Kristofer." Enoch turned to Noah. "Rod was a missionary in India for many years."

How did Nagi know of Noah's connection to India? "What took you to India?" Noah asked, his interest piqued. Those last years in Delhi before his mother died were some of his best.

"God. What made you leave?" Rod asked. Rod turned out to be the frisky octogenarian.

"My mother's death."

Rod nodded knowingly. "You have a mixed dialect in your speech. I would guess French, English, and…something else. Something familiar."

*Hindi.* Noah was impressed. Each country they'd visited when he was young, his mother had encouraged him and his brothers to learn the local language. At least enough so they could play with the local children.

But Noah didn't want to give too much away. "I grew up in Montreal."

"I've never been. Perhaps you'd share a coffee with me this week and tell me about it," Rod said.

"Okay."

Rod fished a wallet out of his pocket, sifted through it with his arthritic fingers, and pulled out a fluorescent blue business card. "One of my grand-children made these for me. This one, Brigid, has decided that blue is my favourite colour." Rod smiled fondly. "It has my home number and address on it. Stop by Tuesday around two. We'll chat."

Noah shrugged one shoulder. "Okay. Cool."

"Miss Hanover," Rod said, lifting the crook of his cane to his forehead as though he was tipping his hat.

"Hello, Mr. Blanchard," she replied.

Had she come to find him?

"Are you ready to go?" she asked Noah.

"Yeah." He couldn't help but smile at her. She *had* come to find him.

Ella smiled back, a little shyly, before she led him back to his CR-Z.

"What did Mr. Blanchard want?" she asked, breaking the silence they'd driven in for the past ten minutes.

"Wanted to talk about India," Noah replied, shoulder-checking before taking the turn onto Qu'Appelle.

"Oh." She lapsed into silence.

"How did Nagi know I'd lived in India?" Noah asked.

Her gaze darted toward the mountainous skyline outside the window. "I mentioned it."

That was good that she was talking about him. As long as she possessed enough discretion not to blab about everything. Probably, since she clearly wanted no one to know about their relationship.

When they reached her house, she turned to him. "I'll, uh, go change."

Noah nodded.

Ten minutes later, she emerged in jeans and a sweater, carrying a backpack.

"I transferred the food into the pack. I thought it'd be easier to carry. Do you want to change?" she asked.

"Would I be allowed inside your house?" he asked, knowing the answer. He'd worn grey lightweight trousers and a fleece sweater over a short-sleeved button-down shirt today. He wore his Keen sandals which were decent hikers. He wore his Keens most of the year. Any day without snow was a Keen day.

"No," Ella replied to his question.

"Then, no thanks." Taking the pack from her, he started toward his car. "Where are we going?"

"Um, uh, I thought I'd drive."

He stopped. "Why?"

"Well, it makes sense."

He spun to face her. *Makes sense if I'm a degenerate who intends to molest you or abandon you as soon as we get outside the city limits.* Anger built, making his chest burn. She was running hot and cold; so changeable he was never sure what her response would be. And he was not enjoying it, not one bit.

He tried to sound calm and reasonable as he said, "You trusted me to drive you to church." But he was clearly unsuccessful, given her response.

Spinning on her heel, Ella strode to the driveway, pulled out her keys and bleeped open the doors of the Element. She dropped into the driver's seat.

Noah hop-stepped-it over, double time. He did not want her to leave without him.

After he opened the rear door, a suicide door, he placed the backpack on the fold-down seat and sat in the front passenger seat.

"Seatbelt," she barked at him.

"Obviously," he muttered in reply.

They drove in a heated silence which he did not understand, until she turned off Columbia and onto Glenfair Drive. Low deciduous lined one side of the street. The other side was bordered by a low, barbed wire fence which surrounded six or seven portables and several white sedans. *Odd.* The rutted asphalt shifted to gravel as they drew ever closer to a sparsely wooded hill spanned by something long and large. A bridge?

"Am I allowed to know where we're going?" Noah muttered.

"Peterson Creek Park," she replied. "It's beautiful."

Given her tone, he guessed that hiking Peterson Creek Park was on par with sucking a lemon.

"The geography of the park centres around a ravine," she added. "A natural creek corridor, they call it. There are lots of picnic tables on various trails. Or we can eat at Bridal Veil Falls."

She forced the gearshift into park and slammed out of the vehicle.

Noah's eyes were drawn to the suspension bridge which spanned the creek bed and led to a grassy field dotted with picnic tables. The brown of winter was giving way to the bright optimism of spring. It reminded him that time was passing. He was no nearer a conclusion to his search for *normal* than the day he'd first set foot in Kamloops. That was why he didn't respond to Ella's march around the rear of the SUV until she'd wrenched open the rear passenger-side suicide door.

Frustrated and even a little angry, Noah slipped out the front door to prevent her escape. When she straightened with the pack in her hands, Noah blocked her way with one hand on the front door and one on the rear. She was trapped.

Fear flickered across her features before she hardened them. "Excuse me," she gritted out.

His anger vanished, replaced by weariness. "We've been doing this for weeks. Every week I wait six lonely days to see you for two or three hours. Then I wait again. Why, you ask? Why would I be willing to put up with that when I see no progress from you?" *Why can't you turn that charm you possess my way?* "You still look at me like my interest is a grand plot to abduct you and have my way with you. How long before you treat me with the barest decency? Eh?"

Ella dropped her eyes while she chewed her lower lip. Did she have any idea what that did to him? Probably not. He sighed internally. She was so skittish around him. And rude. She belittled him...

"I'm sorry."

Her words surprised him. "What?"

"I just don't know what to do with this situation." Her gaze flickered up as far as his chin, then flitted away. "With you."

She fidgeted with the handle of the pack so he removed it from her hands and placed it on the roof of the SUV. He'd seen her with her nephews. She was an affectionate and loving woman. Why couldn't he win her trust enough to have some of that affection shifted his way?

"Thanks," she murmured. "None of this makes any sense. Are you a kidnapper-assassin, a cop with criminal tendencies, or are you the sweet guy who attends church with me every week?"

Those were fair questions. "Probably a bit of each, except sweet."

She frowned up at him. Her expression shifted until a grin quirked the corner of her mouth. "You make it impossible. I thought if I went along with this crazy arrangement, you'd get bored and go away."

Noah's chest squeezed. "You want me to go away, eh?"

"Yes."

Not the response he'd been hoping for. "Listen, I—"

"And no."

Surprised, he moved back a half-step. She snatched the backpack and slipped beneath his arm. Taking a moment to orient herself, she started walking south toward the Tom Moore Trail. Her upper body twisted to swing the pack onto her shoulder.

Noah shut both doors of the Element and jogged after her. He heard the doors lock behind him. Saw her slip the keys into her pocket. When he caught up with her, he slid the pack down her arm and swung it onto his back.

She paused, turning to him. "Look, Noah—"

He placed his fingers on her lips, stopping her. "Don't. Please. For one hour, let me believe I'm here because you want me here, because you like me. Okay?" Her mouth was so soft, damp because she'd been chewing her lip. He traced her lower lip with the tip of his index finger, firm enough not to tickle. On the second pass, he used a firmer touch so he could run his finger along her teeth.

She sucked in a breath. Her larynx bobbed as she swallowed hard. Eyes wide, she turned and continued to the trail. Noah followed her.

The trail started as a gravel path, flanked on the north by a rocky slope and a grassy hill to the south. The snow had melted. The temperature had dropped enough to freeze the mud, making the day perfect for hiking. They trekked past slides of scree and wooden footbridges, up, over, and around to rest a moment at a shallow mine shaft about one hundred metres up the climb. Maybe some lucky adventurer had once found gold inside?

Further on and around a bend, both of them huffing and puffing, the rocks parted to reveal Bridal Veil Falls.

"That was worth the journey." Ella watched water stream over rock, her expression shaped by wonder at the beauty of the location. Her shoulders rose and fell as she caught her breath.

"*Oui.*" It was grand, the rock, belched up from the earth in mountains and trails.

"We could have our picnic on the large rock." Ella gestured toward a flattened outcropping far enough from the falls to be free of spray.

Kneeling on the unforgiving rock, Noah pulled a vinyl-backed table cloth out of the pack, flattened it, and set out the food. He withdrew two water bottles, handing one to her and opening one himself, draining half of it in one gulp. The hike required enough exertion to inspire thirst.

Ella sat cross-legged on the ground across from him. He rested his arm on one raised knee, extending his other leg so that his foot was near her knee.

"You know," she began, peeling a banana that looked like it had not enjoyed the bouncing it received in the pack. "I wouldn't be here if I didn't like you." She bit into the banana, a portion large enough to pouch out her cheek. Good manners would require that she not speak until she swallowed.

"Good to know." Noah took a sandwich, unwrapped it and bit off a portion.

She chased the chunk of banana down with a sip of water. "I'm trying not to make a mistake." She took another bite.

It would take more than church and lunch once a week to convince her he wasn't an error. "I want more."

She stopped chewing, looking like a confused chipmunk. Then swallowed. "More mistakes? What are you talking about?"

"I want more than church and lunch once a week. I want to see you during the week. I want to take you to supper if I want, or to a movie."

"If you want?" she asked, one eyebrow raised.

He caught the humour behind her eyes. "I guess you could offer an opinion."

She laughed. "I suppose there's no reason we couldn't do either of those things."

"Good. After we get back, we should get dinner."

"We'll have just finished lunch!"

"After all this exercise?" He gestured at the trees and hills surrounding them. "I'm sure we'll be hungry."

Her eyes sparkled in her face as she continued to smile at him. "You're incorrigible."

"You must have read my performance evaluation."

She laughed again and he couldn't help but smile back.

"I suppose I would enjoy a coffee when we get back," she conceded, then added in a whisper, "With you."

"Good."

# Chapter 14

Macken Roy closed his laptop and leaned back in the plush brown leather office chair in the conference room of the Sheraton Hotel in Surrey, British Columbia. He propped his three-hundred-dollar cross-trainers on the carved wooden table. All the while, Maximiano Guerra paced. The dude was hyper. He needed some serious Ritalin.

"These plans you make, I like," Maximiano said. "This *tecnología*; it can work?"

"Yep," Macken replied. He pulled out his switchblade, opened it, and spun it by its hilt on his palm.

"This *información* on *asesino de mi padre*—as you say, the murderer—it is good? Solid?" Maximiano asked.

"Yep." Macken flipped the knife up and caught it, blade down, between his thumb and forefinger.

"They know of me," Maximiano said, fiddling with the sleeve of his black silk shirt. "They would expect me to kill this man."

"Mebbe." Macken sat forward, pocketing his knife. So the hyper dude wanted someone else to do his dirty work. "What you gonna do for me?"

"The boy. I find him."

Macken rose, striding swiftly toward Maximiano. The younger man's stance changed, quickly morphing to stillness as he spread his legs and rocked forward on the balls of his feet. He was ready to fight.

"How?" Macken asked. "Ain't been no sign in three years."

"I have—how you say—information, *un informante.*" Maximiano watched Macken warily. "With this, I give you proposal. You kill the murderer, Capital K. I take care of the boy."

With the boy dead, there was not a single person on this green earth who could tie Macken to a crime.

"You've got a deal."

# Chapter 15

The third Friday in June, Ella found herself on the sidewalk in front of her father's house in Langley, BC. It was grey, three stories, and looked like every other house on the street. Within, she'd find a varied assortment of half-brothers, step-brothers, sisters-in-law, girlfriends, boyfriends, a couple nephews, and even one brother-in-law. A family of the twenty-first century.

Ella walked along the front path, past the groomed bushes and flower beds, up the concrete steps to the unadorned grey door that matched every other front door on the street. Welcome to the suburbs.

When Ella had informed Blaine Hanover, the only father she'd ever known, that she was moving from Vancouver, a mere fifty minutes from Langley, to Kamloops, he'd kicked up an enormous fuss. Even when she'd reminded her step-father she was twenty-nine years old and only moving three hours away, he'd acted as though she planned to plumb the depths of the Amazon. For a family comprised of five parents and seven children that hailed from Russia, Pakistan, Belize, Taiwan, and the southern United States, they were surprisingly unwilling to hear of Ella moving to the interior of British Columbia. The drawback of being the only female in a pack of males, she supposed. As a result, she'd promised to spend the entire weekend here for Father's Day this year. Father's Day was the one day that every Hanover and Hanover hanger-on came together to celebrate the man who'd made a family from the scattered remains of ruined relationships.

The front door crashed open and a half dozen teenagers spilled out, surrounding her in profanity and the overwhelming aroma of Axe body wash.

"Hey, Ella!" Her youngest step-brother, Alain Hanover, wrapped her in a bear hug. "You made it. These are my friends. Gotta go. See you."

"Hi," Ella said to their backs.

"Close the door!" That was Gerson Kurtz, two half-brothers and a step above her in age. His voice carried out the door.

Ella finished the journey inside. "Hello?" she called.

Lance Hanover and his husband, Mischa Tabatznik, appeared in the foyer. "Ella," they cried in unison, wrapping her in a four-armed hug.

Lance, the half-brother one below Gerson, stepped back with a broad and welcoming smile.

Mischa kept a firm grip on her arm as he scanned her from head to toe. "That style again." He tisked. "I warned you it draws attention to your puffy cheeks and away from your eyes." He bunched her hair in his fists then released it to arrange the strands around her ears. "Better, sweetie." Before he rejoined Lance, he asked, "What do you think?"

Lance wrapped his arm around Mischa's shoulders. "She's a sight for sore eyes." Lance smiled, though it never quite reached his eyes. "Blaine's in the back yard trying to start the barbecue."

"Trying being the operative word," Mischa muttered. His dark blonde hair was shaved on one side. The other side was styled in a meringue and glued stiff by gel.

"Well I don't know how to do it. Nor do you," Lance said to Mischa and then turned to Ella. Lance's platinum blonde hair was cut close to his head and moussed up in spikes. "Andras and Laszlo are with him. Gerson is upstairs bathing his kids because they got into the downstairs toilet. Like literally got into it." His face contorted into a grimace at the memory.

"Is Perry coming?" Ella asked. Perry Babu was the half-brother just older than her. They shared a mother and had gotten along well as children.

"Oh, don't we all wish he wouldn't," Mischa said, turning away to study the painting on the wall. She wasn't sure why, because he'd painted it. There shouldn't be much mystery left.

"Perry'll be here later tonight. Mischa and I are off to the Club." Lance kissed her on the cheek. "Welcome home, baby sis." He turned away and she could hear him start a whispered argument with Mischa.

Leaving them to their squabbles, Ella climbed the stairs to her old bedroom. The boys had all shared but she'd had her own room, the one bonus of being the solitary female. It was small and painted pale pink, a colour she loathed. But the bed was still covered with her fire-engine-red bedspread and assortment of Star Wars pillows.

"Elly-phant," sounded from the hall followed by a rat-a-tat-tat on the door. "I know you're in there."

"Come in, Laszlo Luu," Ella responded. Laszlo was the son of Nicholas Luu, and Anji Cubillan who later had an affair and another son with Blaine. Alain was the product of that union. People considered Laszlo, as the eldest, the protector of the family. In reality? He was simply nosy.

The door opened and her step-brother entered the room. His black hair was spiked, his eyes dark, his whipcord-thin body clad in jeans and T-shirt, and his arms wide. Why? Not because he wanted a hug. He had an aversion to physical touch. If she stepped toward him, she knew he'd retreat posthaste. "Baby Ella. How are you?"

Ella smiled in welcome. "Fine. How are you doing, Laszlo? How's Beatrice?"

"Beatrice? Don't know who you mean. I'm all about Phyllis now. But she had a hair appointment and couldn't come today. Have you seen Perry?"

*I hope that Phyllis is over eighteen.* Beatrice had only been barely so. "Not yet. Lance said he's coming later." Ella asked it as a question.

"Perhaps." Laszlo dug his enormous phone from his pocket. "I have pictures of you on my phablet. Want to see?" Laszlo always had the latest gadgets.

"Sure." She moved to stand beside him, careful not to crowd him.

With a flourish, he brought up a picture of her walking into the Blenz coffee shop in Vancouver. It looked grainy, like a surveillance photo. Laszlo flipped the screen to an open bathroom door in the coffee shop where she could be seen washing her hands. Her brother was so weird. There was one of her walking back to Laszlo's table. In the picture, Noah Kristofer could be seen watching her.

"How did you get that?" she asked, tearing the phablet from Laszlo's grasp.

"Why, Elly-phant? See something you like?" he mocked.

She pointed to Noah. "This man. How did you get his picture?"

"Is that your new boyfriend? It was obvious he was checking you out. He's a doll. Don't let Mischa see him. Lance will spend another night alone."

"You shouldn't have a picture of him," Ella said.

"Why? Is he a spy?" Laszlo asked in a taunting voice, made to irritate little sisters.

"No, of course not. But he is a police officer. You're lucky he didn't catch you taking pictures without permission," she warned her brother.

Laszlo reacquired his phablet, swiped the screen, and flipped it back to her. "Gone. I've sent you a copy." Laszlo kissed the air beside her left ear and practically danced out of the room. "Glad you're here. Anyone seen Blaine?" He called out to the house as he descended the stairs.

*Great.* Now Laszlo would tell everyone about Ella's "boyfriend". *Groan.* She had no idea what Noah was to her. Acquaintance. Friend. Stalker? Ella chuckled. Then groaned. She did not understand this man who had followed her to Kamloops. He wanted to leap from *stranger* to *boyfriend* when she was just getting to know him. Everything was happening at such an accelerated pace that she couldn't quite get her head around it. And that was making her head ache.

Setting her overnight bag on the foot of the bed, she sank into the softness. Maybe she could just fall asleep and wake up Sunday morning in time for church, escape all the drama to come.

"Ella?" A knock sounded on her door. That was Darla West. "Laszlo said you'd arrived."

Sighing, Ella rose and opened the door to invite Gerson's partner in. She had a freshly scrubbed tot on each hip. As soon as they spied her, the little ones cried her name and reached for her.

"I assumed you wanted to see your nephews. Their clothes are in Gerson's room. We're here together so we're sharing his bedroom and, of course, Laszlo is sleeping on the couch. Or with Alain. I forget." Darla thrust the three and four-year-olds at Ella, dropping them into her arms. *Ready or not.*

"Auntie Ella play with me," Jack said.

"Read to me, Auntie Ella," Gil said at the same time.

Gil was the spitting image of Gerson, round-faced and bronzed. Jack, however, sported bright red hair and a fair complexion which was a mystery to the entire family. Darla claimed a long-distant Irish relative to explain it. Ella had studied enough genetics to wonder. But the Hanover clan was a Heinz 57 family, so one more changeling made no difference.

"Let's get you boys dressed," Ella said, kissing each on the head. They smelled of baby shampoo.

After she dressed the boys, Ella took them down to the basement play room. She read a few books then played bean bag toss. Both activities quickly devolved into wrestling. Ella didn't wonder why everyone scattered when she passed through the house with the little monsters in tow. Oh, she loved her nephews. In doses. When she'd filled her prescription, she convinced the boys to find Pop-pop. Neither Gerson nor Darla were anywhere to be found. Though the curious noises from upstairs were suspicious.

Afternoon bled into evening in a chaos of overlaying arguments and boasting. Supper was eaten and everyone departed for somewhere more interesting. Even Darla and Gerson brought their children along when they went out to the movies.

Ella was finally alone with her step-father. Her biological father was Patrick Silver, the same man who'd fathered Lance. Courtney Clarke was her bio-mom but Lance's was Gert Mikel. Still, Patrick had brought Lance with him into a relationship with Courtney and Courtney had brought both Ella and Lance into a home and marriage with Blaine Hanover. Blaine had given them both his name. They'd stayed when Courtney had moved on to Kaeski Babu, a trader from northern Pakistan. Courtney had returned to drop off their son, Perry, then disappeared into the mists. Well, to be honest, no one, including Perry, was certain whether Perry was Courtney's son from a previous relationship with Kaeski or whether his mother was an unknown. It didn't matter to Blaine, so it didn't matter to anyone else.

Ella sat on the back deck with her arms curled around her knees while Blaine scraped the barbecue clean of the residue of the chicken breasts, veggie-dogs, and tuna burgers he'd cooked to please his children.

"Laszlo says you've found a boy," Blaine said without preamble.

*A boy? It doesn't matter that I'm almost thirty. Blaine never sees reality.* "Sort of, I guess." They hadn't shared more than a greeting since she'd arrived, and then, wham-o, right to the meaty stuff.

"Sort of?" Blaine paused a moment to look at her. At least she presumed he was looking at her. She was busy watching the kids in the next yard trying to start a fire on the pavement. "What does that mean, Pepper?"

Blaine had taken to calling Lance Salt and her Pepper when they'd moved in together. Lance had platinum blonde hair. Hers had been a deep, dark brown but had lightened.

"Ella?" Blaine set the scrub brush down and came to sit beside her. "Tell me, Pepper."

Ella glanced at Blaine. "He's a cop. And I sort of got caught up in one of his cases."

"Sort of how?"

"Another cop arrested me, for suspicion of terrorism."

"Arrested? Ella, why didn't you call? Andras is in law school. You should have called him."

Andras had spent a year in chemistry, a year in marine biology, a year in linguistics, et cetera. Now he was pre-law at Simon Fraser University. Not much help given the circumstances. "It worked out okay." She remembered the cop, Smith, coming to get her. Then she remembered the men kidnapping her away from Smith. "Sort of."

"Pepper." Blaine said her name with such compassion. Leaning down, he brushed her hair back from her face, cupping her cheek. "My poor girl." He kissed her on the forehead. "What happened?"

Tears burned the backs of her eyes. Ella sniffed once and let the tears fall. "Some men came and took me, Dad. They tied me up and knocked me out."

Blaine wrapped her in a hug. Her tears slowed as she enjoyed the warmth of his love.

"Do you want me to find these guys, gather the boys, and deliver a beating?"

Ella chuckled. Blaine offered, but he would never do it. He was comfort, a home base in this turbulent world. But he was not her protector. "No, Dad, it's okay. Noah rescued me."

Blaine pulled back. "So it's Noah, is it? Cute?"

Ella smiled. "Yes."

"How long?"

"Since February. Well, I met him for the first time in December."

"Hm. Is he good to you?"

"He took a leave-of-absence from his job and moved to Kamloops to get to know me better."

"Sacrifice for love? That's good," Blaine commented. "Is he into your churchy things? I've never truly understood what you and Perry find in the Jesus-God thing."

"He goes to church with me. But I don't think he believes in it."

"Friends, then. You don't want to try a life relationship with a person who doesn't share your deepest beliefs." Blaine's face suddenly aged, his eyes reflecting the sadness he usually buried deep inside.

"Friends would be good." Ella leaned her head against his shoulder because she didn't want to see the sorrow. She had tried to explain what God did for her. Perry had too. But Blaine wasn't open, wasn't ready for the information. Ella prayed that someday soon he would be.

"Is he polite? Treat you with respect?" Blaine asked.

Ella glanced up to see that Blaine had hidden his pain away again. "Yes." Noah was a little moody but there was a protectiveness and sweetness about him that she liked. And the way he looked at her turned her all hot and mushy inside.

"I like him already," Blaine said, a smile on his face. That quickly, his concern melted away. "You must bring him home."

"Maybe you could come to Kamloops," she said, hoping.

"Of course," he replied easily then followed up with, "Not now, of course, not with Gerson's boys almost in school and Lance's business struggling. But soon." Blaine patted her head, rose, and gathered the rest of the utensils. "Turn off the lights, Pepper."

"Sure." Ella stayed outside a little longer. She was always welcome home. And her family would sometimes come to her when a need in their own lives brought them close. Like when Laszlo had visited Vancouver to land a business deal for his investment company. But, all in all, she was on her own. She knew her family loved her. They just never loved her enough.

⅄

Ella sighed in relief as she crossed the threshold into her little bungalow on Nechako Drive. It might be the smallest house on the street, but it was her refuge.

The phone in the living room rang. Ella kicked the door closed behind her, dropped her bag on the floor, and answered it on the third ring. "Hello?"

"Ella. It's Noah."

Ella's chest expanded. She was starving after her drive but she didn't want to disconnect. She suppressed the urge to consider why. *Just friends, right?* "Hi. How are you?"

"Better. Where've you been?" He asked the question with concern and Ella melted just a little more. He'd missed her.

Time with her family had made her acutely aware of the sacrifice that Noah had made for her. Their relationship was weird. But, if he was telling her the truth, he had put his career on hold and moved himself to the interior of British Columbia just to get to know her better.

"I was visiting my family," she replied.

"How many brothers do you have, anyway?" he asked.

Ella laughed. "Can you give me two minutes? I just got in the door."

"Do you want me to call back?" he asked soberly.

"No!" She dialled her enthusiasm back a notch. "Just two minutes."

"Okay. Cool." Now he sounded pleased and that made Ella blush.

She placed the phone on the little table beside her cozy chair, ran to the bathroom and peed in record time before setting supper on the stove. She raced back to the phone, pausing a moment to calm her respiration so that Noah wouldn't hear that she was out of breath. "I'm back."

"So you are." She could hear his smile in his voice.

# Chapter 16

It was three o'clock in the morning and Grady Jones was wide awake. Even though his days passed quickly, full of school, indoor soccer, swimming lessons, and homework, the nights were long.

Lillian and Peter had assured Grady it was all right to wake them in the night. But usually, he didn't. So they bought him comic books, a headlamp, and even a flat-screened television. The television stood silent and blank on Grady's chest of drawers, the comics discarded hours ago. Grady lay on his back with his iPhone in one hand and the palm of his other hand on his chest. He counted his heartbeats while he listened to the quiet of the dark.

The creak of a floorboard in the hallway along with a soft huff of breath told Grady that Otto MacDog was at the door. Somehow the ten-year-old Scottish Terrier always knew when Grady was awake, and would come to keep him company.

Grady was sure he hadn't made a sound to attract the terrier because Grady understood the value of silence. Even though these last three years he'd lived with Lillian and Peter Clarke who were the kindest people that Grady had ever met, he had been born into a world where it didn't pay to be noticed. Notice meant attention. Attention garnered violence.

Rolling off his bed, Grady tiptoed to the door. There was no clutter on the floor. Grady kept his room clean. Lillian said he was the tidiest eleven-year-old she'd ever known. But Grady knew Peter worried about it. Grady couldn't change the habit, though, even to ease Peter's concern.

Grady understood that life was unpredictable and you never knew when you'd have to run. So you needed a clear space for a clean getaway.

Grady opened his bedroom door wide enough to admit Otto who trotted in a few steps, looked around the room then sniffed Grady's leg. That seemed to satisfy the little dog. He jumped up onto the end of Grady's tousled twin bed, settled with his head on his front paws and snored softly.

Three years ago, when Grady was moved to Calgary to live with Peter and Lillian, Otto had become his first and only friend. Lillian said the little dog became his on the day Grady walked through the front door. That was cool. Grady had never before had anything that was his.

Turning back to shut his bedroom door, Grady paused. A bright light flashed at the bottom of the stairs and was extinguished. Grady frowned, glancing back over his shoulder at Otto to see if the dog was worried. Otto stared at the door with his dark blue eyes, silent but alert.

Grady peered into the hall. Peter and Lillian's room was right across from his. No illumination appeared beneath their door so they were probably still asleep. If the flashing light was dangerous, they would wake up, wouldn't they?

Grady pressed his palm to his chest, feeling the bump of his heart as it accelerated at the hint of trouble. He needed to decide whether the flash was truly a sign of danger. Grady wasn't so great at recognizing danger. He tended to overreact to threat, that's what his psychologist said, because of his early experiences. Grady had blanked out most of those experiences but he still remembered the fear he'd felt, the terror of discovery.

A black shape moved up the stairs, looked back down, then resumed its upward motion. Grady couldn't see to the ground floor from where he crouched, but that was a human-shaped figure. It was covered in black clothes including a black toque on its head. If that was Peter—it was too big for Lillian—then everything was okay. But Peter wore pale blue pyjamas.

The figure opened Peter and Lillian's bedroom door slowly and quietly. Grady's heart thumped against his ribs. His armpits sweated. Otto appeared at his side. Something bad was happening.

Holding his breath to keep from panting out loud, Grady closed his door the last quarter inch so as not to draw attention to himself. Huddled against the wall between the door and his closet, Grady wrapped his arms around his knees and rocked his body ever so slightly. His vision greyed at the edges so he shook his head to clear it. He gasped in quick, shallow breaths, afraid that the black shapes outside his bedroom would hear the roar in his ears and come and get him.

What should he do? It was too late to run to Peter and Lillian. The dark figure was already there. There was probably another figure downstairs because the first one had looked back at someone.

Were they robbers? Or were they after him? Did his uncle find him again? Did Uncle Macken still want him dead? It was possible after what he'd seen.

Maybe Grady should go to his uncle and tell him he didn't remember anything. His past was an empty book coloured in fear. But he wouldn't be able to tell his uncle, just like he couldn't tell the Mounties. Even if Grady could remember, he hadn't spoken a word since he was four years old. The only words he spoke were through an application on his iPhone that Lillian had purchased and downloaded for him last year. But even so, the words to tell the Mounties never emerged.

Grady's body shook. He scooted away from the door so the shapes couldn't hear the sound the vibrations made. He looked at his iPhone. Should he call the Mounties? He didn't have their number. Lillian did. But it was too late to run to Peter and Lillian's room and too late to go downstairs. He could call 911, but the coppers would take a long time to get here. He could crawl under his bed. But that never worked. Grown-ups always looked there first. Grady would have to run and hide.

When Lillian had realized that Grady didn't sleep well at night, she'd asked the Witness Protection people, the Mounties, why. For a long time, no one would tell. But Lillian didn't give up. One day, a Mountie arrived. Lillian shouted at him for a long time. Grady didn't hear the words. When things got loud, he blocked them out. His psychologist said it was a coping mechanism. However, the very next day, Peter started building an escape route for Grady in his bedroom closet. The emergency hatch was hidden, secret. It made Grady feel safer. It helped him sleep better, most of the time.

Grady crossed the room in silence. The closet door opened without a sound. He grabbed a pair of navy blue cargo pants, put them on, and fastened them with his webbed belt. It was too long, but Lillian said he would grow into it. He added a long-sleeved blue T-shirt and black hoodie to his escape ensemble, pulling them all on over his pyjamas. He put on a pair of high tech merino wool socks before his brown leather North Face hiking boots. Otto stood close by watching every move he made.

A scream started and was muffled. Grady froze. His breath sawed in and out of his lungs. That was the way it sounded when a man covered a woman's mouth so she didn't make noise. Tears formed in Grady's eyes. Lillian was such a fun and kind woman. He didn't want to imagine her eyes bulging as she gasped for breath. Or of the desperate sounds she would make as the man touched her body, hurting her.

Knuckling the tears away before they dropped, Grady grit his teeth. He could not cry. Tears made everything worse. When you cried, your nose got stuffy, making it harder to breathe. Crying only made them madder.

Grady shifted the large carton of cars and blocks that Peter had given him when he'd first moved in. It was Peter's first attempt to interest Grady in play. Then pushed the lower left corner of the east wall of his closet. A secret door clicked and opened toward him. Grady scooted through, ready to close it when Otto's nose pushed through behind him. Grady's chest felt warm. Otto wanted to come. Then Grady wouldn't be alone. So Grady pulled Otto through the secret door and closed it behind him. Peter had built a small area where Grady could sit and still listen to what was happening around him. Usually, Grady listened until the beating of his heart calmed and the terror-filled perspiration dried from his skin, then exited the hatch and returned to bed. Tonight, Grady would dial 911. But he wouldn't hide and wait. Tonight, he would run.

Grady buried his face in Otto's curly white fur, breathing in the familiar doggy scent. Otto poked him in the chest with his cold, black nose.

It was time to move. Grady took a firm grip on the top handle of the navy canvas backpack that Lillian had bought for him and filled with emergency materials. She'd loaded protein bars and fruit snacks, a spare power cord for his iPhone, Para cord, a fire-lighter, a high tech foil blanket, sunscreen, extra socks and underwear, soap and deodorant, a sporf, and a tin cup. Grady wrapped his other arm around Otto, holding the terrier's mouth closed. They descended a ductwork slide to a secret room at the back of the pantry. At this point, he could open another secret door and enter the pantry behind the sacks of dog kibble and cases of pop, or he could unlock the ancient milk door and be outside.

Yelling started, muffled by the walls and doors between it and him. Grady heard two voices aside from Peter's. A funny pop sounded, "sftt", a sound like a silenced handgun. Grady unlocked the milk door and crawled out behind the large juniper bush beneath the kitchen window. Otto followed him out. Turning back, Grady shut the door behind them.

Creeping along the edge of the house, ignoring the painful pricking of the bush, Grady made his way to the window that looked into the living room. There was a nozzle outside there for the garden hose. He used it to leverage himself up to the window, gripping the frame with his fingertips. He peered over the sill into the bright room. Peter was lying on the beige carpet with a pool of blood growing around his head. His head looked warped, all wrong, and Grady thought he was dead. He'd seen *dead* before.

Grady felt his body jerk, like a shock ripped through him. His thoughts got small, sort of like he could think about what was right in front of his eyes but not what it meant. His eyes wouldn't look at Peter anymore. Their gaze lifted until Grady saw three strangers in the living room, each with a handgun, each dressed all in black. One of the dark shapes moved aside. Now Grady had a clear view of Lillian. She was on her knees in her pink cotton nightie with her hands tied behind her back. There was a strip of silver tape over her mouth and her eyes bulged with fear. Tears slid down her cheeks. When their eyes met, hers widened for a moment. She attempted a smile. The tape had caught a few strands of her light brown hair and the movement pulled them taut.

Grady wanted to run. He wanted to rescue Lillian. He was so scared. Lillian smiled again and gave a little nod. Did that mean he should help? Should he run? She nodded again, just a tiny movement of her head. And then she looked away. Grady watched a minute more, wanting her to answer him, to tell him what to do. But she didn't look his way again.

Grady felt a tug on his pant leg. Ducking instinctively below the window, he pushed Otto's mouth away. The little dog wouldn't let go.

**Run.** Grady heard the word inside his head.

Grady didn't want to run. Peter and Lillian were the best people he had ever met. They said they loved him. And gave him things he liked, sat and read to him, never made him try to talk. They'd bought him the iPhone and taught him how to use the app so he'd have a voice. They told him about Jesus, this guy that God sent to save the world. Grady wanted to save Lillian and Peter.

A loud sound came from inside the house. Then another. A sob built in Grady's heart, making his chest burn.

**Run!**

Grady got as low to the ground as he could to peer into the side yard from beneath the juniper bush. No movement. His heart ached like it was crying. His head roared. His body shook.

**Run, Grady.** The voice was deep and gentle.

Grady ran. Otto ran beside him. Fifty running steps to the edge of the woods. Turn right, head north. One hundred running steps to the river. Twenty more steps to the small wooden pedestrian bridge. Run across it. Fifteen strides to the forest. Head west.

Grady ran until his side hurt and his breath sawed in and out of his lungs. Then he walked.

As dawn rose, he crawled into a berry bush in the middle of a forest, laid his head on his backpack, wrapped his arm around Otto, and slept.

# CHAPTER 17

Sergeant Rafael Cortez of the Combined Forces Special Enforcement Unit of the Calgary detachment of the RCMP paced the perimeter of a South Calgary living room. His stride was irregular to avoid the blood on the carpet and to keep out of Constable Myer's way. A wildlife photographer in his former life in Botswana, Myer now took pictures for the police. His keen eye for detail made him a real asset. Given the puzzle of this double homicide, Cortez needed all the help he could get.

"Lillian and Peter Clarke," Constable Eugene entered the room saying. "Nine-one-one hang-up call from a cell around two." Eugene was a new Canadian, having trained as a peace officer first in South Korea before emigrating and joining the RCMP. "She is an accountant who works from home. He is a contractor."

Eugene pointed beneath Peter Clarke's shoulder for Myer to note a scrap of black fabric stuck to the blood there. Rafe reminded Eugene to ensure that the fabric was tagged and bagged once Myer finished.

"Execution-style murder," Rafe murmured. "Hands tied behind them. Shot in the back of the head. Face down on the carpet. Woman gagged. Man not." He liked to hear the facts recited, even if he had to repeat them himself.

"Sergeant." Constable Reed entered the room. Rafe looked up and met her gaze. She was a young officer, but intuitive. "You need to see this."

Rafe followed her up the stairs, scanning the photographs hanging in the stairwell as he ascended. There were a variety of photographs of the dead couple, chronicling their story from wedding day to the present. Several shots showed the Clarkes with adults and children who shared physical characteristics. There were a few school photographs of a young dark-haired, olive-complexioned boy, but none of him at a younger age. No baby photos. No physical resemblance to the occupants of the house. Peter Clarke was of African descent and Lillian was Caucasian.

Rafe followed Reed to a bedroom.

"Did we know there was a child living here?" Astrid Knight, Rafe's partner, asked as she followed him in. She was taller than him at almost six feet, and sturdily built. She kept her long hair in a ponytail or a tight bun. He'd never seen her hair down. Tonight, it was fastened with a pink rubber band, the kind used to bind broccoli.

"Pictures in the hallway with various kids," Rafe noted. "But only the two bodies downstairs."

Reed opened the closet door, shining a light in. "Cars. Building materials. I'd say a boy. Young enough to still have toys."

"Search the house," Knight instructed Reed. "See if there's anyone else here we've missed, particularly someone small."

Rafe nodded and Reed left to search the nooks and crannies in the house.

Knight asked, "You see the pictures near the top of the stairs? School photos of a boy, looks to be about ten. Latino. None of him at a younger age."

Rafe nodded. That was odd. Unless Peter and Lillian Clarke had recently become foster parents or something. He would run a check when he got back to the station.

"There's something else," Knight said, interrupting his thoughts. "When I input the names and address to request details, I found this." She turned her phone toward Rafe. "FWPP has put a seal on the information."

Rafe frowned, looking closer. "Witness Protection?"

Knight nodded. "Whatever these people knew got them killed."

"Inform FWPP. Put out a BOLO for the kid."

Reed returned. "And a dog."

Knight turned to Reed. "What?"

"There's a pet dish in the kitchen and a bag of dog kibble in the pantry."

"Find a good pic of the kid from the wall. Circulate it," Knight said to Reed. "Finish your search. Make sure the kid really is gone and not hiding somewhere."

"Amber Alert?" Cortez asked.

"Not sure," Knight replied. "With Witness Protection involved. Don't want to lead something nasty to the kid."

Constable Eugene entered the room. "Sergeant, one of the neighbours says she's sure she heard the intruders speaking Spanish."

Rafe nodded. "Tell her we'll be by in ten minutes."

Eugene nodded and departed.

"Spanish. Interesting. You thinking The Outlaws? Or Mara Salva 52?" Knight asked.

Was this a revenge killing by one of the local motorcycle gangs or the California-based drug cartel moving into Calgary?

"Not sure," Rafe replied. "We better contact ALERT," the Alberta Law Enforcement Response Teams, "to see if they know what's going on."

"Right."

*What happened here and why? How did an accountant and a small time contractor fall afoul of a motorcycle gang or drug dealers?* Rafe scanned the boy's room, noting the television and comic books.

Knight moved closer to him. "I hope this kid didn't witness the murders."

*Me, too.*

# Chapter 18

Monday evening, Noah pushed his luck. *Fortuna iuvat.* Fortune favours the bold. And fortune had him standing at Ella's open front door, chatting while she smiled up at him. *Bien.* He leaned his shoulder against the door frame, crossing his right foot over his left. He hadn't made it beyond the threshold, but he was here. And she was happy to see him.

"There's a new movie coming to the cinema," he said. The house had an odd odour today, like burnt marshmallows. "And I wondered if you'd like to go see it on Thursday."

Ella's expression offered Noah little hope. "I, uh, am busy on Thursday," she said then added in a murmur. "Though I suppose I could wait until Friday or Saturday to do it."

"So you can cancel Friday's dinner or a Saturday hike or I'm out of luck with the movie?" He jammed his hands in his front pockets. He thought they'd made progress. Before she'd left to visit her family—without a hint she was disappearing—he'd been confined to church and Sunday lunch. Oh, and the occasional coffee. On the phone yesterday, she'd agreed to dinner on Friday and a hike on Saturday. Had he done something wrong? "What's happening Thursday, eh?"

"I have to paint my kitchen. I had a little fire—"

Noah straightened. "A fire? When? What happened?"

"Sunday. I put something on the stove then kind of got busy."

*A fire?* What was so important that it was worth risking a fire? "Doing what?"

A flush spread across Ella's cheeks. "I was on the phone with you, actually."

Brows furrowed, Noah scanned back through the phone conversation yesterday. She'd just returned from visiting her family. They'd talked about the weather, the recent robbery on Columbia Street, favourite vegetables, arranged a couple of dates. "You said, 'oops, I need to go', am I right?"

She nodded. "Flames. Big black stain on my wall."

*A fire.* She'd been in danger and hadn't confided in him. "Why didn't you tell me?"

Ella shrugged and ducked her head. "I don't know. Embarrassed, I guess."

"You should have told me." Her body stiffened. He'd made the mistake of ordering her again. He modified his statement. "I wish you had told me."

Her shoulders loosened, allowing her to shrug, this time with her chin high. "I decided it was a good excuse to paint the kitchen. I ordered a sunshine semi-gloss. It comes in Thursday and I thought I'd paint." She studied his left sandal, shrugging once. "Because ..." Her voice faded.

"Because you didn't want to cancel dinner on Friday?" he asked, hoping.

A one-shouldered shrug. "I guess."

Noah smiled. She wasn't looking, so he could grin his face off. "I can help you paint. If there's a 'big, black stain', you'll need to wash it down first."

She glanced up at him, annoyed. "I know."

"I'll pick up TSP and a bee-mop."

Her forehead wrinkled and then her eyes widened in disbelief. "You want to help me paint?"

"Sure."

"And clean?"

"*Oui.*"

"Why?" Her eyes narrowed.

Was it so unusual to be offered help? "I would rather spend the day working with you than doing anything else away from you." Noah wanted to reach out and smooth her furrowed brows with his fingertip.

Her forehead smoothed without his help. "Really?"

His smile softened. She was so clueless about her power over him. He would do anything to be with her. "Absolutely. Though I'm not allowed inside your house." He let that fact hang in the air.

"I…" She stopped, stepping closer to him. Her chin lifted, the movement raising her eyes to his.

He wanted to touch her, to press his palm against her cheek and feel the softness of her skin. He wanted to kiss her and make her admit that this was more than friendship. But she simply wasn't ready. He was walking on eggshells, hoping to keep her within arms' reach. One wrong move and he'd be out for good.

"You?" He lowered his head a fraction.

She swayed toward him then caught herself. "I would appreciate your help. Thank you."

"El?"

"Mhm." She was distracted by his sandal again.

He waited for her to look up so he could watch the play of emotions behind her eyes. "What colour is sunshine?" he asked.

She frowned. "Yellow. What else would it be?" She sounded defensive. Someone had done a number on her self-esteem at some point. She sighed in feminine pique. "Yellow makes me think of sunshine and warmth and laughter. It's a happy colour."

"Cool. Then that's what you should paint the kitchen." He heard the soft and gentle, positively gooey, tone in his voice.

"You think so?"

"Don't you?"

"Yes. But I assumed…" She shrugged.

"If yellow makes you happy, that's what you should do."

She smiled, reassured. "I like yellow. But red is my absolute favourite colour. It's bright and vibrant. What's your favourite colour?"

He considered that for a moment. "I don't have one."

"You must like some colours better than others."

"I like grass to be green and the sky to be blue. I don't mind if it's grey, though." Noah smiled. "And kitchens should be sunshine yellow."

She frowned at him. "Are you making fun of me?"

"Never." He moved closer, reaching out to slide his fingers down her arm.

She gave her cheek a little nibble. "Maybe...are you free tomorrow? I have Bible study on Wednesday, so I plan to prepare the kitchen on Tuesday. You could help me wash the walls."

"Okay. Cool."

He reached out again, just to slide the edge of his index finger along her cheek. She swayed toward him again. He resisted the urge to lean in and kiss her. He'd made enough progress for one day. An incredible amount in fact. She was going to let him in her house. *Glory be!* As his mother would say.

# Chapter 19

Grady Jones emerged from Fish Creek Provincial Park, a park within the boundaries of the city of Calgary, and onto Canyon Meadows Drive in Calgary south. Otto sat when ordered so Grady slipped his left arm out of his backpack and swung it around to his front. He sat cross-legged on the grass beside the dog to check the bus schedules on his iPhone.

He could take Bus 28 west to the Canyon Meadows Station then hop the 201 north to the Chinook Centre near Meadowlark Park. That would take fifty-two minutes. The 28 only ran every thirty minutes, and he'd just missed it. Grady's thumbs skimmed the screen. If he crossed MacLeod Trail road, he'd hop the number 3 north. The 3 departed every ten minutes and took only thirty-eight minutes to arrive. But Grady was in no hurry. He had nowhere to go and no one to help him, no one but Otto.

Grady rubbed the little dog's head. He would need to take a piece of Para cord from his go-pack and fashion a leash so they could travel on the bus together. Bus drivers never let you on with a dog unless it was on a leash or in a purse. That made no sense to Grady. Why would you ever need a dog so little it fit in your purse?

Between the Chinook Centre mall and Meadowlark Park, Grady figured he should be able to find a large box, gather newspapers, and make a hidey-hole. Food was easy to come by near a mall. There was a Greek restaurant, a burger joint, and a Red Lobster at the Chinook Centre. Lillian had taken him there a couple times to buy clothes for school. They had eaten gyros at the Greek restaurant. Grady closed his eyes as he tried to remember the peculiar texture and taste of the meat.

Pushing aside the memories, Grady rose and whistled for Otto to follow. They crossed the road to settle on the black, plastic bench inside the bus shelter. He also needed to find a public library to charge his iPhone. The battery was low. When you lived on the streets, you found all the public places that had free services like heat, water, and electricity. And crowds. On the streets, it wasn't safe to be alone. The last time he was living rough, Grady joined a mixed group of teens that didn't wear gang colours. As a cute little kid who didn't speak, he was a bonus to keep and protect. Everyone understood that little kids brought in the most money.

But Grady was older now. Even though he was small for his age, he'd started his manhood changes. Lillian acted like it was special and cool that Grady's armpits smelled bad. She bought him deodorant and encouraged him to shower every day. Grady wanted to smile at the memory, but he was too sad and worried. He worried that his smelly armpits would mean he would no longer be seen as cute. Grady wasn't big enough to fight for a place on the streets. Was he little enough to be sought? He needed an angle, something to make him valuable.

He and Otto needed shelter and food for the next few days until he made a plan. Would God take care of him if he was living on the streets?

Once the bus arrived at the Chinook Centre, Grady and Otto scouted through the mall to locate stores and restaurants that might have good garbage. He noted the groups of people in the mall including two groups of teens who might be street kids. There was a vibe detected by others who'd lived rough.

He and Otto made it until almost closing time before a security guard noticed Otto. And even though the Para cord made a good leash, the guard yelled and chased them.

Grady and Otto would shelter in one of the dark alcoves outside the mall tonight. With tomorrow being Monday, it would be easier to spot the street kids. They wouldn't be in school.

Grady sighed. At least being on the run meant that he didn't have to go to school either. School was hard when you didn't talk. Lillian said it was because sometimes the worst bullies were the tall ones who were meant to protect you. Grady already knew that. Adults were in charge and they were supposed to keep you safe. But Lillian and Peter were the first grown-ups Grady knew who tried.

Grady prayed. *Dear God, thank you for no school. Please give us food for today and a safe place to sleep for the night.*

That settled today. Tomorrow was for tomorrow's thoughts, that's what Lillian said.

# CHAPTER 20

When Ella opened the door to him on Tuesday evening, Noah held up two bee-mops in greeting. "Present and ready to work," he said. He readjusted the newspapers beneath his arm when they slipped.

"Come on in." Smiling, Ella stepped aside and gestured him into her house. For the first time. Without hesitation. One small victory.

It was a nice house, a little dated. The front hallway branched to the right into a living room. There was an eclectic assortment of furniture, blue plaid couch, beige overstuffed chair and ottoman, a wooden rocking chair. The centrepiece of the room was the bow window where someone had fashioned a seat, and scattered cushions. A flat-screen television sat in front of the window on an old-fashioned Clairtone cabinet-stereo system.

Noah leaned into the living room far enough to glimpse a dining set in the room beyond. He assumed that the hallway to the left of the front door led to the three bedrooms and second bathroom advertised with the house.

"The kitchen is this way," Ella said.

He removed his Keens and followed her down the hallway past the living room, a closet, and into a vintage 1970's kitchen. The stove was a hideous green which matched the walls. The white refrigerator looked newer as did the scarred oak kitchen table and three of the chairs. The fourth chair was a dark-stained pine of a different design. Cheap plywood cabinets hung on the walls over counters of butcher's block melamine.

Through the kitchen window, he saw a small elevated deck accessed by patio doors off the dining room. An antique dining set filled the dining room. And he was right. There was an excellent view of the mountains beyond.

"I brought newspapers to cover the cupboards," he said as he dropped them on the counter. *Though it might be merciful to paint them.*

"I have a couple of old bed sheets we can use to cover the furniture."

"Cool."

"Do you want a drink or something before we start?" she asked.

"No. I'm good."

Ella nodded, unfolding a cream-coloured sheet, tossing the other end to him. He grabbed it and together they moved it over the kitchen table.

There were stains on it. Coppery. Was that what it looked like? "Is that blood?"

Ella ducked her head. "Probably."

He tugged the fabric closer to study the stain. "You were bleeding? What happened? When?"

"Noah!" Ella's face turned a royal crimson.

Blood. Blush. Noah's mouth formed a silent "oh". His ears burned.

Noah wheeled about and began taping newspapers over the upper cabinets, keeping his mind carefully blank. Ella was still and silent. She was probably as embarrassed as him. What a dope he was.

Ella giggled. Noah spun. She was definitely blushing, but she was also laughing at him from her perch on the counter beside the sink. Her humour was infectious.

"You think this is funny?" he asked in mock indignation.

"Well, isn't it?" she asked, a grin on her face.

Noah paced toward her. Her uncertainty grew as he approached. He lunged, grabbing her around the middle and tickling.

Ella squealed, blocking his hands with one arm as she turned on the kitchen tap and squirted him with the hose. Noah pushed down the tap handle, cutting off the flow. Ella dropped off the counter and ran from the kitchen. He caught up to her in the hallway but she wriggled away and turned into the living room. When he crossed the threshold, she smacked him in the chest with a cushion. He wrenched it from her grip.

"Ow! Hey!"

*Cool it*, he told himself. This was play. *Settle.*

Ella grabbed a different cushion and hit him again, this time in the face. He hit her back with the cushion in his hand, being careful not to hit too hard. She backed away, grabbing a stuffed brown rabbit and two stuffed angry birds and flinging them at him. The birds' maniacal giggle fit the mood. Noah deflected them, tackling Ella onto the couch. She wrapped her arms and legs around him, trapping him.

They froze, eye to eye. Her eyes sparked with laughter, morphing into a growing awareness. He had no idea what expression his face held as he felt himself growing hard. It was time to back off, before she noticed.

Reaching behind him, he unwrapped her legs and sat back on his heels. Ella grinned at him, breathing hard. He grinned back. She was flushed, tousled and happy. His chest felt lighter, as carefree as he'd felt as a child, before life had taught him about grief and duty. Ella tapped a joyfulness within him he'd thought he'd lost when his mother died.

"All right," she said, tucking her legs up and twisting off the couch. "Back to work."

Noah agreed, following her back to the kitchen. He used his pockets to adjust himself, glad he'd worn overalls today.

"You look cute in overalls," she said over her shoulder.

Was she reading his mind? "Cute?"

"Like Huckleberry Finn."

"I remind you of a child?"

She paused in the doorway to the kitchen, glancing coyly over her shoulder. "You don't look anything like a child, Noah. Nuh uh. Not at all."

He smiled. "*Bien.* Good."

She hesitated as if she had more to say. Instead she grabbed a stack of newspapers and roll of tape and climbed up on the counter. To prevent any mishaps, Noah covered the antique table in the dining room with the second sheet, studiously ignoring any altered coloration in the fabric. It was only a couple of bleach stains, but still.

"Now what?" Hands on her hips, she surveyed the room.

Noah put two bottles of TSP on the counter. "Spray the walls. Wait a few minutes. Wash with the mop. Then rinse with warm water." He glanced around. "We need a bucket for water."

"There are buckets in the basement."

"I can get one."

"Okay. Bring the grey one. The green one is my puke bucket."

His steps slowed as he glanced over his shoulder at her. "You have a puke bucket?"

"Sure. If you have the stomach flu, eventually it gets too hard to drag yourself to the toilet. My father always brought a puke bucket to our rooms so we didn't have to walk to the bathroom anymore. So I have a puke bucket."

He pursed his lips as if considering her words. "Makes sense."

"Thank you." Pride glinted in her eyes.

He descended to the basement. It was dry and bright, with large windows overlooking the sloping back yard. A painted steel door opened onto a covered patio. Linoleum covered the floor, light oak panelling the walls. It was about half the size of the upstairs and built into the side of the hill.

Noah spotted the buckets in the laundry tub in the corner. He grabbed the grey one as instructed.

Upstairs, he filled it about halfway with hot water, dipped the bee-mop in, used the lever to squeeze out the excess water, and rubbed it over the walls. Then he sprayed the TSP. Noah spent extra time on the huge, black, carbon stain up the wall beside the stove hood. Whatever she had burned had made quite a mess. It bothered him she hadn't said anything. A fire was a significant event.

Ella grabbed the other bottle and started at the opposite end of the kitchen. "I was embarrassed."

"*Par-don?*" He turned toward her.

"I keep telling myself that you and I are just friends, just casual friends. But then I was so preoccupied by our conversation I forgot everything, even the pasta cooking on the stove. I put oil in the water so the pasta won't stick so when it boiled over and then boiled dry, the oil caught fire." She huffed a laugh. "It was stupid."

"You could have told me," he said. He continued to work because she was avoiding eye contact every time he looked over.

"I didn't want you to laugh at me. Or scold me. It's not like I did it on purpose."

"El-là." He stopped working and waited until she finally looked at him. "No one has ever been so distracted by talking to me that they've started a fire, not unless I was holding a gun on them."

She seemed discomfited by that statement.

"I would not have laughed at you," he insisted. "Or scolded you."

She nodded.

They finished the walls. Ella took the bucket and carried it to the kitchen sink.

"Don't dump it down there." Noah stopped her with a hand on her arm. "It will corrode your pipes."

"Oh. I didn't think of that."

"Is there a spot outside to dump it?"

"Yes. In the back corner of the yard. Just be careful. There's a fairly steep slope." She held the bucket out toward him. "Thanks."

"*Pas de problème.*"

"I'm hungry, but I need to wash. That chemical is bugging me. When you get back inside, can you order pizza if I leave the flyer on the counter? The phone's in the living room on a table beside the cozy chair."

"Am I invited for supper?"

She smiled, a twinkle in her eyes. "Yes, of course. You think I'd make you order food then kick you out?"

He lifted a brow comically. "Depends."

She sobered. "I'm just trying to be cautious. I don't mean to hurt your feelings." She looked sad. For him.

But he hadn't meant to make her sad. It was her smile which had enchanted him. Contrite, he said, "I didn't mean anything by it, El. I'd love to stay for pizza."

Her fingers brushed his arm. "Thank you for your help. I couldn't have managed without you."

He kissed her on the cheek, just a quick peck. But still, she blushed hotly.

"I would do anything for you, El."

He carried the bucket out before she could respond.

Ella washed her hands and changed her clothes. She brushed her hair before admitting that she was nervous. The more time she spent with Noah, the more she liked him. Sometimes he was moody, but usually funny and warm. He made her feel good about herself. Was she falling for this near-stranger who'd followed her to Kamloops?

As she stepped out of her bedroom, she heard his voice. He was getting more and more agitated by the sound of things.

"Well, what is your best deal?" She heard him say. Oh, yeah, he was ordering pizza for supper. "How am I supposed to know what you have on your menu?" he asked.

Bemused, Ella accelerated along the hall to the living room. Did the man seriously not know how to order pizza?

Noah was hunched over the small table with the phone. His clenched fist tapped the pizza menu on the little oak table as though he was in a slow motion fistfight with the restaurant. "Why would I want extra cheese? Don't you put enough cheese on it already?"

A giggle escaped her and he turned to scowl. The lilt in his voice flattened out when he became angry. It was the opposite of what she would have expected.

Ella put out her hand for the phone, wiggling her fingers for him to pass it over. He put it in her hand and walked away to stand in front of the bow window. He shoved his fingers into his curly brown hair.

"I would like a large supreme pizza, please. And a family-sized Caesar salad," she said.

The man on the other end sighed with relief. "Would you like a dipping sauce with that?"

"Yes, please. Creamy garlic."

"For delivery or pick up?"

"We'll pick it up."

"No we won't," Noah said, appearing beside her.

She suppressed a smile. "Could you deliver it, please?" She gave the man her address, and he told her "forty minutes."

Ella hung up to find Noah pulling two twenty-dollar bills out of his wallet. He placed them on the table beside her hand.

"Are you telling me that after nine years as an undercover police officer, you never had to order pizza?" She rubbed her upper lip to cover her smile.

"They're idiots." He scowled. "Am I responsible for that? How much cheese? What kind of sausage? Do you want mushrooms with that?" He mimicked a high-pitched, truly irritating voice. "*Idiot*."

A laugh sputtered out. "Poor Noah." She stroked her hand up and down his arm. "Poor Huck."

He propped his hands on his hips, learning toward her. "You're taking your life in your hands, *chérie*."

She hesitated only a moment before grinning at him. Somehow, she didn't think he'd take out his annoyance on her. Not for pizza. Or coffee. Or drug-dealing terrorists. "Next time, I'll order the pizza."

"See that you do." He was as cranky as a toddler without a nap.

She skipped away, stopping short at the kitchen doorway. "It'll be difficult to get dishes. And it smells in here." She turned to him, scrunching up her nose. "Picnic on the coffee table?"

"Sure." He still sounded belligerent but his expression was clearing. "If you have paper towels, we can use them as plates."

"Hm. I do." She pulled them from a lower cupboard. "We can eat the salad out of the container. Split it in half and each take one. No plates necessary." *Because there is no way I'm sharing a fork with a guy I barely know.*

Ella retrieved two sodas from the fridge and held them up as if to ask what he wanted.

"How about a beer?" he suggested.

*Is he a drinker?* "I don't have beer." She opened the fridge again and said, "There's grape juice, water," then straightened and showed him the pop again.

"Cola's fine."

This pizza supper was moving things to a more intimate level. Except there was no reason for that to be so. Friends shared pizza. Friends asked for beer. Alcoholics asked for beer, too. And she had no interest in spending time with an idiot who used booze to escape from life, a guy who became unhappy and accelerated his drinking to cope. She'd seen it far too often, alcohol used as a coping mechanism for pain or anger or disappointment. She wanted to know that she could count on her friends to be sober.

Ella set up the picnic in the living room, setting out doubled-over paper towels as plates and folding single sheets to use as napkins. She retrieved two forks from the utensil drawer and set them beside the "plates".

What did she know about this guy? He was an undercover officer, and he liked coffee. He carried a knife and knew how to remove a carbon stain from a kitchen wall. He drove a fancy sports car and had a weird determination to eat with her.

"El?" Noah touched her arm. "Everything okay?"

"Sure. Yes," she replied too quickly.

"Right." He looked and sounded doubtful. "I'll, uh, wash up now if you don't mind."

"Sure. Yes." She nodded toward the other room. "You can use the bathroom off the kitchen." It was a half-bath with a sink and toilet.

"All right." He was watching her carefully.

"Thanks for paying for the pizza."

"*Pas de problème.*" He nodded once then walked out of the living room toward the kitchen.

Ella slumped down on the couch. What was she fussing about? There was no need to plumb the depths of his neuroses on the first supper date, no need to examine every psychological issue he might or might not display.

Or hide. Because it wasn't a date, it was simply two friends sharing a chore and a pizza.

Ella paid the pizza delivery man when he arrived and then set the pizza and salad out on the coffee table. Noah joined her on the floor. He picked up the can of cola and seemed to be reading the ingredients.

"I don't have beer," she blurted.

Noah rotated his body, lifting his left knee and resting his arm on it. "Yeah. I got that."

"Okay." She nodded for no apparent reason. *What am I doing?*

"Is there something you want to ask me?" he said, his brows conveying his confusion.

*Remember, neuroses can wait.* "No, uh, not really. Let's eat."

Noah turned back to the coffee table, opening the can of pop and taking a sip. He dropped it back to the table. "*Dégueulasse.*"

"What?" Surprised at his response, Ella turned to him.

"This no-name cola tastes like buffalo urine."

Astonished, she laughed. "How would you know what that tastes like?"

Noah smiled crookedly. "Got anything else?"

She sobered. "I still don't have beer."

Noah furrowed his brows. "El? What's the deal with the beer?"

"Are you an alcoholic?"

"Seriously?" Noah's eyes widened in astonishment. "Asking for a beer makes me an alcoholic?"

"No, of course not. I—well, I know next to nothing about you except that you're obsessed with going to church with me. I don't know you."

"Isn't that what we're doing here? Breaking bread together to get to know one another?"

"Like dating?"

"I assume so."

"We're friends."

"Nice to know." Noah opened the pizza box and stared at the contents. "My family—I've seen a lot of hurt caused by the careless use of alcohol."

"I'm no drunk, Ella." There was no mistaking the irritation in Noah's voice. "Occasionally, I enjoy a beer. And Bourbon from time to time. I never *need* to drink alcohol. And I don't overindulge. That's a death sentence in my job."

"Right. Of course." Ella nodded again a few times. That made sense. Even though police officers were at risk for addictive behaviours because of the stress level of their jobs, an undercover officer would need to be sober and aware at all times to protect his life and the lives of those depending on him. Or her. No reason to consider female officers less diligent.

"Um." Noah's focus was on the pizza again. "Those mushrooms?"

"Yes?"

He pursed his lips, reaching out to finger one.

Ella couldn't help but smile. "Don't like mushrooms?"

"Hate 'em. They're all shriveled and grey and yuck. *Dégueulasse.*" He stuck his tongue out in a show of disgust.

His expression amused her, and she felt her mouth twist as she fought a laugh. "You can put yours on one piece and I'll eat them."

"Bless you, *chérie.*"

Ella laughed at the blatant relief on his face.

She finished her first piece in the time he took to harvest his. Another sip of cola confirmed his opinion of the cola. It was gross.

Removing the offending beverages, Ella returned with water. "I put on coffee. Would that be better?"

"Much." Leaning in, Noah kissed the corner of her mouth. "*Merci.*"

She nodded to hide the shudder that rippled through her body at the unexpected and yet sweetly tender gesture.

Noah bit into his pizza slice with glee. Then disgust. "*Pizza foutaise!* It tastes like baloney on a cardboard crust. Is this the only pizza joint in town?"

"Um, I don't think so." She took her second slice and sampled it. Maybe only her first piece had been good. But, no. "It's not so bad."

He took a smaller bite this time. "Have you been to Calgary?"

"Through it, but not to stay."

"The best pizza in the world." His expression morphed to near-ecstasy. "The Blue Ox, truly meat-tastic!"

"What were you doing in Calgary?"

Noah hesitated a moment before responding. "I was undercover there one winter looking for an embezzler who was using his position to funnel funds to crime. He'd run, but we knew he was in Calgary, and we knew that he was a pizza connoisseur."

Noah finished the one piece and then started in on the salad, knocking the croutons off before leaning over to fork a bite.

Without considering, Ella brushed her fingers through Noah's hair to remove strands of cobweb. The sides and back of his hair were short but there was still a length of looping, walnut curls on top.

"I love your hair." She twined a curl around her finger, testing the softness with her thumb. "It has a mind of its own." Her fingers sifted through, the warmth of his scalp heating her fingertips. "It's so soft. And there are flecks of red mixed in with the brown." She brushed her thumb over his eyebrow. "Your eyebrows are much darker." The backs of her fingers smoothed over his cheek to his jaw. "But your beard is so light, almost auburn."

Colour rose in his cheeks as he watched her closely, his body perfectly still. Startled by the intensity of his stare, Ella pulled away. He caught her hand and pressed the backs of her fingers to his lips. They were so soft. And warm. He straightened her fingers and tugged, kissing her palm. He worried the pad of her thumb with his teeth for a moment and then kissed the skin, licking lightly. Placing one final kiss on the centre of her palm, he lowered her hand, continuing to hold it.

Ella drew in a breath as intensity speared through her. He felt so good, smelled so good, the spicy scent of his aftershave blending with the pleasant, woodsy scent of his shampoo. She felt hot and cold all over.

"I should go," he said.

"Why?" Her eyes were droopy, her thoughts sluggish.

"Don't you want me to go?"

*Go? Do I want him to go?* "No. Um, there's a new comedy streaming. You could stay and watch an episode."

His gaze lightened. "Okay. Cool."

With her free hand, she used the remote to turn on the television and scroll to the new show. She shifted close enough that their shoulders touched. Though she wasn't sure why. Except that it felt nice.

# CHAPTER 21

It was nine-thirty at night and the Chinook Centre had been closed for half an hour. A few late-night shoppers exited by the west door, their heads down against the unseasonably cool breeze as they found their cars, got in and drove away. They might be driving home to put their kids to bed. Or maybe they would stop at the grocery store and pick up milk and bread and then go home. Or they might be planning to pop popcorn or boil water for hot chocolate to drink while they watched television before they crawled into their soft, warm beds.

Grady shivered and Otto whined, pressing his little body closer. It was the end of June, summertime. Why was it so cold? The cardboard crate they'd claimed for the past few nights was just a little too big to keep warm. Yet it was too early to go searching through the rubbish for newspapers to stuff around them for insulation. There were still too many people around to spot them and maybe call the authorities.

Grady squeezed his arms around his knees, pressing against his belly. He was so hungry that his stomach hurt. Peter said that God feels our pain and hears our thoughts. Grady wished He'd hear him now and order Chinese takeout. Grady loved chicken *soo guy* with almonds and chicken *lo mein*. But the Chinook Centre didn't have a Chinese restaurant.

Lillian said that God was not a vending machine, only around to give us treats when we ask. *Treats.* Like chocolate bars. Grady's favourite was Mr. Big. His stomach squeezed. It was a bad idea to imagine food.

There were plenty of boxes and crates at the loading bays to the mall so there was always a place to sleep. But food was a problem. There was a shelter in the city that had bartered a deal with the local restaurants to take their leftover food. Grady was glad for the shelter, but not for his empty belly. Even though he and Otto had haunted the mall and the park across the street for eight days, Grady hadn't found a group of youths that seemed safe enough to approach. Soon he might have to risk the kids in gang colours if he didn't find a source for food.

Tomorrow, he needed to take the bus to the Alexander Calhoun Library to charge his iPhone. He put it off because Otto didn't like to be tied to the seldom-used bike rack out back. But Grady needed the information and safety of his device.

Otto's head lifted as a man walked toward them. Grady shifted to a crouch so he was ready to run. He patted Otto's head to keep him calm and close. The man kept coming. There were only a few stragglers left at the mall. Even the employees had gone home. Not one of them even looked at Grady. He was invisible to everyone but the man moving closer.

"Hey, kid."

Grady settled his gaze on the man's face. He was Latino, broad but not too tall, with black hair and scruffy whiskers all over his chin and cheeks. He wore a dirty white apron over his large belly.

"Kid. Can you hear me?"

Grady nodded.

"Seen you here a few times." The man frowned when Grady didn't respond.

"Right." The man stepped closer.

Grady shifted to the balls of his feet to be ready to run away if the man tried to grab him. Releasing a low woof, Otto stood beside him.

Halting, the man looked back and forth between Grady and Otto. Then he shrugged. He dropped a brown paper bag on the ground at his feet. "Church on Tenth has a shelter. Probably don't care about the dog."

Grady watched the man walk across the parking lot to his rusty brown Volvo and unlock it. He removed his apron and tossed it into the back seat before he got in the car and drove away. He waved to Grady as he passed.

Once Grady was sure the man wasn't coming back, he crouched down to examine the paper sack. Otto sniffed, his nostrils flaring. Grady pushed his nose away and opened it. Grady drew in a deep breath that contained the scent of meat. Otto whined. Reaching in, Grady pulled out two plain hamburgers in buns and one naked meat patty. His stomach growled so loudly that Otto gave a start before turning his attention back to the paper sack.

Grady took a huge bite out of a hamburger. "Mmmm." The sound coming from his throat startled him.

He took out the naked patty and dropped it down for Otto who scarfed it in three bites. Grady took a little longer to finish his meal. It was the first food he'd eaten all day.

*Thank you, God, for this food.* Grady heard Lillian's voice in his head sounding just like she had when she'd taught him the prayer they said before eating. Maybe God did give us things sometimes. But he was better than a vending machine. He was free.

*Tenth Street.* Grady wasn't sure if the shelter was a good idea. Just in case, he folded the paper sack and placed it in his backpack. It still smelled of hamburgers and would be good to chew later.

# Chapter 22

Thursday evening, Noah stood on Ella's stoop again and rang the doorbell. He rang again when she didn't respond. Had she forgotten that they were painting tonight? After that intense moment they'd shared on Tuesday, perhaps she was hoping he would forget. Not a chance. He wasn't likely to forget an opportunity to spend time with her or pass up the possibility of coaxing this relationship to the next phase.

Ella opened the door with a groan, pulling her blanket tighter around her shoulders. "Hi." She tried to smile but sneezed instead.

"You're sick." Noah reached out and rested the backs of his fingers against her forehead. "Fever, too."

"I can't paint tonight," she croaked miserably.

"No, I don't suppose you can." If he walked away now, would that put them back where they'd been prior to Tuesday? He didn't want to lose that ground. She'd touched him, voluntarily put her hands on him. And working together had been fun. Relaxing. A chance for her to see him holistically as a man rather than the weird-o who'd chased her to Kamloops. He wanted to stay.

Inspiration lightened his outlook. "You can still boss me around."

"Boss you? Huh?" Ella sniffed.

"Want me to leave you with newspaper chic?"

She huffed. "Not really, but..." Then shrugged.

Taking her by the upper arms, Noah shifted her and stepped inside. Grabbing the overstuffed chair from the living room, he moved it to the hallway near the kitchen. Then he shifted the ottoman to sit in front of it. He gathered the roller, pole, paint tray and paintbrushes he'd bought for the occasion.

"How did you get all that in your tiny car?" She wiped her nose on a tissue as she held the door open for him.

Instead of answering, he took her hand and led her to the chair he'd moved. He snugged her in. "You sit here and tell me what to do. Okay?"

"You sure?" she asked on a sneeze.

He kissed her on the cheek. "I'm sure."

Noah opened a can of sunshine yellow and poured it into the paint tray.

"Music," Ella said gruffly. Gruffly only because her throat was sore.

"Your wish," he replied. She told him how to hook her iPad into the speakers and find her play list.

"Can you please get me a ginger ale?" she asked.

"*Oui*." There was a Brita water pitcher, name-brand cola and ginger ale, and a carton of flavoured iced coffee in the fridge. She was trying to find him something to drink that didn't taste like buffalo urine. He smiled at the gesture as he reached beyond the coffee to find a ginger ale for her. He delivered it with a glass and two Tylenol.

Within an hour, Ella was snoring gently in the chair. Filling his roller with sunshine yellow, Noah covered the walls, transforming the bland room into brightness. If he was prone to maudlin moods, he might consider that Ella had brought the same transformation to his life.

Growing up as the child of a diplomat had been exciting, unpredictable, always an adventure. The ability to move at a moment's notice, to never attach too quickly or securely to people or places, had perfectly prepared him for undercover work. But it had also created a sense of dispossession, of never having a home. His mother had been his touchpoint. That was why, when she'd died, it hadn't seemed so bad to be sent away. Without his mother, nowhere seemed home anymore.

But Ella, she drew him to her like no one had in his adult life. With her bright smile, inner joy, and her strong convictions, she tugged at his heart. She grounded him, made him want to be a better and more stable man. He'd never have guessed that one day he'd give up his career and his bachelorhood to follow a woman across the country. But then he'd never met a woman like Ella Hanover.

Noah put the last stripe of paint on the wall and stepped back to survey his work. Not bad. He turned to Ella who snorked as she shifted in her chair. He chuckled. She was adorable.

After he'd cleaned up the kitchen, he washed out his brushes and roller and left them to dry in Ella's basement. Once upstairs, he took a moment simply to watch her sleep. She shifted in the chair seeking a more comfortable position.

"Come on, *chér*." Noah kissed her hand and then her forehead.

She stirred. "Dad?"

"Nope."

Her eyes flickered open. "Noah?"

"*Oui*. Time for bed."

"Hm. Did you paint my kitchen?"

"I did."

"Thank you," she sighed. "You're the best."

Her words warmed him. With the blanket snugged around her, he used it to tug her to her feet. "Off to bed." His arm around her shoulders, he led her down the hall. There were two bedrooms at the back of the house, a bathroom, closet, and another bedroom at the front. Hers was the only bedroom decorated.

"Go do your bathroom thing." Once she'd closed the door, he called in to her. "Where do you keep your bedsheets?"

"What?"

"Never mind," he murmured.

He located her linen closet, the narrow door between the bathroom and front bedroom. Within, he found a complete schmozzle of fabric, a riot of colours. She had serious issues folding bedsheets. He found a matched set.

At the threshold of her bedroom, he felt an unexpected reluctance. This was her sanctuary, her place of peace and escape from the world. And he wasn't sure he belonged. A faded pattern of pink and red roses decorated the wallpaper. There were a few paintings and family pictures on the walls. A few of these he recognized from his brief survey of her Vancouver apartment when he'd searched for her the day after Longford had snatched her. The bedframe was a double with a wooden spindle design. The mirrored dresser set matched the oak of the bed. A feather duvet covered in bright dots and swirls lay in a heap on the bed. An antique quilt was discarded at the foot on top of a wooden chest. She had created a reading alcove with a bronze velour chair and three mismatched IKEA-style bookcases that was lit by a rear-facing window. A flexible floor lamp hooked around the chair.

Noah changed the sheets on her bed and went back for pillowcases.

She emerged from the bathroom clad in cotton pyjamas with yellow bunny rabbits on them. Her face was damp as were the bangs on her forehead. She looked uncertain.

Noah gestured her over. "Let's go, *bébé*. Into bed."

When he pulled back the covers, she turned to him and said, "You changed my sheets? Why did you change my sheets?"

"In."

She climbed into bed with a frown on her face and pulled the covers up to her chin. Wary, she studied him.

"Does it feel good?" he asked.

"Mhm."

He tucked her in and kissed her on the forehead. "Good night."

She cupped his cheek, stroking his beard with her thumb. "Thank you." She still seemed pensive.

"I'll lock up when I leave," he said.

Her entire visage brightened. So he'd passed some sort of test. *What did she think? That I'd try to get it on with her when she was sick?*

"Mm," she replied, already falling asleep. "Thanks."

"You're welcome."

# Chapter 23

The shelter on Tenth was closed when Grady arrived with Otto. It took all day to decide to go there. He thought so long and hard they missed the last bus and had to walk, only to find that the shelter was closed for the night. That was okay. It was a warm night.

Grady led Otto around to the back of the building and huddled there. He slept a bit. Otto didn't sleep at all. Instead, he spent the night sniffing the air and growling at every little thing. Grady tried to tell him it was only rats in the dumpster across the alley, but dogs were dumb that way.

Grady and Otto spent the morning at a park nearby and then joined the line for food at lunchtime. No one questioned him about Otto.

*Soup.* Grady sighed. They always gave you soup at shelters. At least it was chicken soup, not tomato. Lillian made tomato soup once. Grady had taken one look and thrown up on the kitchen floor. Because it looked like blood. Then he'd run and hidden in the bushes at the side of the house. It had taken Lillian two hours to find him but when she'd taken him by the arm, he'd followed her back into the house. Once you were caught, it was usually better to accept the beating. It was only worse if you ran away again. If Grady stayed hidden for twenty-four hours, the adults usually forgot why they were so mad. Especially his guardians who had to call the Mounties when he went missing. If they showed up, and he was bruised, the Mounties sent him to a new house and the guardians didn't get paid. That was how Grady had gotten away from Durvan Henden and his wife, Tamzin.

Lillian hadn't beaten him though. And she'd cleaned up his sick before she brought him back to the kitchen. She hadn't mentioned the soup, never served it again. She'd made him grilled cheese sandwiches for the first time that day.

Grady tore the white bun that came with the soup in half and slipped a piece to Otto beneath the plastic table. Then Grady finished his soup and ate the other half of the bun. The shelter had juice boxes so Grady popped the little straw in and sucked back the apple flavoured liquid within it. The drink was very acidy but helped fill his stomach.

Once he'd eaten, Grady led Otto out of the dining area and down a hall. He walked toward the sound of children playing. Usually, he had little success interacting with kids, but it might be worth a try in exchange for a steady supply of food, and a bed. At least until he was ready to continue his journey west.

"Hello."

Grady spun at the unexpected greeting. A slender blonde lady stood behind him. She wore a plain blue dress and white sneakers on her feet. She looked tired but happy.

"Can I help you?" she asked.

Grady whistled for Otto to sit. So the lady didn't notice his shaking hands, he squeezed his trousers. Sometimes adults got mean if they thought you were scared.

The blonde lady's face got serious, and she bent down so she was closer to him. "Are you okay, honey?"

Grady pointed to his throat. He'd learned in one of the books that Peter had showed him about the human body that your voice came from your throat not your mouth. Peter had bought the book to help Grady understand his manhood changes.

"Are you sick?" she asked as she reached toward his head with the back of her hand.

Grady flinched away before she made contact, shaking his head. Otto rose but Grady snapped his fingers, instructing the dog to sit. The lady straightened up again. She wasn't a lot taller than Grady, not like Lillian who was five-foot-seven. But Grady knew she could hurt him if she tried.

"Excuse my poor manners. May I touch your forehead to see if you have a fever?" she asked. Folding her hands in front of her, she waited.

Grady felt his forehead crinkle in a frown. Would it do any harm if she touched him once? *Probably not.* Grady nodded slowly.

"Thank you," she said then placed the backs of her fingers gently against his forehead. "You don't feel warm. Are you feeling sick?"

Grady shook his head.

The lady pouted her lips and tapped her chin a few times. "Do you have a place to stay?" she asked.

Grady shook his head again. He knew he could use his device to answer her questions, but he didn't want anyone to know he had it. Any electronic device was gold on the streets. He didn't want it stolen.

"Would you like to stay here for a few days?"

Grady thought about that for a little while. He was on his way to Vancouver to find his Uncle Macken and show him that he didn't remember anything about the night his uncle and his father had a fight. He'd decided that was the best plan. But Vancouver was a long way from Calgary. This place had food and a roof and beds with mattresses. He and Otto could be warm and fed for a few days. That would be okay, wouldn't it? This seemed like a good place to find sanctuary.

Grady pointed at Otto who sat obediently at his side watching the woman.

"Your little dog is welcome to stay with you, though I'll expect you to watch over him and clean up after him. Does that sound fair?"

Grady nodded.

"Good, now that's agreed. Welcome to Bethsaida." She held out her hand. "My name is Rosalie."

Grady thought she wanted him to shake her hand, but he wasn't sure. It could be a trick to grab him. Grady looked around the hallway. People were coming in and out of rooms but no one was paying attention to them. If she grabbed him, he would kick her. His hiking boots had a heavy tread. They would hurt. Then he'd run out the front door before anyone stopped him.

Grady looked back at Rosalie and then shook her hand. She released his hand and led him back the way he'd come, but rather than sending him out the front door with the other people who'd come to eat, she led him up the stairs.

# Chapter 24

Noah parked his CR-Z in Ella's driveway. He was taking a chance, showing up unannounced. Over the past few weeks, they'd spent more and more time together. However, each dinner, hike, or movie was carefully negotiated.

Noah gathered the food he'd purchased, locked the car, and made his way to Ella's front door. She opened after his second ring of the doorbell.

"Hello," she said, surprised. "Did we make plans I forgot?"

"Nope. Just thought I'd pop by," Noah replied, lifting the bags in his hand. He moved forward to enter and she moved aside to let him. *Excellent.* Step one achieved, *got inside the door without an engraved invitation.*

"You can take those into the kitchen. We can eat in there. I love spending time in there since you painted it for me," she said.

"So you're happy with it, eh?" he asked, setting the bags on her scarred oak kitchen table. He ran his palm across the top. One of these days, he wanted to get her something nicer.

"Oh, yes." She smiled happily. "I love it. I'm thinking I should paint the rest of the house." Her expression dimmed for a moment and then she surprised him. She wrapped her arms around his chest in a brief hug. "Thanks. For painting." She released him before he got his arms up to return the embrace.

"You're welcome," he murmured. He couldn't look away. She was beautiful even when the smile dimmed from her eyes. Why had he ever thought her plain? "I'm glad you like it. And you know where to find me when you want to paint."

"Curlew Road," she replied. "I drove by your apartment building yesterday."

That was a good sign. He was on her mind even when out of view.

"What's for supper?" Ella scanned the assortment of Styrofoam, paper, and plastic on the table.

Noah dropped his gaze to the table and opened the containers. "German food," he replied, adding, "Kamloops-style. I found a restaurant near Victoria Street. I got chicken schnitzel with creamy mushroom sauce, Applewood smoked beef, Bruschetta, Asiago Cheese Crisps, and artichoke crab dip." He revealed the *piece-de-resistance*. "Apple strudel with whipped cream for dessert."

"Oh, this looks sumptuous. Thank you." Ella retrieved two dinner plates from the cupboard and assorted cutlery from the drawer. "See. I told you that Kamloops was big enough."

He lifted a brow in a stern expression. "Pizza *foutaise*, though. *Dégueulasse*. I thought I'd have to drive to North Vancouver to get anything good."

She shrugged but her mouth quirked up in a smile. "There might be places with better pizza. I don't know. I've only lived here two months longer than you."

"I guess we'll find out if you're determined to stay here."

Ella paused as she forked a piece of schnitzel onto her plate. "What do you mean?"

"If you're here, I'm here. Haven't I made that clear?" he asked.

"I…just…" Her voice faded. Her cheeks darkened and she averted her eyes.

"Just what?" he asked. She didn't understand. He was here, in this tiny corner of nowhere, for her. To be hers. He was aiming higher than *friends*.

She met his gaze, her face pinched in confusion. "You hate it here."

Was that true? He didn't like the city. It was small with few of the amenities he was used to. Her bungalow had promise, though. The hiking trails in the city and surrounding area were abundant and, frankly, amazing. "I don't hate it. It's just small."

"What will you do? I mean, you were an undercover cop. There can't be much need for that here."

"I got a job at Thornton's. You know it, the garden centre at the eastern edge of town?"

"Bob Thornton? He goes to my church."

"I know that," he said, trying not to sound irritated by her comments and questions. "It was Nagi that put me in touch with him."

"Enoch?"

Noah nodded. *How many other Enoch's were there living in this century?*

"You're doing what for Bob Thornton?" She took a handful of the cheese crisps and placed them on her plate.

"Landscaping. Lugging dirt, carrying rocks, whatever."

"That's a very different job than what you had before, chasing terrorists and infiltrating criminal organizations. Do you like it?"

"I like being outside. The grunt work will keep me fit. So, yeah, it's all right."

Ella chewed her lip for a time while Noah resumed filling his plate.

"If you planned on staying, would that be enough to satisfy you?" she asked. "I mean I can see wanting something different for a while. But long term?"

He shrugged casually. "It will do for now. I have over a month until I need to decide."

Ella took out the mushroom sauce and poured it over her schnitzel. When she offered it to him, he shook his head.

She asked, "So if you decided to return to undercover work, you'd be leaving soon?"

He was heartened that she at least seemed ambivalent at the prospect. "I don't know what I want to do. Though I do know I want to be with you."

"But, Noah, for how long? How long will it be worth it?"

"Always, *chérie*." Noah placed his plate on the kitchen table then cupped her cheek with his palm, forcing her gaze off the food and onto him. "I'm not looking for something temporary. If you kick me to the curb, I guess I will have to find a different future. But I've lived long enough in the company of liars and villains. No matter what, I'm not going back to undercover work."

Ella resumed filling her plate but kept sneaking surreptitious peeks at him. "If you hate it here in this *teeny, tiny town*, then you're not going to be happy staying here long term."

"Are you planning to stay long term?"

"Yes. I've been looking for years for a place to work exclusively with children. Because the counselling practice covers such a wide geographical area and demographic, I get to do what I love most. I'm not saying I'll never move, but I came here to settle down."

"Okay. Cool. That's fine with me. I'm not asking you to move."

She set the plate down hard enough to clatter on the table. "But it's not fine. You can't just hang around for months lugging rocks."

He huffed out a breath loaded with garlic. "Ella. We are going around in circles. What do you want to know, eh?"

"Nothing. Just think about it."

"Ella." Impatience bit into his voice. There was no denying they were growing closer. She liked him, he was convinced of the fact. He saw it in her eyes, read it in her posture. What was all the fuss about?

Grabbing an empty paper bag, Ella crushed it brutally in her hands. She dodged his arms and strode to the sink, opening the door beneath it to shove the bag into the garbage pail. Her movements brusque, she turned on the water and washed her hands. "What is the point of falling—all of this if you're just going to leave in a month or so?"

In one step, Noah moved to her side. His hand gripped the counter hard enough to whiten his knuckles. "I'm not going to leave. Isn't that what I just said?"

"No." She met his gaze, a mix of emotions swirling in her eyes. Those beautiful eyes lowered to his chest again. "You said you hated this small town. You said you were only staying for six months and you've already been here for nearly five. I don't see what the point of investing all this time if you're going to pull up stakes and leave in a month."

"That is not what I meant." Noah straightened, releasing his hold on the counter. He stepped closer, right into her bubble of personal security. "Ella," he whispered. "*Chérie.*"

When she still wouldn't look at him, he cupped her chin gently. She pulled out of his grip. He turned to face the opposite wall, crossing his arms over his chest as he leaned back against the counter. "I said that they had pizza *foutaise.* That the variety of restaurants was small. You live in a small city, three hours, minimum, from civilization. But this is the digital age. I googled German restaurants and found this one. I also found a pizza place across town that sells New York style pizza. Next week, I'll check it out. I am not leaving in a month unless you make it plain that I have no hope. Even then, I might stick around and try to change your mind."

She gulped the whispered, "Hope of what?"

"El." Frustration rose within him. He was falling for her. How did she not know? Was she obtuse? Or was she playing with him?

"But what would you do about your job?" She peeked up at him.

Huffing out a breath, he flung his arms wide as he turned to face her. *She will not listen.* "Ask for a transfer here? Get a job with the local police? Set up a private security business. There are lots of options. I have a little money set aside." He tapped his knuckles on the counter. "I will find something to do."

Her eyes searched his face. "This is just all so weird."

"Weird and wonderful?"

"I guess."

Ella moved the rest of the half-emptied cartons and bags to the counter and then sat at the kitchen table. Noah sat across from her.

"Do you want something to drink?" she asked. She was trying to sound calm and comfortable but there was still an edginess to her manner. "I think I'll have water. So I don't spoil the flavours."

"Water's fine. I'll get it." Noah retrieved a couple glasses and filled them from her Brita pitcher. He placed one on the table in front of her and placed the other beside his own plate.

"Do you have family, Noah?"

He groaned inwardly. So this was her agenda for the evening, annoying him into leaving? "Some."

"Tell me about them."

He sighed. "Mother, father, two brothers." He took a big bite of schnitzel. It was succulent, the breading the perfect blend of spice and crisp.

"And?" She huffed a laugh as she gestured for him to continue. "Where are your Mom and Dad? And your brothers? What do they do? And where were you born anyhow?"

"Burkina Faso."

She stilled, her eyes widening. "Very cool. That's in Africa, isn't it?"

"West Africa, between Mali and Niger."

"Oh." She squinted at him as if trying to divine his connection to Africa. "Um, where are your parents from?"

"Smooth," he said.

She frowned at him.

"You were trying to figure out how a Burkinabe was born so pale."

She grinned and then laughed. "You think I was trying to avoid offending you? Noah, my family contains every shade of brown there is. I can't figure out how you got Canadian citizenship if you were born in Burkina Faso."

"Shade of brown?" he asked.

"Well, yeah." She gestured between them with her fork. "Every human is a shade of brown, Noah. It's all in the melanin. I've never understood why people talk about red and yellow, black and white. We're all just brown."

Noah smiled. It was a genuine smile that started in the warmth of his belly and spread throughout his heart and mind. "So we are."

"How did you end up a Canadian citizen?"

"My father is in the diplomatic corps. I was born in Burkina Faso because he was stationed there at the embassy in Ouagadougou. My mother was the child of missionaries in Burkina and, I guess, she'd asked my father to request station there so she could reconnect with her parents."

"Cool." A genuine smile had taken up residence in Ella's eyes. Noah couldn't look away. "Where were your brothers born?" she asked.

"Frank Junior was born in Finland during a vacation. Sammy was born in Morocco."

"That's neat," she said, smiling. "What about your Mom?"

"She died. When I was fourteen."

"Oh, Noah." Her expression softened. She had such a kind heart. "Fourteen. That's such a difficult age. I'm so sorry. How did your father cope?"

"He sent us away." Noah shrugged one shoulder. "We were living in New Delhi. Frank was seventeen, so he stayed to finish out his education. My father sent me to live with my mother's brother in Montreal. Sammy, my younger brother, was sent to Philadelphia to my father's parents."

Ella's eyes widened in shock. "It must have been so awful to lose your mom and then be sent away."

"I was used to it. We'd lived all over the world." Noah rose to place their dishes in the sink.

"That's a blithe reaction for a grieving fourteen-year-old."

"My mom was gone, El. It didn't much matter after that."

Her eyes were full of such sorrow that he looked away, out over her back yard. There wasn't much to see at this time of night. But it was better than watching her grieve over something he'd put behind him a long time ago. He had loved his mother, still did. Part of her, his memories of her, would always be with him. But she was gone. And a river of tears wouldn't bring her back.

"Was your uncle good to you?" Ella asked. Her voice was soft and full of some emotion he couldn't quite guess.

Noah dropped his gaze from the window to the sink. He filled it with hot water, squirting soap in. "Define good."

"Loving, caring, supportive."

"Then, no." He rubbed the dishcloth over the surface of his plate.

Ella moved to stand beside him. She put her hand on his back, between his shoulder blades. "Your aunt?"

"Mm." He pretended to think about it then turned to her, repeating, "no."

"Was there anyone kind in your life? After…" Her voice drifted.

Noah looked down at her, seeing compassion brimming in her eyes. "Mrs. Patel, a lady who'd grown up in Mumbai. When things got bad at my uncle's, I'd knock on her door and she'd feed me real tea, rather than the English kind, and *jelabies*. They are these saffron-coloured pastries cooked in ghee and smothered in a sugary syrup. Greatest food I've ever tasted."

Ella's deep brown eyes swam with care and concern. "With all this against you, how did you get to be so nice?"

*What?* "Nice?"

"Well, sweet."

"Sweet!" he replied indignantly.

Ella laughed, her sad mood breaking with the act. "Never mind," she said. She retrieved the box of strudel and brought it to the table.

Noah dried his hands. "Want to share it out of the box?" She'd shared Caesar salad with him. Although there'd been a clear delineation between his portion and hers. Would she share strudel?

"Um, sure. Can you get clean forks? I don't want to mix mushroom sauce with whipped cream."

Noah complied. "Want coffee with dessert?" He asked the question slowly, expecting the chuckle he received. Because he still had not mastered the use of her single-cup coffee brewer. It required him to grind beans and fill a small basket with the grounds and then place them in the correct position on the coffee maker. He was unable to produce a drinkable cup of coffee using it.

"Can't order pizza," she murmured with mock-disgust, "Can't make coffee." Then her face brightened in an all-consuming smile. It sparkled with joy in her eyes. "If you press the power button, I'll make the coffee when it heats."

Noah returned her smile. It burst from his chest and took over his expression. "Great. Thanks." He pressed the power button.

"Oh, this is wonderful." Ella moaned in pleasure at the first spoonful of strudel. Noah shifted to make himself more comfortable. She had no idea the effect she had on him. She was so innocently sexy.

When she held a forkful for him, he took it into his mouth, agreeing, "It is good."

They ate in silence for a few moments, a silence that was finally relaxing and comfortable.

Ella took the last bite, stealing it right off his fork.

"Hey." He protested just to make her laugh.

"Let's play Scrabble," she suggested, smiling around the whipped cream. She swallowed. "English words only, though."

"Bigot," he accused without any heat.

Ella looked uncertain a moment and then relaxed into a laugh.

They played the game. Ella soundly trounced him. Even though she yawned her way through the final few turns.

"Next time we play French Scrabble," Noah proclaimed. "Then maybe I can win."

Smiling, Ella walked him to her front door. "Good night, Huck," she said. "I had fun."

This time when Noah said good night, he kissed her. Before he asked permission. Before he reconsidered. He pressed his mouth against hers, keeping the kiss light. He'd kissed her before, on the cheek and on the forehead. He'd kissed her knuckles, her palm. But this was different. So much better. Her mouth was so soft. Before he thought better of it, he licked out to get a better sample. She tasted like coffee and cinnamon. Ella parted her lips and reciprocated the action. All the blood in his body shot to his groin. She tilted her head to kiss him from a different angle and he was lost. He tasted her deeply, testing the surfaces in and around her mouth, licking, suckling, tasting. She wrapped her arms around his neck, pressing closer.

With her back pressed against the front door, he spread his legs to get closer. One hand cupped the back of her head. His other hand gripped her waist, sliding down to cup her bottom.

*Oh. Need to stop. Don't go too far.* He pulled back slowly, releasing his hold on her.

Ella's eyes slowly opened to meet his gaze. "Wow," she breathed the word on a sigh, wonder in her voice.

"*Oui.*" His voice was husky, even to his own ears. Noah stood straighter, allowing the movement to increase the distance between them.

"I knew it would be like that," she whispered as she rested her forehead against his chest.

One hand slid to her shoulder while the other settled at her waist again. "I hoped."

"I'm—Noah?" She rested her palms on his chest, meeting his gaze directly. "I'm not ready for this. I need more time."

He released her as frustration jacked through him. Raising his arms to tangle his fingers in his hair, he turned away. "Why? Why is it always a problem for you?"

He felt her hand on his back, caressing him between his shoulder blades. "Is it a big deal to continue on as friends a little longer before we move into romance? You say you've come all this way to be with me. Am I not worth a little patience?"

Her sweet voice touched him in a heart that wasn't used to holding and staying. Turning, he pulled her into his arms. She responded by hugging him around the waist, resting her cheek against his chest.

"I guess," he said, begrudging the need.

She spoke softly. "I like you, Huck. I've never been in such wonderful relationship."

"I want more."

He felt her smile widen against his shirt. "You always want more."

Noah grunted in reply, pulling away to stand against the opposite wall. He shoved his hands into his front pockets.

Ella stood across from this man who had come to mean so much to her, and waited. She waited until she was sure she was strong enough to resist his petulant need. "All I'm asking for is a little more time." She kept her voice even. "We hardly know each other."

His brow furrowed darkly.

Firming her lips, she held in her bemused smile. "You're behaving like a cranky toddler."

"So?" he retorted.

"So, it's unattractive." Which was a barefaced lie. He looked adorable standing there pouting and demanding she love him. "Noah." She reached for him but he pulled away, crossing his arms and averting his gaze.

What did this complex man need from her? He was belligerent and demanding and yet sweet and loyal. And, really, all he demanded was space in her life. Or, a piece of her heart. *Yes, that's what he wants.*

But did she trust him enough to give him that piece?

*No.* Because he didn't believe what she believed. They were good together in the short term, their friendship grew stronger every day, but the differences between them would destroy their relationship in the long term. The realization saddened her. It worried her. Affection. Friendship. Passion. Humour. These were not enough to hold a marriage together. You had to have common goals, common beliefs, common ambitions. They had none of these in common. In time, that would tear them apart.

"We need to have a conversation," she said. *I thought we would have more time to figure these things out. It's all moving faster than I expected.*

"Another conversation?" He scowled at her. "What else do you want to know? Did I cry when my mother died? Have I ever sought 'closure' with my father?" He used air quotes and an obnoxious intonation to emphasize his disdain at the idea.

"What sent your grandparents to Burkina Faso to serve as missionaries?"

Noah straightened against the wall. "What?"

"Why did they go?"

"I don't know." He looked thoroughly confused.

Ella regrouped. This wasn't going to get her the answers she wanted. "Did your mother take you and your brothers to church?"

"Sometimes. She was never much for organized religion. Why?" He shoved his hands in his pockets. "What exactly do you want to know?"

She chewed her cheek. That was becoming a bad habit. She spent far too much time gnawing her own face these days. "Are you a Christian?"

"That's what this is all about?" His dialect flattened-out. Noah strode the two steps to the front door then turned on her. "You've been stringing me along for months so you can fill your quota of converts?"

And that was that! Anger and betrayal surged within her. In a sudden movement, Ella forced herself between Noah and the door. She gave him a hard shove. "How dare you? How dare you accuse me of subterfuge? You're the one who put me under surveillance. You completely violated my rights to privacy, not to mention I ended up arrested. Arrested! Because of you! Then those guys grabbed me."

Ella opened the front door, grasped Noah's shirt and tugged him toward the opening. She was about as successful as if she'd tried to move a hundred-year-old Douglas Fir. "I changed my mind. Get out." Who was she kidding? They had no future together. Her ridiculous fantasy was just that.

"El." Noah closed the door before she ejected him. "Calm down."

"No." Tears flooded her eyes but she refused to let them fall. Not for him. "You're a jerk."

"I know that," he acknowledged, his voice soft and tender. "I'm sorry."

She glared at him. "Go away." Then wrapped her arms around herself.

"I was a jerk." Noah bent his knees, bringing him down to her level as he tried to catch her eye. He was so much taller and bigger than she was. She often forgot that. "I've only been thinking about what I want and what I need to do to get it," he said. "I didn't stop to ask what you needed." He tapped her chin gently with his finger. "I'm asking now. What do you need?"

"I don't know," she whispered. She kept her gaze down so he was talking to the top of her head. Because she didn't want to see the caring in his eyes. She didn't want him to sway her. Not when the stakes were so high.

"I think you do." The sweet and tender pull of his voice called to her. "I think you have a clear idea of what you want from me."

"Maybe. But I don't know how to ask for it."

"Do you want sex?" he asked, his voice soft and sweet.

Her head jerked up. "No! No, no, no." She couldn't let him think that. She repeated the word again so there was no mistake.

Noah's eyes widened in astonishment. "Okay. Well. That's a negative." His bronzed cheeks darkened to an intriguing shade of crimson.

It was nice to know that she wasn't the only one who ended up embarrassed at the topic of sex.

"What is it then?" he asked.

"I don't want sex. That's what I want."

His face contorted in confusion. "What?"

She sighed heavily. "My family is a product of sex."

"Isn't everybody's?" Noah asked, still looking confounded.

Ella couldn't resist chuckling. "I guess. What I mean is that my family was brought together because too many people thought that sex was only for pleasure, that commitment was unnecessary, or an outdated cultural restriction. I've seen the pain that results from sex without love and commitment. And the pain that leads to indiscriminate sex. I don't want that."

"Uh huh." His words said, "yes" but his expression said, "what on earth are you talking about?"

"I've had sex." She said the words softly but they only seemed to ramp up his confusion.

"In this day and age, that doesn't surprise me, El," he replied. "I didn't expect you to be a virgin."

"Oh." That disappointed her, more than she expected. "When...when I was seventeen..." Her voice trailed off, her cheeks darkening. "I thought it was disappointing because we were so young, you know?"

Ella looked up to meet Noah's gaze. He nodded slowly though he clearly didn't understand. The words perhaps, but not the meaning.

"The next time, I waited until I was sure it was someone I cared about, someone who had more experience. But it—it's not the physical part of the act that's the problem. It's the emotional. Every time I was intimate with a man, it was like I gave a piece of myself to him. Now those pieces are missing. The men moved on. I moved on. But they will always carry a part of me with them. And I," she gulped, "I have to carry a part of them with me. I will always have the memory of the acts, this intimacy I shared with a man who is no longer a part of my life. Does that make sense?"

"I suppose."

"Is it like that for a man?"

He stroked his beard as he thought about it. "Perhaps it's easier for a man to ignore that part of things. But, yeah, to some extent." He frowned a moment. "Maybe it's easier for a man to compartmentalize emotions and events. Yet, I suppose, when you have to purposely forget things, you lose more than just a few pieces of memory. It could be, perhaps, you lose a small piece of yourself."

"Um hm." The thought made her sad.

"But if I could go back and replace those women with you, El, I'd be good with that."

She ignored his comment because she didn't know how to respond. "If sex is about physically sharing your body, which, of course, it is." Her face flushed hotter than the sun. "And it's also about sharing a piece of yourself emotionally with another person, then it makes the most sense to be with one person for life." She sighed. She was not explaining this well at all. "What I'm trying to say is that I understand why God put sex inside marriage and why He decided on monogamy as a means to bind families together." She slowly twined her fingers together to demonstrate. "If *she* gives to *him* and *he* gives to *her*, then nothing is ever lost. They gradually grow together into one person with two parts."

"Makes sense."

"So you'd be interested in monogamy? With me?"

His gaze sharpened. Darkened sensually. *"Oui."*

"But would you be willing to wait?"

"Wait for what?"

"Marriage. I want to wait."

"Kissing isn't sex, *chérie*." Noah reached out and cupped her cheek. The lilt was back in his voice.

Ella closed her eyes a minute, absorbing the sweetness of the gesture. "I know. But I didn't know if you understood that. I want to wait for marriage."

Noah slipped his hand down to her shoulder then down along her arm to link his index finger with hers. "Most people say a trial run is important to test compatibility."

"I know. But I don't believe it. Do you?"

"Honestly?" Noah released her finger and pushed his hands into his front pockets. "I haven't thought it through. Sex was a pull I answered when it drew me. Feels good. I was never looking for commitment, just a temporary connection." He seemed to consider something before he shrugged one shoulder. "I don't think I broke any hearts. I looked for women who didn't want commitment either."

"You realize that doesn't make it any better, don't you? And saying you don't want commitment doesn't make it so. Everybody wants to be loved. Only dysfunction leads to a self-identity which protects itself by saying 'I don't want, I don't need'." Ella tugged on Noah's shirt, just as a gesture of connection. "I do want commitment. I want marriage then sex."

"To be clear, you're saying you won't have sex until you're married?"

"Yes." She sighed in relief, a hint of a smile in her eyes. "And I'm asking you not to have sex with anyone else either. In fact, I'll emasculate you if you're unfaithful."

He looked startled a moment and then pensive. His lips pursed. And then his gaze softened. "All right, sounds fair." He tilted his head. "So you're not kicking me to the curb?"

"No," she replied. "I'm, uh, glad you found me in that coffee shop. Glad you followed me."

"Even though it put your life in danger?" He spoke quietly, his eyes searching her expression. After all the trouble she'd given him, he was probably looking for the "but…".

"Yes. Our relationship is rather bizarre, but…well…I'm glad."

He smiled, his eyes soft and warm. "Glad," he repeated.

"Yeah. To be your friend."

"Friend," he repeated that word with less enthusiasm.

She rested her palms on his chest. "All I'm asking for is a little time before we move from friendship to romance."

He drew in a breath. And because she figured he was going to protest, probably vociferously, she kissed him. She pulled back before the intensity ramped up. "I'm not looking for a way out, just a slower pace." Tip-toeing up, she linked her fingers behind his neck. His arms came around her. "More is coming." She pulled back enough so she could see his face but remain in his arms. "Can you wait a little longer?"

Noah slipped his hands up to her wrists and pulled her arms down to press her palms against his chest. He rested his forehead against hers. "Ella, I get the sense that there is something you are not telling me, something that if I don't guess right, you *are* going to kick me to the curb."

An expression of guilt took over her face. She knew it because she felt it deep inside. Not that she was trying to fool Noah. She simply didn't think telling your boyfriend—friend—that you wanted him to become a Christian before you would move into a romantic relationship with him was such a bright idea. How would she ever know if he was sincere?

Ella tried to tug her hands free but Noah held firm, pressing her palms to his chest. He didn't hurt her but it was a no-nonsense hold nonetheless.

"So I am right. What is going on, Ella? Are you seeing someone else? Who is more important than I am?"

She curled her hands into fists within his palms. Gulping, she admitted, "God."

"What?" His grip slipped to her wrists.

"I can't—I won't get involved in a romantic relationship with someone whose beliefs are so different from mine. But I like you, Noah. I don't want to lose a chance with you. I don't know what to do." Her conscience pricked her. "Well, that's not true. I know what to do, what's supposed to happen."

His expression hardened. "You want me to be a Christian. If I'm not a Christian, then I'm out? Is that right?"

She dropped her gaze and leaned into him. "Yes. And no."

"And that means?" Noah dropped his head back against the wall, his eyes heavenward. Or at least aimed at the ceiling.

"Noah, a romantic relationship means that the man and woman are headed toward marriage."

He dropped his chin, meeting her gaze. "Marriage doesn't frighten me."

"Okay." She nodded. "Good. But what about jobs, home, career, children, finances, all those things that go along with marriage?"

"We'll figure it out."

"Famous last words, Noah. How many marriages fail because no one bothered to talk about things beforehand?" She swallowed. "What is the most important thing in your life? What means the most to you? It's not your family."

Noah flinched at that. "True." He paused a moment before responding. That was good. It meant that he was taking this seriously. "I guess it's duty."

"Duty to who?"

"You, I guess."

Disappointed, she replied, "That's really not the right answer. You don't even know to whom your duty belongs. You keep telling me you're going to stay here until I 'kick you to the curb'. If I did, would you leave?"

"I'd stick around and try to change your mind."

"And if I didn't?"

He shrugged.

"You'd move on just like you did after your mother died?"

He tensed, his shoulders rigid with anger. "What is that supposed to mean?"

"Do you have the skills to commit and stay? You're an undercover police officer. You absorb yourself in a task and then move on when it's completed. If you were good with attachment, you'd be unable to do that."

"I'm done with that. As I said. I've moved on."

"Exactly."

His brows furrowed. He fixed his gaze intently on her. "No. Not exactly. I moved here to get to know you, Ella. Are you saying I lack commitment? Following you around doesn't count? Is that it? What sort of commitment are you looking for?"

Ella sighed. "You're getting upset."

"Gee, I wonder why?" The sarcasm in his voice was obnoxious.

"So move on," she said. She realized she was goading him, but it was better to find his true mettle now than later.

"I don't want to move on, Ella. Though at this exact moment, I'm not sure why I'd want to stay."

*Exactly my point.* "So then, answer the question. What is most important to you?"

Noah shoved his hands into his pockets, paced to the kitchen then returned to the front door. "Doing what's right?"

"How do you know what's right?"

"Helping people, protecting the innocent, putting scumbag criminals in prison, stopping bullies and other terrorists, those are the right things to do."

"Who taught you that those were good things?"

"My mother." He slumped back against the front door.

"Who taught her?"

"God?"

"Really?" His answer surprised her.

"Yeah. My mother was a Christian. She had little patience for formal religion, but did have a personal relationship with God. She used to tell us that Jesus was her best friend. I remember her saying that people would always let you down, but God never would."

"Do you accept those ideas?"

"I don't know." His response was belligerent.

"Are you willing to think about it?"

"Think about what my mother believed?"

"Yes."

"How do I do that?"

"Go to church. Read the Bible. Read books by learned men and women. Think."

Noah reached out, took Ella's arm and pulled her closer. "You believe all that stuff that Enoch says about forgiveness and redemption?"

"Yes."

"My mother used to tell me stories, about King David and Noah and Elijah. She told me about Jesus."

Ella glanced up, but his face was averted as if he was remembering. "What did she tell you?"

Noah took her wrists again, sliding his palms up to flatten her hands against his chest. "For God so loved the world that He gave His one and only son that whoever believes in Him should not perish but have eternal life." Noah tilted his head down to her. "It's a children's story."

"It's the truth." *Wait a minute.* "Your mother was a Christian. Was your father?"

Noah studied Ella's face. She felt his intensity like heat. "I don't know. My father gave the impression of being a good, hardworking man, but he was not. He drank too much. He was a bigot, a critic, no one ever measured up." Noah's face darkened as he spoke about his father. "When he wasn't ignoring us, he was berating us." The lines and furrows softened. Brightened. "But my mother was lovely. And I don't mean that only as a compliment to her looks. She was like you, El. She was kind and forgiving and she always had a smile for me, no matter what mischief I'd gotten up to with my friends."

Silent, Noah stroked his thumbs over Ella's knuckles. Finally, he spoke with that distant look in his eyes. "I can see why a Christian shouldn't marry a non-Christian. Your priorities *would* be seriously mismatched. The way you approached finances, child-rearing, family and work relationships, eh? Even if you loved each other, you'd be setting yourself up for certain conflict and heartache."

Ella's heart lifted within her. "And what about kids? Would you teach them that money or ambition or self-fulfillment were their goals? Or a relationship with the God of the universe who loves them? The God who loved them enough to send his son to earth to let him die so that we have a God who understands what we're going through. The God who is so powerful that he raised his son from the dead in triumph."

"That's compelling." He leaned his forehead against hers and closed his eyes.

"Yeah," she replied, smiling. God's love meant everything to her. It was her present, past, and eternity. She wouldn't let anything or anyone interfere with her faith. "What do we do?" she asked.

Noah pulled back to meet her eyes. "I can't make a decision like that for sex, El, not even for you."

Inside, Ella cheered for joy. Noah was a good man who would stand on his principles. "I don't want you to, not for that reason. If you'll keep an open mind, we can be friends for now. Friends that don't date other people."

Noah chuckled. "So friends but not friends. We could keep going the way we are."

"I can't. I mean, I can't—with the kissing and such. I'm falling for you, Noah. I can't risk—more—if—it's too risky."

"And I'm not worth that risk."

Ella jerked as if he'd slapped her. Tears filled her eyes. "I'm not saying that."

Noah cupped her cheeks. "Okay. All right."

Noah pressed his lips against her temple, to the corner of her eye, beneath her eye. Ella's fingers clenched in his shirt, her head turning into his caress. Kissing across her cheekbone to her ear, he slid his hands down her neck to cup her shoulders. His thumbs traced her collar bones over the cotton of her shirt, the sensation soothing and exciting.

"Noah." His name came out more as a groan of encouragement than a request for him to stop.

He pressed closer, kissing her ear, licking around the shell. Ella shivered at the sensation, her body tightening in response.

"It's okay. Just needed to taste you," he murmured.

"N-kay," she replied, her eyelids at half-mast, her voice throaty.

While pulling back to meet her gaze, he caught her chin between thumb and forefinger. "Not sure I can agree to the no-kissing thing." He kissed her lightly on the mouth then tapped her chin with his knuckle. "Counter offer. Kissing but no sex. But lots of kissing." He grinned at her with a hint of lasciviousness, wiggling his eyebrows comically.

She smiled even as she blushed.

He continued, sobering, "I will keep going to church and I'll think about what you said about God. Good?"

"Yes. Very good."

Noah kissed her once more, a quick peck. "I need to head home. I'll pick you up for church. Okay?"

Ella nodded. "Okay."

"Cool."

# CHAPTER 25

Grady walked along the upstairs hallway at the Bethsaida shelter with Otto trotting along at his side. When he heard the adults talking about him at the bottom of the stairs, he stopped and listened. He didn't bother to hide. Adults forgot about you, thought you were stupid, if you didn't talk. He wasn't stupid, just mute. That's what Lillian said. She told him he was smart, extra smart since he did things the hard way; most people took the easy way out and talked. Grady rubbed his chest. The force of Lillian's love warmed him and made him feel good.

"He and the dog have come and gone from here for days but we're no closer to knowing who he is. I sent pictures of the dog around but no one knows him. The boy won't let me take his photo."

"Do you think he's retarded or something?"

*Why did some grownups think it was okay to use that word? Rosalie never used it. Neither had Lillian or Peter.*

"I don't think so." That was Rosalie. Grady trusted her. "He's bright but I'd guess he's running from something terrible. It might be better not to know where he's from."

"You can't assume that, Rosalie." That voice was Burton. He seemed to be the secretary for the boss of the shelter, Mrs. Plummer. "There may be someone out there searching for him."

"But for what purpose?" Rosalie asked.

"I…" Burton started to answer.

Grady moved away from the stairs. It was time to go.

# Chapter 26

"I've been thinking about what you said, El," Noah said from his position reclined on Ella's couch. He placed the book he'd just finished reading aside and crossed the living room to sit on the ottoman facing her.

Ella shifted upright in her cozy chair and tucked a bookmark into her novel before closing it.

"I finished the book of John. I read the Acts, too. Very interesting." Noah smiled as he spoke. "Talked to Rod Blanchard. He's bright for an old guy."

"Did you watch the Billy Graham video I told you about?" Ella placed her novel on the table beside the phone and stretched her legs out on the ottoman beside him.

"*Oui.* That was straightforward and yet insightful. What's next?" he asked.

"Um, what do you want to know?"

"You believe the events in these books are true, that they really happened, eh?" He dropped his hand to rest on her bare ankles, stroking his fingers absently over her skin.

"Yes."

"If what the books say is true, then there is no alternative but to accept that Jesus is God's son."

"I agree." She slipped her feet out of his grip, resting the balls of her feet on the edge of the ottoman.

Noah returned his hands to his lap. "If the events are true, then Jesus died and rose again then went to heaven."

"Some books deal with the historical proofs for Jesus. There's Lee Strobel's *The Case for Christ,* and *History and Christianity* but I forget who wrote that. There's also Josephus who provides historical record of Jesus. The writings of Billy Graham, Calvin Miller, Max Lucado, Phillip Yancey and many others who talk about what the Bible tells us and how it makes a difference in our lives. Um, there's also a book called *The Ring of Truth* which talks about the veracity of the Bible."

"Ring of Truth?" Noah's mouth quirked. He leaned forward, resting his elbows on his knees. "Not another Lord of the Rings reference?"

"Nope. But if you try to google it, that's where the title will take you," Ella replied, smiling.

"I'm not struggling with the idea of a historical Jesus. And I accept there is a grand intelligence, a creator god. There are too many miracles in the world, too many times when something happens that cannot be explained away by those who'd like to be able to. There is too much complexity in the natural world to allow for any explanation of nature but an intelligence that's behind it all. None of the pagan gods can explain life because they're selfish, vindictive, and largely clueless of humanity. I keep coming back to the idea of God being the god who is described in Genesis." Noah paused, shifting in his seat. "I accept that Jesus existed and He was either the son of God or a liar. Or maybe a lunatic. But Jesus as liar and lunatic don't work logically." He stopped talking for a moment.

Ella looped her arms around her knees. "So God made the world. Jesus is His son. Jesus lived, died, and rose again. Does that sum up where you're at?"

Noah tipped his chin up, meeting her gaze and nodding slowly. "So what does that mean for me?"

"It means this: this Jesus who died and rose again for you, offers eternal life. If you confess with your mouth Jesus is Lord and believe in your heart God raised Him from the dead, you will be saved."

"That's childishly simple."

"Because, in many ways, children are smarter than adults. They are not limited in the same way that adults are by unfulfilled imagination and disappointed expectations. They get hope. As in, they understand it."

"I don't. Get hope, that is."

Ella's eyes widened. "Are you kidding me? You're an incredible hoper. You saw me and hoped I'd be someone worth knowing. You left your job and moved to a teeny, tiny city in the middle of nowhere," Noah chuckled at her words, "because you hoped we could have a relationship. You get hope."

"Is there a special prayer or something I should use?"

Her eyes widened and her heart sped. "You mean if you want to ask Jesus into your heart?"

He looked thoughtful. "That is an odd phrase. I want to tell God that I believe him, give him my life. How do I do that?"

"Tell him."

"But isn't there some magic formula or special prayer I need to say?"

"No. Just talk to him."

"Will you stay with me, *cher*?"

"Yes." Ella's eyes filled with emotion. "Come." She tugged Noah's hand to the couch then knelt down, resting her elbows on the cushions of the seat. Noah knelt beside her.

"Why are we kneeling?" he asked. "Seems very catholic."

"A show of respect."

"Don't need kneelers or an altar?"

"Nope. We have the direct route to the God of the universe."

Noah nodded once. "What do I say?"

"I started with asking for forgiveness."

"For what?" he asked.

"Have you always made the right choices? Have you ever lied, cheated, manipulated others for your own purposes, hurt another person physically or psychologically—"

"Okay. Right. I get the idea."

"Are you sorry? Do you want to do better?"

"*Oui*."

"Tell God. Then ask forgiveness. Believe that He gives it. Hand over control of your life."

Noah gripped Ella's hand hard. He closed his eyes and bowed his head. "God. Uh. Please forgive me. I've done plenty of wrong things in my life, disappointed people who care about me. And there are plenty of wrong things I'd do if I could get away with it." He paused as though gathering his thoughts. "From the time I became a man, I've tried to make a difference. I've tried to live by duty and diligence. But, somehow, it never seems enough to fill the empty spaces in my heart. I thought that falling in love would fill the emptiness, would make me feel good. And it does." Noah squeezed Ella's hand. "But it's not enough to fix what's wrong inside me. Kind of like King David. He tried to use a woman to solve his disappointment. He made a mistake. But you loved him, anyway. That's one of the things I like about the Bible. You tell the truth about people. And that makes me think that if you can love and make use of the people there, then you can love me. I've read about the kind of man you respect. That's who I want to be, God. Someone you would call a 'good and faithful servant' at the end of time. I'd like to go to heaven when I die and see my Mom again."

Noah brushed the back of his free hand across his eyes. "Take my life and show me how to live for you. Amen." A sigh shuddered through his body.

Ella opened her eyes and turned to him. "How do you feel?"

"Light." He smiled, a bright smile that lit his eyes from within. "Easy."

"Easy?"

"Like a weight has been lifted from me. I could get used to this."

"The feelings will come and go, but God won't. He'll always be there. God always keeps His word." Ella hugged Noah around the shoulders. "You look so happy."

Noah pulled her close. "I feel good. Though I didn't expect to. After looking at the evidence, I had no choice but to accept Christ. If you accept personal responsibility for your actions and the fact you can never do enough good to outweigh the bad we do, there is no other logical choice. Now I know it was real. I didn't need to feel anything. I made the right choice. But God gave me peace and joy like He promised."

Noah hugged her tightly, a smile on his lips, and wonder in his eyes.

# CHAPTER 27

Grady Jones was cold and hungry. In this campground away from the city, the nights were not as warm as he'd expected. Huddled together in the shelter of a leafy bush while the iPhone charged, Otto's little body provided comfort as the two watched the families in the campsites around them. Moms and Dads sat around campfires while their children roasted marshmallows or played Marco Polo in the dim light. *Isn't that supposed to be a water game?* His swimming teacher had let them play it on the last day of his lessons.

He missed Bethsaida, the shelter on Tenth Street in Calgary. The food had been boring, but it had been nice to sleep indoors. Crowded, though. People everywhere. Kids always snooping into his stuff. Then, a week ago, the adults started asking questions and it had felt like a good time to go.

He and Otto had ridden the city bus after lunch Friday as far west as possible, and then walked from Signal Hill to Banff Provincial Park. It had taken five days to get here, just in time to melt in with the Canada Day revellers.

Even with the food and juice boxes he'd taken— Rosalie had once told him it was okay to take extras while he was staying at the shelter—he was hungry. The smells of chocolate and graham crackers floated over from the campfires. Even though the odour made his stomach hurt and his heart sad, it was nice, too, because it reminded him of baking with Lillian. If Lillian was dead, he would never again sit on a stool in the kitchen while she baked him his favourite cookies. Chocolate chip. She thought chocolate chip cookies were his favourites. She was always so happy to make them for him. Grady liked them all. Chocolate. Butterscotch. Gingerbread. They were all good. But what he liked the most was the time Lillian spent talking to him, smiling at him. She always said she enjoyed his company. That's what he liked about Baking Day.

Thinking of cookies made his stomach cramp with hunger. But he'd been hungry before. Grady had once gone three days without food when a guardian decided that Grady would talk if he was hungry enough. He'd collapsed at school on the third day, during gym class. Then woken in the hospital and gone to another new house with another set of guardians.

Grady had learned the word "guardian" by reading a comic book. Guardians were crazy, irresponsible people who didn't do anything right. That about fit the people he'd met because of the Mounties. Some of the guardians wanted to be called Mom and Dad, some wanted to be called by their first names or last names. Some were nice, but Grady had met a lot of nasty people in his short life. Nobody nice wanted a boy who wouldn't talk, a boy who stole food and didn't sleep.

Until he met Lillian and Peter. They took care of him even when he wouldn't talk. Fed him even when he didn't do his chores. They gave him Otto, a bed, a family, an escape route. Now it was gone. Peter told Grady that God was always with him. So he wasn't alone. He and Otto weren't alone.

But Peter might be dead. The blood around his head had leaked out, so much had leaked out it could never be replaced. Grady might never go camping like Peter had promised. Thinking about Peter made Grady's thoughts get small. He could feel his brain getting narrower until a noise jerked him out of his closing-down mind.

A man and a woman walked by Grady's berry bush, talking loudly and laughing. "That tent was doomed," the man said. He was skinny and had blonde hair that stuck up all over the place. "The new one will work much better."

The lady laughed. "What did you do with the old one?" She hugged the skinny guy around the chest. She was skinny, too, but had dark hair that hung in a long braid down her back, and dark brown skin like Grady's. They were both wearing shorts, T-shirts, and flip-flops.

"I threw it and the old sleeping bags over by the dumpster," the skinny man said. "Someone will pick them up tomorrow."

Grady's mind ding-dinged. That was what Lillian always said when Peter came up with a good idea. She would say, "ding, ding, you got it" and then point at Peter. Peter always laughed.

If the skinny man's tent was by the dumpster, then maybe Grady could take it and use it. He could use the Para cord in his pack to make up for the broken tent poles by tying the sides to a tree.

Waiting until the skinny people walked out of sight, Grady unplugged his iPhone and crawled out of his hiding place. He shushed Otto when he whined. The terrier was probably hungry and cold, too, just like Grady.

There was a big green dumpster behind the bathrooms and another one near the change rooms at the beach. Grady would check near the bathrooms first because it was closer. Maybe he and Otto would get to camp, after all.

# Chapter 28

Warm August rain pelted the road as Ella made the return journey to work, southward on Highway 5, the Southern Yellowhead. To the left, the ground rose in grassy slopes with here and there a stand of stubby conifers. The green of the pines contrasted with the burnt brown of the grass and weeds, all darkened by the moisture in the air. To the right, the ground was flat, today affording a blurry view of the Thompson River. Utility poles lined the highway, their wires making a cross-hatched pattern of the overcast sky.

There wasn't much traffic on the road; only one vehicle had passed her, heading north. One of those large pickup trucks with the extended cab had been behind her since Vinsulla.

The weather had been dreary but calm when she'd left her office at Thompson Rivers University to drive north to McClure to meet Toby Jasper. He was an eight-year-old boy experiencing difficulty with what his parents termed "getting along" after witnessing a fight outside his parent's restaurant over the Easter weekend, four months ago. Toby had heard one of the fighting men tell the other, "this ain't over", and taken the threat personally. No one in young Toby's life had bothered to talk over the incident with him and quell his fears. Knowing that he had misunderstood the man's intent had visibly altered Toby's demeanour. Ella would meet with him a few more times, but it looked like he'd be fine.

Ella turned the knob to activate her windshield wipers. Then rotated it further as the rainfall became more intense. With the increased frequency, the wipers stroked a rhythm that didn't mesh well with the music on the radio so Ella switched to a classical music station. Bach blended better with precipitation. Noah preferred Dvořák. Something about the folkish rhythms of Moravia touched him. But she preferred the bright and happy tunes of Bach.

*Noah.* She spent more and more of her time thinking about him. Was it only eight months ago that he'd rescued her from that motel room on East Hastings? Six months since he'd followed her to Kamloops? Which meant that he'd run out of time to decide. Would he stay or would he go?

She didn't want him to go.

When had that happened? When had she fallen for this guy? While painting her kitchen? Chasing each other through the bungalow with pillows? Kissing on the couch? He'd been sincere when he warned her there'd be "lots of kissing".

Ella chuckled. Kissing Noah was wonderful. Passionate. Heady. And though he probably wanted more, he never pushed. So she trusted him. Because of that, and his loyalty, his kindness and care and humour and hard work and patience, she was falling in love—*whoa*! It was far too early to talk about love. She liked Noah a lot. Thought about him all the time. But, love? Surely not yet.

Though she imagined a future with him. She envisioned them married with little curly-haired Kristofers running around the bungalow on Nechako and up the mountain across the gulley from their house. Her house.

Something was in the road ahead. Ella decelerated. She'd noticed nothing on the highway on the way to Toby's. In this direction, through the rain, it was difficult to tell whether the shape was something lying on the road or a part of the road itself, like a speed bump or a pothole. Except that it was rather large for a pothole. She tapped the brakes.

Wham!

The seatbelt caught her, steeling her breath. Her foot slipped from the brake to the accelerator. The Element surged forward. The front wheel dropped with a jarring thump and Ella fought to retain control of the steering. She slammed both feet on the brakes. Her stomach dropped as if she was hurtling forward. Looking down, she ensured that her feet were pressed to the brake. Looking up, she saw the pickup that had been following her whiz past and take the right onto Edward Road. It skidded on the corner but continued away, vanishing into the gloom. The speed of the truck racing past had created the illusion of movement. But she was still. Stopped.

Scanning the area through the windows and mirrors, Ella realized that she was alone on the highway. She moved the gearshift into park. Her hands shook as she flipped down her vanity mirror to examine her face. She wasn't bleeding. Nothing was broken. She was okay. If only her heart would get the memo. It raced in her chest.

The Element started with ease. She hadn't even realized it had stalled. Putting the gearshift in reverse, Ella backed out of a hole with some tire-spinning and slipping, and onto the asphalt. Shifting into drive, she rotated the steering wheel to the left to move around the tire-capturing canyon. But as she inched forward, the car refused to follow her steering, pulling to the right. Was it her nerves making the car's response seem sluggish? Well? Maybe? No?

The closer Ella got to Kamloops, the heavier the traffic. Her nerves jittered and her heart raced. Her mind was unfocussed. The Element limped along. At this rate, she would not make it back to the office in time for her afternoon appointments. How was she going to navigate the city streets with only minimal control over the trajectory of the vehicle?

With tears in her eyes, she pulled into a turnout on the side of the highway. This was ridiculous. Why did she feel so weepy and sluggish?

Her hands shook as she pulled out her cell phone. "Noah." She whispered his name out loud. She wanted Noah. Then she should call work and BCAA. But, first, she needed Noah.

She pressed his number into the phone and waited.

"*Bonjour,* Ellà," he greeted her. "What's up?"

"I…I was in a car accident. I'm okay. But-but the c-car won't go s-straight."

"Where are you? Are you hurt?" Noah's voice was grim.

"No. I'm okay. A little sh-shaken. I'm on Highway 5, southbound. I pulled off beside the river, the North Thompson."

"That highway parallels the river. Can you narrow it down for me?" he asked. His voice was patient and steady. "What do you see closest to you?"

"I-I don't know." She glanced around, seeing the railway tracks beside the road. "Railway tracks." And then she realized the pullout was a unique feature on the road. *Duh.* "I pulled into a little rest area. But it's not like a rest area with picnic tables or toilets. The trucks sometimes stop here. But I'm the only vehicle here now."

"What was the last side road you passed?"

"Um, I haven't seen Cn Road yet, you know, with a capital C and a small n on the map on the computer. It should be soon, though."

"Great. I know where you are. Have you called BCAA?"

"No. Not yet. And I need to call work to let them know I'll be late."

"*Chérie*, you tell them you won't be in today. Call BCAA first then work. Is the Element still working? It's warm today."

"Yes. I can use the air conditioner if I need it."

"I'll be there in fifteen minutes."

"Really?" Even though she still felt shaken, her entire being settled at the idea.

"*Oui.* See you soon. Lock your doors. Stay inside."

"I will. Thank you."

"*Pas de problème.*"

She disconnected then took a moment and a few deep breaths to calm her voice. She didn't want to sound weepy and weak when she called, but she also didn't want Indira's parents to drive all the way in from Logan Lake for a cancelled appointment.

After ordering a tow truck from the British Columbia Automobile Association, Ella called into work. She asked the Case Coordinator,

Ephraim, to reschedule Indira's play therapy session and Joshua Greyeyes' counselling session.

Noah arrived thirteen minutes later. Ella spotted the little white sports car as soon as it came into view, following its progress as it made a U-turn across the highway and into the turnout. Ella gave a little wave as Noah pulled to a stop beside her. He was out of the car with her door open in a flash.

"Are you all right? Are you hurt?"

He steadied her as she exited the Element. Then took the opportunity to examine her. He cupped her cheeks in his hands, tilting her head up and easing it from side to side to check her pupils.

His concern drew the corners of her mouth up. "I'm okay," she said. "It's weird, though. I can't think. I keep running through the sequence of events in my mind."

"You're in shock."

"It was only a little accident."

Noah shrugged. "Doesn't matter. Your brain and body got a significant jolt. Your shoulders will be stiff tomorrow."

Noah kissed her, a quick peck that soon deepened. She pressed forward, sliding her palms up to cup the sides of his neck. When she pulled back, he tucked her against his chest.

"I called the mechanic," he used the English word with the French pronunciation, "and he's expecting your Element."

Ella pulled back to look up at him but Noah cupped her head to keep her close.

"I don't have a mechanic," she said.

"I called Enoch to get a name. He's a handy fellow to know."

"Hm." Ella smiled against Noah's shirt. "I'm glad you came for me."

"Any time. Anywhere."

# Chapter 29

Four days later, Ella stood in Noah's kitchen in his apartment on Curlew Road. She set out six slices of bread and slathered on butter. "There was a guy looking at your fancy little sports car when I got here this morning."

Noah grunted in reply.

Ella retrieved the honey mustard, mayonnaise, and deli meat from the fridge, and tried again, "I can't say I enjoyed having to use the transit system to get here this morning. I miss my Element."

"*Zut.* You should have told me someone rear-ended you," Noah groused.

He had ignored every attempt she'd made to shift his attention from that fact. Had been sweetly irritating ever since the accident. Well, if truth be told, she'd never felt as cared for as she had these past four days. Noah had ridden to her rescue like a knight in shining armour and then wrapped her in a cloak of protection all weekend. But there was no point in trying to chase down some poor driver who'd panicked.

Ella layered turkey, roast beef, and Swiss cheese on their sandwiches. "I didn't see who it was. And I guess I thought it was partially my fault. I was preoccupied," *I was thinking of you,* "and, with the rain, I didn't see that hole in the road until I was right up to it. There was this other shape on the highway. I think. I didn't notice it later. Anyway, the other driver probably couldn't see well either."

"The guy hit you and drove away."

"It could have been a woman. Let's not be sexist here." So that Noah didn't see how humorous she found his protests, Ella kept her chin down and her eyes on her task as she placed the sandwiches into zippered bags then opened the fridge. "You want the left over Caesar salad packed?"

"Hm. No croutons," he replied, though the shift in conversation did not deter him from his topic of choice. "You had an impact from the front and rear of the vehicle. No wonder your shoulders were so sore. Are you sure you don't still have a headache? We can forget going out and watch a movie or something."

"I'm okay, Huck. I was off Thursday and Friday. I've done nothing all weekend but pop ibuprofen. I think I can handle a little picnic."

"Whiplash can be quite serious." Noah's frown deepened.

A chuckle escaped, but she camouflaged it with a cough. At least, she thought she'd camouflaged it.

"You think this is funny?" Noah asked. His indignation was not in any way subtle.

Ella reached across his counter, grasped the front of his red-checked cotton button-down, and tugged him closer for a kiss. "I'm fine. Come. Let's go have this picnic before the weather changes." She let her fingertips stroke over the soft technical fabric of his undershirt which peeked out at the open neck of his shirt.

Noah grunted at her but still stole another kiss before piling the sandwiches, bottled water, apples, and homemade cookies inside the wicker picnic basket.

"What did the méchanic say?" Ella asked, using Noah's odd hybrid pronunciation, as she propped his apartment door with her hip. The picnic basket occupied her hands because his arms were full of dirty laundry.

"Tierod's broken. Wheel's bent. Should be ready in a couple days," Noah replied, shifting the laundry basket in his arms. "Had a few jobs ahead of your Element." He set the laundry on the floor in the hallway before locking up his apartment.

"A couple days as in Sunday, Monday? Or what?"

"Wednesday morning."

Ella led the way down the hall to the stairs. "Oh, crappolla. What am I going to do about getting to work tomorrow and Tuesday? I've got a home visit assessment near Pinantan Lake on Tuesday afternoon. That's forty minutes in good weather."

"Off for a picnic, Mr. Kristofer? Beautiful day for it." Mrs. Rooster was an elderly lady who lived on the third floor of Noah's building. She had taken a keen interest in Noah.

"An afternoon with my sweetheart," Noah replied. His pronunciation always flattened to neutral when others were around.

Ella gaped at him. He'd never declared anything like that before.

Mrs. Rooster scowled, squeezing past them in the corridor. The woman took every opportunity to speak to Noah but never spoke directly to Ella, blatantly ignoring her. She seemed to think that if she ignored Ella, she would cease to exist, and Noah would thus be free to marry her granddaughter, Wilma.

"Told you," Ella whispered over her shoulder.

Once Mrs. Rooster had rounded the corner, Noah winked at Ella. Then nodded down the stairs for her to continue. "I told you it makes no difference what plans Mrs. R has for me. I'm all about Ella," Noah replied.

Smiling, Ella paused on the landing until Noah moved in close enough to fulfill her unspoken request for a kiss. He was very in tune with her kissing desires.

Descending the last few stairs, Ella held the front door of the apartment building open, waiting for Noah to catch up. She was letting him do his laundry at her house rather than the laundromat in the basement of the building because it gave them time together in a more comfortable setting than the concrete-walled room below-stairs which held the decades-old washers and dryers.

"I can borrow a truck from the nursery for a couple days," Noah said, glancing down around his large and awkward burden to see the last few steps.

She'd insisted he bring his bedding and towels today. *Every now and then* didn't seem frequent enough to give them the full-wash treatment.

"You can borrow my car."

"Really?" Her eyes widened in astonishment.

Noah was particular about the little sports car. He never refused to let her drive. But without fail, he found reasons he should drive instead.

Noah rebalanced his load to fish his keys out of his pants pocket. "You can practice today."

Grinning, Ella accepted the keys, rebalanced her load, and stepped up her pace. She was excited to sit in that plush leather driver's seat and shift it forward until her feet nestled on the pedals.

When Noah stopped to check his mailbox, Ella glanced at him before accelerating toward the car, hitting the key fob to unlock the trunk.

"I guess you really do like me."

Fwoosh!

A rhino punched her in the chest. The world exploded around her. Then winked out.

"*Sacre bleu!*" Noah raced out of the building and across the lawn, leaping over the scattered remnants of the picnic basket to skid to his knees beside Ella. Flames flickered on her pretty yellow blouse, obscene next to her precious skin. Whipping his cotton shirt over his head, Noah patted out the flames, heedless of the heat. He was thinking only of Ella.

As he passed his right hand over her, he retrieved his phone with his left and called 911.

"Ella? Wake up, *chérie.*" Noah checked her pulse. Steady.

"Fire, ambulance, police," the dispatcher said.

"Ambulance." Noah scanned Ella's body. His hands followed, testing her respiration and pulse. She was so pale and still. "Send the police." Noah glanced at the flickering remains of his CR-Z. "And a firetruck."

There was a beep and a click and then another operator came on the line. "Ambulance services. What is the nature of your emergency?"

"An explosion." Trunk blasted open, the fire in the CR-Z guttered. "My girlfriend is injured. Burned."

"Are *you* in danger, sir?"

"Nah. The car is smoldering."

"Can you safely remain where you are, sir?"

"Not sure. Could be another explosion. But I don't want to move her when I don't know how badly she's hurt."

"Be certain you are safe."

"I don't care if I'm safe," Noah's voice rose with his frustration. He tucked the phone between his shoulder and ear to check her pupils and pulse at the same time. *"Chérie.* Wake up, *bébé."* He brought her left hand to his mouth, kissing it. "Let me know you're okay."

"The ambulance is on its way."

Noah ignored the dispatcher, leaning forward to kiss Ella's forehead. Her skin was too hot. "Wake up, El."

Checking over his shoulder, he registered his neighbours gathered on the street and lawns in front of the white stucco apartment building. More neighbours stood on the balconies. Now he'd noticed them, he heard their chatter over the distant sirens. Not interested, he blocked it out though he warned them, "Stay back. Ambulance is on its way."

Mrs. Rooster approached. "What happened? It sounded like thunder." She glanced up at the clear sky. "But it's not raining."

All at once, she noticed Ella. "Is everything all right?"

*Duh.* "No, ma'am," Noah replied, waving her away. "Stay back. There could be another explosion."

"Your car is on fire." She kept advancing, glancing down at Ella. "Try this." She thrust a disposable water bottle in Noah's face. "To rouse her."

"Thanks." Noah prised off the lid and poured a little over Ella's forehead and cheeks.

"Uhn." Ella groaned. It was the most musical sound Noah had ever heard. Her right arm came up to guard her face. "Head. Hurts."

*Thank you, God.* Noah leaned over her. "Stay still. Ambulance is on the way." He brushed her hair off her forehead, the damp tendrils sticking to his hand. His shaking hand.

"Can't hear you. Lots of static." Ella opened her eyes. She reached out to stroke his beard. "Don't look so worried."

Noah grabbed her hand, pressing it to his mouth. "Ah, *bébé*. I've never been so scared in all my life."

"Pardon?" she said.

Noah shook his head, grinning stupidly. "Nothing. Nothing."

"Okay." Ella closed her eyes. She groaned, mumbling, "Rhino," as she rubbed her breastbone.

*Rhino?* Noah tapped her cheek. "Stay awake, *chérie*."

"Kay." Ella fluttered her eyelashes a few times.

"She seems to be all right. Good," Mrs. Rooster said.

Noah looked up at her. "Thank you."

Mrs. Rooster gazed down the street. "There's the fire guys. And the ambulance."

Noah glanced over to see two fire fighters in turn-out gear unrolling a hose while another fit a wrench to the fire hydrant across the street. His attention shifted to the blue-uniformed man and woman approaching from the ambulance. Noah moved to kneel at Ella's head, trying to stay close while shifting out of the paramedics' ways.

They started by checking her blood pressure, pupils and pulse. "What happened?" the man, Dhaliwal, asked. He was short and stocky with a black crew cut.

"There was an explosion," Noah replied. "Something in the trunk of my car. I should have rented her her own car. Stupid. But I didn't know."

"Sir." The woman, Seymour, laid a firm hand on Noah's arm. "This is no time for recriminations. Who are you?"

"Noah."

"Tell me what happened, Noah."

"Yes. Of course. Sorry." Noah drew in a breath then released it. "She, Ella, used the remote to open the trunk. To put the picnic basket in, I suppose. When the lid released, there was an explosion. She was walking toward the car from the front door." Noah turned and gestured toward the door. "The explosion knocked her backward and knocked her out. Her clothes caught fire. I used my shirt to put out the flames." He gestured at the remnants on the ground beside Ella.

"How long was she unconscious?" Seymour asked, making notes in a black notebook while Dhaliwal examined Ella. He lifted her blouse enough so Noah saw blisters forming on her belly. The sight made him ill.

"Sir?" Seymour prompted him. She was slender, with long raven-black hair pulled back and captured by a leather hair roach. She had a ruddy complexion and dark, almond-shaped eyes that squinted at him when his attention faltered.

"A minute or two," he replied. "She roused with a few drops of water on her face."

"What did Ella say?" Seymour asked.

Dhaliwal was talking to Ella now. "Ella? Can you hear me? What day is it?"

Ella mumbled a response but Noah didn't catch her words.

"Sir?" Seymour sought his attention. "Noah?"

"She said her head hurt. And she couldn't hear very well."

Seymour called in the information while Dhaliwal retrieved a back board and neck brace. Once Ella was transferred to the gurney, they loaded her into the ambulance.

Noah followed them to the rear doors of the vehicle. "Wait," he said. "I want to come with you."

"I'm sorry, sir," Dhaliwal replied. "You can meet us at Royal Inland Hospital."

Anxiety tightened Noah's chest even as he nodded. *How?* Ella's Element was in the shop and his car had just exploded.

Nearby, sirens sounded. The police?

Noah felt a soft tap on his arm. He looked down to see Mrs. Rooster beside him again. She had another water bottle. And a set of keys. "Take my car. It's the green Ford Focus over there." She pointed to the curb across the street. "You can leave the keys in the flower basket that decorates my apartment door if it's late when you get back. That's what I always tell my granddaughter to do." She winked at him.

A police car peeled onto the street. *No. No way.* He wasn't getting trapped here talking to the police when Ella needed him. "Thank you, Mrs. Rooster. Can you—do you think you can do me a favour and gather up the laundry?" When she nodded, he added, "I owe you one. Please tell the police I'll be at the hospital with Ella."

"Of course, honey. Hurry now." She smiled at him conspiratorially.

*Groan.* Noah was certain Mrs. Rooster would collect on her favour.

# CHAPTER 30

E lla was lying on a hospital bed in a curtained-off section of the Emergency ward at Royal Inland Hospital in the centre of Kamloops. She'd been here since the paramedics had off-loaded her. A nurse had taken her details, checked her blood pressure and pulse. One of the Residents had sent her for X-Rays to rule out fractures of the head and neck. Then they'd finally removed the brace thing she'd had to wear in the ambulance. Now Ella waited for the doctor on call.

"...fiancé. Husband then. I need to see her. Please."

Ella smiled as she recognized Noah's voice through the racket inside her head, a high-pitched tone with a background of white noise and a persistent deep bass thrum. She shifted to sit on the edge of the bed, planning to get up and go to him, but a ripple of vertigo kept her in her seat.

"Nurse." She couldn't tell if her voice was an appropriate loudness but it must have been a little too loud, given the prompt response of the nurse on duty. "That man, Mr. Kristofer, can he come back here?" Ella asked.

"Mwum bap bwum?"

"Pardon?" Ella said. Her eyes were gritty and she struggled to focus her attention.

The nurse, whose nametag read, Shaniqua, repeated her sentence but she still sounded like Charlie Brown's teacher. Then she smiled, leaned out through the adjoining curtains, and waved.

Noah promptly arrived. "Ella." He sat on the bed beside her and wrapped his arms around her. "Ah, *bébé*." He muttered more words against her neck.

Ella tugged at the back of his soft grey T-shirt until he finally pulled back enough to meet her gaze. "I can't hear properly. My ear drums ruptured."

Noah cupped her face with his hands. His expression was bleak. "I'm so sorry."

"Why? My head hurts and I feel kind of fuzzy," Ella said. In fact, it felt like her head was floating above her shoulders. Like her neck was missing. Or maybe it had gone on safari in Africa without her.

"Ms. Hanover, I'm Doctor Wunsch." The doctor faced Ella and used a firm, clear voice. "I understand you've had an accident."

The doctor was plump, in her early thirties, with long, baby-fine, strawberry-blonde hair. She examined Ella and sent her for a CT scan. Once all of the results were in, Dr. Wunsch pronounced Ella fit to go home with a prescription for painkillers for the likely whiplash that would appear by morning, antibiotic and analgesic cream for her burns, and a warning to buy ear plugs for showers until her ear drums healed. Dr. Wunsch finished with a referral to an Ear, Nose and Throat specialist, an Otolaryngologist, who would monitor her ear drums and her hearing.

Dizzy, Ella accepted Noah's support as he led her to an unfamiliar green Ford sedan. "Whose car is this?"

"Mrs. Rooster's, believe it or not. And, in the interest of full disclosure, I now owe her a favour," Noah replied.

"As long as it's not a date with Wilma." Ella scowled.

Noah chuckled, the first sign of relief he'd shown, as he helped Ella into the front passenger seat, fastening her seatbelt for her. He crossed around the front of the car and slipped behind the wheel. Even with his seat all the way back, he looked large in the small car.

Ella leaned her head back and shut her eyes, trying to relax into the uncomfortable seat.

"I need to call her and see if she minds if I keep it until tomorrow," Noah said.

"Why?" The flashing headlights of passing cars was accentuating her headache even through her closed eyelids.

"I, uh, want you to stay at a hotel tonight," he replied.

Ella frowned then flattened her expression. Frowning, smiling, it all felt weird. "Why?"

"Exploding car," was all he said in reply.

"Whatever," Ella replied. She was too woozy to care where she slept tonight.

"Okay. Good."

Either a long or a short time later, Ella wasn't sure because she wasn't certain whether she'd fallen asleep, Noah pulled into a Howard Johnson's. "Do you want to wait in the car while I get a room?" he asked.

"Hm. Yeah."

Noah changed his mind. "No. Not a good idea. Come with me. I'll help you."

"Don't ask if you don't want to hear the answer," Ella muttered. When he appeared at her open door, she said, "Sunglasses."

Her voice sounded weird with holes in her ear drums. Rupture of the tympanic membranes, Dr. Wunsch had said. Ella thought of tympani drums exploding, then stopped. That only made her queasier.

"You okay?" Noah asked, placing a pair of sunglasses in her hand. Where had they come from?

"Just a little nauseated," she replied. It was dark outside but even so the sunglasses helped to cut the glare from the streetlights.

Gingerly, Noah helped her out and across the parking lot to the registration desk. He lowered her into a soft chair by the bay windows and went to the front desk. Across that distance, Ella couldn't hear anything of what was said except a persistent buzz.

Noah soon returned with a key-card. "The room's not far. If you can walk to an elevator, I'll take you up and then move the car to a proper parking space."

"N-kay," Ella replied.

Holding Ella firmly around the waist, Noah helped her to and into the elevator at the Howard Johnson's. The elevator rose and her stomach dropped. Her lunch tried to make an appearance. She swallowed hard to keep it down.

"Did the doctor say I have a concussion?" she asked Noah.

"A mild one. Why? Head hurt?"

"A little queasy."

"Breathe in through your mouth and out through your nose."

"Kay."

When the door opened, Noah led her a short way down the hall. He kept his hold on her as he opened the door and led her in.

"Keep the lights off, please," she said when he reached for the switch.

"Come to bed." Noah led her to the nearest double bed, pulled back the covers and helped her lie down. He removed her shoes and socks and pulled the blankets over her. "I'll be right back. Okay?"

"Mm. Water. Please."

"I'll bring you some cold water when I come in from parking the car."

"Thanks." Ella reached up and patted his face, sliding her hand down his cheek to run the backs of her fingers along his beard. "Soft."

Noah kissed her fingers. "I'll be right back."

"N-kay."

# CHAPTER 31

**M**rs. Rooster released her Ford Focus to Noah for as long as he needed it, saying she would call a taxi if she needed to go anywhere in the meantime.

After moving the car from the front check-in area to the rear parking lot of the Howard Johnson's, Noah visited the Denny's next door to purchase a chilled bottle of water for Ella and a strawberry mango pucker for himself.

When he returned to the room, however, Ella was already asleep. He left the drinks on the table beside her. Because before he considered pucker lemonades and sleeping arrangements, he needed intel.

Noah went into the bathroom and called Mike Rainer. It took ten minutes of jockeying with dispatchers and secretaries before he could finally speak to his team commander.

"How much more time do you expect us to give you?"

Noah ignored Mike's brusque greeting. "There's been an incident."

"What kind of incident?"

"My car exploded."

There was silence on the other end of the line. "Interesting." Mike's response lacked inflection. "Anyone hurt?"

"Ella Hanover."

"Hanover? The lady who curtailed your career?"

"Knock it off, Mike. She could have been killed."

"Was she?"

"No. Ruptured her eardrums. Mild concussion. A few first-degree and second-degree burns."

"So, she's okay." Mike's voice was cheerful. "Good to hear from you. Bye."

"Mike." Noah interrupted before he disconnected. "What's going on?"

"You're on leave. Weren't you trying to convince me to accept your resignation?"

"Mike." *Give me a break.*

"Let me look into it."

"Look into it? And then what?"

"Take care of it."

Noah gritted his teeth in frustration. "What do you know?"

"Many things, my friend, many things I would share with you if you were not on some kind of erotic adventure."

Mike's flippancy angered Noah. "It's neither erotic nor an adventure, Mike." Actually, it was both, but not in the way Mike meant. "I'm in love with her." Noah paused a moment. *I am in love with her.* He pushed aside that discovery for a more convenient time. "I need to know if this explosion was deliberately set, and if it was set because of me."

"In love," Mike muttered. "So your plan worked?"

"My plan to have a normal life? Maybe not. My plan to get to know Ella Hanover, to have a chance with her? Yes. Help me, Mike."

A knock sounded on the bathroom door. "Hello?" Ella's voice filtered through.

"Just a minute," Noah called to her. To Mike he said, "Please."

"Meet me," Mike replied.

Ella knocked again. "Noah? I need to pee." Since the explosion, her voice sounded weirdly loud and lacking intonation.

Noah covered the phone. "Coming, *chérie.*" He rose and quickly ended the call with, "Text the time and place." Then he opened the door.

Ella looked battered and exhausted as she limped her way over to the toilet. "Um." She turned to face him with her hands on the waistband of her pants. "You need to leave."

Noah's phone beeped a text received. *"Oui. Excuse."*

He stepped out of the bathroom and into the little hallway between the front door and the bedroom, closing the door behind him before he read the text: McD Pk, 30m. Mike was in Kamloops. And what would bring the undercover officer here? A bomb perhaps? Set to eliminate an off-duty officer?

After a few minutes, the bathroom door opened behind him. Noah moved aside so Ella could shuffle out.

"How you feeling, *bébé*?" he asked.

"Ugh," she replied. "My clothes are filthy and itchy. Why are we at a hotel? I want to go home. My clothes are at home." She slumped down on the foot of the bed she'd been sleeping in.

"Here." Noah had used his button-down shirt to put out the fire on her—his stomach quivered at the memory of flames on Ella's body—leaving him in his grey technical shirt. He pulled it off over his head. "You can wear this. You'll feel more comfortable."

Ella looked at the T-shirt dangling from his fingertips then up to his face. "I…hm."

"Are you hungry?" he asked, setting the shirt on the bed beside her.

"Ugh." She grimaced. "Just thirsty." Shifting around the bed, she reached over and picked up the now empty water bottle he'd left on the night table. The lemonade cup had been emptied, as well. "Can you please get me more water? From the tap is fine."

"Okay. Sure." He took the bottle and filled it in the bathroom, returning it to her. Had it only been a few months ago she'd gone thirsty rather than trust the cup of water he offered her? "While I'm out, I can get clothes."

"All right." She picked up his shirt and pressed it to her nose, inhaling. "It smells of fire."

"I suppose it would. Probably sweat, too."

She sniffed again. "Not too bad. All right, I'll wear it. But I can't change until you leave. I can't face another walk to the bathroom."

"Do you need help?" His question was sincere but the ruddiness of her cheeks deepened to a hot pink making it plain where her mind had gone.

"I'll manage."

His imagination ran riot for a moment before he pushed the image of her slipping out of her clothes aside. He needed to keep her safe. Meeting Mike was the next step in that process, not climbing into bed beside her.

"Okay," he said. "I'll be back within two hours. Put on the deadbolt. Let no one in. I'll knock three times when I get back."

"What do you mean?"

"I need to go out for bit."

"But you can't sleep here," she said, rising. She held his T-shirt in front of her like a shield, even though she was still fully dressed.

"I'm not leaving you alone, El. If this wasn't important, I wouldn't go now. My car exploded. I need you to be safe. So, yes, I will sleep here."

"You can't, Noah. We're not married yet. We can't sleep together."

*Yet?* Interesting. Definitely something to pursue later. "We won't be having sex, *chérie*. I'll use the second bed. All perfectly moral."

"I…just…what will people think?"

"That I want to keep you safe?" Noah gestured, palms up. "Who cares what they think, eh?"

"It matters a little." Ella gripped her forehead. "Oh. My head hurts. I can't deal with this right now."

*Good.* Noah picked up her purse and retrieved her house keys from it. "Fix the deadbolt after I go."

Ella shuffled to the door where he pulled her into his arms. He massaged her neck in light compressions. She felt so good against his bare chest, her cheek pressed warmly against his skin. Which reminded him his first stop on the way to meet Mike should be a Wal Mart or someplace to buy a shirt.

"I won't be long." He tipped her chin up and kissed her mouth. Then he left, praying this explosion had nothing sinister behind it, and if it did, that she'd be safe for the couple of hours he needed to discover the plot behind it.

# Chapter 32

Noah found Mike at the band shell in McDonald Park. Without a word of greeting, Mike handed Noah a printed document. It was a forensics report on the contents of his trunk. The chemical residue, the wires and other components all clearly said, "bomb".

"Triggered by the trunk opening," Mike said. "You were lucky."

"How'd you get this so quickly?" Noah asked, glancing up from the report.

Mike didn't bother to respond. When you had the right connections, the wheels of justice moved post-haste.

Noah shifted his topic to something he needed to know more urgently. "Who put it there?"

Mike shrugged. "Classified."

The pose looked casual but Noah wasn't fooled. There was something serious happening. And Mike knew about it. "Don't feed me that bull-spit," Noah growled. "You know and you can tell me."

Mike maintained his unflappable stance. "You're on leave. You are not part of any active cases. My hands are tied." As if to illustrate his message, Mike clasped his hands in front of him.

"Was it Alex Treherne?" Noah asked.

Mike lifted an eyebrow. "Think further back."

Noah wasn't sure what game Mike was playing; he was offering information with one hand while blocking Noah's search with the other. For now, Noah had no choice but to play along. Mentally, he tallied the individuals from his past who might have somehow broken his cover. "Zidane? Rutgers? Howard?" The list of cases he'd worked over the past decade was too long to search. "Who?" His identity had been solid until six months ago when he'd started his leave. Had something happened since then?

"Think ten years ago. The op that never happened."

*Ten years. Plausible deniability.* Something clicked in Noah's mind. "Maximiano Guerra? You're telling me a kid did this?"

"He's not a kid anymore. He turned eighteen six months ago."

"But...how? Why?" Noah asked. He paced away then back again. *This doesn't compute.* "The death of Chenche Hernandez-Guerra put Augustus Sander in control of the cartel. He was cooperative, isn't that what we were told? Why would Sander send the kid after me now?"

"Sander died of an unexpected deadly snake bite in his bathtub three months back—Coral snake from what I hear—placing Maximiano at the head of the cartel. Maxi has officially taken over the reins of his daddy's business." Mike released his hands and crossed his arms over his chest. That was the only sign he gave that the topic had shifted to something more sinister. "You were instructed to leave no witnesses."

Noah flung his arms wide as if to encompass the entire land. "Our motto is no collateral damage."

"The son of a Mexican drug lord is not collateral."

"He was a kid, Mike. I wasn't going to shoot and kill an eight-year-old child."

"Now your girlfriend pays the price."

The accusation pierced Noah's heart. He had failed to protect the woman he loved. His past had returned and hurt her.

Mike had more to say. "You walked away from an opportunity to protect this country from the child of a dangerous man, a criminal bartering deals with one of the most vicious gangs in Vancouver."

"I have to stop him." Noah heard the determination in his voice.

Mike raised an eyebrow. "You're on leave."

And Noah finally understood what Mike wanted. "Fine. Take me back." His voice conveyed the weariness of every year he'd spent in the company of liars and villains. Because he did not want to return to police work. He wanted something new. With Ella. He was falling in love with her and, if she was using terms like, 'not married *yet*', then she might be falling in love with him. He didn't want to lose the precious gift of her love by disappearing into the mists. Yet he had to keep her safe.

Too many sides of the argument to consider.

He'd get her settled at home. Make sure she was safe. Explain, tell her briefly why he had to leave, promise to catch the young man who'd put her life in danger, and then promise to return. He would hold her and kiss her and tell her he loved her. Because, who was he kidding? He'd been in love with Ella Hanover since that first smile. From the moment at Bridal Veil Falls when she'd admitted she liked him, he'd been hooked. He'd stop Maxi. And then he'd retire and return to her little house in Kamloops, marry her, and never, ever leave.

Mike nodded once, accepting Noah's capitulation. "Treherne's arrest left a gulf in the drugs trade which Maxi has the backing to fill. We have word he's been in talks with the Dark Coast Warriors," Mike said.

"Just like his papa," Noah murmured.

"If Maxi's not stopped, we're looking at an all-out drug war on the streets of Vancouver. People are going to die, K. We have a brief reprieve while he tries to take you out."

"If I help you take down the *Pandilla*, what then?"

Mike's expression was inscrutable. "Meet me tomorrow. I'll text you a location."

"I'll be there." He would go. Do his job. And then he would find a way out whether Mike wanted to release him or not.

# PART 3

# CHAPTER 33

Ella left her final meeting with Sergeants Ray and Bonnie, the detectives investigating the car explosion, drove to the ENT clinic and completed her final audiological assessment, passing with flying colours. Her ear drums were healed, her hearing normal, and there was absolutely not one speck of evidence as to who had tried to blow her up exactly one month ago. Case still open. Investigation stalled. No further action taken.

And Noah was gone. Haunting coffee shops and chasing down pizza terrorists or whatever he was up to. He'd been gone for a month, or forever. She wanted things to be the way they used to be, back to normal. And today? *Normal* meant Noah home in Kamloops.

▲

*Sacre bleu!* Noah Kristofer woke in a haze of pain. The agony wasn't localized to any one region of his body and he couldn't convince himself to move. So he slept.

When he roused again, it was night. Though his right eye was swollen and throbbing painfully, he could make out the silhouette of trees and the bright points of stars above. Through his left eye, he saw nothing but red.

*Where am I?*

Flashes of memory, snapshots of violence, returned him to moments or days before. Four men. Fishing vests over crimson-ink spider tattoos. A Makarov, a .38 Special. Bull neck, square jaw, overbite. Fighting for his life in the belly of a helicopter skimming the tops of the trees in the interior of British Columbia. Far from civilization. Alone in the Canadian bush, alone because the bullets meant to end his life had skittered around the metal shell of the copter, pinging off the seats and through the skin to puncture the fuel tank and damage the rotor blades. Whirring, pinging, screaming.

Bright light exploded behind his eyes. A void opened beneath him. And he fell in.

Waking hours later, Noah rolled gingerly onto his back. *Zut!* Propping himself against a nearby tree, he took stock of his body. Something was wrong with his left eye, his face throbbed, agony pulsing in time with his heart, and his head ached viciously. His left side bled sluggishly where the flesh had been scraped raw by the rough pine bark of the trees. A chunk of broken branch protruded from his thigh, the sight making him ill. But he had to cope. Walk out. Because no one was coming to save him. No one knew he was here.

The helicopter was down. When it didn't arrive in Prince George, B.C. as scheduled, Search & Rescue would be alerted. As long as Artus Black, the pilot, had filed a flight plan. Even then, how far from the crash site would the searchers venture? Only Mike Rainer knew that undercover officer, Noah Kristofer, had been aboard, traveling north up the interior of British Columbia to follow the trail of Maximiano Guerra. No one knew that four thugs had held hostage the pilot, a retired RCMP officer who flew tour groups to the remote lakes of B.C. for a living. Nor that the helicopter had exploded after Noah had been shot at and ejected. Or that he had been forced to cling to the foliage, falling and scrabbling for purchase, scraped and beaten by the trees until he'd finally landed in the isolated bush, miles from anywhere. Kamloops, even Monte Creek, would have been a welcome sign of civilization this far into the interior.

Noah searched his pockets, finding his one litre collapsible Platypus bottle in the side pocket of his cargo pants. Only partially full, it hadn't popped when he'd landed. He pulled it out and took a sip. The warm liquid brought temporary relief. His fingers were slick with blood and sweat but functioned well enough to prise his Gerber pocketknife out of his front pocket. He needed to get that chunk of wood out of his leg before he passed out again. Then he needed to stop the bleeding. About his left eye, he had no idea what to do.

His body protested every movement as he removed his shirt. With shaking fingers, he cut the sleeves off and then put on the ravaged shirt. Using a strip of cloth created from his sleeves as a sweatband on his forehead to keep perspiration from dripping like acid into his damaged eye, he snugged the other around his leg above the wound. Gritting his teeth, he pulled the shards, one. At. A. Time. *Groan.* The world turned grey, shimmering at the edges.

He resigned himself to oblivion.

Noah roused again as the sun rose, the bright orange rays glinting off the billowing clouds in the pale blue sky. Coniferous trees, pines, birch, larch, surrounded him where he lay at the base of a tall yellow pine, curled in a ball around his wounds. Blinking rapidly, he tried to clear his vision. He could see through his swollen right eye though it felt like he had a first class shiner; like he'd gone three rounds with Muhammad Ali and led with his face. His left eye was still giving him nothing but a red wash. His left leg was hot around the wound but the bleeding had stopped. Loosening his makeshift tourniquet, he refashioned it into a bandage. The effort sapped his strength.

*God, help me.* Why had it seemed so important to find Maximiano Guerra? Why had he let Mike draw him away from Ella? Ella.

**Get up. Walk.**

Noah struggled to his feet, limping forward two steps and then two more. *Ella. Home.* He set the goal as the tree straight ahead, one step closer to Ella and home. When he reached there, he leaned against the tree and vomited. Taking a sip of water first to clean his mouth, he set his sights on the next tree and walked. *Ella. Kamloops. Good pizza, and fresh, cold water.* Except the pizza in Kamloops sucked.

On and on he shuffled from one tree to the next, scoring every tenth with an X to mark his path and progress. Every fifty trees, he rewarded himself with a sip of the lukewarm water in his Platypus. His blood pulsed in his veins. His head throbbed. The vibrations of his body repeated, "Ella. Kamloops. Pizza *foutaise*," with every step.

*Oh, God, help me. Take me to Ella.* He held his knife away from his body because he knew that eventually he would fall and he had no desire to land on the point. Though he wasn't sure it was possible to hurt any worse.

# CHAPTER 34

When the telephone rang, Ella removed the pasta from the burner and turned it off. Proof she learned from her mistakes, she never answered the phone with supper on the stove. Although, that fiery mistake had led to an evening of fun with Noah and had definitely been a turning point in their relationship. *Noah.*

She sighed, answering the phone in the living room. "Hello?"

"Ms. Ella Hanover?"

She didn't recognize the voice. "Who is this?"

"My name is Revan Yu of the B.C. Parks Commission. Am I speaking to Ella Hanover of Kamloops?"

"Yes, that's me."

"Ms. Hanover, I was part of a team investigating the crash of an aircraft in the interior of British Columbia."

Ella replied because he seemed to expect it. "Yes."

"A hiker called in a report of a survivor within the boundaries of the Mt. Seymour Provincial Park. The man was alive though injured and ill."

"I heard on the news there was a hiker found up north." Ella circled her fingers in the air in an "and so" gesture.

"I was the individual who located the survivor in the bush."

"Okay," she replied. Why had this man called to brag to her?

"He, the man, was unconscious for most of the time I was with him as we waited for an air ambulance to take him to Vancouver General Hospital.

However, he did come-to on a few occasions." Yu cleared his throat. "He repeated the name Ella Hanover several times, then the city of Kamloops and," Yu cleared his throat again, "pizza footays. That last one was odd, though I'm certain that's what he said."

*Footays? Foutaise. Baloney on a cardboard crust.* Ella stifled an absurd desire to giggle while her heart sped in excitement and her stomach bottomed out in dread. Laugh or cry? Both. Neither. "Did the man have any identification on him? Because that sounds like my Noah."

"That is interesting. Noah. The man was carrying no identification."

Ella's palms dampened. Was it Noah? Was he hurt? How did he wind up in a crashed plane? "What did he look like? The man you found?" She was proud of how calm she sounded. Because inside she was a roiling mass of confusion, dread, and hope.

"His injuries…around the face…it was hard to say. He was tall, over six foot, two-twenty or so, curly brown hair. He had a beard. You know, one of those on the chin only. A goatee, I think it's called."

"It sounds like Noah." Ella's throat tightened. "His name is Noah Kristofer. Where is he? I need to see him. Is he okay?"

"With the crash and everything happening here, it's taken me some time to get in touch with you. Mr. Kristofer was air-lifted to Vancouver General several hours ago."

"Thank you, Mr. Yu." Tears burned the back of her eyes. "Thank you so much."

"My pleasure. Ms. Hanover? Good luck."

Ella hung up then called into work, taking an emergency leave. Dylan Meeker, a fellow psychologist who specialized in treating traumatized youth, promised to cover for her.

Three and a half hours later, Ella pulled into the Vancouver General Hospital. She wasn't sure how she'd made it without driving her Honda Element into a tree or a logging truck. But here she was.

Ella walked through the front doors of the hospital, spotting the information desk located off to the left of the entryway.

"Hello," Ella read the woman's name tag: Hello, my name is Jacintha. How may I be of service? "Jacintha. I'm here to see Noah Kristofer. Capital K-r-i-s-t-o-f-e-r."

*Capital K? Really?* Ella's mind flitted to the smelly Detective Longford and then returned to the present at the woman's response, "We have no one registered here by that name."

"He came in as a survivor of an airplane crash," Ella explained. "I got a call from someone at the B.C. Parks Commission. He might still be a John Doe."

"Yes," Jacintha said, studying the computer screen in front of her. "We have two John Does. One is approximately sixty years of age. He was found on Cambie Street three days ago, suffering from hypothermia and other complications. The second was brought in by helicopter this morning. Age approximately mid-thirties."

"That's him." Ella's heart beat harder.

"Are you a relative?" Jacintha finally looked up at Ella.

"Not yet," Ella replied.

"Well, he's not in the ICU, so it's probably okay." Jacintha retrieved a pen from the Mickey Mouse mug on the counter and wrote the room number on a yellow Post-it.

Ella found the elevators. She pressed **5**, waiting impatiently as the metal car rose before she debarked to find the number on the page. But her feet wouldn't carry her across the threshold. She couldn't just rush in. It might not be Noah. Instead, she looked through the window in the door. The room was modern, sterile, white. A large bank of windows let in the grey of the sky, suffusing the room in Vancouver dull. The lone occupant of the room looked large in the hospital bed. The pale blue blanket and industrial white sheet were pulled up to his chest. He—because he was obviously male—was turned away from the door, but Ella saw white bandages covering his head and half his face. Even from this distance, she could tell the man was battered and bruised.

"Can I help you?"

Ella spun. A woman stood there wearing deep purple scrubs, a stethoscope, and a nametag that read, Lorene. It didn't say, Dr. Lorene, so she assumed it was a nurse.

Ella gestured vaguely toward the room. "I'm here to see if I know the man in there."

Lorene pursed her lips as she gave Ella a once-over. "Are you family?"

"Close friend," Ella replied. "Very close."

Lorene nodded once then opened the door, gesturing for Ella to follow her in.

The man in the bed was tall and broad-shouldered like Noah. But with the damage and bandaging around his face, it was difficult to pick out specific features. He looked like he'd gone ten rounds with a grizzly. That's what Revan Yu had said, that the survivor of the crash was injured beyond recognition. No, not beyond recognition, just that his features were hard to distinguish.

Lorene touched Ella lightly on the arm. "He was unconscious when he arrived, battered and badly dehydrated. He's been down for an X-Ray and is waiting for his CT scan."

Ella reached out to touch his hair, letting her fingers slide from his dirty locks along the whiskers on his cheeks to the longer auburn hair of his goatee. The man—because she still wasn't certain if she recognized him—turned toward her, unconscious.

"Noah?" Ella slipped her hand down along his arm, skirting the bandages, to his hand. She lifted it and studied his fingers. His knuckles were scraped and raw, his fingernails ragged and torn. But this was definitely the hand that had held hers, the hand that had stroked her face so tenderly.

"Honey." Ella gasped out a sob she hadn't anticipated. *Oh, Noah.* "What happened to him?" she asked, pressing her lips to his battered knuckles.

"As I said," Lorene replied with calm patience. "He has been unconscious since he arrived. No one knows for certain what happened, but it seems he was involved in an accident in the interior, and then hiked out alone."

"The bandages." Ella nodded toward Noah's head and arms.

"I cannot discuss his injuries with you unless you are a family member." She sounded sympathetic. "You can stay through visiting hours." Placing a hand on Ella's arm for a moment, Lorene turned to go.

"His name is Noah Kristofer with a capital K and an f," Ella said over her shoulder.

"I'll let the doctor know."

Ella put the nurse out of her mind. Leaning down, she kissed Noah on the cheek and then on his ear. "Noah. Can you hear me?" She leaned over his face, stroking her fingers through locks of hair not covered by white gauze. "It's Ella. Please wake up, honey. I'm so happy to see you."

The words caught in her throat. She was happy to be near him again but her heart ached at the pain she saw on his body, the evidence of a battle. She bit her lip to keep from crying.

"Please, be okay."

# Chapter 35

Ella woke after a fitful slumber on the lumpy mattress in the Ramada Inn nearest Vancouver General. After a barely warm shower and an uninspired continental breakfast that consisted of orange juice, toast, and strawberry jam—not a muffin in sight—she returned to the hospital.

When she arrived at Noah's room, she heard voices within, a husky male voice and a female voice. She didn't recognize either and couldn't detect the words they said, but neither individual sounded pleased.

Ella knocked then pushed the door open.

"Get your hands off me."

"Excuse me," Ella said, hoping to reach into the midst of this argument and bring a little peace.

"This is not a good time. Wait outside." The owner of the female voice was clearly this woman in pale yellow scrubs and bearing a nametag which read, Magda. She was sturdy, fair-complexioned, and not to be messed with.

"Move, lady," the male voice snapped at Magda.

"He needs to take his medication," Magda insisted. "Please wait outside."

The man snorted derisively. "I'm not taking anything to make me sleep. I've been out too long as it is." Though the voice sounded off, the message was all Noah.

Ella stepped around nurse Magda and kept going to his side. He was lying almost flat on the bed. However, that submissive position didn't seem to translate to acquiescence.

"It is not only to help you sleep but to help with the pain," Magda replied, hands on hips.

"Find me something that does one and not the other," Noah insisted. And then told her in no uncertain terms, "We're done."

His focus shifted completely to Ella. Magda gave up with a gesture of disgust, and departed. Noah didn't even mark her exit.

"Hi," Ella said, her voice soft and gentle.

"El." Noah's voice was as tender as it had been irritated. "I can't believe I made it. You're here." He tugged her hand until she sat on the bed beside his hip.

"I missed you," Ella said.

"Yeah," he whispered.

"What happened? When you left me you were planning to find Max Guerra and arrest him."

Noah closed his eyes—though she only saw the one—and then opened them to stare at the ceiling as though it contained the answers he needed. He remained still and quiet for a long moment which grew longer as Ella waited.

*Why doesn't he kiss me?* "Should I paint a mural up there so you have something more interesting to look at than the bare white ceiling?"

The tiniest hint of a smile pulled at the corner of his mouth, the corner not obstructed by pristine, white bandages. "Ella by Rubens. I would enjoy that."

Ella's brows furrowed. "I'm not sure what that means but I'm going to assume it's flattering."

He turned his head to the side to scan her face with his one good eye. Though, to be honest, the eye looked purple and swollen rather than good. What did that indicate about the one they'd covered with a bandage?

"I missed you," he said.

"I missed you, too," she replied. "Did you really fall out of an airplane?"

"Helicopter. And I didn't fall. I was pushed." There was no lilt in his voice at all. His speech and language patterns were neutral. "I got a tip that Maxi, the little turd, was in Prince George. Mike, my handler, hooked me up with a retired RCMP officer who runs tourists up the interior. He picked up four fishermen, planning to drop them at Anahim Lake. It was a little off the path, but, hey, everyone needs to make a living." Noah's visage darkened on these last words.

"They weren't fishermen?"

Noah made a disgusted sound. "Gangbangers. They got the drop on me. Planned to shoot me and drop my body in the bush."

"Oh, Noah." Ella's heart squeezed at the violence he'd experienced, violence that was printed all over his body in black and blue and crimson.

"I can't remember all the details. Gunshots. Wrestling for my life. I'm certain the helicopter exploded not long after I fell into the canopy."

"Canopy?"

"The trees. Artus managed to get us low enough."

"So you could climb down a tree?" she asked. How was that possible?

Noah huffed a laugh that held not one whit of amusement. "Think ping-pong ball. Pinball may more accurately describe my descent."

She tried to imagine. But failed. "What did the doctors say?"

His gaze slipped away again. "Skull fracture. The gash on my leg is infected. No surprise there."

"What about your eye?" Ella touched the white bandage gently.

"Which one?"

"What do you mean?"

"Right one, orbital fracture, they called it. Have to operate to stabilize it or something."

"And the left?" she asked.

"Too much damage. Blind." He gulped loudly.

"Oh, Noah. I'm so sorry. But so glad you survived."

"You don't understand." Noah shifted to his elbow.

All the colour leeched from his face. Groaning, he dropped back to the mattress and curled onto his side. "Gonna throw up," he gritted out between his teeth.

Ella scanned the room for a waste basket or kidney tin or something.

"Hurry," he moaned.

Running into the bathroom, she grabbed a plastic basin and returned to hold it in position. His body contracted in a spasm as he tried to resist the impulse to vomit. He retched twice then threw up his breakfast. When he finished, he flopped onto his back, spent and aching.

"Do you want me to get a nurse?" Ella asked, resting her palm on his pale, clammy forehead.

"No."

"I'll empty this." She took the basin into the bathroom, emptying the foetid contents into the toilet. She rinsed the basin in the sink and deposited the fouled water into the toilet before flushing.

When she sat back down beside Noah she placed the basin on his bedside table, just in case they needed it again.

"Feeling better?" she asked, stroking her fingertips along his forehead to the edge of the bandage and back to his temple. She caught the sharp bite of bile on his breath. "Do you want a drink?"

"Yeah. Something to get rid of the taste."

By the time, she returned with a can of ginger ale and two of those ridiculously tiny straws, Noah was back on his side, retching. He was pallid, sweating. His body convulsed. Agony tightened his muscles and he groaned pathetically. This was more than a little nausea.

"Nurse? Nurse!"

Magda took one look in the room and called for assistance. A second nurse arrived, insisting Ella leave. Two doctors followed the nurses into the room.

Wasn't this an overreaction to a little vomiting?

Ella heard the words, "emergency surgery". And then he was gone.

A flash of white pierced Noah's brain, propelling him into consciousness. Groaning aloud, he jackknifed up. A giant fist punched him in the stomach, his cry of pain blocked by a wave of nausea large enough to fell him. He heaved and curled into a ball on his side, clutching his stomach. Light flashed behind his eyes, so brilliant he was blinded. Pain ricocheted through his skull. He cried out, gripping his head in his hands. It was so bright he couldn't see anything. He tugged at his bandages, pressed his fingers into his eyes. His head exploded in agony and he cried out again and again, guttural sounds of pain, a gorilla amongst the leaves, a boar rooting in the dust.

Voices sounded. Hands grasped. Pain. More pain. Lethargy that stole his ability to fight the pain. Numbness to soothe the edges of his agony, to dim the brightness.

A black spot emerged in the centre of the blinding white. It grew, filling his vision.

Ella. *Where are you?*

# Chapter 36

By moving his tent around the forested areas of the Provincial Park and scavenging small amounts of food from campsites while their owners were off touring or at the beach, Grady and Otto survived several weeks without being noticed. They might have lasted all summer, right through Labour Day weekend, if the dude with the Rottweiler hadn't stayed an extra week. He'd complained about Otto to the park ranger, just because Otto refused to run scared when the jerk's filthy brute came tearing out from beneath the man's camper-trailer when Grady snuck onto the campsite to get a cola from the cooler. *Jeesh!* What had he expected? He left the cooler on the picnic table twenty-four-seven. Adults could be so stupid.

Grady knew they shouldn't chance another encounter with the man. He would yell, the dog would bark, a ranger would be called, and then Grady's escape would be over. The Mounties would arrive and send him off to another set of guardians.

Grady was done with guardians. If Lillian and Peter couldn't be his parents, then he'd make it on his own, just him and Otto.

Checking the mapping app on his iPhone, Grady planned a route. He needed to get to Vancouver. In Vancouver, he'd find Uncle Macken. Or disappear into the streets. He wasn't sure yet which was the best idea. But he had grown up in Vancouver and lived on the streets. If he decided to stay away from Uncle Macken, he could survive there and be free.

The clatter of packing and the calls of an older couple across the road made Grady look up. Otto woofed low in his throat. The old people who drove the dark green camper-pickup truck were loading it. Their truck had a **Beautiful British Columbia** licence plate.

"Let's hike to the Upper Hot Springs and take one more soak," the man suggested to his younger wife. At least she looked younger. Her hair was black while the man's hair was grey. They both looked kind of wrinkly so Grady wasn't sure.

The man put the last lawn chair into the camper and closed the door. He didn't lock it. Instead, he put a baseball cap on his head and took his wife's hand. They walked away toward the Upper Springs trail.

*Ding, ding.*

The hot springs were not more than a kilometre or so away from the start of the trail. Old people sometimes found them too hot and didn't stay long. If Grady wanted a free ride to beautiful British Columbia, two steps closer to Vancouver, he needed to get inside with Otto quickly.

He made a quick accounting of their food and drinks, took Otto to empty his bladder, and then emptied his own against the same tree. He waited until no one was looking and then slipped into the camper.

# CHAPTER 37

"*Andhērā.*" Noah's voice was raspy and faint. But it filled Ella with joy.

Twenty-four hours ago, Ella had been ejected from Noah's room while he was taken for emergency surgery. Surgery. For vomiting? When she'd finally been allowed back to his side, she'd known, without a doubt, that something terrible had happened. She asked, she begged, she pleaded for information, but because she was not family, she had no rights aside from any Tom, Dick, or Mary off the streets. No one would tell her what was happening.

Both of Noah's eyes were bandaged now, a path of white gauze that covered the upper portion of his face and his left ear. They'd secured his wrists to the bedframe.

"Thirsty."

Ella pressed a straw between Noah's lips. He sipped, but the action seemed to exhaust him.

"S'dark."

"I know, Noah. Relax." Ella brushed her fingers through his hair and leaned over to kiss his cheek, low down over the angle of his jaw, one of the few unbruised spots on his face.

"*S'est passé?* Em' I?" He sounded groggier, as though he was already falling asleep again.

"There was an accident. You're in the hospital. Your face is bandaged." Pressing her face into the crook between his neck and shoulder, she kissed him again, hoping her even breathing would calm him. "Go back to sleep."

He turned his head so his cheek rested against hers. "Kay." He drifted back to sleep.

Ella was left alone with her fear.

▲

"El-lá?"

"I'm here, Noah." She stroked his cheek and gripped his hand.

He flailed, groping, pulling against the restraints. "*Foncé. Pourquoi*? Why z'it so dark?"

"Everything will be okay." She tried to pour every ounce of reassurance into her voice, to convey confidence and comfort through her fingertips.

"Turn on the light. It's too dark."

This was the third time in the past thirty-six hours Noah had awakened confused, speaking in multiple languages, and complaining of the dark.

Ella used the call button to summon a nurse. Unfortunately, Jenny was on rotation. Ella pressed the button to no avail.

"El-lá! *Zut!* Turn on the light! *Prakāśa!*"

She gripped his fingers. "Calm down, honey. It's just the bandages. Everything will be all right." She moved over him, pressing his shoulders into the bed. If he didn't stop flailing around, he would injure himself. "Noah. Settle. Please. Calm down." Her heart jerked in her chest. He was miserable. Terrified. Her eyes filled with tears.

Finally, Jenny arrived. "What can I do for you?"

"You can call the doctor," Ella snapped at her. "He's in the dark. He's frightened. Help him."

"I'll get a sedative," Jenny said, sniffing like a cat whose favourite sleeping spot was occupied.

"And the doctor," Ella insisted. They might not care to share anything with her, but they seemed to care about Noah.

Another sniff from Jenny. "Then I will contact the doctor."

Ella turned back to Noah. Her heart squeezed at the torment printed on his face. He struggled, reaching for something she couldn't give him.

"It's okay, sweetheart. Close your eyes and rest." A sob blocked her airway. She swallowed it back.

Jenny returned and the sedative she administered sent Noah back to sleep. But sleep was a poor solution for this problem.

Before long, the Ophthalmologist arrived. Doctor Gill was an Indian man, born in Yavatmal in Central India. He had trained in the Christian nursing school nearby and then trained as a physician when he arrived in Canada in his early twenties. He was bright and kind and talkative. And had found a way to explain the procedure he'd performed on Noah's eye socket fracture without divulging any facts about Noah's case. Ella liked him.

Dr. Gill checked Noah's heart sounds, respiration, pulse, and blood pressure. Then he moved the bandages on Noah's face and Ella got her first glimpse of his injured and operated on eyes. His right eyelid was bruised and puffy, the purpled tissue around it also swollen. There were stitches below the eye, their black, cross-hatched pattern looking all wrong against his skin. Noah's left eyelid was marked by a raw-looking scar.

When Dr. Gill lifted the right lid to flash his light in, Ella saw a familiar, rich brown eye. The pupil did not react to the light. With extra care, the doctor pried Noah's left eye open and Ella's first impression was *pain*. The sclera was red, like it was seriously bloodshot, but the coloured part of his eye was all black. The pupil was blown, the doctor had said, meaning it had dilated fully because of the damage the flying branch, or whatever had ruined it, had done.

"What do you think, Dr. Gill?" she asked, her heart aching in pity for the list of things Noah had lost. What would be added to the list?

"Hm," the doctor replied, turning to her. "He regained consciousness again?"

"Yes."

"Tell me what he said."

"He said it was dark. Asked me to turn on the light." She didn't know whether to tell them about the way he was mixing his languages. Noah was usually so careful to camouflage his background.

"Hm," the doctor repeated.

"What do you think is going on? He seemed okay yesterday morning. I mean, as okay as you expect someone to be who was pushed out of a helicopter. Until he started vomiting. Is that normal after an accident, the vomiting?"

"I'm ordering a high resolution CT scan. Eye and ear." Dr. Gill replaced the chart in its pocket on the wall.

*Eye and ear?* "Doctor? Please?"

Dr. Gill's dark brown eyes dropped to meet hers. "I don't like to speculate. In a few hours, we'll know more." He turned to go, surprising Ella by patting her on the shoulder first. "It's good you're here for him."

"I am," she replied.

Tears filled her eyes.

# CHAPTER 38

The next morning, Ella sat in Dr. Gill's office in a faux-leather chair, waiting for news. The doctor entered after a few minutes.

"Good morning, Ms. Hanover."

Ella rose and shook his hand. "Good morning."

As Dr. Gill rounded his desk, he said, "We need to wait for one other person."

"Who?"

The doctor looked above and beyond her, toward the door. "Ah, come in, Mr. Rainer."

Ella turned to see the man she had met as Mr. Smith, the man who had rescued her from Longford only to lose her to Treherne's villains.

"You. What are you doing here?" Ella rose, ignoring Smith/Rainer's hand. She swivelled her head to meet Dr. Gill's gaze. "Why is he here?"

The doctor gestured for them both to sit. "Mr. Rainer has Noah Kristofer's power-of-attorney."

Ella gaped at Smith. Rainer. "You do? Are you a relative or something? And I thought your name was Smith." Why would this man hold Noah's POA rather than his father or one of his brothers?

"I'm his boss." Mr. Rainer flicked a glance at the doctor, hesitating over the word "boss" as though he'd been planning to use a different term.

"At the RCMP?" Ella asked. Was this the handler Noah had spoken of, his team commander? "Are you Mike?"

"He has been loose-lipped." Rainer frowned. "What else did he tell you?"

All at once, she was reluctant to speak. "Nothing. Just that he was a police officer and you were his," she hesitated a beat like he had, "boss."

Mike's smile was unpleasant. "Right." Mike ended the conversation, turning to Dr. Gill. "What have you found, doctor?"

"Are you comfortable with Ms. Hanover attending this meeting?" The usually pleasant expression was absent from the doctor's face. He had picked up on the tension between them. Not that it was subtle, Ella supposed.

Mike passed his eyes over her. "Yes. Noah seems to trust her."

"Seems to—" She slapped her hands on her thighs, appalled at the man's nerve. "I'm the one who's been here for him for these horrible days. Where have you been?"

"Busy." Mike turned to the doctor again who looked back and forth between them, nonplussed by the situation. "Carry on," Mike murmured, gesturing for the doctor to do so.

Ella pressed her lips together to keep silent. Noah had said the bad information he was given or the bad chopper pilot or something had come from his handler. Mike.

"Very well," the doctor replied. "Initially, we were dealing with two separate issues: vertigo and vision loss." Dr. Gill took a sip from the mug on his desk and continued. "The vertigo seems to have resulted from a fracture of the temporal bone suffered during Mr. Kristofer's accident. A fragment of bone penetrated the inner ear, introducing air from the middle ear to the inner ear. Dr. Bernard performed the surgery to repair the inner ear. The accident Mr. Kristofer suffered also caused a traumatic injury to the left eye. We were able to save the eye but not his vision in that eye. The impact which caused the temporal fracture, or perhaps a secondary impact, caused a fracture of the bones supporting the right eye. What we call an orbital fracture. Sometime before or during surgery, the bone fragments shifted, injuring the optic nerve."

Ella's stomach clenched at the image. "What does that mean? How does that explain why he's complaining of the dark?" Ella asked, but suddenly she feared she understood.

"There may be some residual vertigo which Dr. Bernard will monitor. As to his vision, we will have to wait and see when he regains consciousness. It is likely, though, that his vision will be affected, perhaps permanently."

"So he's blind," Mike said, the word harsh in Ella's ear.

"I'm sorry."

# Chapter 39

Contrary to the pace of the well-known saying, Rafael Cortez was getting nowhere at glacial speed.

A married couple was murdered in the living room of their urban Calgary home. A boy and a dog were missing. No fingerprints. No witnesses. Except one neighbour who thought she'd heard Spanish coming from the vicinity of the house when she let her cat inside just after one in the morning. As if the language had been produced from the ether to float along the airwaves to her ears. Even more puzzling? Everyone remembered the dog, a white Scottish Terrier. No one had ever spoken to the boy. He'd appeared one day. No one knew whence he'd come. No one seemed concerned that he had disappeared.

The Federal Witness Protection Program was being typically obstructive and uninformative. They seemed unconcerned that two people had died, a couple under their care who should have been safe.

The murder had all the markings of an execution but Rafe had found no evidence—and not even rumours—of the involvement of any of the local gangs. His partner, Knight, kept harping on about rumblings from the streets that a new cartel was moving into Vancouver from Mexico. But what could that have to do with Calgary? With Lillian and Peter Clarke? Nowhere in their background checks—which had all the markings of an authentic history rather than one created by analysts as he would have expected from witnesses in protective custody—was there any connection to drugs or Mexico. Where had this well-liked and clean-living couple come across the means to their murder?

Frustrated, Rafe flipped open the case file and looked again.

# CHAPTER 40

Blind.

Because he'd dropped out of a helicopter in the middle of nowhere. Because wooden splinters had punctured the orb of his left eye as he'd fallen through a forest to the earth. Because impact with a tree branch had shattered the bones around his right eye. He was blind.

"Hello? Noah?"

Noah jerked to awareness. The movement set off his vertigo and he flattened himself against the mattress to quell the nausea. He swallowed twice, to force back his breakfast.

When he was no longer in imminent danger of vomiting on his guest, Noah turned his head toward the voice at the door. "Who is it?"

"It's Enoch Nagi. I heard you'd been in an accident." The voice was closer now.

Noah braced himself for a touch but none came. People were always touching him, nurses, orderlies, volunteers. It drove him crazy.

"Do you mind if I sit?" Nagi was closer still but he hadn't touched him or invaded his personal space.

Relieved, Noah gestured vaguely toward the side of the bed. "Sure. There's a chair somewhere. How did you hear?"

"When Ella called in to ask for time off work, Dylan passed the information on to me," Enoch replied.

"Dylan who?"

"Dylan Meeker works with Ella. He also attends our church."

"Does he? I've never met him. Why should he care about me?"

"Well, truthfully, I think he was worried about Ella. When I heard you had been injured, I wanted to see if there was anything I could do for you. You don't have many contacts in our community, yet."

Noah snorted. That was an understatement. He had the total of one contact. Ella. And that's all he wanted in that puny burg. "I don't need anything," he grumbled. Noah kept his head in line with his body. The posture minimized dizziness.

"All right," Enoch replied. "I can offer the chance to tell me what happened."

Noah wasn't interested in gossip. "You know I used to be a cop?" *Used to be.*

"Yes."

*Well, there you go, then.* "Details are classified."

"Oh. Okay. Were you able to tell Ella?"

"Of course," Noah sneered. As if he wanted to tell everyone what happened. But of course he told Ella.

"That's good," Enoch said, his voice reassuring. "As long as you had someone to talk to about it."

That surprised Noah. Weren't ministers and priests usually nosy people who wanted to butt into your life and tell you how to live?

"Have you been to Vancouver before?"

"Yeah," Noah replied belligerently. "I've lived here a few times."

Enoch didn't respond to Noah's angry tone. "I've only visited once before. I come from out east, the Maritimes. Outside Halifax. When I was eleven, my family moved to Ontario. After university, I attended Tyndale Seminary in Toronto then headed out west after I graduated." Enoch shifted in his seat. "I attended a Foundational Theology conference a few years ago in Vancouver. It was an incredible experience."

"Why would you live in Kamloops if you had an opportunity to live in a real city?" Noah said, stopping short of sneering at the man.

Enoch chuckled. "Ella told me your opinion of Kamloops."

*Hm.* He complained about Kamloops by habit more than anything. The city was too small. Right? He'd thought that once. But now? It was the one place Noah wanted to get to. Because Ella lived there. And Noah desperately wanted to go home with Ella. "I guess it's growing on me."

"It has the diversity of a city with the sense of community usually found in a small town. I like that about it."

"Lousy pizza. *Dégueulasse.*"

Enoch laughed outright. "You know? I've never been much of a fan of pizza. It's a lot of dough with a sauce I'd rather have on spaghetti, and toppings that, normally, I'd cook in the sauce."

"Calgary has some of the best pizza in the country," Noah replied.

"Really? My wife wants to take the kids to Calgary for the Stampede next year. You can tell us where to get some truly tasty pizza."

"Yeah. Sure." Will I ever taste good pizza again? Will I ever do any of the things I enjoy?

"You're young, Noah." The pleasant tone left Enoch's voice. It grew serious. "So much life left to live."

"I'm blind." Noah had no idea why he'd blurted that out.

"I'm sorry. That will take some getting used to," Enoch replied.

"You think that God has a plan for our lives." It was a statement Noah had heard often enough in church, even though he'd only been a Christian for a short time. "I was a cop, a good cop. I helped put away a lot of scumbags. That's over now."

"But, Noah, life is about so much more than that. Being a police officer, a firefighter, doctor, pastor, teacher, scientist, ditch digger, bottle washer, it's only a part of what life is all about. What we do outside our jobs is sometimes the larger part of how God uses us in the world." He cleared his throat. "Fanny Crosby was blind, yet she penned some of the most beautiful and meaningful songs in history. Beethoven was deaf for part of his life but created musical works of art. Jim Elliott gave his life as a missionary only to be killed by the very people he wanted to help. From his ministry sprang the opportunity of transformation for a people group that was isolated and incarcerated by the evil of their culture. Noah," Enoch said, shifting in his seat. "Do you mind if I touch your arm?"

Noah grunted his assent. Soon, a warm hand gripped his forearm.

"'He is no fool who gives up what he cannot keep to gain what he cannot lose.' Jim Elliott said that." Enoch placed a cool hand on Noah's forehead, a brief gesture of comfort. "Life isn't about what we think it is. It's about so much more. Sight, hearing, eloquence, none of these matter to God. He loves us, he uses us to be his love in the world. He doesn't need your vision. God needs you, Noah. He loves you, as if you were his one and only love. Never limit God to healer, matchmaker, scientist. He is so much more than that."

Noah was fixated by Enoch's voice. No, not by his voice, by his message. Brightness filled Noah's mind and he heard a voice inside him telling him he was loved.

Enoch continued. "First Corinthians two tells us, 'No eye has seen, no ear has heard, no mind has conceived what God has prepared for those who love Him.'" Enoch gave Noah's arm a light squeeze. "Paul says, in Romans twelve, 'therefore, I urge you, brothers, to offer your bodies as living sacrifices, holy and pleasing to God which is your spiritual worship. Do not conform any longer to the pattern of this world, but be transformed by the renewing of your mind.'"

"What does it mean there, be transformed?" Noah asked.

"What does that mean to you?"

"Me? I'm so new at this, what do I know about God?"

"What do you think it might mean?" Enoch persisted.

Noah thought about that for a while, conjuring a picture in his mind of a dark room illuminated by the simple act of flipping a switch; a room transformed from darkness to light. But that verse wasn't talking about anything so simple as a lightbulb. It was talking about people. And how they reacted. So what was normal and what was a transformation? "It's normal to be angry when something good is taken from us."

"Yes," Enoch replied, encouraging him.

"It is normal to hate our enemies. To fear evil. It's normal to blame other people when things go wrong. So there's no transformation there, no change from the status quo."

Enoch chuckled. "Once you have children, if you choose to have children, you'll quickly discover that blaming others is truly status quo."

Noah was so deep in thinking he barely heard the attempt at humour. "So if I embrace the dark, I would be transformed." He paused. "No, that's not right. I have to allow God to transform me so I can embrace the dark."

Enoch stilled. The room became eerily quiet.

"What? What's wrong?" Noah said. He couldn't read Enoch's expression so he couldn't figure out what was creating the silence.

"That is the most insightful idea I have ever heard. You are a born theologian, Noah. Wow," he said the final word on a breath, wonder in his voice. "May I use that analogy?"

Noah shrugged. He didn't care. He didn't need ownership, just vision. And Maxi Guerra in a prison cell. Along with whoever sent the gangbangers after him. And they could rot there forever, too.

Enoch said, "Darkness is often used as an analogy for evil. But God's light penetrates even the darkest night. Darkness is no barrier to Him."

"Thanks." Noah slipped his hand up and squeezed Enoch's fingers briefly. Then he crossed his arms over his chest.

"Thank you, Noah."

They were both silent for a time, even as a nurse came to check Noah's vitals and change his IV.

"Is there anything I can get you before I go?" Enoch asked.

"Nah. I'm fine. Ella brings me what I need."

"She's a special person."

"Yeah." He refused to even consider life without her.

"Rod Blanchard would like to come and visit you. Would that be all right?"

"Yeah. Sure. I, uh, don't know when I'll be," *home* "...what will happen."

"It is difficult for him to travel, but when he's determined…" Enoch didn't bother to finish his thought. The chair scraped on the floor. "I should go. I need to check into my hotel. Do you mind if I come by tomorrow?"

"Sure. That'd be good," Noah replied.

"All right, then. See you tomorrow, Noah."

"Bye."

"Hey. I'm back."

Noah's heart picked up at the sound of Ella's voice.

"Hello, Enoch," she said. She sounded surprised to see the man.

"Hello, Ella. How are you keeping?" Enoch said.

"I'm all right. What are you doing here?" she asked.

"Dylan brought Noah's name up for prayer. So I came to see him."

Noah heard a rustle of clothing. "You hugging my woman?" Noah asked, partly joking and partly envious. He couldn't stand up and hug her because of the vertigo.

Ella laughed. "Jealous, Huck? Don't worry, I save my best hugs for you."

Enoch laughed at that. "Goodbye, Ella. Call if you need anything. Noah, I'll see you tomorrow."

The door closed. Noah heard Ella approach the bed.

"My turn," Noah said as he patted the bed beside him. He shifted over carefully so as not to agitate his system.

"Happy to oblige," Ella murmured, curling gingerly against his side. She cupped the side of his neck, pressing her cheek into the space between neck and shoulder. Noah wrapped his arms around her.

# Chapter 41

"Okay, Mr. Kristofer, we're going start building your tolerance for sitting today."

It was the sadist, Nurse Jenny. She was skinny and mean. He knew from the times she'd moved him around in the bed, adjusting his bedding. As slender as her form was, her humour was more so. She never said "please" and she spoke to him like he was brainless rather than simply sightless.

Noah heard the motor running to elevate his bed. He'd managed about forty-five degrees on his elbows while Ella was kissing him. That had been great.

This did not feel great at all. Noah gripped the sheets as the bed tilted up closer to fifty. Nausea welled up within him.

"Stop," he commanded through gritted teeth.

"A little further," Jenny said in her sing-song voice.

Noah breathed sharply in through his mouth and out through his nose, fighting to keep his breakfast down. If he'd known this was on the schedule for the day, he would not have eaten.

The head of the bed continued to rise. Noah groaned. He swept his arm out, connecting with something that clattered to the floor.

"Mis-ter Kris-tofer." Jenny reprimanded him. He pictured her standing there with her hands on her hips, scowling at him.

Noah rolled to his side, gripping his stomach. "I'm gonna hurl," he warned her.

"Breathe deeply…"

The rest of her words were lost as Ella's voice joined it. "Noah. Sweetheart."

He heard her steps. In fact, he concentrated on her footsteps to suppress the urge to vomit.

"What are you doing?" That was to Jenny the sadist.

Ella's cool hands cupped his face.

"Down," he ordered on an inhale.

"Lower the bed, please."

"Ms. Hanover," Jenny began indignantly. "Doctor's orders. He needs to sit up. He has been on his back for nearly a week. We risk further complications if we wait any longer."

"Down," Ella snapped at her. Noah heard a rustle and rush and then the head of the bed lowered. "Tell me when it's okay, baby."

Noah inhaled deeply. The sensation was retreating. "Okay. It's okay now."

Ella's hand reached from the opposite side of the bed to pet his hair. "Breathe evenly now. Do you need a drink?"

"Maybe." He slowly released his death grip on his belly, returning to his back.

"What did you think you were doing?" Ella's hand left his hair. "It hasn't been a week. It's only been four days since his surgery. Did the ENT clear this? He said it would take time for the vertigo to go away. And he's still so sore, his head, his ribs, his leg."

"The doctor—"

"Which doctor? Because I can't believe Dr. Bernard okayed this."

"The doctor covering rounds."

"Call Dr. Bernard," she used the French pronunciation, "and ask his advice. Please." Dr. Bernard was apparently one of the best in the country at dealing with vertigo.

Nurse Jenny huffed away. "Keep him at this elevation," she ordered haughtily.

Ella lowered the bed a few degrees and then went to fetch a ginger ale to settle Noah's stomach.

"No Name?" Noah groused after he took a sip through those idiotically tiny straws.

"Yes. Sorry."

"I could use a beer." Noah lay back against his pillow. "This vertigo is worse than anything."

Ella stroked his arm. "I'm sorry."

Noah shook her off. "Don't pet me. I'm not a dog."

"Sorry." She gritted her teeth to keep from snapping right back at him.

"And you can stop apologizing. It doesn't do me any good. It's irritating."

"Noah," she snapped then drew in a deep breath. He was a unique blend of pathetic and annoying these days. When she trusted her voice she asked, "Do you want me to get some Canada Dry?"

"No." He swung his arm out toward her, groping the air to locate her. "El?"

She grasped his hand and brought it down to the bed. "I'm here."

"Mr. Kristofer."

Ella turned to see Dr. Bernard enter the room. He was tall and slender with dark hair and fair skin. He wore thin wire-rimmed glasses perched on the end of his beak-like nose. As he moved across the room, his lanky frame reminded Ella of one of those inflatable balloon characters you sometimes saw on the roof of car dealerships.

"Who is it?" Noah asked.

"Dr. Bernard, the ENT." So Jenny had called the doctor.

The doctor took Noah's wrist, checking his pulse.

Noah flinched from the unexpected contact. "ENT? What's that?"

"Ear, Nose, and Throat. Otolaryngologist," Dr. Bernard replied. "Mr. Kristofer, are you comfortable with me examining you with Ms. Hanover in the room?"

"Of course." Noah scowled.

Dr. Bernard didn't react to Noah's surliness. "I'm going to check these stitches." He moved to Noah's side and lifted the bandage, palpating the skin around the incision. "Any pain?"

"No," Noah replied.

"Good. The site is healing well. I understand you're still experiencing nausea?"

"Yeah." Noah sounded so petulant, like a sixteen-year-old denied the keys to the family car.

Even so, Dr. Bernard directed his conversation to Noah. Ella thought that was great. She had already noticed that many people, orderlies and volunteers to name a few, ignored him once they realized he couldn't see, as though in losing his vision, he had lost all cognitive ability.

Dr. Bernard continued, "We expect there to be some lingering nausea. I'll order another high resolution CT scan if things don't resolve in a day or so."

"All right," Noah replied.

Dr. Bernard made a note in the chart and departed.

Noah crossed his arms over his chest, his head tilted to the ceiling again. Ella remembered the comment he'd made about a Rubenesque Ella mural. Oh, how she wished she'd painted it for him. Anything to give him more memories of pleasant sights.

"Ella?"

"Yes. I'm here."

"I'm sorry I'm being a jerk."

She was about to tell him it was okay when he said, "I'm so scared."

"It's going to be okay," she replied. *Oh, please, God, let it be okay.*

Noah's hand shook as he lifted it toward her face. She clasped it against her cheek, kissing his palm.

"Don't leave me, El."

"I'm here, Noah."

He tugged and she moved closer. "Hold me," he said then added in a whisper, "Please."

Ella lay down on the bed beside him, resting her arm on his chest and her leg across his thigh, careful of the healing injury on his left.

"Tighter," he said.

She shifted closer and pressed her body against his. "I'm here."

"El?"

"Yes."

"Pet me."

Ella pet him as requested, stroking his arm and shoulder, brushing the hair back from his face, stroking the backs of her fingers across his neck and cheeks, his scruffy beard.

"Don't leave me."

# Chapter 42

Ella found herself sitting in the hospital psychologist's office the next morning. Noah had called in a lawyer and given Ella his power-of-attorney, making it clear in his grumpy and voluble manner that she was his family. It had opened the world of medical and allied health services to her.

"Thank you for meeting with me," Dr. Eveline Cryderman said.

"Dr. Bernard suggested it," Ella replied.

"Tell me a little bit about your relationship with Noah Kristofer."

"We were dating," Ella replied.

"Dating with a view to marriage or as friends or friends with benefits?"

A small smile pulled at her mouth. "We were dating. And we had talked about marriage a little bit. But there were no 'benefits'." Ella used air quotations.

"So marriage was something you were moving towards."

"Yes."

"Tell me what you understand about Noah's injuries."

"He had a skull fracture, the temporal bone, which caused damage to his inner ear, the part that deals with balance. That's what's causing the vertigo. Dr. Bernard repaired that but I guess it can take time to fully recover, so Noah still has some nausea. He's also—there was an orbital fracture to his right eye. The left ... a branch or something else damaged it ... can't be repaired." Ella was struggling to produce the word she needed to say out loud. "He's ... he will be ... he's blind."

"Yes." Eveline nodded. She flipped through a file. "His left eye was damaged during the accident. Dr. Gill—he's one of the best—operated on Noah's right eye socket to stabilize a fracture."

"Fragments of bone sliced," Ella gulped, "the optic nerve. So he's totally blind."

"Yes." Eveline looked up from the file. "Are you aware of any changes in Noah's personality?"

Ella gulped back her emotions to. "He's grumpy, edgy. But he was kind of like that when I met him."

"But since then, his personality had changed?"

"Only settled a little. He had become calmer, less prone to argue."

Eveline cocked her head, interest in her expression. "To what do you attribute this change?"

"He became a Christian."

Eveline nodded, making a note in Noah's file. "With such a traumatic and life-changing injury, we expect to see changes in personality. Noah will need time to grieve, to come to terms with his loss."

"I know," Ella replied.

"What does that mean to you?"

"I—" Ella shrugged.

"I'm not here to press you for a right answer, Ella. I merely want to help you understand your emotions."

Ella pressed her lips together firmly then relaxed them to sigh. "I'm scared. Noah and I were moving toward marriage. I spent a lot of time thinking about having babies with him. But now? Could he even have children?" Ella met Eveline's gaze.

"As far as I'm aware," Eveline flipped back and forth within his chart, "his reproductive abilities were not affected by his accident."

Ella blushed lightly. "I don't mean that, not physically. I mean, how would he even care for a child without his vision?"

"Many blind people have children."

"Yeah? I suppose." Ella dropped her gaze to her hands, thinking out loud. "I always thought I'd work part-time or quit work altogether when my children were born. But if my husband can't work, then how can I?"

"The blind and visually impaired find employment."

"How can he be a police officer when he can't see?"

"A police officer. Yes, I'd forgotten." Eveline flipped through his file again. "That would be difficult."

"If we were already married, I'd stick by him for sure. But we're not. And I don't know what to do. I feel guilty for asking these questions. But I'm scared. What if I have to give up everything I've always wanted to be with him?"

"That's a fair question to ask. You need not feel guilty about it." Eveline folded Noah's file and set it to the side. "You have two decisions to make. The first being whether you want to participate in Noah's recuperation."

"Oh, yes. I can't walk away. No matter what happens, Noah is my best friend. I care about him." *He is so frightened.*

"That leaves the second, a question about your future which simply does not need to be answered yet."

"No?"

"Are you a spiritual person, Ella?"

"I believe everyone is. Every person has a spiritual dimension to their beings. Some people try to fill it with material things, others try to fill it with nothingness."

"Where do you look for spiritual fulfillment?"

"Jesus."

"Can Jesus help you make this decision?"

"Yes." A flutter of peace entered Ella's mind.

"You don't need to decide today what your feelings are for Noah nor what your plans for the future are. Everything has changed. If you're able to move forward from here, you will likely find it easier to decide. Take the time you need. There's no reason to hurry."

"Thank you."

"Any time. My office is always open." Eveline stood and shook Ella's hand.

"I'll be back."

# Chapter 43

Noah awoke with a start, his bladder full to bursting. Because his vertigo had finally abated, he was on his own now to see to his biological needs. Unfortunately, he was still stone blind. And groggy from the medications they had him on to help him sleep.

Noah flailed his arm through the space beside him, trying to reach the bedpan.

"Ella?" No response.

His fingertips grazed a hard, metal object that clattered when it landed on the floor. "*Zut!* El-là!"

Where was she? He pressed the call button clipped to his pillow. "Nurse!"

No response.

Noah reached over the side of the bed. He had no idea where the bedpan had fallen. And, other than the fact the bathroom was off to the left, he had no idea how to get there. The world around his bed was a black chasm.

His muscles groaning and his head pounding, he pushed himself up to sit on the edge of the bed. "Ella, please." His voice softened. He didn't want to wet the bed.

"Noah. What's wrong?"

*Ella.* His entire body relaxed. Then he had to tense again before he lost control of his bladder in relief. "Bedpan," he said, gesturing at the floor around his feet.

"Got it." Her voice was muffled, like she was bending over. She thrust the cold, metal contraption into his hands.

"Is everything all right in here?" Nurse Magda said from a distance. Near the door, he supposed.

"Get her out," Noah muttered. He didn't know how loudly to speak because he didn't know exactly where everyone was in the room. "Hurry." He was going to lose control and hose down the place if he didn't get this done now.

"Thank you, Magda," Ella replied. "I've got it all in hand."

Noah huffed a laugh at the implied suggestion even though he knew Ella hadn't meant it. His countenance fell. She would likely never mean it, never want him now. Because he was blind. The villains had taken his vision though they'd neglected to take his life. They might as well have. If Ella didn't want him, what good did life do him?

"Noah?"

A hand gripped his shoulder, making him flinch. He struggled to control his bladder. "Gotta whiz."

She took his hand holding the bedpan and positioned it.

"Let go. Is the witch gone?"

"Yes, Nurse Magda is gone. She is not a witch, either, Noah. She's very nice. Don't be a jerk."

Noah grunted at her. "Turn around."

When he moved his hospital gown out of the way, it fell back onto his lap. Finally, he yanked it off, ripping the ties at the back, and dropped it. Where it fell, he didn't care. He adjusted his shorts and…relief. He sighed loudly. He was glad Ella had brought him boxers once they took out his pee-on-demand tube.

Ella giggled.

"Are you watching, Miss Hanover?" he whispered.

He heard her sharp intake of breath. Embarrassment. She was embarrassed at his suggestion.

"Of course not." Her indignation rang false.

The misery of his life lifted a moment and Noah chuckled. He imagined her blushing hotly and ducking her eyes as she always did when he embarrassed her. "Liar."

"It's not a lie when I only peeked because...Noah!"

He laughed outright. "Like what you saw?"

She jerked the bedpan out of his hands. He heard the liquid sloshing around inside, the faint hint of urine in the air.

"Careful, *bébé*," he warned, still laughing.

"Humph."

He loved it when she humphed him. She was sexy when she was mad. Though he had learned it was unwise to comment on it.

"I didn't mean to peek," she muttered.

That started his laughter again. In spite of the ache it caused in his ribs and the distant thrum it set off in his temples, it felt good to laugh, to bicker with Ella. To have the darkest days of his pain and fear and confusion lifted for a moment.

He reached for her then thought better of it. "Have you put that thing down yet?"

"Yes."

He'd heard the contact of metal on laminate that indicated she'd placed it on his bedside table. The sharp scent diminished. He'd need to remember not to put his coffee there later. That thought prolonged his chuckle.

He opened his arms in invitation. "I think it's sexy you peeked," he said.

"Uh, Noah? You're practically naked." He heard the renewed blush in her voice.

The fabric of the hospital gown was soft when she placed it in his hands. Complying with her unspoken instruction, he pushed his arms through.

"You ripped it," she said.

He shrugged. He didn't care. The idiotic things were annoying. "Now, come here," he said.

She walked into his arms, wrapping him in a hug. "Don't tease." There was no heat in her warning.

He hugged her as tightly, sighing at the blissful sensation of her body, of her soft hands on the skin of his back. "Glad you're here."

"Mm." She kissed him on the neck then pulled back to kiss his forehead. His headache disappeared for a moment. "Do you want to walk to the bathroom, anyway?"

He should have grabbed hold and pulled her close before she got her hands on that ridiculous hospital gown. If he wasn't getting a kiss on the mouth, he could have had more skin-to-skin contact. "Why?"

"You…you just went to the bathroom. You need to wash your hands."

"I only touched my—"

She slapped her palm over his mouth.

He laughed again, the sound muffled against her palm. Sometimes, she was a sex kitten, kissing his breath away, touching him and driving him out of his mind. *What will sex be like when we finally get to it?* But at other times, she was positively prudish. He liked that about her, the contrast.

Sometimes he wanted to forget the agreement they'd made about waiting for sex. He was tempted to seduce her, to make love to her, to bind her to him so she would never leave. But he wouldn't do that. Going against her beliefs would change her. And, to be honest, as much as he longed to be certain of her commitment to him, he wanted her to choose him because she loved him. He didn't want her choice to be born of guilt or remorse or even lust. He wanted her to want him, all of him and all that meant. Unless she didn't. Then he would take what he could get.

"Come." She tugged his hand until he stood.

He sure hoped he'd tucked himself back into his shorts. No cool breezes down there. But, without the ties, the gown slid forward down his arms.

"Arms out," she ordered him then removed his gown. "I'll grab a new one. And then apologize to the nurses because you destroyed this one."

What would he do without her?

Ella returned with a new gown, tugging it up his arms and tying it at the back. "I left it loose so you can take it off easily if you want to. Without ripping it."

"Can't you get me some T-shirts or something?" he complained.

"Sure. I can do that. But I better check with the nurses first, make sure it's okay."

He grunted. They weren't the ones who had to flap in the breeze without being able to see what was on display.

Her sweet scent filled his nostrils as Ella took his left arm by the wrist and placed his palm on the bed. "Use your touch to find the end of the bed." She moved away from him. Silent.

"El? Is this necessary? My ribs ache. My leg aches. My head aches." His voice faded. "Are you still there?" he asked, feeling a spurt of panic.

"I'm here," she replied but she didn't come close enough to touch. "Find the end of the bed."

*For her.* He complied for her, shuffling unevenly forward until his hand connected with what he supposed was the faux-wood footboard.

Ella secured his hand to the footboard by placing her palm over the back of his hand. "You need to move perpendicular to the end of the bed. Keep your hand on it so you know when you reach the end." She released his hand.

Noah's breathing accelerated. She was his anchor to the earth. Without her touch, he was adrift. He had no confidence he wouldn't walk off the edge of the world into a pit as black as the darkness behind his eyes.

"El," he growled at her.

"You're okay. I'm here. Move around the end of the bed."

"You been plotting with the occupational therapist or something?" he asked grumpily.

"Maybe. Stop stalling. And stop growling at me."

He hadn't even realized he was making a sound, but a growl about matched his level of frustration and, to be honest, his fear.

Noah slid his palm along the top of the headboard. He shuffled forward in tandem with the movement. His right hand sifted the air around him.

He limped for the first couple steps. The ache in his leg from the infected wound had seemed so minor compared to the vertigo and losing his vision. Now that his headaches were manageable with medication—mostly—and he didn't need to worry about falling off the edge of the earth every time he moved, the knitting flesh where a tree branch had once been lodged itched and ached. It was still tender to the touch and Ella described it as angry-looking. Yet it was no bother as compared to navigating an unfamiliar room in the dark.

When he reached the end of the footboard, he jerked to a stop. He was breathing heavily as if he'd just chased down a suspect. Or was fleeing for his life.

"Wait there," she said.

Noah jumped when she placed her hand on his right forearm. His skin tingled from the contact. Probably all the adrenaline pumping through his system.

"My fault," she said as an apology. "I forgot to warn you. I'm going to pace out the distance to the bathroom door."

He heard the soft patter of her feet.

"Five steps," she said.

She retraced the route.

"I'm going to touch you." She gripped his forearm again. "Five steps, just normal-sized steps." Then she released him.

"Aren't you going to help?"

"Help you walk? You know how to walk, Noah. Five steps."

*Right.* He could do this. She was right, it was simply walking. Sweat dripped down his sides and dampened his gown. One step. Start with one step. He forced his foot to move. One.

"One," she said.

He moved the other foot.

"Two."

And then he was adrift. He had to release the footboard to move forward. Noah waved his arms around his body but she was out of reach. "El."

"I'm here. Keep going. I won't let you walk into anything. I promise, love. You can do this."

"Right." *Love.* She'd called him "love".

With herculean effort, he took the third step. All thoughts of throbbing leg wounds, headaches, and sore ribs were forgotten. He was cast adrift in the dark. Then he took the fourth step, and she was there, stopping him by placing her hands on his upper arms. She was in front of him. How did she get there? He'd been concentrating so hard he'd not even heard her move.

"I guess it only takes four of your steps, not five."

She slipped her hands down his arms to his wrists, lifting his arms and placing them against the wall. No, it couldn't be the wall.

"You are standing in the doorway to the bathroom. Nice job."

He heard the pride in her voice. Because he walked. What would she sound like when their children took their first steps? *Whoa.* Way ahead of the game. She hadn't even brought up marriage again since his accident. There may be no babies between them. Ever.

"Now, a step and a half to the toilet. It's on the right-hand side of the room. The sink is," he heard her pace when she released him. "Two steps across and a half-step to the right of the toilet. Did that make sense?"

"Don't need the toilet," he reminded her.

"Okay. Hm." She was silent a moment. "One step in, a quarter-turn and take two steps or so to the sink."

"El." He said her name but decided not to ask for anything. She wanted him to do this on his own. So he did.

Waving his arms, he shuffled forward, imagining a hundred things he could stub his toes on during the journey. He turned and finally his stomach hit the cold enamel of the sink. He gripped the edges and dropped his chin to his chest. His breath huffed in and out of his chest.

"Wash your hands," she commanded from beside him. Close, but again, not close enough to touch. However, her scent filled his head. She smelled of talcum powder and sweet flowers. She smelled of determination and love. He would know her anywhere, by her scent alone.

He washed his hands, fumbling to find the handles of the taps and the soap dispenser. The whirr and clunk of the paper towel dispenser followed and she thrust the wad of paper into his hands. He dried and dropped it into the sink.

"I need an iced coffee, sweet as it gets," Noah said.

"Okay, now back," she said.

Was she kidding? "El," he protested. He was exhausted. No way could he do that again.

"I'm here," she said sweetly, slipping her arm around his waist. "Why don't we work on walking in tandem? The Blind/Low Vision Specialist said that is a skill to cultivate. Put your hand beneath my arm."

He connected with her head and then found her shoulder. He slipped his hand between her arm and her body where he could feel the softness of her breast against the backs of his fingers. Ella squeezed her arm tight, trapping his hand in that haven of softness, and then shifted her position to be slightly in front of him. She moved and he followed.

She walked slowly. Even so, he was unable to keep pace. With an irresistible urge to explore the space with his hands and feet.

When they reached the bed, she removed his hand from her body and pressed it to the familiar footboard. Except it didn't feel familiar. From this angle, it felt different. Noah remembered her instructions and slid his palm along the edge then turned a quarter-turn. He fumbled to press his hand into the mattress.

"Use your leg," Ella said. "Stand tall and walk close enough you can feel the edge of the bed with your thigh. You know it's safe because it's just a bed."

Noah straightened, reluctantly lifting his palm from the mattress. Inching closer, he pressed his leg against the bed frame. He shuffled forward until the bed angled. Reaching down to touch the mattress and feel around, he positioned his body and sat. Then he reclined.

He was done. Toasted. *Tout fini.* His body ached and his head thrummed.

Ella perched beside him on the bed and then leaned in slowly to embrace him. "I'm so proud of you. You are amazing."

"For walking," he replied caustically.

"So much more than that," she replied and he realized she was crying.

He brushed the hair away from her neck and then slipped his fingers beneath the thick fall to massage her nape. "Hey, it's okay."

She burrowed into his chest. "I think you're amazing."

But did she love him? *Could* she love him, like this?

A knocking sounded on the door.

"I'll get it," Ella said, sniffing loudly.

She pulled out of his arms and he missed her immediately. She grounded him to the earth.

"Oh, it's you," Ella said. Definitely someone she did not like. "Noah, Mike Rainer is here." Her voice chilled several degrees. What was that all about? "I'll go get some coffee so you two can talk."

So she had heard him ask.

"Hello, K," Mike said once the door had closed.

Noah wiped the perspiration from his face as he tried to orient to the sound of Mike's voice. "What are you doing here?"

Mike ignored his question. "She doesn't look like the sort of woman to set a thousand ships to sail."

"She floats my boat." Shifting released the sharp stench of sweat. *Too bad.* Mike would have to deal. "Did you find Maximiano?"

Noah heard a sigh and then sounds which he interpreted as Mike approaching. Metal scraped along the floor as Mike shifted it. The bed dipped near Noah's knee.

Noah shifted his knee to find the offending footwear then pushed. "Get your feet off my bed."

"They told me you were blind," Mike replied, bemused. "Doesn't seem to have impacted your charming personality."

Mike flung the word callously in Noah's face. Fear and anger seized Noah. He pushed it aside to deal with later. Crying on Mike's shoulder was a no-go scenario as was shaming him.

The door clicked open. "Here's your water, Mr. Kristofer," Magda cheerily told him as she entered. Noah tried to track her progress across the room. "Do you want a drink now?" she asked.

"No, thanks," Noah replied.

He jerked in surprise when she touched his wrist. She never warned him of what she was doing.

He settled while she took his pulse, resisting the urge to shift away from the cloying scent of her body spray. Lemon Pledge.

He felt a light pull on the bandages around his ear as she checked the incision site. The stitches should dissolve soon.

"Everything looks good. Call if you need anything." Magda patted his shoulder.

Would he ever get used to unexpected touches? "Thanks."

He waited for the door to close then returned his attention to Mike. "You told me Artus Black was clean."

"He was."

"Then why did he pick up the gangbangers? They had weapons, Mike. Handguns."

"Why didn't you guess they weren't tourists? Use some of that intuition you were famous for?"

"I thought I was safe. I was thinking about the case." *I was thinking about Ella.*

"Black didn't know you were on an op. I told him you were a colleague who needed time in the bush to clear his head."

Noah snorted. "I got plenty of that."

"Yeah, K. How did you walk out of there? I visited the crash site, saw the bodies."

"You want to know how I survived? I prayed. Every step I took, I prayed that God would get me out of there." *So I could see Ella again. I prayed that God would protect Ella from Maximiano.* And now that he was back with Ella, what next? How long was she going to stay with him?

"I've spread the word you were incapacitated by your injuries. Out of the game. As good as dead."

*Out.* Noah was annoyed Mike had made the decision without consulting him. However, *out of the game* to Maxi was good. But *out of the game* also meant that he was out of a job. The case was unresolved. As little as he wanted a return to police work, he wanted Ella safe.

The door clicked open again. "Hi, I'm back." It was Ella. "I see Magda brought you some water. You must be her favourite patient. I never see her spend this kind of time in other rooms. I don't know why, though." She chuckled. "You were so rude to her at the beginning." He heard the smile in her voice, a smile he wanted to taste.

"I get it," Mike said quietly. "It's the smile." His voice was so soft Noah didn't think it carried to Ella who he heard moving around near the bathroom.

Mike clapped his shoulder, startling him. "I'll be in touch. Be careful." The door closed.

"He gone?" Noah asked Ella. In listening for the door, he'd missed the softer squeak of her sneakers as she approached the bed.

"Yes. Can I sit on the bed?"

"*Oui.*" He smiled again. She was finding less obvious ways to warn him of her movements.

"I've got your coffee. Do you want it on the bedside table, the tray, or in your hand?"

And offering him choices, to give him some control over his life. "Hand. I'm thirsty. Didn't want to waste my liquid intake on Nurse Magda's lukewarm water when I knew I had you coming."

Ella took his hand and lifted it to receive the cold plastic cup. "Lid, straw," she said.

Droplets of condensation slid over his fingers. "Thanks." He drew on the straw, a cool hit of caffeine. Just what he needed. "Perfect."

She closed her hand around the cup so her fingertips touched his thumb. "I'll put it beside you on the bedside table, on your side of the phone."

"All those secret meetings with the occupational therapist and the psychologist are paying off," he said. The words spilled out, carrying accusation with them. Noah sensed her sudden stillness.

"Why do you say secret?" The smile was gone from her voice. "You know they're consulting with me. They would meet with you, too, if you'd let them."

He hadn't made a good impression on his occupational therapist and he'd flatly refused to speak to the psychologist. But he had an idea what they were telling Ella: all the things he was unable to do. "Don't need that kind of help."

"They're giving me ideas of how to help you adjust," Ella said.

"And what you can expect of a future with me?" he asked, suddenly angry. No, not angry. He was afraid.

"Sometimes," she replied. "We do talk about your prognosis. And other stuff."

"Stuff like how long before you can walk away?"

She gasped, and he heard the truth within it.

But he didn't want to hear the truth. *Nope. No truth. Don't want to hear it.* He was hoping her kind heart would keep her from saying the words out loud. *"I'm leaving you."* Or, *"I can't see a future with you."* And if she didn't say it, she wouldn't do it. He was fairly certain Ella wouldn't simply disappear on him.

Ella collapsed against his chest, the suddenness of the movement startling him. And hurting a bit. "Oh, Noah, I'm sorry."

His blood ran cold. Fisting her hair, he tugged her head back from his chest. "Sorry for what?"

"That your life has changed so much."

He held her still when she tried to pull away from his grip. "How will my life change?"

"Um." She sniffed, tugging against his hold. "Let go of my hair," she said, annoyed.

He released her. "Ella, how is my life going to change?" *Are you leaving me?*

"You're blind. You may never see again." She sounded confused, perplexed, as though the answer should have been obvious.

She didn't understand his question. He needed to know, didn't want to know, needed to ask, needed to get used to the words he never wanted to hear. "Are you leaving me?" His voice rasped weakly.

"What? No!" She landed on his chest again. This time he wrapped his arms around her and held on.

He positioned her body to lie alongside his. "You're staying with me, right?"

"Yes, sweetheart." She sounded exasperated at his twice-asked question.

A selfish man, he didn't care that it would derail her life to stay with him when he was rendered virtually useless by the vengeance of an angry adolescent. He wanted her in his life forever.

"I'm scared, El."

"I know."

Noah breathed deeply. He was blind. He would likely never see her face again, never see a sunrise or the faces of his children. Children? How could he even consider having children when he couldn't see? How did you keep a child safe when you couldn't see the danger? Tears stung the backs of his eyes.

Ella shifted her head to his shoulder and petted his beard. He loved it when she did that. His beard had gotten out of control since the accident. But her soft hands felt so good, her fingers tenderly sifting through the hair, that he might never shave again.

"It's okay to cry, sweetheart," Ella said. "To grieve."

*Cry?* What was she talking about? A sob shuddered through his chest, surprising him.

"That's it, darling. Let it out."

He opened his mouth to correct her. He wasn't going to cry—but a sob broke free. She tightened her grip on him, her leg coming over his legs to give him a full-body hug.

Somehow he'd been able to hold it together when every moment he'd feared her exit from his life. But now he knew she was staying, he lost it.

He grabbed on, pouring out his grief, his grief that was so much larger than vision loss. It encompassed the death of his mother, the miserable years with his aunt and uncle, and an adulthood of death, duty, and loneliness.

Somewhere in there, the Lord had brought him love and redemption. But in this moment, he needed to cry out his grief. Ella held him while he did.

# CHAPTER 44

"Well, son, you look mighty beat up."

Noah jerked awake. He'd been dozing in bed, worn out by his crying jag with Ella that morning. "Who's there?" he asked. The voice sounded old, weak and little wobbly.

"So, young Enoch was right. You've lost yer sight?"

"Who is this?" Noah turned his head toward the door.

"How many old men you know, son?"

"Mr. Blanchard?"

"Yup. That's me." Noah heard the extra tap a cane made on the linoleum floor as the octogenarian walked from the door to his bed.

"There should be a chair." Noah gestured in a wide sweep beside the bed.

"Thank ye, son." There was much grunting and groaning until Mr. Blanchard settled. "You call me Rod. You know better. I hear ye had some kind of run in with an airplane an' a bunch o' drug dealers."

"Helicopter." Noah paused. His frown pulled at his face. "What makes you think drug dealers were involved?"

Rod laughed his familiar croaky chuckle. "Because I'm a smart old man. What happened, son?"

"Can't. Can't tell you. Classified."

"And who am I meant to tell?"

"I can't."

"Not the details, no. But, this. You got in a helicopter with people you thought you could trust. And then—" Rod paused with an expectant tone to his voice. "Sorry, son. I'm gesturing like you should continue."

Noah's eyes widened in surprise at the old man's insistence. *His eyes widened; so that still happens when you can't see.* "Huh," he muttered thoughtfully. Then he answered Rod obliquely. "It would be interesting, for instance, if an undercover officer was chasing up a lead and he trusted the wrong pilot who stopped and picked up a group of fishermen who turned out to be gang members."

"I would think that man was not paying attention when he should have been."

"Maybe he was distracted thinking about the woman he loves."

"Ah." Rod lengthened the syllable. "Women ain't nothin' but trouble. But I tell ye, the right one's worth every single bit of trouble she can cause."

Noah smiled. "Yes. Yes, she is."

"Now, what I don't understand is how you wound up on the ground."

"These gang members, if they existed, might have tried to disappear the cop by shooting him and dumping his body in the bush."

"But you—this copper, fought back."

"Yep. I fell through the forest canopy. More of a ping-ponging motion than a straight fall, though, with lots of hanging from branches and slamming against tree trunks. That sort of thing."

"You walked out of the wilderness in that condition?"

"Walk or die."

"Gonna pat your shoulder, son." Rod did so. "I think you're one of the bravest men I know. Now, women. Few braver than my wife."

"You've never spoken of her."

"She walked by my side through a decade in a tiny village in the jungles of India. Gave her life to rescue little girls from child marriages."

"That's amazing." Noah was humbled simply by the bare facts Rod provided. Had his own life ever counted for so much?

"I miss her. The man who murdered her, blinded her first. Wanted to prevent her from helping anymore children. But it wouldn't have stopped her. She would have found a way."

*Sort of puts a little perspective on my situation.* "How did she die?"

"Blood clot formed. She stroked out."

"I'm sorry."

"I wanted many more years with her. But I wouldn't have traded what I had for anything." Rod shifted position. "These are very uncomfortable chairs. Gonna touch you again." He squeezed Noah's shoulder. "You're a baby still in the Lord, but you got so much to offer the Kingdom. Don't let a little thing like blindness stop you." Rod coughed then drew a few breaths before he continued. "Jesus doesn't walk away from his children. He grieves. He loves. He holds 'em dear. You remember that story as told in Matthew 14 where Jesus walks on the water?"

"I read it as a child."

"The disciples were in a boat on the Sea of Galilee when a gale came up. Jesus walked out through the storm to them. Now, many people say to God, 'take away the storm'. But Peter, he says, 'I want to walk with you'. After Peter steps out, he takes his eyes off Jesus and sees the waves, the danger, and starts to sink. And do you know what Jesus did?"

"I don't remember."

"'Immediately Jesus reached out his hand and caught him.' Jesus doesn't always take away the storms of life. But he always walks through them with us. Keep your hand in Jesus'. He will see you through."

Rod groaned as he stood. "I'll see you when you get home. Get well. Don't give up."

"Thanks. Thank you for coming all this way."

"Next time you tell me when you need a friend, son," Rod reprimanded him. "There's no need for you to get through this alone."

"Ella's here."

"Yes, she is," Rod replied.

# CHAPTER 45

Lying as she was, half on the hospital bed and half on Noah, Ella sensed his inattention as she read to him. One of his arms was up behind his head while the other was wrapped around her waist, his fingers lazily stroking the small patch of bared skin between the hem of the B.C. Lions T-shirt she'd picked up at the Real Canadian Superstore on Marine Drive when she'd run out of clothes, and the waistband of her soft cotton slacks. But his mind was far away.

Ella stopped reading, closed the book and tucked it between her hip and the bed. "Noah?"

"Hm."

"What book are we reading?"

"Huh? Uh, something by Davis Bunn?"

"We finished that yesterday."

"Oh." His body was humming with tension.

"Noah, what's wrong?" She rolled onto her side, taking some weight off his body, propping her head on her hand.

"Huh?"

"Noah," she said sharply.

His hand clenched on her flesh. "Jeez. What?"

She lowered her voice again. "What is wrong?"

He increased the tension in his arm to tip her back onto his body. Removing his hand from behind his head, he tucked her hand beneath his T-shirt and then propped his arm behind his head again. She nestled her face into the crook of his neck, her fingers lightly brushing his skin until they tangled in the hair on his chest. The pleasant sensation hummed through her body.

A small grin pulled at the corner of his mouth, brief and then gone in a frown. "You really want me to stay here while you go back to Kamloops?" he asked.

"This program they have sounds amazing," she replied, rubbing her cheek against his neck. "It's a good opportunity. You heard them explain, there's a maternity leave and so they can't have services in place in Kamloops for another two weeks. If you stay here, you can participate in this new rehab program in the meantime."

"Yeah. Maybe. But you'll be in Kamloops."

Her fingers stilled. "I know," she said, lifting her head to watch his expression, "but the doctor seems to think it would be best for you to start rehab right away. Not to wait until the new person is in place at home."

He frowned, his muscles tensing. "Stay with me then."

"I can't."

She pushed her hand up through the neck of his dark green T-shirt to tangle her fingers in his beard. He hadn't shaved since he'd been injured and it was getting thick and long. "You can contact your father. He could visit."

Noah shook his head. "I don't need him here. I need you."

"How about Sammy? You were close to him."

"He just got married. I'm not asking him to interrupt his honeymoon to sit by my hospital bed. I want you to stay."

Ella sighed. She couldn't give him what he wanted. "I need to work. After the past two weeks off, I need to get back to work." She shifted up to look into his face then realized he couldn't see her expression, anyway. "I don't want to lose my job, Noah. I really like working there. I like Kamloops."

His frown deepened into a scowl. "I'm supposed to move into a fake house which is really a nursing home while you move on with your life?"

"It's not a nursing home," she protested. She released his chin, pressing her palm to the centre of his chest. "It's a residential rehab centre, a place where people who've suffered traumatic injuries go for specialized care. They'll teach you how to start being independent."

"And why do I need to be independent? So I don't need you?"

She gasped in a breath, shocked. "How can you say that?" To her consternation, tears burned the backs of her eyes. Okay, yes, she had considered getting him through rehab and then moving on with her life. But every time she thought of facing a day without him, she felt hollow and sad.

"Then why are you trying to get rid of me?" he asked.

"I'm not." There was no reason to walk away from him, so she would stay. Maybe the love they shared would fade away in time. Maybe it wouldn't. "I want you to have the best life possible. If living here for a few weeks without me makes that happen, then I think you should stay. It will give me time to get things set up for you at home." Ella kissed a line up his neck, across his cheek and to his mouth. "I'll miss you."

"Yeah?" His breath tickled her lips.

"Oh, yes."

Then he kissed her, imprinting his flavour on her body and mind; he kissed her like he never wanted her to forget him.

# Chapter 46

Ella alternately fidgeted in place and paced the platform at the Kamloops train station, nervous and excited all at once. It had been three weeks since she'd last seen Noah. They chatted on the phone most evenings but she'd been so busy getting caught up at work, she hadn't been able to visit.

The intensive training program Noah had attended was offered through the Canadian National Institute for the Blind, the CNIB. It was designed to give those newly diagnosed with vision loss the tools they'd need to begin to adjust to life in the dim or dark. Because of a gap in service created by budgetary cuts—also called, 'not filling a maternity leave'—Noah had been given the opportunity to participate in a new program in Vancouver. He was to learn the rudiments of cane travel, navigating a living space, and the basics of Braille. Now his service would be delivered on an itinerant basis at home.

A volunteer from the program in Vancouver was traveling with Noah on the train and then continuing to Edmonton. Noah would disembark at Kamloops on his own. And then she'd take him home to Nechako Drive.

With Enoch and his wife, Ilse's, help, Ella had packed a suitcase of clothes and necessities from Noah's apartment along with what Enoch termed 'more masculine items to offset the transparent femininity of her home' and transferred them to her bungalow. Because it simply hurt her heart to think of Noah recuperating in the cramped apartment.

The rehab program was a great start to his new life, but it couldn't possibly cover everything he needed to know to navigate the world sightless. That would take months, possibly even years. He'd need to meet with Mobility Specialists, Independent Living Specialists and many others. The house would afford him more space and freedom to adjust. With access to the gulley behind the house, and the mountain trails beyond, he'd be able to spend the time he was accustomed to outdoors.

Ella had packed a suitcase of her own things and transferred it to Noah's apartment on Curlew Road. That way they could spend most of their time together but still maintain separate residences. Until they married. If he still wanted to marry her. Because she absolutely wanted to marry him. Three weeks apart had clarified that for her.

Ella searched through her purse for a piece of cinnamon chewing gum, tried three times before she popped it out of its packaging, and then tossed it into her mouth. She coughed. The stupid thing had gone back too far, gagging her. If she couldn't chew gum, how was she going to convince Noah they had a chance at a life together? She didn't care if he was blind. She loved him. Wanted to marry him and make a family together. She was more sure of that than she'd ever been. Life wasn't right without him.

Ten minutes later, the train pulled to a stop at the station. Ella scanned the length, at least eight cars. Finally, the doors opened and passengers disembarked.

Noah descended with a hand from the coach attendant, wobbling on the metal step. His right foot landed on the concrete platform. He released the attendant's hand. The man reached back in and placed a bag on the concrete beside Noah. He looked so handsome in a tailored blue suit over a white shirt. No necktie. His full beard was neatly trimmed and his hair freshly cut but slightly disheveled. Sunglasses covered his eyes. But she would recognize him anywhere.

An older lady descended to stand beside him. She was statuesque, dressed in a blue pantsuit, her iron-grey hair in a bun. Taking Noah's arm, she bent at the knees to lift his bag. He retrieved a folded white cane from a blue holster at his belt and extended it. The tall lady said something to him and he moved forward slowly, sweeping the cane across his path.

"Noah." Ella called his name and waved to him, belatedly realizing how stupid that was.

He paused at the sound of her voice and grinned. The lady immediately shifted his trajectory to move in her direction. Noah continued slowly, tapping and occasionally stopping to explore the space in front of him with the toes of his black leather dress shoes.

Ella met him halfway, shy and gloriously happy to see him. "Hi."

His smile brightened his face. "Hello, *chérie*. You miss me?"

"Very much," she replied.

"That is my cue to exit," the lady said. "Good luck, Noah."

"Thanks, May."

"Thank you," Ella said, but May was already moving away. She re-boarded the train and was gone.

"You ready to take me home?" Noah asked.

"Absolutely." And when she threw her arms around him, he enveloped her in a tight embrace.

Ella roamed the kitchen of her little bungalow, referring between the suggested layouts for the blind and visually impaired she'd found online and the instructions Darrell, the Independent Living Specialist from the CNIB, had provided when he'd made his first contact visit with Noah today.

This was the reality of Ella's and Noah's lives now. Things, including furniture, dishes, food, everything, had to be maintained in a predictable and orderly manner. Dinner plates on the bottom shelf in the cupboard to the left of the sink, dessert plates beside them. One shelf up, she placed the cereals bowls and coffee mugs.

Noah scanned the kitchen as she worked. Ella paused. He couldn't see. He wasn't scanning, he was listening. Noah was sitting at the kitchen table listening to her move around the kitchen.

"I can't believe that you've been home for a week already. Are you getting used to the house?"

She typed "bowl" into the braille label-maker she'd bought. Noah was underwhelmed at the prospect of learning a new written language, but he'd started on it during his time in the rehab program in Vancouver.

His head jerked in her direction. "Why are you living in my lousy apartment while I live in your house? You bought this thing with your hard-earned cash and credit."

Ella shrugged then remembered he was unable to see the gesture. "It makes the most sense for now." She turned on the coffee maker. If he had something to drink, he'd look less like he was brooding and more like he was on a break.

"I got the agenda for my conference, The Psychological Effects of Prenatal Substance Abuse on the School-aged Child," Ella said. She pulled two mugs back out of the cupboard where she'd placed them. "It looks like it'll be very interesting."

"Conference?" Noah froze, then started tapping his foot on the floor.

Ella glanced at him. His body was tense, his fingers fidgeting with his white cane which was folded on the table. The scar across his left eyelid was still angry and red, but the doctor had assured her it would fade to white in time. And when Noah looked at her—she needed to stop doing that—she still found the appearance of his left eye disconcerting. With the pupil blown, it looked a dark and fathomless black as compared to the rich, warm brown of the other eye. She supposed in time she'd get used to that, too.

"Remember? I told you," she said patiently. She was very proud of how patient she'd been this entire week, given his rapidly shifting moods. "My work is paying to send me to a three-day conference in Calgary next week."

"When?" His voice was terse.

"Wednesday to Friday."

His brow furrowed and he narrowed his eyes. "That's six hundred kilometres, pretty far to commute."

Ella placed a K-cup in the holder and a mug beneath the spout before lowering the lever on the coffee maker. She had given up the basket cups and grinding her own beans to fill them, realizing that buying the pre-filled K-cups would make things easier for Noah. The hiss of hot water forced through coffee grounds followed and Ella inhaled the comforting aroma.

"Ella."

She glanced at Noah. What was this about? Noah looked so intense, almost angry. But she had told him about this. Twice. Once during their first conversation in the Element after she'd picked him up at the train station—*You want to take me home, chérie? he'd said*—then again on Wednesday when she was given approval to attend. "We're staying at the Radisson."

"We?" Noah clenched his jaw.

Ella turned her back on the coffee maker so she was facing Noah. She steadied herself on the counter behind her. "Dylan Meeker, one of the other psychologists I work with. Remember him? He covered for me while I was in Vancouver with you. Anyway, Dylan and I are driving there together on Tuesday night."

Noah gripped his cane, extending it. He rose and, using his cane, crossed the room to stand toe-to-toe. He reached out with an open palm until he made contact with her shoulder, probably a little harder than he should have, and gripped it.

"And what am I supposed to do for four days?"

As tense and angry as he sounded, he wasn't hurting her. Still. His temper was erratic since his accident.

"I don't know. Whatever you want, I guess."

Releasing her, he strode away from her. His cane arced through the air and hit the edge of the fridge. He smacked it twice then seemed to find the space beside it which led to the hallway. Sweeping his cane across the floor while feeling the air in front of him with his other hand, he shuffled away from her.

"Great. So I can wander around this forsaken house all day and then again all evening." He turned right toward the bedrooms. Ella heard his cane connect with either side of the corridor. His voice increased in volume the further from the kitchen he moved. "Instead of eight hours of acute boredom, I'll have seventy-two hours plus of continuous boredom."

"You could go out—" Ella followed him.

He paused. "Out?" His voice rose a few more decibels. "I can't even make it past the front steps. I can't remember if there's three steps or four. There's no railing, nothing to hold onto. There's no bus stop on Nechako so I have to walk out to Qu'Appelle. And there's no bloody sidewalks on this forsaken street."

Noah reached her bedroom, his bedroom now, pausing only long enough to turn the doorknob. He shoved the door open. It banged against the wall. He kept his arm out to catch the rebound. A precaution he'd learned from experience. Tap. Tap. Tap.

Ella's eyes tracked his movements, her heart thumping and her throat clogged with tears.

"I can't do it." He went from speaking angrily to shouting in an instant. "So go to your damned conference! Get out. Go!" He slammed the door in her face.

Emotion swamped Ella. Fear. Anger. Regret. Guilt. Remorse. Frustration. He'd never sworn at her before. From the moment they'd connected in that hotel room on East Hastings, he'd offered her the respect of clean language. She realized that profanity was a part of his vocabulary, had heard him use it with others, and noticed he didn't flinch when it sailed his way. But he had never lost control with her.

Ella turned away. But where could she go. Her bed was in Noah's room. Her clothes and other things were at his apartment.

Eyes full of tears, she walked away.

Noah stood in the centre of his bedroom, his body vibrating with fury. *What if Ella leaves me?*

Frigid fear swamped him, dousing his anger like a shower of glacial water. What if she took him at his word? What if she decided it wasn't worth being around a grumpy blind man who could not come to terms with his loss?

He didn't want her to leave. He *really* didn't want her to leave.

Noah wrenched open the bedroom door. "El. Don't go!"

Using his cane, he retraced his angry steps, his new steps full of fear and self-loathing.

"Ella?"

He reached the front hallway then paused, listening. Had she left? He hadn't heard the door. But he'd been so consumed by rage that maybe he wouldn't have.

"Ella?" His voice sounded desperate now.

"I'm here."

Relief flooded him. Noah moved across the hallway and beyond the threshold of the living room. *Ah, zut!* She was crying.

"El." All the anger and loathing drained out of him, replaced by remorse. "I'm sorry. *Bébé. Excuse.*"

"It's okay," she replied. She was still crying but trying to stifle the sounds with her hands.

Noah listened to locate her. She was on the couch at this end, probably curled in a sad ball.

He took the last steps to the couch and dropped his cane on the floor by the arm. Then he scooped her up in his arms and sat back down with her on his lap. It was a lot harder when you couldn't see where anything was. But he knew her body, and her weight felt right in his arms.

"Sh," he said. "Don't cry."

Ella sat on his lap, her body rigid. "I'm sorry." She drew in a shuddering breath. "I didn't realize."

"Everything is fine. You did tell me about the conference. I remember now. It's fine. Stop crying. Please."

"I'm so sorry. I stupidly thought everything was going well. But of course you wouldn't be content to sit around doing nothing. After years of service, chasing bad guys and going undercover. I'm sorry."

Noah pulled her hands away from her face and slipped them around his neck. He leaned in to nuzzle her cheek and neck. "Don't cry anymore, El." He tightened his grip on her. "I'm sorry I yelled at you."

She huffed a wet laugh. "I'm not crying because you yelled." She punched him on the shoulder. "That's for yelling at me." She punched him again, harder. "That's for swearing at me. Don't do it again."

"Ow. Jeez." He rubbed his shoulder. "Blind man here," he complained.

"Suck it up, big boy."

Noah chuckled as he pulled her close, nuzzling the side of her face. *She is amazing. Super fine.* "I'm sorry. I just—blind—don't know—"

"I'm so glad you survived. And I don't care if you're blind."

"Yeah?" *Can it be? Is it possible?*

"Yes."

"Well, good, then." Something hideous slipped out of his heart and peace settled in its place.

# Chapter 47

Something was off in the house. Noah noticed it as soon as he entered the kitchen the morning after Ella left for Calgary. Folding his cane and setting it on the table—he was getting better at navigating the house without it—he explored the kitchen with his hands and feet. The chairs which were usually left square to the table were shifted out of place. Noah traced the countertops and then opened the refrigerator. The food was arranged in the fridge differently. Not by much, but the cheese was out of the drawer and sitting on a shelf beside the sour cream. The milk was shifted behind the Brita water pitcher instead of beside it.

Ella hadn't done this. Ever since she'd started meeting with the instructor from the CNIB, Ella had become orderly about how she kept the house. With that realization, fear swamped Noah. Because it meant that someone else had been in the house, someone he couldn't see.

Had Maximiano come for him? How did he protect himself when he couldn't see the danger headed his way? Should he call the police? Noah snorted aloud at the idea. And tell them what? *Someone moved my cheese?*

*Non.* What he would do is deal with this problem himself, tonight. He would get his SIG and stake out the kitchen. There were advantages to being blind. He had a mental map of where everything should be, how things should feel and smell and sound. He was able to operate in the dark with all the advantages that brought.

It was time to make a plan.

Fourteen hours later, Noah sat in Ella's cozy chair which he'd placed in the corner of the kitchen, in the deepest shadows between the fridge and the bathroom. That had been a feat, moving furniture in the dark. When the fridge was opened, he would be completely hidden from view. Every light in the house was off, though Noah heard the electricity buzzing in the halogen lamp in the living room. It always carried a trickle charge. He had his gun and his cane with him as well as a flashlight. The light, he hoped, would disorient the intruder while he got the drop on him.

Sometime past midnight, Noah alerted to the soft sound of footsteps accompanied by the clickity-clack of claws on the linoleum accompanied by the cloying scent of wet fur. Was there an animal in the house? A raccoon?

Noah slowed his breathing, maintaining motionlessness. He heard the intruder walk to the fridge then open the door. Cold air teased Noah's bare feet.

The light from the fridge would have helped the intruder's eyes adjust to the light. The flashlight would now be useless. Noah slipped it into the seat beside him, nestled between the edge of the cushion and the arm of the chair, so it wouldn't fall when he rose.

Movement created an air current that shifted the cold air, and Noah guessed that the intruder was closing the fridge door. Noah pounced. He imagined the position of the intruder and then wrapped his arms around that space. But instead of a torso, Noah gripped a head. This intruder was even shorter than he'd expected. A woman?

The head tried to bite him. He gripped the smooth jaw with one hand while he slipped his other arm lower around the torso. Definitely not a woman.

A dog barked—so not a raccoon—the timbre of his voice giving away its small size. It sunk its teeth in his pant leg above his ankle. Noah grunted at the shock, kicking the dog away, not willing to risk losing his hold on the mini-intruder by grabbing the little beast. He heard the dog's body slide along the linoleum and impact the wall. It yipped in surprise.

His mini-intruder fought. He kicked Noah in the shin. When he reached back to grab hold of Noah's vulnerable bits, Noah was glad he'd chosen to wear jeans. He shifted out of reach, pinning the boy's arms to his sides. Because that's what he was. A preadolescent boy. Skinny. Nine or ten years old.

"Settle down, kid," Noah ordered then tried to bring a more soothing tone to his voice. "I'm not going to hurt you."

The boy flung his head back, nearly connecting with Noah's nose. Instead the brusque movement brought the back of his head in contact with Noah's cheek. *Zut. That hurt.*

Noah shook the boy, hard. "I'm not going to hurt you," he repeated, angry at the pain now vibrating up the side of his face. It wasn't so long ago that those bones had knit.

The dog was back, tugging at his pant leg and growling. "I won't hurt you unless you give me no choice. Call off the dog. Now!"

The boy stilled abruptly in Noah's grip. He whistled and the dog released. His little claws ticked on the linoleum and then his butt hit the floor.

"Who are you? Why are you in my house?" Noah asked, keeping a strong hold on the kid.

The boy's breathing sped but he didn't respond. Noah changed his hold, grasping both of the kid's wrists in one hand and raising them high above his head. That should have put him on tiptoe and should keep him enough off-balance to provide Noah some protection.

Noah patted him down, the kid wriggling all the while. It felt like a wad of cash in his rear right pocket. Noah tossed it toward the kitchen table. A phone or something in the side pocket of the boy's cargo pants, Noah extracted with finger and thumb. He explored the device to the best of his ability with one hand.

"What's this? Phone?" Noah asked, giving the kid a little shake when he didn't answer.

The kid tugged his right hand, trying to free it from Noah's grip, but he still didn't make a sound. The dog was up again, growling low in his throat.

It was large, like an iPhone. "Hey, kid. If I gave you this, who would you call?"

The boy went still. Shuddered. Noah experienced a pang of concern. The kid was small. Noah slowly brought him down to his heels, released his wrists, anchoring him to his body with an arm around his chest. As he suspected, the boy swiped at his face as if wiping away tears.

Noah shoved the phone into his own front pocket and brushed his fingertips over the boy's features. The boy was crying quietly. Silently. As in, the boy made no sound. *Bizarre.*

Noah placed his palm across the kid's forehead. "Can you talk?"

The boy shook his head, sniffing loudly.

"Is that phone yours?"

The boy nodded. The shuddering in his body was lessening.

"I could use it to call your parents," Noah said, trying to sound firm and authoritative.

The boy's narrow shoulders shuddered under the force of his grief. It was odd, the nearly silent weeping.

"Hey, kid. Did something happen to your parents?"

He nodded.

Noah noticed the dog's growls had changed to whines and he felt the furry beast rubbing between his legs and the kid's, as if he was trying to comfort the boy.

"Was there an accident?" Noah asked.

The boy shook his head. This silent crying was disconcerting. The kid twisted around and tugged his phone out of Noah's pocket. Noah had a strong hold around his chest so he let him move and waited to see what would happen.

Suddenly, he heard words. But they sounded like they came from the phone not the kid's mouth. "Parents dead."

*Okay.* "I'm sorry, kid. How did they die?"

"Don't remember."

"You type in what you want to say? And then the device reads it out loud?"

"Yes."

The voice and intonation were all wrong. It was a man's voice, spoken in disjointed phrases. Weird. But better than no speech at all. If only they'd invent a way for him to see electronically.

"Did you run away?" Noah asked.

"Yes. Do not want to be shot like Peter and Lillian."

Was this some kind of joke? "Shot?"

"Yes." The boy's body shuddered.

It figured that Noah's prowler would turn out to be a kid with shooters on his tail. "Who are you, kid?"

"Grady."

"Grady who?"

"Grady Jones."

"Peter and Lillian, were they your parents?"

"Gardens."

Noah frowned. That made no sense. "Seriously?"

"Garfish." Grady stiffened. Blew out a breath.

"Guardians?" Noah asked.

"Yes."

Noah understood. "That device has a predictor function? It guesses what you want to say as you type?"

"Yes."

"It's not always so helpful, is it?"

Grady laughed, a near-silent puff of air escaping. The reaction seemed to surprise him as much as it surprised Noah.

"So your parents died and Lillian and Peter were your guardians?"

"Yes. Wanted to adopt me."

*And they were shot.* "Ah, kid, I'm sorry. Why are you here in my house?"

"Run away. Lights never on. Though no one lived here."

"*Thought* no one lived here?"

"Yes. Came to find food. Sleep inside. Cold."

"How long have you been running away?"

"Long time. Cold. Hundreds." Grady blew out a breath in frustration.

*Hundreds? Cold and hun? Hungry?* "Hungry and cold. What do you want? Grilled cheese and hot chocolate?"

Grady stilled a moment and then he shook. But this vibration spoke more of excitement than fear or grief. "Yes. Please."

"Okay. Sit at the table." Noah realized the dog had gone quiet when his claws abruptly tip-tapped across the floor, again in tandem with Grady's soft footsteps. "Is the dog hungry, too?"

Noah sensed movement and assumed the kid was patting the dog's head.

"There's tuna in the cupboard beside the stove." Noah oriented himself in the room then pointed in the general direction. "Open a can and give it to him. Careful not to leave sharp edges."

Noah opened the fridge and pulled out the cheese. Crossing the floor then feeling along the counter, he located the cutting board. Tracing the edge of the wooden board, his fingertips encountered the wooden knife block. He drew his index finger up the block until he encountered the plastic handle of a knife. Using that knife as a place marker, he traced left to the last knife in the row, his favourite cheese cutting knife. Lifting it out, he set the knife parallel to the top margin of the cutting board, knife edge pointed toward the wall.

"Everything okay?" Noah asked. Sensation crawled between his shoulder blades. The kid was silent, watching him.

Movement started again. The sound of running footsteps, the clatter of something on the table. "Yes. Are you blind?"

Noah choked in an oath. Nothing was ever going to be normal again. He flipped between outright terror at the thought of leaving the house and confidence in his skills within Ella's house. But nothing he did was normal.

"Yeah." His voice was husky with emotion.

"Cool."

Grady jogged back over to the tuna cupboard and then, from the sounds he made, climbed onto the counter, opened it, and retrieved a can of tuna. Soon Noah heard the whirr of the electric can opener.

The click-clack of claws followed the path Grady had taken and soon the sounds of a hungry dog eating filled the air. Grady filled a bowl or something with water and set it on the floor beside the dog's food. He hoped it wasn't the ceramic bowl that was Ella's favourite, the one her brother, Perry, had brought her from Pakistan. Too late to worry about it now.

Noah returned to his task, opening the cheese package and positioning it to cut off slices. He felt a light touch on his arm, nearly propelling him through the roof in surprise. Adrenaline coursed through him. "Kid! Don't do that! Don't sneak up on me. Make a sound. Cough. Something."

Silence met his tirade. Even the dog had stopped eating.

Noah regretted his reaction immediately. The kid was scared and hungry. He didn't need Noah hollering at him. He might take Noah's temper a lot more seriously than Ella did.

"Sorry, Grady. You surprised me. I need a little warning, okay, bud?" Noah worked to gentle his voice.

"Sorry." The voice was bright and robotic but when Noah reached over to lightly skim the boy's face with his fingertips, he sensed that Grady was crestfallen.

"I'm sorry, too. I overreacted."

There was furious movement beside him followed by, "I over react too. My sy—py—therapist said. Because of what I see."

Noah processed that and then found a likely translation. "Your psychologist said you overreact because of what you saw?"

"Yes."

This time when Noah brushed his fingers over Grady's face, he detected happiness. Almost glee at being understood. "You're a whiz with that device, kid. Good job."

"Thank you."

Noah ruffled the boy's hair. "What did you see, Grady?"

The energy in the room shifted.

"They tell me Uncle Macken kill my dad and his girlfriend and the other people."

"That's why you were in foster care?" Given that Grady had guardians instead of parents and that his father was dead, it seemed a reasonable assumption.

"The Mounties want me tell what I see. But I do not remember."

*Mounties?* The RCMP was involved with this kid? Noah wondered, "Are you in Witness Protection?"

"Yes."

And somebody shot Peter and Lillian. This poor kid was in danger. And he'd run to a blind man to help him.

# CHAPTER 48

Grady and Otto MacDog—what a goofy name—were settled in the spare room next door to his. He was pretty sure the kid was asleep.

Noah settled in the kitchen with his cell phone, one of his burner phones left over from his days on the force. He wasn't sure why he felt he needed the protection of anonymity, but his instincts were screaming at him. So he listened.

Who did he know in Witness Protection? Eric Nguyen.

Noah found the zero key and asked the operator to connect him to the RCMP head office in Ottawa. When he gave his clearance code, he was connected to Eric's voicemail. At least Mike hadn't cut him off when he'd told the world he was incapacitated.

"Hey, Eric. Noah Kristofer here. I've got a question to ask you about a little witness. Give me a call as soon as possible." He left the number of the burner. Nguyen wouldn't recognize it. But Noah expected him to reply. They'd worked on a case together a couple of years ago. Nguyen should remember him.

Two minutes later, the phone rang. Noah connected. "Noah Kristofer speaking."

"Kristofer, man." Eric sounded astonished. "How are you? Long time."

"Yeah. Five or six years I think." He'd enjoyed working with Nguyen. He was bright and able, with a carefree attitude that made him fun to be around. "The Vincenzo case."

A little boy had been abducted from his safe house by his gang-leading, drug-dealing papa. The mother had agreed to testify against her one-time lover, but had made the all too common blunder of calling the man to apologize. *Ridiculous.* The man had been violent and disloyal. What need had she to apologize? Noah had gone undercover in the gang's neighbourhood as a convenience store clerk until he'd located the boy. Poor little mite had been left with an elderly aunt who was half-blind and all mean. Eric had been Noah's contact with Witness Protection during the operation.

"Good times," Eric replied, a hint of wryness in his voice. "What can I do for you? You said you have a witness?"

"A kid. He showed up at my house. Says his foster parents were murdered."

"Hold up." Eric's voice was grim. Noah heard computer keys clacking in the background. "You know where he was?"

"No, sorry."

"Physical description?"

"Um. Short. About ten years old. Has a small dog with him."

Eric's annoyance laced his voice as he responded. "That's a lousy description for a cop, Kristofer. What's wrong with you?"

"I'm blind. I can't see him." Noah muttered the words darkly.

The clacking sound ceased. "Sorry, man. I heard about your accident. Good to know you're not out of the game. But I didn't realize—"

Noah thrust the emotion away. "Whatever. You got any kids in Witness Protection who fit that situation?"

The clacking resumed. "Yep. Whoa." The word came out on a breath. A flurry of noise followed, voices, a shutting door, the squeak of a swivel chair.

"What? Nguyen."

"Sorry. Give me the kid's name."

Noah hesitated. But he'd trusted Nguyen in the past. He would again. "Grady Jones."

Nguyen whistled, the sound soft and introspective. "This kid's file is flagged. Something's definitely wrong here. Can you keep him for a little while, K? Give me some time to follow up. Keep the kid and keep him safe. If he is who I think he is, then his life is in danger. Death has been dogging this kid his whole life. Can you do that?"

"Sure. Yeah. He's anonymous here. Where's he from?"

"Vancouver? Then…whoa."

"He got all the way to—"

"Don't tell me! Kristofer, don't tell me where you are. Destroy this phone and get a new number. Contact no one." Nguyen typed some more. "Blast it all! This is a mess. Keep him close, buddy. No one knows where he is. Keep it that way."

"His name. Is his name a flag?"

"No. They've changed his names a few times. The last foster parents were going to adopt him and give him their surname, but he's still here as Braeden Roy. Bio-dad was Scottish-Canadian, white. Bio-mom was Latino, Colombian."

"Okay. How are you going to let me know what's going on?"

"I'll set up a website with an email option. Check the drafts folder from time to time. I'll use a modification of the web address we used on our last case together. Got it?"

"Cryptic, but yeah, I got it."

"I'll be in touch."

# Chapter 49

**N**oah stood on the flagstone patio outside Ella's back door and waited. He reached out with his senses. The crisp aroma of freshly mown grass laced the air. Cars moved on Nechako behind him. Small children giggled and cried in the neighbours' yards to either side. Above, a helicopter beat the air with its characteristic whup-whup-whup. A dog barked, the sound echoing off the mountain across the gulley. But of Grady Jones, there was no sign.

Noah's pulse pounded. His hands shook. Sweat trickled down his temples to soak into his beard. *Zut.*

A walk. That's all he'd meant to do. Take the boy and his dog for a walk. Simple. He and Ella walked the path along the gulley every evening together. It made sense to bring Otto out here. There was no vehicle traffic, unless you counted bicycles and the occasional quad-bike. Both easy to navigate around because you could hear them coming a mile away.

Sweeping his cane in front of him, Noah took a step and then another until he detected the edge of the patio with his foot. He froze again.

"Grady!"

Another dog barked, a smaller dog than the last. Footsteps pattered across the soft ground. A hand touched his side, took his free hand. He flinched.

"Grady?" Noah smelled the familiar woodsy scent of his shampoo on the boy's head.

A furry body pressed against his lower leg. *Otto.*

"Don't wander off, okay, kid?" Noah was pleased he managed to say that without sounding pathetic.

Grady pressed his head against Noah's side and nodded.

Noah's heart rate slowed to approach normal. "Good. Let's walk." As if that wasn't what the kid had been doing when Noah called him back. Pathetic. When a simple walk made him feel weak. Unmanned.

Using his cane and his grip on Grady's hand, Noah made it down the sloping yard to the gulley and along it for a couple of miles. Then back to Ella's house.

For the next two days, Thursday and Friday, Noah kept Grady busy watching television, playing computer games on Ella's laptop, going for walks, and preparing meals. He showed him where Ella kept her stacks and stacks of books, hoping that at least some were age appropriate.

Noah flipped through the available programs streaming on television. He needed to ask Ella how to activate the Descriptive Video features again. He hadn't bothered to listen the first six times she'd explained.

Without warning, the couch cushion shifted. The kid moved stealthily.

"When is Ella coming here?" Grady asked through his device.

Noah had explained to Grady that Ella was his girl and that she owned the house. "She said that she and her co-worker were leaving Calgary at three-thirty, so she should be here soon. You want to watch television?" Noah asked.

"I live in Calgary."

*Calgary? Eric said the kid was from Vancouver.* "Oh, yeah? With Peter and Lillian?"

"Yes."

"That's a long way for a kid to travel. How did you get from Calgary to Kamloops?"

"Find safe place close to the mall. Not cute anymore so streets not good. Stay at a shelter. Got sus—" The voice stopped.

"Got what?" Noah stilled, suddenly fearing what the boy would say next.

"Not know how to spell it."

"Got sick? Got rickets? Got suspicious? Got pickles?"

Grady laughed, a nearly silent puff of air. "Not pickles."

"Suspicious?"

"Yes."

"You got suspicious of them. Did someone hurt you, G?"

"No. Man wants to call police. Maybe Uncle Macken find me then. One time he sent a cop to kill me. I go. Take bus. Walk to camping park."

"You walked from Calgary to Banff Provincial Park?" This kid was amazing.

"Yes. Riding in a camper to Kamloops. Has lots good place to stay." He typed for a while then. "Peter said he takes me camping. No time." More typing. "You go camping?"

"Yeah. I have been camping. Not since the accident."

"You take me and Otto? I help you walk on grass. Not wander off."

The words were so hopeful that Noah couldn't refuse. He also didn't want to give the boy false hope. Life was uncertain for both of them at the moment.

"We can try, kid. You'd have to help me put up the tent."

"Yes. I help. I know how to make fire. I learn on streets."

"When were you living on the streets?"

"Six years old. My cousin take me away from a garden. We live on the streets for—" Grady paused. "Six months. That time. He got caught selling drugs. Cops take us both. I go back to the Mounties."

"How old was your cousin?"

"Sixteen."

"Why did he take you?"

Grady must have shrugged because his clothes rustled.

"You've led an interesting life, kid," Noah commented.

"Teaching me how to survive."

"Did someone tell you that?" Noah asked.

"Lillian said bad is bad but God used even bad stuff to make good for us."

"God brings good even out of bad? That's a cool idea, G."

"Bible says so."

"Thank you. I needed to hear that." Noah groped with his hand until he found Grady's head, then he ruffled the boy's hair affectionately.

Grady flinched and Noah thought he'd hurt or frightened him, but then he heard the front lock open. Grady's ears were even keener than Noah's were becoming.

Otto barked then came to sit against Grady's leg. Noah guessed. He heard the dog and felt the warmth of his body pushing between them.

"It's okay, Grady," Noah reassured him. "Only Ella has a key to the house. She's good and kind. Trust me."

The front door opened and then closed, sending a jet of unseasonably warm air into the room.

"Hello! I'm home." A thud marked the spot she dropped her bag. "Brother, what a lot of blowhards. I mean some of the sessions were excellent but a couple of those presenters used it as an excuse to toot their own experimental horns. They only spent the last fifteen minutes on treatment. Bother, I say!"

As though drawn by a magnetic force, Noah started moving as soon as the first vibration left her throat, and continued until he gripped her shoulders. He pulled her tight against him. This woman was the centre of his world.

She embraced him tightly around the chest. "Hey. How are you?" she asked. He heard the smile in her voice, calling up the picture he kept in his mind of her happy, sparkling eyes.

"I missed you," he murmured.

"I missed you, too. So much."

Otto growled low behind him.

Ella stiffened and pulled back. "Um, who is that?" Ella shifted to look around Noah. "There's a dog in my house?" Then she tilted her head up, Noah assumed so she was looking at his face.

Noah moved aside, keeping her linked to him with an arm around her shoulders. "This is Grady. And the dog is Otto. They're staying with me."

Ella said nothing for a time, but he sensed her movements by the play of muscles across her shoulders. She was looking back and forth between the three of them. "Um, hello, Grady. My name is Ella."

"Hello." Grady's app replied for him.

"Is that your dog?" she asked. She was truly amazing. Confused, but trying to catch up.

"Yes," Grady replied. "His name is Otto MacDog."

"Hello, Otto. That's a great name." Ella sounded like she was smiling as she leaned her cheek against Noah's side. "Did you name him?"

"No. Peter."

"I'll fill you in later," Noah murmured to her. No need to make Grady go through all that again.

"Okay," she murmured back. "Um, okay. Welcome."

Noah felt her turn toward him.

"I brought you a gift. But I forgot to bring it in, I was in such a hurry to see you. It's in the Element."

"Did you park in the driveway?"

"Yes."

Noah held out his hand. "I'll bet Grady can get it for you."

Otto yipped as though he'd understood the words, except interpreted them as "bone for Otto".

Ella dropped her keys into Noah's open hand. "It's a white plastic bag behind the passenger seat."

"You hear that, G? Can you get the bag for Ella?"

"Yes."

"Okay." Noah pressed the unlock button.

Grady skirted Ella then opened the front door and jogged out with Otto at his heels.

"What on earth, Noah?" Ella asked.

Noah kissed her temple. She tilted her chin up and he kissed her mouth. "Love you. Tell you later."

"Okay," she said, accepting his desire to wait but concerned about the need.

Soon, Grady jogged back into the house. Noah pressed the lock button twice, listening for the double beep that signalled the vehicle had locked. "Close the front door and lock it, kid." Grady complied by the sounds of it and given the fact that Ella didn't say anything or move away to help him.

"Thank you, Grady," Ella said, imbuing the boy's name with warmth.

Noah heard the bag rustle and felt the boy's body heat close to him. He hooked his arm around the boy's shoulder.

"I think I have a gift for each of you." Ella pulled something out of the bag and handed it toward Grady. "Here is a cookie I saved from lunch in case I got hungry on the way home. You can share it with Otto. And here's a stylus I won as a door prize. You can use it on your device."

Noah prompted, "What do you say, bud?"

"Thank you."

"You want to watch a movie in your bedroom?" Noah asked.

"Yes. Can I use your computer?"

"Sure. Does Otto need to go out first?"

"No. He peed on wheel of the car."

Noah chuckled. "Good."

Noah tracked the clacking of Otto's nails as he followed Grady down the hall toward the bedrooms.

"Now, you come and sit with me." Noah took Ella's arm and led her to the couch. He sat without releasing her and then pulled her onto his lap. "I missed you."

Ella wrapped her arms around his neck and kissed him, long, luxurious kisses that took his breath away. When she pulled back, she said, "I have something for you, too. Two somethings."

Noah skimmed his hands across her shoulders and down her arms, up her back. "Mm. I like the sound of that."

Ella chuckled, stopping his exploration to place an item in his hands. "I attended a session on responding to trauma. There was a conference room set up with products and catalogues. I saw it and couldn't pass up the opportunity to do a little shopping. Anyway, they had lots of good ideas. Like this." She prompted him to open the box. "It's a cell phone specially designed for the visually impaired. It reads texts to you. There is Braille on the letters and numbers. And other features I haven't figured out yet."

Noah's stomach bottomed out. Is that all she thought about him now? He was blind, sum total of his existence? He would have bought her a book or chocolates or something she liked.

"I sent you a text," she said. "You might want to listen to it before Grady comes back."

Noah skimmed his thumbs over the face of the phone until he thought he found the *Read Text* button. He pressed it and it said, "One text received. From Ella."

"I programmed my numbers in."

"To hear text, press again." It was another automated voice like Grady's, except it was a woman's voice. But as robotic and odd.

Noah pressed again.

"Home soon. Can't wait to run my fingers through your hair and kiss you until you pass out from lack of oxygen." A beep sounded. "To hear this text again, press one. To save this text, press two. To delete this text, press three."

"Two. Find two, El." Noah rushed to say.

Ella chuckled as she removed the phone from his hand. "My pleasure." *Pleasure. Yeah.* Noah's mouth quirked in a smile. That was awesome.

"You like it?" Ella asked.

"Ah, *oui.*"

"I also bought you a watch." She placed another box in his hands. "It reads the time to you. And it has a GPS in it so, if you ever get lost, I can find you."

Noah scowled. "I'm not a child, Ella."

Ella opened the box and slipped the watch on his wrist, fastening it. "I know that, Huck. I promise you that I know that." She kissed him on the cheek. "I promise that it's a butch watch, very tough looking."

Even though the idea she thought she had to rescue him was depressing, Noah couldn't resist the humour in her voice. He replied, "Butch, eh?"

Ella pressed her palm to his cheek, turning his face into her kiss. She shifted to rest her head on his shoulder. "Now, tell me about this boy and his dog."

"Fingers first while he's busy. Who needs oxygen?" Noah replied, un-fastening the buttons on his shirt and slipping Ella's hand inside against his chest. Her fingers sifted through the hair there.

"Oxygen? What?" Ella's fingers still a moment as she figured out the reference, then she laughed outright. "I missed you so much." Then she didn't speak again for a while. Instead, she explored his mouth with her own and he let her for as long as she pleased.

# Chapter 50

"**It's. Just. Odd.**" Ella enunciated each word.

She'd been home from the conference for two weeks now and made a habit of coming over for breakfast on Saturdays. Today, she'd made banana-pecan muffins with Grady, and was now watching the boy frolic in the backyard with his dog.

Then she'd hit him with this.

"Exactly what are you accusing me of?" Noah sounded annoyed because he was. Had she come over this morning to berate him for taking in the boy? After her absence, this was all that occupied her mind?

"Nothing. Of course, nothing," she replied. "If I thought you were the kind of man to interfere with a child, I would have nothing to do with you."

"Interfere? Psych-speak."

"Hardly surprising since I am a psychologist." Bemusement sounded in her voice.

But he found nothing bemusing or amusing about her accusations. "If you know what's going on, and what's not, what's the problem? I wouldn't hurt the kid."

"I know that." He noted the change in timbre which indicated she'd turned toward him. "The problem is how it looks."

His face distorted in a scowl. "Why do you always worry so much about other people's opinions?"

"I'm not worried about other people's opinions. But if I want people to see me as a moral person, I have to appear to be moral. We have to appear to be moral."

If she was so anxious about appearances, there was a simple solution as far as he was concerned. But he knew she'd never do it. No way was she ready to marry him. So he flung it out there as a challenge. "If you're so worried about appearances, move in with us."

"I can't." Her voice drifted as she turned her face back toward the window. "Noah. I love you. There's no way I can move in and pretend we're simply housemates, ignore the passion between us. I'm not made of marble."

"What?" All the air rushed out of his lungs.

"I'm not hard as stone. I am determined to stand firm but—"

"Say it again." Had he imagined her words?

"Say what? Made of marble?"

"No." His face pinched in frustration.

"I don't understand."

"I love you, Ella."

Ella's voice got all gooey. "I love you, too."

Noah crossed the room in two steps and pulled her close, burying his nose in her hair. "That's it. You've never said that before."

"Oh. Really?"

"I would have remembered. Trust me."

Ella rubbed her face across his shirt then kissed his throat. "I thought you knew."

"I didn't."

She pulled away but not out of his arms, twisting in his embrace, presumably to hug him and monitor Grady at the same time.

"So if we were married, you'd move in?" Noah asked.

"Of course."

"Then marry me." Noah spread his arms wide in a gesture of completion, smiling broadly.

Silence.

"El?" His arms dropped.

She pressed her palms flat on his chest and shoved.

Okay, not the response he'd been hoping for. "Ella?"

She strode away from him. *She's angry?* Noah strode after her. "Ella? Wait. Come on, *bébé.*"

Her steps sounded equally as angry on the return journey. "That was the least romantic proposal ever made. You want me to marry you so I can be your live-in nanny?"

"No. Jeez, El. I want you to marry me because I love you. I can't imagine my life without you. I've wanted—I've wanted to marry you since the first time you humphed me. But you—you've said nothing about marriage since the accident. I—don't want to lose you." He exhaled, forcing out all the sorrow in one breath. "I have nothing to offer you. I should let you go find a life with a whole man. But—"

She rapped him on the chest with her knuckles. "Don't say that!" Her voice grew softer. "You are a whole man."

"El, I—" He stopped because he simply didn't know what else to say.

She pressed her forehead to his chest. "I did think of getting you through rehab and then breaking things off."

"I know that."

"You do?" She tilted her head up, sounding so surprised.

"It's what all the therapists were telling you to do."

"No. Sweetheart. No. They were teaching me how to live with you, showing me the possibilities of life with a spouse who is visually impaired." She gulped. "They were helping me look beyond the way your life had changed to see *you* to help me decide if I wanted to marry you. So I wouldn't have to make a decision based on pity or fear."

"So why get angry when I propose?" He cupped her shoulders.

"Because," tears laced her voice, "I love you. I want you to propose because you love me not to serve as a temporary solution to a problem. I think I deserve a little romance. You treated me like a crutch when I've tried so hard to be your companion." She gasped in a sob as she shoved away from him.

*Zut.* Noah reached for her, walking toward her voice until he pulled her back into his arms. "I'm sorry, El. *Excuse.*" He stroked her hair, holding her close, kissing her temple, her tears. "I love you, *bébé.* I've wanted to marry you forever. But I don't want you to be my companion. I want you as my lover and my friend. My wife." He wrapped his arms around her shoulders, pulling her closer, resting his chin on her head. "I didn't think you'd want me like this. Blind. I assumed I needed to persuade you."

She punched him in the ribs, not even hard enough to hurt.

"Ow. Jeez. You're a violent little thing."

"I'm not little," she laughed. "And I know that didn't hurt." She reached between them to wipe her eyes.

The outer basement door opened and soon the rubber tread of size 5 hiking boots raced up accompanied by the tiny thump of little paws. The kitchen door opened and Grady was there, breathing heavily, his face flushed from the exertion. Otto passed him, his claws clicking on the linoleum until he came to sit on Noah's bare foot. A whiff of wet fur rose on the air. Noah released Ella to crouch down and pet the dog who, in gratitude, stood and shook the light layer of water he'd likely picked up from the puddle at the bottom of the gulley.

"Gak!" Noah replied, startled by the sudden cold liquid on his bare feet.

"Did you have fun outside?" Ella asked Grady. Her voice sounded artificially bright, but Noah didn't think the boy would notice.

"Yes," Grady replied through his app.

"Did Otto enjoy chasing the ball? He looked really happy."

"Yes. Ella. Are you sad?" Grady asked.

Perceptive little guy.

Ella's sharp inhalation spoke of surprise. "Um, Noah and I had a little argument but it's all over now."

Things were silent a moment.

"Noah needs a hug, too," Ella said conspiratorially.

Noah prepared for the contact, returning the boy's hug.

"And Noah?" Ella said. "If you ask me properly, then you'll know. I'm thinking a game of Monopoly would be perfect. Who agrees?"

"Me," Grady replied in the app's oddly adult voice.

"*Oui.*"

# Chapter 51

Rafael Cortez answered his phone on the first ring with his usual gruff and basic greeting, "Cortez."

"This is Eric Nguyen of Witness Protection."

"About time." All of Rafe's frustrations about this case rang in his voice. "I've been trying to get a response from you lot for the past three months. Do the lives of your witnesses mean nothing to you?"

"You have?" Eric asked, baffled by the vehemence directed his way. "I'm sorry. I'm not calling in response to your inquiry. I'm calling to see what you know about a Lillian and Peter Clarke of—"

Rafe cut him off impatiently. "That's who I'm talking about."

More silence. "The Clarke's are not registered with us as witnesses."

"Then why are you calling?"

"The boy. Placed with the Clarke's. He didn't come up in your investigation into their deaths?"

"Only incidentally."

"Their deaths were suspicious?"

"Clearly murder. Executions if you ask me."

"Gang-style?"

Rafe's brows furrowed. "No. Mexican. Looking more and more like *El Cartel Pandilla* is involved."

"What? I can't…why would they go after the boy?"

"What boy?" Rafe asked, irritated by this directionless conversation.

"Never mind. Can you meet with me?"

"Sure. Anything, if you'll explain what this is all about."

"I can be in Calgary in five hours. And Cortez? Don't talk to anyone about the boy."

"You are the first person who has even asked."

"Good."

"Good? That's all? I'm trying to solve a murder here. The boy is a missing person."

"If you talk about him, I can guarantee you'll be solving one more murder."

"See you in five hours."

"Find a discrete place for us to meet. And be careful."

"Right."

# CHAPTER 52

Willing his mind to shake off the effects of his sleep medications, Noah emerged slowly from the twilight between sleeping and waking. He hated taking the meds, hated anything that messed with his vigilance. But he couldn't relax enough to sleep without them. And the headaches. He could deal with the intermittent pain during the day when he was upright and moving. But once he settled on a horizontal surface, tension banded his forehead. The doctors told him it was a result of his brain coping with his vision loss. Then they usually added some other psycho-babble to explain post-traumatic reactions and coping with loss, et cetera. He was willing to listen to Ella on the subject but he didn't need any other professional trying to tell him why he was unable to sleep at night.

Opening his eyes was a futile gesture to determine what had awakened him, so he stilled his body, reaching out with his other senses. A rustle of sound, a wisp of breeze, an unfamiliar scent. An itch between his shoulder blades. That was it. His scalp prickled with awareness. Someone was in his room. And they were watching him.

Noah focussed on a soft shuffle at the door, at the same time reaching beneath his pillow for the sheathed knife he kept there. The tread was light, too light for a man. Unless he was a ninja. Noah hadn't done anything to tick off any ninjas recently, so it must be Grady. Noah tucked the knife back beneath his pillow.

"That you, kid?"

All motion ceased. Then there was the patter of bare feet running away from his room. The click-clack of claws followed. Then returned.

"You asleep." Noah heard Grady's *voice* make the statement and repeat it with an interrogative intonation. "You asleep?"

"I'm awake," Noah replied. *Obviously.* "What's up?"

"Cannot sleep," Grady replied.

This wasn't the first time Grady had come prowling in the middle of the night over the weeks since he'd arrived. The poor kid obviously didn't sleep well either and he had no medications to help him. Maybe Ella was right. Perhaps the psychological effects of living most of his young life in danger had caused sleep issues. And quite possibly losing your vision after being shot at and dumped out of a helicopter could have a commensurate effect on a grown man.

Once again, Noah wished he and Ella were already married. She would know what to do to help the little guy feel safe. But Noah wouldn't make the mistake of asking so clumsily again. She wanted a proper proposal and he planned to give her all the romance he could manage. Somehow.

"You want to get the laptop and watch a movie?" Noah asked Grady.

"Yes." The boy's "yes" always sounded the same.

"In here?" Even though the voice asked the question confidently, Noah was certain Grady's voice would have been tentative.

"Yeah. No problem. It's not like the flickering lights will bother me."

Grady's light footsteps jogged down the hallway and then hesitated. Noah hollered after him, "Turn on whatever lights you want, kid. Won't bother me."

Otto gave a little woof.

Noah heard the subtle buzzing of the power connecting to the switch in the hallway. He opened his eyes, seeking a flicker. To no avail.

Otto at his heels, Grady returned after a few moments, moving slower with the extra weight of the laptop.

"Move the chair wherever you want it. There's an old quilt in the bench at the foot of the bed. Grab that as well."

Grunting and scraping followed as Grady pushed the chair closer to the bed, close enough to impact the bed frame. Grady's bare feet pattered to the foot of the bed and the lid on the bench creaked open. Fabric rustled.

"Use the quilt to keep you warm in the chair," Noah instructed. "Hold the computer on your lap."

"Hm," Grady replied. Was that his real voice? It was huskier than the voice on the communication app.

"Do you have headphones?" Noah asked.

Movement ceased for a moment. Fabric brushed Noah's side. He sensed a flurry of movement retreating and returning. Grady had dropped the quilt in a heap on the bed, run to his room and returned. Otto whined and then jumped. Noah never felt the impact, suggesting the dog had leapt to the chair not the bed. After more commotion, Grady settled. Noah pictured the dog snuggled up beside him on the chair.

"Good night, kid."

"Hm."

When Noah awoke again, the room was silent. No, not quite silent. He heard the whirring of the computer and a light breathing. There was no prickle of sensation so Grady must still be asleep.

Slowly, Noah rose from bed. Sometimes if he moved too quickly before he had his morning coffee, he got dizzy. Leftover effects from the temporal fracture.

Otto tip-tapped into the room, sniffed Noah's leg then carried on to jump up beside Grady.

Trying to picture his bedroom with the chair placement he thought Grady had chosen and the lump the boy must form in the seat, Noah navigated around the space to gather his clothes. He carried them to the bathroom.

After showering, Noah brushed his hair and combed his beard. In some ways, he liked the convenience of a full beard because it precluded the need to shave. But he missed the style and refinement of his goatee. Ella had bought him an electric razor when he'd complained about the uncontrolled nature of his facial hair. He had a long-term hatred of the stupid things, though. They never gave you a close enough shave. However, he had no desire to risk learning to use a blade when he couldn't see. Ella said the CNIB guy would help him learn. But, really? Did he want to feel fourteen again?

When Noah re-entered the bedroom, he stumbled then pitched forward. When his feet tangled in something soft, he landed on his hands and knees. Humiliation flushed through him. The quilt. How had it ended up here?

"You've got to put things away, dude," Noah snapped. He pushed back to sit on his heels.

Fabric rustled. Little hands patted his back.

"Sorry. Fixed it."

Noah was hotly embarrassed. The simplest things tripped him up. Literally. He hated being blind.

"I am sorry, Noah." Grady's voice sounded like it always did, like a half-robotic half-grown man. Noah suspected, however, that he'd find a crestfallen expression on the boy's face if he saw it. He swallowed his irritation and calmed his voice. Grady was just a kid, a lonely little boy who'd spent most of his life in the company of strangers and villains.

"It's all right, G. Have a shower and get dressed. You can help me make pancakes. Sound good?"

"Yes."

Noah rose from the floor, crossed to the dresser, and retrieved his retractable white cane from its spot there beside his box of cufflinks. Like he'd ever use those again.

In the kitchen, Noah added milk to the pre-measured Bisquik Ella had left for him. Once mixed, he poured batter into her large Teflon-coated frying pan. In the old days, he'd rarely taken time for more than a coffee in the morning. Since his accident, he'd found that making breakfast filled some of the vacuum of time

Noah poured a second scoop of batter into the pan. He had no idea whether the circles of batter were intersecting or even if they were round.

The butter popped in the pan and Noah inhaled the scent of the cooking batter. His mouth watered. It didn't matter what shape the pancakes were, they would taste the same.

A shuffle at the doorway warned Noah that Grady had entered the kitchen. "Hey, kid. You clean?"

There was a pause as Noah imagined Grady typing into his handheld device, but no words came. Abruptly a wet head pressed against his side. Noah flinched but kept from moving away. Why had Grady done that? What did the boy want him to do? The butter popped again in the pan and Noah inhaled to test the air and see if the pancake was burning. Along with the scent of cooking batter, he caught the clean scent of shampoo. *Ah. Okay. Cool.* Noah patted Grady's head where it was still pressed against him, making his shirt damp. "Good job," Noah said as if he was approving the proof that Grady had washed. Grady seemed satisfied by that, moving to the kitchen table. Lillian must have developed the habit with him.

A chair squeaked and the laptop tapped against the table. It whirred to life. Grady had set it down and turned it on.

"Does it need to be charged?" Noah asked.

"Hm," Grady replied.

That usually meant "yes" so Noah asked him to plug it in. "There's maple syrup in the fridge and butter in a dish. Get those out, will you?"

"OK." The app had taken over as Grady's voice again.

Noah flipped the pancake out of the pan. From the motion, he was fairly certain it landed in a semi-formed mass on the plate. He flipped out the other one.

Grady appeared at his side again. The kid moved stealthily. "Smells good."

"Thanks. What shape is it?" Noah asked.

"Hm." Grady's voice, a thoughtful sound. "Igloo," Grady replied via the app.

Noah laughed aloud. "You want those or want to wait and see if the next ones come out round?"

"This."

Noah poured more batter into the pan, hoping to go for one giant pancake this time rather than trying to make two distinct shapes. "Go ahead and eat, kid."

"Ask the blessing?"

"You want to ask the blessing before eating?"

"Yes." There was a pause and Noah sensed the furious typing Grady was engaged in because he was still standing so close. "Peter and Lillian talked to me about thanking God for our food before we eat. I like them. I liked them. They were nice."

Noah looped an arm around the boy, squeezing him tightly around the shoulders for a moment. "I'll bet they loved you, too, bud. You miss them?"

"Yes." A pause. "Lillian made flat pancakes."

Noah laughed aloud. "Can you get us each a glass of milk to go with these?" He flipped the pancake.

"OK." Grady's bare feet padded across the linoleum to the refrigerator and then to the counter.

"Knives and forks, too, please."

"OK."

After Grady retrieved the blessing from the phrase bank on the app, they ate in companionable silence. Then Grady took the dishes and placed them in the sink. Lillian had taught Grady good manners.

"So," Noah began once the dishes were washed and sitting to dry on the counter. "I was thinking you could help me with an important errand today. You up for that?"

"OK. What?" Grady replied via his app.

"I need to buy a ring for Ella. I'm going to ask her to marry me."

"Peter and Lillian are married."

Noah wasn't sure how to respond to that. Did he say, "good"?

"Ella is nice," Grady said through his device.

"Yeah." Noah felt his mouth quirk up in a smile. *Nice. And he so wanted to give her a nice and romantic proposal.* "So you think you can help me?"

"Yes."

"We need to brush our teeth. You better use the toilet. Get our boots and jackets."

"How do we get there?"

"We can take the bus." As terrifying as Noah found that idea, he was determined to get a ring and make the proposal Ella wanted. With the kid along, he planned to make it happen. Grady had lived on the streets. He'd managed to bus-it, hitch-it, and walk-it from Calgary to Kamloops. Surely he could get Noah to a jewellery store. Perhaps it was cowardly to rely on a child to get around, but Noah wanted to marry Ella. His sense of pride paled in relation to that.

"We need to get to Aldo's Fine Jewellery on Valleyview off Highland. Can you find the best bus to take using your device?" Noah asked. He would call the bus company if Grady couldn't map it.

"Yes."

Noah found his wallet in the top drawer of the dresser in his bedroom. It felt like his credit cards were inside along with a few bills. Which denomination, he had no way to see. But, wait. Wasn't there some tactile feature added? Didn't matter. Grady could check. Noah had a bus pass Ella had bought him when he was released from the rehab program. He'd never used it before. At the last minute, he donned his sunglasses. Sunglasses and white cane were the code for *blind*. As little as he wanted it to be so, he might need the protection they provided.

Noah sent Grady to find change for the bus in the little drawer in the phone table where Ella kept it. Then to pick out the house keys from the hooks beside the front door.

"You ready?" Noah asked.

"Yes. Otto ready."

Ella had purchased a proper leash for Otto the day after she'd returned from Calgary, along with dishes, kibble, balls, and chew toys. She'd taken Grady along to get his hair cut and buy him a few things she thought he needed like clothes, books and board games.

*However,* "We need to leave Otto here, G," Noah said, his voice surprisingly gentle, even to his own ears.

"No. He comes."

"He can't, bud. The store won't let him in. Maybe one day we can get you a service dog. They wear little vests to let store owners know they're working dogs. I learned about them at this rehab program I went to in Vancouver. But, for now, Otto has to stay here. We should be back in a couple hours. He'll be okay."

Silence greeted his pronouncement.

"You can put out food and fill his water dish. He's emptied his bladder so that should be fine." What else would make Grady more comfortable? "You can leave your bedroom door open so Otto can nap on your bed."

"Leave the television on."

"Great idea."

Grady took off. Noah tried to track the boy's movements, but it was easier to follow Otto's. His claws tip-tapped from room to room until, finally, Grady appeared at Noah's side. Taking his hand, Grady tugged him to the front door.

"Ready to go?" Noah asked, chuckling at the boy's eagerness.

"Yes."

"Okay."

Otto whined and scratched at the door when Noah and Grady moved outside without him.

Grady took off across the lawn, his hiking boots crunching in the thin crust of snow, while Noah locked the front door. He was worried about the boy's emotional state. Had he run away because of Noah's demand to leave Otto behind? Or was he excited and waiting at the curb?

Noah extended his white cane and used it to descend the three front steps—Ella had assured him there were only three—and walk across the lawn, his movements laboured. He didn't even want to think about what he looked like and how many neighbours were staring at him as he swept the air with one hand, tapped his cane, and shuffled his feet. Everything familiar had become new when he'd lost his sight. Things he'd done a hundred times had become insurmountable challenges, terrifying obstacles.

When he reached the curb, Noah sighed his relief, catching the crisp scent of snow in the air. He missed his Keen sandals, but with the light snow, he'd had to settle for shoes.

Where was the kid? "Grady?" Little footsteps approached him. Noah smelled the familiar woodsy scent of his shampoo. "Grady?"

"I waved to Otto to the big windows. Told him to stay," Grady said through his app.

Noah's mouth quirked in humour. "Good idea."

Grady gripped Noah's free hand. When Grady moved forward, Noah followed. His tension eased an increment. "Thanks, buddy," Noah murmured.

By the time they reached Qu'Appelle, Noah was sweating, his shirt sticking to his back. How could such a simple activity be so stressful?

Noah reminded Grady of the information the boy himself had found and then trusted him to get them on the correct bus and off at the right stop.

Soft music played in the background as they entered Aldo's. Classical. Bach. Ella would have enjoyed this piece, some fugue or other. Noah preferred the Nationalistic tone and the heavy influence of folk music in the tunes of Dvořák.

As soon as they stepped over the threshold, Noah noted a change in Grady's manner. He was cloaked in intensity, possibly nervous, definitely silent, even more so than usual.

"Hello, sir. Can I help you?" The man spoke slowly and a little louder than was necessary.

Noah suppressed an impulse to snap at the man: "I'm blind, not deaf or simple."

"Son, you can't take pictures in here." The man's voice had taken on an edge. "He needs to put his phone away. We don't allow pictures in here."

Grady pressed his body against Noah's side, gripping his hand tightly.

A fierce wave of protectiveness surged through his chest. "It's not a phone to him. He doesn't speak, so it's his voice," Noah explained, then insisted, "He keeps it out." If the man persisted in his complaint, Noah would take Grady and find another jewellery store. Somehow. The difficulty of that washed over him, weakening his knees.

Stiffening his resolve, Noah asked, "Are we understood?"

"Yes, of course, sir. There have been some robberies in the neighbourhood recently, but I can clearly see your son has no ill intentions." The man sniffed, the arrogant affectation belying his generous attitude. "How can I help you?"

"I need a ring, for a woman. Sapphires with diamonds."

"For a special occasion?" the man asked.

"Um, who are you?" He'd never even given Noah his name. It's not like Noah could read the name tag.

"Mr. Collins," he said then went silent.

Noah frowned. What was happening now?

Grady pushed Noah's hand forward. Mr. Collins gripped it. The unexpected touch startled Noah but he had the presence of mind to clasp in return. He quickly retrieved his hand and wiped the palm on the leg of his trousers. Then realized how offensive the gesture had been.

"Engagement ring." Noah wanted them back on topic.

Collins sniffed again. "Of course, sir. Come this way."

Mr. Collins evidently gestured because everything went silent again.

"Where?" Noah asked. At least there was no one else in the store to witness his humiliation. He hoped. But there could easily have been someone chuckling silently in the corner. How would he know?

Noah smelled the cloying musk of cologne, heavy on the cloves, a moment before he felt an unfamiliar touch on his elbow. He jerked back.

"Sorry. Over here," Mr. Collins said. Collins gestured, moving his hands in circles, creating turbulence in the air.

"Grady," Noah said. And the boy understood.

"OK," he replied through his app, taking Noah's hand and placing it on his shoulder. Then he led Noah across the room. The kid was a good guide. Noah only bumped his hip once on a display of some sort, something that rattled. Better than crashing, he supposed. He didn't miss Mr. Collins' gasp, though.

Feeling exhausted, Noah wondered again how he expected to be a husband when the mere act of taking the bus had worn him out. They hadn't even accomplished anything yet. Except to discover that Mr. Collins had no clue how to deal with people with different abilities. Noah should have called the CNIB counsellor Ella had been communicating with. Darrell would have helped. Or Noah could have contacted Carlie, the Mobility Specialist assigned to expand his use of the white cane. But Noah was too stubborn. His chest felt tight and heavy, making it hard to breathe. His palms dampened.

"Are you determined to have sapphires and not a solitaire diamond, sir?" Collins asked.

"*Oui.*"

"Most of our sapphires are set in white gold. Some in platinum. Were you hoping for yellow gold?"

Did Ella care? He had no idea. "Uh, white gold should be fine. We'll get bands to match."

Noah heard Collins set three boxes on the counter and Noah felt almost completely unmanned. How was he going to choose a ring for Ella when he couldn't see? He should have brought her along. Except, she'd asked him to buy a ring.

*Zut!* He hated being blind.

Grady took his hand and pressed it flat to the counter. The glass counter was cold and smooth, a rim of metal at the edge.

Noah sensed a flurry of activity beside him.

"White ring with 8 diamonds around a big blue stone in the middle." Grady moved Noah's hand to the right and pressed it flat again. "Three small blue stones. Kind of like a flower." He moved his hand to the right again. "Three stones. One blue in the middle. A white one on both sides. Nice."

"You're amazing, kid," Noah said. The weight on his chest shrank and he breathed easily.

Noah tapped the counter with his index finger. "I want to touch this one." He turned his hand over, palm up.

"Of course, sir." Collins went on to recite the assets of the stone, the clarity and quality and carats of the diamonds and the gold.

Noah took it in his hand. He collapsed his cane and handed it to Grady to explore the ring with both hands, trying to create a picture of it in his mind. "You like this one, kid?" he asked.

Grady's hands were full so he responded with, "Hm."

"How much?" Noah asked Collins.

Once they'd discussed price and Collins had given him the speech about returns and refunds, Noah bought the ring, using his credit card. He got Grady to check the amount for him before he signed. Then tucked the velvet box and receipt into his front trouser pocket. He felt like he'd run a marathon.

"Sir, are you certain you don't want to have the young lady come in and size the ring?" Collins asked.

"She'll need to come in and pick wedding bands. She can deal with it then," Noah replied.

Now, he needed to organize flowers and food. He'd get Grady to use Canada 411 to get the number of a florist and restaurant. Noah would order and Grady could type the credit card number into his device and have the app read it over the phone. He could do this. Together, Grady and he would do this.

"Let's go home, kid. Maybe we'll call a cab."

Collins offered to call one for them and Noah swallowed his pride to let him.

# Chapter 53

The day had been long and Ella was tired. Joshua Greyeyes had been suspended from school for fighting and Indira Chapakai's parents were considering arranging a marriage for her. She was only ten years old. Ella's heart hurt for the children. She wanted to go home, soak away her sorrow in a bubble bath and sleep until morning. Or possibly the morning after.

She couldn't, though. She wouldn't do that to Noah. Now that she understood how lonely and frustrated he was sitting around her house, she tried to spend as many hours as possible in his company. So she took the turn onto Qu'Appelle and then to Nechako.

He was right about one thing: life would be a lot simpler if they were married. However, since his pathetic attempt at a proposal last month, he hadn't brought the subject up again. And neither had she.

Parking in the driveway, she locked her work bag in a covered box in the trunk of the Element, grabbed her purse and walked to the door. It opened before she got her key out.

"*Bonjour.*" Noah's voice came out of Grady's device.

"Uh. Hello," Ella replied. "You look…nice."

Grady wore a white T-shirt, blue cargo pants, dark socks, and, if she wasn't mistaken, one of Noah's vests. A silk tie that was much too long hung loosely around the boy's neck. Grady bowed, gesturing her into the house. Ella stepped in. The aroma of roast chicken filled the air along with other subtler aromas. She inhaled deeply. Candle wax? Flowers? Possibly roses? Grady tugged her purse from her hands and then knelt to tug her boots off her feet.

The chuckle that bubbled up in her was irresistible. "Thank you."

When Grady took her hand, she followed him through the living room and to the dining room. Two vases laden with white roses decorated the table along with two tapered candles, their delicate flames flickering. He left her there and skipped across the room to press *play* on her iPad, filling the room with music. He lowered the volume to a gentle murmur.

Otto scrambled into the room as if he'd been held and then released. After pausing a moment to sniff at Ella's legs, he charged over to Grady who knelt to hug the little dog.

"El."

Ella turned away from Grady toward Noah. His left hand skimmed the tops of the dining chairs as he approached. He was wearing a tailored black suit, the one he'd worn the first Sunday they'd attended church together. The fabric hugged his body, emphasizing his good looks. His white shirt was a little wrinkled and his tie a little crooked, but he looked gorgeous.

"*Cher.*"

"Noah. This is…beautiful. You look so handsome." She glanced at Grady and Otto. "You, too, Grady. You look wonderful."

Grady grinned shyly and hid his face in Otto's fur.

Noah moved closer, placed his hands on her shoulders, slid them down her arms to her hands. He raised them and kissed her knuckles, first one hand then the other.

*Can this be…did he…?* She was afraid to wonder.

Keeping her hands in his, Noah lowered himself to one knee. "Ella. The first time I saw you smile, I was a goner. But that was simply the spark, the beginning. I observed. I listened. I found the most amazing woman inside a beautiful body. I fell in love with you. Ella, will you marry me?"

"Oh, Noah." Ella squeezed his hands.

Grady appeared at Noah's shoulder, reaching inside his suit pocket and retrieving a blue velvet box. He offered it to Ella.

"That the box?" Noah asked.

"Yes," Ella replied, her eyes brimming with tears.

"Yes, you'll marry me or yes it's the box?" Noah asked.

Grady offered the box again and this time Ella took it and opened it.

"Yes to everything, Noah. I love you, Huck. Yes, I'll marry you."

Noah rose and pulled her close. Grady clapped and jumped up and down. Ella pulled him into the hug.

"This is wonderful. Beautiful. Everything is so romantic," Ella said.

"Back a step, dude," Noah said, setting Grady back a step. Then he wrapped his arms around Ella and dipped her. His mouth fell unerringly on her lips.

He set her back on her feet. "Good?"

Ella laughed, tears of joy in her eyes. "So good." She linked her arms around Noah's neck and kissed him. "I love you."

Grady smiled brightly, joining the hug again.

"Good."

# CHAPTER 54

Ella heard the tap-tap of Noah's cane as he walked down the hall from their bedroom. *Their bedroom.* Ella grinned and blushed, hiding the heat in her cheeks by leaning over the game she and Grady were playing on her iPad. Yesterday, after a three-week engagement, she and Noah were married in their church by Enoch, with Grady as Best Man. Enoch's wife, Ilse, Rod Blanchard, Blaine Hanover, and her brother, Perry, had attended. Perry had stood with her as her Best Man of Honour. Soon after, Perry had flown off to Thailand and Blaine had returned to Langley to deal with some crisis with Andras. Noah had agreed to email his father and brothers "once we're settled".

Ella loved that he and Grady had taken the bus downtown to buy her an engagement ring. They, all three of them, had returned the next day to choose weddings bands and have the rings sized. After that, Ella made sure Grady had a bus pass and a map of the bus routes. She found out about the paratransit system in the city and programmed the information into both Noah's and Grady's phones. She wanted Noah to feel independent and Grady to feel safe.

"Where are you guys? And what is that sound?" Noah asked.

The sleeping pills the doctor had prescribed made him groggy in the mornings, so he often resorted to his cane to get to breakfast. Once he'd imbibed his morning coffee, he was able to abandon it until it was time to leave the house.

Grady looked over at Noah, retrieved his iPhone from the side pocket of his camel-coloured cargo pants, and typed. "Zombies."

Otto jumped off the couch and pattered over to Noah, giving his pant leg a sniff. Noah tapped his cane gently against Otto's body before he crouched down to pat the dog's head. Otto seemed satisfied by that, trotting back to Grady's side. The little dog rested his head on the boy's lap.

"What?" Noah replied.

"I'm playing zombies with Ella on her iPad," Grady said through his app. "You get flowers and nuts to smash zombies."

Noah's brow quirked as he reached the couch. He explored the space with his hand before sitting beside Ella. "And this is worth your time?" he asked, skeptical.

Ella suppressed a grin. "It's fun. I'll show you." Once the game was paused, she curled Noah's right hand into a point. *Hm,* her mind drifted, *what this hand did for me last night.* Her eyes rose to his face. *That mouth.* Her eyes dropped, her body tightening in remembrance. She squeezed her legs together, sighing happily.

"El?" Noah sounded confused. He lifted his left hand to her forehead, resting the backs of his fingers there. "You're warm. You feel okay?"

Grady looked up in concern. Even Otto lifted his head.

The attention made Ella's cheeks burn. "I'm fine," she stated clearly.

Grady accepted her words, returning his gaze to the screen, waiting expectantly for her to continue. But Noah still frowned.

Ella pushed up to whisper in his ear. "Just remembering."

And then he understood. His gaze heated. Leaning in, he kissed her on the cheek. His lips lingered long enough to let her know he was remembering, too.

With no small amount of effort, Ella refocussed on the game for Grady's sake. Restarting the level, she tapped Noah's index finger on the screen of her iPad. "Here's a leek. It punches things." She moved his finger along the line. "These ones are all pea shooters and these here are walnuts that act as barriers." She moved his hand to the other side of the screen.

"The zombies come from here. They stumble across the lawn toward the plants, eating them as they go. If they get to the end, a lawnmower releases and mows them down."

Noah let her manipulate his right hand while stretching his left arm across the back of the couch to tousle Grady's hair. Ella took in the boy's shy grin at the affectionate gesture.

"So there's no way to lose?" Noah asked. He cocked his head toward her.

Ella found it interesting which of his gestures and responses were changing since his blindness, and which remained the same.

"You got one lawnmower in each row," Grady replied via the app.

"So they eat all the plants twice to...what?" Noah asked.

"Eat your brains," Grady said. The voice from the app was neutral but Grady's eyes sparkled with glee.

"My brain is already missing parts." Wry humour laced Noah's voice.

Ella stilled, searching his face. But when Noah winked at her, she relaxed. "I guess you better not lose," she said, patting his cheek.

Noah laughed, leaning in to kiss the side of her face. His aim was getting better. She supposed all the practice from last night had been greatly beneficial.

Smiling, she started the level. "Okay. Here we go." She used Noah's finger to plant the flowers and collect the little suns that appeared, explaining what was happening. Grady shifted onto his knees, leaning into Ella. His little body bounced and shook with excitement.

After a while, as the pace of the zombie attack increased, Ella fell into silence.

"Suns?" Noah asked as she swept his finger across the screen.

"Yep." She tapped to the left then in the middle.

"Leek or Brussel sprout?" Noah asked.

"Leek," Grady typed then pressed the speaker icon on the yellow button to make the app read his message.

She'd had him show her how the device and app worked this morning while they waited for Noah to wake.

"Yep," Ella agreed. "Just behind the walnut. So it punches around the barrier and stays safe."

"Power-up. I can hear it," Noah said, excitement filling his voice.

Ella glanced up to see an expression of wonder on his face. Grady reached across her when she was too slow to respond. "Oh. Thanks, Grady. I didn't see that." She tapped the next power-up and then the fiery pea shooter. *Zoot.*

"I heard that," Noah said, as thrilled as he'd ever been.

"Punch things." Grady reached across her again.

Ella used Noah's finger to plant a Brussel sprout so it would fling the tiny cabbages at the approaching hoard of zombies.

"You play this crazy game, kid?" Noah asked.

"Yes," Grady replied through his app. Then he typed and hit the yellow button. "I never see this one before. I played the original one. Ella show me today."

"I *haven't* seen this one. You need to remember your grammar, bud. I think you're both crazy. Killing zombies with trees. Bizarre idea."

Ella laughed and soon Grady joined in. Laughter was one of the few times they heard his voice. It was new, a little hint of progress in showing that they were helping the boy feel a tiny bit safer.

"I never would have imagined spending my honeymoon playing zombies," Noah murmured in her ear before kissing it.

Ella squeezed his leg, tilting her head to kiss his whiskered chin. "I love you," she whispered. "I'm very happy to be married to you."

When she handed the iPad to Grady, he took over gleefully.

"Yeah?" Noah asked.

"Oh, yes." She turned to Noah, embracing him around the chest. She tucked her face into the space between his neck and shoulder, breathing in his scent.

"Me, too."

# Chapter 55

Ella Kristofer was drowning. She couldn't breathe. Couldn't move. Something heavy pinned her legs to the ocean floor. Struggling against the weight, she tried to swim to the surface. Up, up, she reached.

"Ow! *Bébé?*" Noah's groggy voice floated down to her.

Ella kicked. Harder. Stroked. Faster. She clamped her lips tight over a scream.

"*Chérie*, what's wrong?" Noah always sounded groggy in the mornings.

So it was morning. But in the sea?

Something clamped on her face. *Noah, help me!* Ella twisted in the watery depths, trying to break free.

"Breathe. El. Breathe."

Hands grasped her, shook her. She gasped at the assault.

"That's it, *cher*. Breathe."

The dark waters parted and, suddenly, Ella was awake. "Noah? It's dark. I'm wet." She reached for him.

"You're not wet, *chérie*. You're dreaming." Noah's voice was still thick and slow, but it sharpened when he asked, "What's that smell?"

One finger at a time, she released the death grip she had on Noah's sleep shirt to explore his body for injuries. He was whole. Well. She inhaled deeply. "Something smells funny."

"Smoke." Noah stilled Ella's hands, listening, testing the air. "There's a fire. Grady and Otto."

"Come." Ella rolled out of bed, dragging Noah after her. He surrounded her with his body, shadowing her movements.

He snatched her hand away when she reached to grasp the doorknob. "Wait. Test the heat," he admonished her.

She passed her hands over the door, not quite touching the surface. "It's cool. It doesn't matter, Noah. We have to get Grady."

Wrapping his arm around her waist, he moved her aside then tucked her behind him. "Let me go first."

"Noah," she protested. *You're blind.*

In that moment she realized that her sight was of little added value in the hazy darkness created by the smoke. His sense of smell, his hearing, his sensitive touch, was worth more than her limited vision.

Noah ignored her anyway, opening the door. He paused a moment, sniffing.

"Grady! Otto!" Noah whistled for the dog.

Muffled barking sounded from the room beside theirs, Grady's room, and then was cut off.

Ella surged around Noah. "Grady! Come out! Hurry!"

Noah grasped her arm and stopped her. "Grady, there's fire. El! Get something for our feet."

Ella raced back into the bedroom and found their church shoes under the edge of the bed, black patent leather loafers for Noah and low-heeled black suede boots for herself.

"Hurry, El. Tell me what's happening. Where's the fire coming from?"

"The smoke seems to be coming from the front of the house. The door to the front spare room is closed but I can see flickers beneath it." She looked back over her shoulder and then crushed her body against Noah's back, instinctively increasing her distance from the flames licking at the living room doorway. "There is definitely fire in the living room. And it's coming this way."

"We get out the back," Noah said. "Grady's window opens onto the patio roof."

Cautiously, Noah moved forward, passing his hands over Grady's door before opening it.

"Grady!" Noah called out sharply. "We're coming in."

Otto shot out, yapping, jumping up to push his front paws against their knees before running back into the room, returning to jump at them again.

"Good dog," Noah said, not bothering to stop and pat him.

On his next pass, Ella dropped to her knees, scooping the small dog into her arms. Otto wriggled and barked. "Where's Grady, pup?" she asked Otto as if he could answer.

"Grady?" Noah's voice was gentler now. "Come out, son. I know you're afraid, but I'm not leaving without you." Noah shut the door behind them. He moved further into the room, his arms clearing the way before him. "Come here, now!"

Ella scanned the room to see Grady's head appear around the door of the closet. He'd been hiding inside, but somehow Otto had not. "He's there, in the closet," Ella told Noah. She crouched lower, keeping her voice gentle as she spoke words of reassurance to the boy, trying to coax him out.

Noah turned to the wall, patting along it until he located the window. He unlocked, opened, and removed it then set it aside against the wall.

Once Grady's body had fully emerged from the closet, Ella grabbed him. She pulled him close for a hug. "It's okay, sweetheart. We're getting out."

His little body shuddered in her arms. With his cargo pants over his pyjamas, hiking boots on his feet, and backpack in hand, she suddenly understood why he insisted on keeping his every possession in his bedroom. This poor child had done far too much running in his short life.

"He out?" Noah asked.

"Yes. We're ready to get out," Ella replied. Ella helped Grady don the backpack.

Rising, Noah groped his way forward, testing the air with his hands until he enclosed his arms around them a moment. He followed up by cuffing Grady lightly on the ear.

"Noah," Ella admonished him.

"You come out when I call you, dude," Noah reminded Grady gruffly. "We love you, kid. How we gonna get out without you?"

"Uhn," Grady replied, his eyes glimmering in the dark

The growl and crackle of the flames in the hallway grew louder, heat shimmering through the air.

"Out the window," Noah said. "Now."

"Come on, Grady," Ella said, keeping one arm around him and one clasping Otto to her side.

Ella helped Grady out the window and then handed Otto to him. She stepped out after him, scooting with them to the edge of the overhang. "Drop your pack down."

Grady did, flinging it out toward the edge of the yard.

"Hang off the eaves trough and let go. When you hit the ground, roll away from the house. Okay, honey?"

"Hm," Grady replied.

"Okay, honey. Go. I'll pass Otto down once you're there."

As she watched Grady lower himself over the side, Ella checked over her shoulder to find Noah standing inside the room at the window, clutching the lower ledge. The air in the room was hazy.

"El." Grady called from the ground. "Otto."

Ella grasped Otto by the scruff of the neck and lowered the wiggling dog down. Otto yarped indignantly as he fell.

"Noah," she called to him over her shoulder. He hadn't moved.

Scrabbling back across the roof, she grabbed him by the arm. "Come. Climb out." She stroked his face. Kissed him. His mouth was taut and sweat soaked his moustache. He was pale, paler than she'd ever seen. "Baby, you can do this."

"El! Noah!" Grady hollered, his voice throaty and hoarse.

"Grady's waiting, sweetheart," Ella said. "He needs you to come." She eased her way backward on her knees, one hand holding her balance on the shingled roof and the other firmly enmeshed in Noah's sleep shirt. Once they were close to the edge, she turned to face him. "You need to crawl to the edge and lower yourself down. Grady is at the bottom." Taking his hands, she placed them on the eaves trough. "You can do this, Noah."

Noah's face was taut and sweat poured off him. "You go first." He spoke through gritted teeth.

"No. Can't do it. You first, then you can help me."

"Can't see."

She stroked his hair. "I know." The growl and crackle of flames reached Grady's room. The glow flickered in the open window. "Hurry." Sirens sounded close by.

"Noah," Grady said. The moon shone on his round, terrified face as it stared up at them.

Muscles shaking, Noah lowered himself over the edge.

"Grady, step back, sweetheart. Call out so Noah can hear you."

"Come. Hurry," the boy said, walking backward down the slope of the yard. Otto barked as he circled his young master.

"That's it," Ella encouraged Noah. "Now, let go."

Noah groaned and released. Ella watched him land in a heap and roll awkwardly. Grady jumped to his side, rolling him onto his back. Relief soared through her. *Thank you, Lord.*

"Here I come." She forced herself over the edge, held her breath, and released her hold. The ground rushed up to meet her, forcing her knees into her chest. She pushed off and rolled until she stopped on the gravelled dirt in the gulley at the bottom of the yard. Eyes open, she breathed through the shock in her system. Stars spun overhead.

"El. Ella!" Noah called her name over and over.

She tried to inhale so she could answer, but her diaphragm spasmed and wouldn't allow it. It was Otto's frantic licking that finally forced her to gasp in a breath. "I'm here."

"Get her, G," Noah barked the order.

Grady ran over and helped her to her feet.

"Are you okay, Grady?" she asked, tilting his face up to hers.

"Hm."

Noah yanked her into his arms, passing his hands over her body. "Are you hurt? Are you all right?"

Ella stilled his hands, pressing them to her cheeks. "I'm safe. Are you okay?"

"Fine." A muscle ticked in his jaw. Noah groped beside him until his hand landed on Grady's shoulder. "You okay, G?"

"Hm." He adjusted his backpack on his shoulders.

"He's safe and very brave." Ella wrapped an arm around Grady's shoulder, pulling him close again.

Grady smiled shyly. Distressed, Otto ran around their feet.

"What's that?" Noah asked, raising his head and turning it to locate the source of the sound.

Running feet. Shouted orders that meant a fire truck had arrived on Nechako. Two firefighters appeared from her neighbour's yard. She supposed that there was no other way to get back here.

"Ma'am, are you hurt?" The first firefighter reached them, a tall man with a heavy eastern European accent.

"We're fine."

The firefighter took hold of Noah's arm. Noah pulled back, widening his stance defensively.

Ella pushed between Noah and the fireman. "Noah. It's a firefighter. He's trying to help." She turned on the fireman. "You cannot grab him like that. He's blind. He doesn't know what you're doing."

"Sorry, ma'am. Excuse me. I need you to come away from the house. Can you walk?"

A second man, thinner and shorter than the first, arrived.

"Yes," Ella replied.

Otto ran at the two firefighters, barked, then returned to Grady several times. Grady finally knelt and cuddled the little dog, rubbing his face on his sooty fur. The soot left more streaks on Grady's filthy face.

"We'll walk around through your neighbour's yard and up to the street," the thin guy said. "We can help you." He motioned between himself and the other firefighter.

"All right." Ella took Noah's hand, holding Grady around the shoulders. Otto trotted along at Grady's side.

Paramedics met them halfway up the neighbour's yard, wrapping blankets around their shoulders and leading them the rest of the way to an ambulance. One of the paramedics, a blonde woman named Miller, set Ella on the edge of the open doorway and shone a light in her eyes. Another, a husky man with an Irish lilt to his voice, reached for Grady who shrank back against Noah.

"What, kid? What's going on?" Noah's head tilted, as if he was trying to interpret the air around him.

Ella tried to see past the penlight in the paramedic's hand to Noah. She just couldn't. This wasn't going to work. "Wait," Ella said. "I need to help."

"Ma'am, please look straight ahead," Miller said as she gently turned Ella's chin forward.

Noah shucked the blanket to give him freedom of movement to search for hazards and barriers with his right arm as his left pulled Grady in protectively. Grady's arms gripped Noah around the waist as he buried his dirty face against Noah's side. Otto yapped, alternately sitting on Grady's feet and circling man and boy.

"Please…" Ella used the paramedic's shoulder for leverage and stood. The blanket slipped from her shoulders. She didn't even notice. "This will have to wait," she told Miller and then asked the male paramedic, "What do you need?"

"The boy. I need to check him over."

Ella scanned his uniform, her eyes resting on his name badge. Riley.

"Grady," Ella said, gently easing him out from under Noah's protective embrace and commanding Otto to, "Sit."

"Grady, please tell Mr. Riley where you're hurt." Ella reached down and tapped Grady's side pocket, the one which held his device.

Grady's wide eyes met hers for a long moment, searching for something he needed from her. Satisfied, he retrieved his device, scrolled to the app, and typed two words. "Not hurt."

"I need to check for burns, listen to his lungs," Riley explained.

"What's that thing?" Miller asked, indicating the iPhone.

"Grady doesn't speak. He uses a communication app to get his messages across."

"That's cool, Grady," Riley said. He palpated around Grady's neck and shoulders. "Does this hurt?"

Grady looked up at Ella for help. The paramedic's arms were in the way. He was unable to activate the device, couldn't respond.

"Sir," Ella began. "You need to let him use his hands so he can answer your questions."

"Makes sense," Riley murmured, then, "Sorry."

Grady pulled the device up between Riley's arms. "Not hurt."

"Are you dizzy or sick to your stomach?"

"No."

"You okay, kid?" Noah asked.

"Yes."

"He's fine," Noah said.

Riley nodded in response.

"The paramedic, Mr. Riley, he nodded, Noah," Ella said.

Riley looked chagrined. "Sorry," he murmured. "You, sir." He stood and reached for Noah. Ella intercepted his arm.

"Noah, the paramedic would like to check you now."

"No." Noah took a step back. "I'm fine." He cocked his head as if tuning in to the chaos around them, hoses, sirens, orders, alarms. As Ella followed his turning head, she saw her neighbours and a host of reporters lining the street and filling the yards. No wonder Noah was finding the situation overwhelming. So much noise and chaos.

"You should all be checked out at a hospital," Miller said and Riley uttered his agreement.

"Maybe—" Ella began. Miller placed a blanket around her shoulders again, handing her an extra for Noah.

"I'm not going to the hospital," Noah insisted.

She guessed that he was thinking of the days he'd spent there after his accident. It had been such a miserable time she wasn't surprised that hospitals had become anathema to him. But, still.

"Are you sure?" Ella asked Noah, placing a blanket around his shoulders. "Even Grady?"

"He says he's fine," Noah replied.

Miller stepped closer. "After smoke inhalation, fluid can build. Cause problems later."

"We'll watch him," Noah said.

"Is there something I need to sign?" Ella asked. Not that she had any legal right to sign anything for Grady. But they wouldn't know that.

Miller asked her to come to the ambulance.

"I'll be right back," Ella said to Noah. She chucked Grady on the chin. "Wait here, honey. I'll be right back." She shifted her gaze toward Noah.

Grady nodded in understanding. *Watch out for Noah.*

"Are you sure, ma'am?" Riley asked her.

"I'm sure. We're fine and we will watch Grady for signs of smoke inhalation. I can look the symptoms up online."

"Your husband..." Miller shrugged.

"I'm sure you can imagine what my husband has been through. He lost his sight after an accident." *When bad guys tried to shoot him and blow him up with a helicopter.* "His time in the hospital was miserable."

"If you're sure."

A firefighter came over. He introduced himself as "Captain Lee" and asked Ella to describe the sequence of events. She did her best.

After he'd handed her his card, he asked, "Do you have a place to stay tonight?"

"If I can use a phone, I can call our insurance company. They can find us a hotel or something."

"Try a neighbour. Let me know where you're staying so we can connect."

"All right. Thank you. Thank you for all your help." Ella glanced around to include all the emergency personnel.

# CHAPTER 56

Ella woke to an empty bed in the Super 8 in Kamloops. Grady was asleep in the second bed. Otto lay against his side, awake and watching a figure silhouetted at the window. Noah. He stood at the gap between the curtains as if looking out. Except he couldn't see.

"You awake, *chérie?*" he whispered.

"Yeah." *How did he know?*

Ella crossed to him, wrapping her arms around his waist and pressing a kiss to his back. He was so tense it was like hugging a brick wall. "How do you know..." *where the window is?*

He released a huff of air. "Why am I not staring at a wall?"

"I didn't mean that."

"El." He tilted his head toward her, skepticism printed on his features.

"You're right." She kissed him between the shoulder blades. "I guess that is what I wondered."

He turned his head back to the window. "I can feel the cool convection currents coming off the glass."

"That's amazing."

When he remained silent, Ella stayed silent, too, holding him. In time, his tension eased.

"What's wrong, sweetheart? Why can't you sleep?" she asked. It was past dawn but still too early to start the day. Even though there were a million things to do. They needed to call the insurance company, get dog chow for Otto, get Noah's prescriptions refilled…the list went on. "We can get you some meds later today."

"It's not that. It's—That was the most terrifying thing I've ever done."

"What?"

"Letting go."

"Of the hospital?" Ella twisted around his body to see his face. *They would have given him a prescription. Why didn't I think of that?*

"Of the roof." Noah hooked his arm around her shoulders and pulled her to his chest. "I couldn't see. Everything's black. I had no idea what was below, how far it was…" His voice faded. "I would rather have faced the fire than that chasm."

Ella propped her chin on his chest, looking up at him. "What made you?"

Noah tilted his head down, kissing her on the forehead. "I knew you were still on the roof. Knew you wouldn't leave me. I had to jump or you'd die."

"Perhaps." She squeezed him hard enough to make him grunt. No one had ever loved her that much, so much that they faced their worst fears to protect her. "I probably would have pushed you."

Noah chuckled. And that summed up the reasons he wanted to spend the rest of his life with her. When he was unable to see his way, she pushed him.

"I love you." He drew her up against his body, closer than a kiss.

"I love you, too, Noah."

He sucked in a rapid breath and held it. But he was unable to stop the emotion coursing through him.

"Baby, what's wrong?" Ella gripped his T-shirt. "Tell me."

Noah swallowed but he couldn't hold back the words. "I want to see, El. I hate being blind." His voice shook, though he tried to control it. "I'm missing…everything. I want to see the sky, the grass. What does Grady look like? How would *I* know?" He gulped, trying to push down the fear that was trying to strangle him. "I want to see you smile again. I want to watch your face when I make love to you."

Astonishment trilled through her. He felt the electricity of it. "Wh- what?" she said, her voice husky and warm.

"All of it. All the things I've never seen."

"You've seen me smile. And laugh."

"But not the other. I've never watched your face when we're together."

"I...you can feel it." Ella's voice was soft. Sweet, and a little embarrassed. He loved that about her. She was passionate, willing to explore her sensuality, but so sweetly embarrassed when they talked about sex.

"Noah?" She prompted him when he didn't respond.

"It's not the same."

"No, honey. That's not what I mean." She paused a moment, forming a new thought. "You can feel it in my body, in the way I move. That's all it is for me, too. My eyes are closed. All I can feel is your body. I can hear you gasp, moan, laugh."

"Maybe." His grip loosened and he buried his face against her neck, kissing her there. Then he gripped her harder. "I hate this."

"It's okay, honey. We're coping."

*Coping? Is that the best life now has to offer? Coping with the crap?* Noah pulled back. "And if it was you?"

"Noah." Her voice beseeched him.

*I want to hear the truth.* His hands shifted to grip her upper arms. "I don't want platitudes. It's not weak to feel..."

"Weak?" Ella clutched Noah's T-shirt, shaking him lightly. "You're the strongest man I know. You and Grady, you amaze me. If I had lost my vision, I would be cowering under the covers. I would be a quivering mass of fear. I don't know how you face each day."

Her whispers were fierce enough that Otto gave a little woof. Ella whispered "stay". The dog must have obeyed because Noah didn't hear him move. But the itchy feeling between Noah's shoulder blades told him that Otto was watching him.

"I don't like it. It makes everything harder. I'm sorry," Ella said. "I know that doesn't help, but that's how I feel."

*Difficile. Oui.* Noah sighed in relief. "I'm glad I'm not the only one."

"I'm sorry." He sensed the sorrow in her voice.

"I don't need you to be sad for me, *bébé*. But I do need you to be honest. Don't pretend."

Ella rubbed her face against his chest. "I'll try. I love you." She hooked her hands up and over his shoulders.

"As long as you're with me, we can do this."

"I'm with you."

# CHAPTER 57

M acken Roy connected the face-to-face video request from Maximiano Guerra. "Bon-jour-no." He purposely mispronounced the Spanish greeting then enjoyed Maxi's scowl. The kid was easy to prick.

"Something you must see." Maxi flipped the camera on his device and pointed it toward an article in the Vancouver Sun. "You recognize the people in this picture?"

Macken leaned forward. It was difficult to decipher the greys, oranges, and browns of the photo. "Send me the link."

Once Maxi did, Macken clicked on it and watched as the picture loaded. There was a single-storey house, flames in the windows. A woman in a nightie was talking to a police officer while a man in a T-shirt and shorts was checked out by a paramedic. A child, a boy, stood beside the man, wrapped in a blanket.

"You know the face of this boy?" Maxi asked.

Macken looked closer, zooming in on the photo. Something dark unfolded in his chest. "Aside from the dark hair and dark skin, he's the spitting image of my brother." *My dead brother.*

"The other one? The man?"

"Noah Kristofer," Macken read from the article. Recognition flashed. "K. It's Capital K. Doesn't look injured to me. Your sources got it wrong."

"They tell me lies."

"Who started the fire?" Macken asked. "Not you?"

"My men, they tell me the fire was Alex Treherne. From the prison, he ordered it. It is said that he blames the woman for his arrest."

"Convergence of opportunity."

"*Que?*"

"Let's get them." Macken said. His mind burned with ideas. But there was one small problem. "Where is Kamloops anyway?"

# Chapter 58

Ella returned to the miniscule round table where Grady and Noah were finishing their complementary breakfast at the Super 8. Otto sat at Grady's feet. It hadn't been easy to convince the manager that the little dog needed to stay, but he'd finally agreed. After Noah threatened to sue. What he would have sued them for he'd never said. But the ploy had worked.

"I called the Fire Marshall and he said we can go to the house today with him to get anything that survived," Ella said. "But the house—it's pretty well destroyed. It will have to be rebuilt." Her beautiful little bungalow. She'd already had a good cry in the shower after hearing the news.

"Right," Noah replied.

"Where are we going to live until then?" she asked.

"We can stay at the apartment. The lease isn't up yet. Have you called the insurance company?"

"Yes." The insurance company had cut a cheque for living expenses and couriered it to the motel late last night. Before breakfast, Ella had cabbed-it first to the only Blenz coffee shop in town to stock up on coffee and muffins, then to the nearest Wal Mart for clothes and toiletries. She'd made a stop at the 24-hour Shoppers Drug Mart for a new folding white cane for Noah and a refill of his prescriptions. She had explained that all the medications were lost in a fire, insisted she was telling the truth, and even then, the pharmacist had only agreed to contact the doctor to inquire into the matter. He hadn't committed to giving them the meds. What did he think? That she'd make up such an outlandish tale?

"They're sending out their adjustor in a few days who will estimate building costs. Then we can either let them hire a contractor or hire one ourselves and submit receipts." They could upgrade the house, refashion it, or rebuild it to the same plans. It would be like new. But still be the same old house.

"Hiring a contractor? What a headache," Noah replied with asperity.

Grady looked up from his chocolate chip muffin, glanced between them, and then ducked his head. Otto shifted to press against his leg.

"Grady's worried," Ella said, tapping Noah on the hand.

Noah sighed. He wasn't ready to move on from the conversation to meet the boy's needs. But he did, anyway. He found the back of Grady's chair and then settled his hand on the boy's shoulder to give a light squeeze. "It'll be okay, kid."

"What's bothering you, Grady?" Ella asked.

Grady peeked up at her through his bangs and then fished his device out of his pocket and typed. When he finished, he pressed the yellow "speak" button. "Was it Uncle Macken?"

Ella glanced at Noah's face but he was turned toward Grady. "I don't know, G. I suppose it might have been. But it could have been the guys who took my sight. Chenche's boy's been after me for a while. Or any number of enemies coming after me now they know I'm helpless."

"Noah, you're not helpless," Ella protested.

Noah turned his head toward her though his eyes never lighted on her face. Why would they, she asked herself?

"My point is," Noah turned back to Grady, moving his hand to the nape of the boy's neck and massaging gently. "It could have been anyone, even punks from the neighbourhood. I assume even tiny Kamloops has crime."

This was aimed at her. "Of course."

Grady typed furiously for a few moments. "Uncle Macken talk to man named Chinchay. Chinchay tell him to kill my papa."

*Chenche.* Noah looked thoughtful at the information. "Whoever started the fire, we're in this together. You, me, and Ella, we're a team, G. Oh, and Otto." Noah chuckled when the little dog woofed at the sound of his name.

Grady reached down to pat Otto's curly, white head.

Ella reached across the table, taking Grady's hand and then Noah's. "I agree, Grady. You're with us now. Whatever happens to one of us, happens to all of us."

Grady's eyes grew wide and filled with moisture he didn't let fall. Removing his hand from Ella's, he typed again. "Lillian and Peter are dead?"

Even though the device read the words, Grady flipped the screen to show Ella what he had typed, she assumed so that there was no mistake what he was asking. His eyes begged her for a response. And Ella's heart cracked a little more. She glanced at Noah but of course he didn't see her plea for assistance. Her throat tightened over the words she needed to say, so she cleared it.

Noah's head snapped toward her, seemed to calculate something, and then he leaned his head over Grady's in a gesture of comfort. "I'm pretty sure, bud. But that doesn't mean you don't have a home. You can stay with me and Ella for as long as you want."

Grady's body shook. It was an odd thing to watch. Rather than dissolve into tears, his eyes widened, his pupils dilated. The tremors that started in his hands traveled up his arms until his entire body was shuddering. His natural olive complexion paled. And then his eyes rolled back in his head.

"Noah, catch him." Ella was up and around the table. It happened so fast.

Noah dragged Grady bodily sideways until he lay partially across his lap with his head tilted at an odd angle on his chest and his legs folded against the side of the chair. "El."

Ella slipped her right arm under Grady's legs and hefted him more securely onto Noah's lap. Otto yipped, ran around the table and then returned, hopping in place.

"Ma'am, is everything all right?" A tall, spare man with a shaved head, who had been eating at another of the tables, came over.

"Our boy fainted. Can you please get a member of staff?" Ella asked.

"Sure."

She heard him move away but didn't bother to watch. Ella felt Grady's forehead and took his pulse. His skin was clammy but his heartbeat was strong.

"Ma'am, is there a problem?" the desk clerk asked as she approached. She was blonde, medium-build, and wearing a black dress with the hotel chain's logo.

The man who'd fetched her returned to his table for his coffee then departed quickly.

Noah murmured words of comfort in Grady's ear as he chafed the boy's arms and cheeks.

"Do you have a doctor or nurse on staff?" Ella asked.

"No, I'm sorry. Would you like me to call an ambulance?"

"No," Noah replied. His voice was sharper than Ella expected.

"Maybe we should," Ella replied. *After the fire, he might have trouble breathing.*

"No. Help me get him to our room. I'll check him over," Noah insisted.

"Can you get me some orange juice or apple juice?" Ella asked the clerk then said to Noah, "If you can carry him, I'll get us to the room."

"I can carry him. Grab my cane, would you?" Noah replied.

Standing, Ella commanded Otto to heel, took her bearings to note all the potential obstacles for Noah, and then guided him to stand.

Noah shifted Grady to sit in his arms like a toddler with his legs straddling his waist and his head against his chest. The boy looked large in this position but not ungainly. The position would give Noah some freedom of movement. Hefting Grady higher, Noah asked for his cane. Ella handed it over and then accepted two plastic tinfoil-covered cups of orange juice from the desk clerk.

"Ella?"

"I'm here." She turned Noah's body a few degrees to the left and said, "Straight to the bottom of the stairs then about three paces left to the elevator. No obstacles."

Noah blew out a breath then hitched Grady up once more. Sweeping his cane across the floor in front of him, Noah started forward. Ella hooked her hand in his elbow, sandwiched beside Grady's leg.

They made it to the room without incident. Ella pulled the covers back on the nearest bed and Noah laid Grady down. Then Ella removed his hiking boots.

"Cover him. He's in shock," Noah said. "We need to warm him up."

Ella doubled the quilt and laid it over Grady, then added the quilt from the other bed. She reclined on the bed, enfolding the boy in her arms.

Noah ordered Otto onto the bed where he snuggled close, his damp, black nose on Grady's shoulder. Noah stretched out beside him. He patted the mattress until he found Grady's arm, then slipped his hand down until he held Grady's hand through the covers. Tucking a pillow beneath him first, he placed his other hand on the top of Grady's head. "You'll be okay, kid. I promise."

Noah tilted his head toward Ella. "I don't understand what happened. He knew Peter and Lillian died. He saw Peter's body."

"Though he knew it, his heart only now figured it out. It's a simple defense mechanism when you're faced with something too terrible to acknowledge."

Noah looked thoughtful for a moment. "You're very smart, Mrs. Kristofer, for someone who uses psych-speak."

Ella's heart softened. "I love you." She reached across Grady's body to stroke Noah's cheek with the backs of her fingers.

He grasped her hand, kissing her fingers. "Love you, too, *chérie*."

They remained in that position for twenty minutes or so until Grady came around.

Grady looked startled when he opened his eyes and found himself the centre of attention. He accepted a hug from Ella and then shrugged out of the blankets and dropped to the floor to play with Otto as if he'd woken from a simple nap rather than a faint. And perhaps that's what he'd done, checked out until he could cope.

Ella and Noah scooted to sit side by side at the head of the bed. She lifted Noah's arm around her shoulders. "I think he needs to see a doctor, sweetheart."

"He's okay now. Like you said, everything simply caught up with him," Noah replied.

Observing Noah, she would have said that he was watching Grady try to teach Otto to fetch the newspaper provided by the motel except, of course, he was unable to see.

Noah blew out a breath. Pressed his thumbs to his eyes. "You could be right. Maybe I'm reflecting my reluctance onto him." Noah blew out a breath, making an unusual enough sound that both Grady and Otto looked over at him.

"Come on over, Grady," Ella said, opening an arm in welcome.

Grady glanced back and forth between her and Noah before crawling onto the bed between them. Otto trotted over at his heels then jumped onto the bed at their feet.

"I thought I'd drop you and Noah off at a walk-in clinic so a doctor can check you out while Otto and I meet with the Fire Marshall."

Grady touched Noah's shoulder, two light taps. Noah must have expected it, because he didn't flinch away from the contact.

"Yeah, bud. I think Ella's right. I'd hate to find out you needed something we didn't give you," Noah said.

Grady tapped Noah's shoulder again with more force. His expression reflected a determination Ella couldn't quite interpret.

Noah reached out, tapping his fingers against Grady's chest before settling his hand on the boy's nape. "I'm all right. I don't need to see a doctor."

Grady's lips firmed and he shook his head.

"I thought of something," Ella interrupted before Noah made some kind of declaration that would do none of them any good. "Do you have a health card, Grady?"

Grady slipped from beneath Noah's hand, crawled across his legs, and ran off to retrieve his little blue Velcro wallet from his backpack. He flipped it open and presented it to Ella. She took it and looked through to locate a special laminated card she'd never seen the like of before. On the back, it said the bearer was eligible for health care in the provinces of British Columbia, Alberta, and Ontario, but not Québec.

"This should work."

# CHAPTER 59

The doctor at the Columbia Walk-in Clinic had been good with Grady. He had taken the time to explain what he had to do and why. He'd given Grady time and space to respond using his app. It still felt like a waste of a morning, however. The kid said he was fine. The doctor confirmed it.

By the time their two-and-a-half-hour wait was over, followed by the six minutes they actually spent with the doctor, Noah was exhausted. It took so much energy to be alert to the environment when you couldn't use the shortcut of vision. He was grateful for his fancy blind man's cell phone that enabled him to call Ella to say they were finished and waiting out front. She promised to be there in fifteen minutes. Probably a little optimistic given the traffic at this time of day. It was warm for early winter and not windy, so they'd be fine waiting outside in the heavy sweaters Ella had picked up for them with the insurance advance. There was only a light layer of snow on the ground.

Grady tugged on Noah's sleeve.

"What is it, dude?" Rather than standing here on this sidewalk in front of the walk-in clinic, what Noah wanted to do was crawl into bed with Ella. Grady could watch a movie or play zombies on his iPhone while they took a nap.

Who was he kidding? He wanted to do more than sleep with his wife. And there was no privacy for that in the motel room. It might be time to move out and into his old apartment. It was a one-bedroom, but they'd partition a section for Grady until they came up with a more permanent solution. Noah was grateful now that the landlord hadn't let him out of the lease when they'd married. It was a good backup location. And Mrs. Rooster would surely give up on him when he showed up with a wife and a boy. And a dog. How were they going to sneak that past the landlord?

Grady tugged his sleeve again, this time with more energy.

"What's up, G?" Noah reached around Grady's shoulders, pulling him close. The kid was still traumatized by the whole sequence of events, the fire and finding out that his foster parents were dead. Grady was shuddering. Everything stilled inside Noah, his attention suddenly focussed. "What's going on?"

"I would guess that he is *muy preocupado* with the gun which I am holding."

How had he missed the gunman's approach?

"I have been looking for you, Capital K."

"Maximiano Guerra." Noah fought to find his professional demeanour, his cop instincts that seemed to have failed him so decidedly of late. "I've been looking for you."

"Hello, baby Braeden." Macken Roy's voice was cold and cruel.

Grady whimpered, the sound low and pathetic. The shuddering increased its tenor.

Noah heard a slap and felt Grady jerk in his arms.

"Back off!" Swinging his cane in an arc around him, Noah gripped Grady tighter, shifting him behind his body. The boy plastered himself against Noah's back, his hands grasping fistfuls of Noah's heavy, Sherpa-lined sweater.

Noah's head snapped back as a palm connected with his cheek; the force drove him back a step and he tripped over Grady's body, nearly taking down the both of them. Humiliation flushed through his body. He widened his stance, shifting to the balls of his feet in preparation.

Grady shadowed his every move even as his body quaked in terror.

"Dude's blind, Max," Macken said.

"Sir, is everything all right?" A female voice said.

"What's happening here?" A male voice.

Chattering increased in volume with murmurs of 911 thrown in. Noah couldn't distinguish individual words, was unable to follow the rapidly shifting voices while trying to track the movements of his enemy, and Grady's as well.

"You're going to shut up and move along," Macken ordered, adding foul words which created images of vile deeds.

Noah heard the *schook* and *click* of a Glock being cocked. "You got two seconds, lady."

"G," Noah whispered. "Call 911."

Grady's shuddering didn't change but the boy gripped his sweater tighter, pressing his face into Noah's back hard enough to hurt. Noah knew that with both hands occupied holding on, Grady couldn't use his phone. If Noah got out his own phone, they'd knock it away and it would be lost.

"Get the van, Max."

"First," Maximiano began.

Noah staggered back at the force of the blow that landed on his jaw; his head snapped back and his cane went flying out of his hand. Only Grady's grip kept him upright. Maxi followed up with a punch to the gut. The air forced out of his lungs, Noah dropped to his knees. He felt the weight of Grady on his back as the boy held on as though his life depended on it. And, Noah supposed, it did.

"Now, I get it."

Noah heard movement, engines, murmurs and shocked exclamations all around him. Drawing in breaths, deeper each time, he fumbled to get a grip on Grady and pull the boy into the protection of his body. Grady's shuddering eased somewhat, though his body was chilled and he was utterly silent. If he hadn't felt the boy's vibrations, Noah would not have been certain Grady was still alive.

"What are you doing?" a man asked.

"Get back," Macken replied. "Their lives ain't worth yours."

A second handgun cocked. Feet shuffled.

Noah heard more murmurs and quiet cries, but in that moment he realized they were on their own. No one was going to step up and prevent the abduction of a child and a blind man. This was his last opportunity to fight back.

Shifting to the balls of his feet, Noah prepared. He couldn't see, but he could hear and smell and feel. Pushed down, his fear settled, allowing him to reach out with his senses. He tuned into the murmuring voices around him, then pushed them to the background where they became a hum of white noise. Tuned to the sounds of traffic, he picked out the vehicle approaching and then stopping a few feet in front of him. Even though he whispered a plan, it was unclear whether the boy heard or would obey when the moment presented itself.

The vehicle door slammed, the sound followed by the *shush* of a van door opening. Footsteps approached. A hand reached for his shirt. He felt the heat of it, felt the air the movement shifted.

Noah sprang. He tangled his left hand in fabric, clenched his right into a fist and struck. He hit and kicked even when Grady's body was ripped from him. The boy cried out. Noah turned instinctively toward the sound. Something heavy struck him on the side of the head. White streaked across his vision and Noah watched it in fascination as he slipped toward unconsciousness.

But he couldn't let go and chase it. He wouldn't leave Grady alone.

Letting the white go, Noah groped upward into the night. Rolling away from the bodies entangled with his, he called out, "Grady!"

A small body hurtled into his arms, small hands clutched and holding around his neck. Noah gripped him, succumbing to the dark of night.

# Chapter 60

Ella arrived at the Columbia Walk-in Clinic to a scene of chaos. Two police cars guarded the entrance to the plaza. A crowd gathered on the sidewalk in front of the clinic, spilling onto the asphalt. She was unable to see Noah or Grady anywhere, even though Noah had assured her they'd wait. She tried Noah's and Grady's cell phones. Straight to voicemail.

Otto stood with his back feet on the passenger seat of her Element and his paws on the dash. His tongue lolled, giving him a carefree expression, like he knew instinctively they were on their way to Grady.

Parking, Ella snapped the leash on Otto, grabbed her purse, and approached the scene. She honed in on the nearest uniformed police officer.

"What's happened here?" she asked. "I need to get inside to see if my husband is still here."

"Ma'am, please stay back." The police officer looked beyond her, gesturing for her to step aside and join the crowd on the snow-scattered lawn between the street and the parking lot.

"You don't understand. My husband is blind. This chaos out here will be confusing for him. He has our boy with him and—"

"Wait a minute." The officer took her by the arm, his attention focussed on her. "Your husband is blind?"

"Yes." Ella chilled. "Why?"

"He had a boy with him?"

"Yes. Why?"

"Wait here a moment." The officer spoke into his radio.

"What's happened?" Ella asked. Her voice rose in tension. "Where is my husband? Noah! Grady!" Ella craned her neck to see around the police officer and through the window of the walk-in clinic. She scanned the faces in the crowd but spotted no one familiar, no hint to Noah and Grady.

"Ma'am."

Ella swung her gaze to two men approaching from the direction of the street. They were short men as compared to Noah's six-two. Both were dark-haired and olive complexioned. Though one sported a three-day growth of beard on his angular features, the other's face was smooth and round.

"My name is Eric Nguyen of the Federal Witness Protection Program." This was the smooth-complexioned man. He flashed a badge at her. RCMP. Then indicated the man beside him, the scruffy one, who also showed her his badge. Same. RCMP. "This is Rafael Cortez. He's a detective with the Calgary detachment. Who are you?"

"Ella." *Hanover.* Nope. "Kristofer." *She wasn't used to introducing herself by her married name yet.*

"Could you please come with us," Nguyen asked, though it wasn't truly a question. When he reached for her, Otto barked at him, two serious woofs.

"It's okay, Otto," Ella murmured, patting him. The little dog quieted but, when Nguyen took her by the elbow and started leading her away from the crowd, he sniffed the man's pant leg. Momentarily appeased, he released a huff of air.

"I need to find my husband and our boy," Ella insisted.

"Who is your husband?" Cortez asked.

They flanked her. Still, they didn't make her feel intimidated.

"Noah Kristofer." She hesitated before bringing Grady into the conversation too much. From the little Noah had told her about him, the boy was being chased by his uncle, some sort of career criminal. These men beside her weren't criminals, they were police, RCMP, just like Noah. But, still.

"I worked with Noah Kristofer several years ago," Nguyen said.

Astonished, Ella halted, turning to him. "You did?" What were the odds of a former colleague appearing at this location at this moment in time? *What is going on?*

"Yes. I was his contact on an operation involving a mutual person of interest."

"Okay."

"K—Noah—called me a couple of months ago saying that a young boy had shown up at his door."

Cortez seemed to be scanning the environment. When one uniformed constable approached, Cortez waved him away.

Ella turned her attention to Nguyen, feeling a little more settled in the privacy. "Why did he call you?"

"He said that the boy had been under the protection of the FWPP. Witness protection," Nguyen explained. "He wanted to know who the boy was and why he felt pursued."

"Grady," Ella breathed his name.

Nguyen nodded. "Grady Jones."

Cortez met Nguyen's eyes a moment and then nodded, some sort of nonverbal message passing between them, before he returned his attention to their surroundings.

"When I investigated, bells went clanging all over. What do you know about Grady?"

"Mr. Nguyen—"

"Sergeant."

"Sorry. Sergeant Nguyen. What has happened here? Today. Where is Noah?"

"I would like to get to that in a moment. Trust me that taking the time to talk to us will not slow things."

"All right. Um, Noah told me Grady was on the run from his uncle who is a career criminal. He said Grady had told him that his foster parents were killed."

Cortez suddenly pinned her with a glare. "Who were they?"

"Um, Lillian and Peter Clarke. I think Grady may have seen something, possibly their attack. But when Noah told him they were dead, he responded with shock. So it's unclear what exactly happened and what he understood of it. It makes me think that though he saw something terrible happen to the Clarkes, he hadn't processed the certainty of their deaths."

"You talk like a psychiatrist," Cortez commented, frowning.

"A psychologist, actually," Ella replied.

Cortez and Nguyen exchanged a glance. Cortez spoke next. "Does your husband know who killed the Clarkes?"

"No. I don't think so," she replied. "He monitored Grady closely, afraid his uncle would find him. Or me."

Cortez turned to Nguyen. "It couldn't have been Roy, though. The DCW were pulling a series of home invasions in Vancouver at the time."

Nguyen turned back to Ella. "Grady's real name is Braeden Roy. He's the son of Monroe Roy, former president of the Dark Coast Warriors, a pacific gang. Very violent. Monroe was murdered seven years ago. Braeden, Grady, witnessed the murder." Nguyen closed his eyes a moment. "It was carnage. Monroe, his girlfriend, and four others who were unlucky enough to be toking with them at the time, were slaughtered. The officers who responded to a 911 call by neighbours found Braeden in a cupboard. He told the first officers on the scene, 'I saw it. He killed my daddy.' And then he never spoke again. Witness Protection took him into custody and waited for him to start speaking once more so they could put the killer away. Everyone suspected it was Macken Roy, Monroe's youngest brother. But there was no proof except the boy's testimony. This Roy's been tough to pin down. The Crown Attorney's desperate to get something on him, put him away."

"Poor Grady," Ella whispered, her heart clenching in pity. All that carnage. All that pressure.

"Lillian and Peter Clarke were the last in a line of foster parents solicited by the FWPP to care for the boy. They'd asked permission to adopt him." Nguyen rested his hands on his hips. His white cotton dress shirt gaped at the neck. A wide brown belt held up his brown slacks.

"What's happened to Grady? And where is Noah?" Ella asked.

Cortez stepped closer and Nguyen fell back a step as though to take over surveillance. Cortez wore a wrinkled black suit with a dark grey tie and dove grey silk shirt. He looked as though he hadn't slept in days.

"The police were called to the scene here. Witnesses reported that masked gunmen attacked and abducted a man and a boy."

"No," Ella whispered. The world greyed at the edges and Ella swayed.

Cortez gripped her elbow, shaking her lightly. "Mrs. Kristofer," he said her name sharply.

Otto woofed in a low voice.

Ella drew in a deep breath and the colours returned. "What happened? Why are you two here?" She shook off the grip on her arm, breathing deeply again and pulling herself together. "I'm all right."

Cortez exchanged a glance with Nguyen. "I am with the criminal investigation division in Calgary. I'm investigating the homicides of Peter and Lillian Clarke. Your husband contacted Nguyen," Cortez nodded toward him, "who has since been investigating the Braeden Roy case. What we cannot understand is how the two intersect. We understand why the DCW would want to get their hands on the boy. Why would someone want to harm your husband?"

Something clicked in Ella's mind. "Max...ah...Guerra. I'm sorry, I don't remember his proper name. But a few months ago, someone put a bomb in Noah's car. It blew up in my face. But I wasn't hurt, not really. Noah said it was the son of a Mexican drug dealer. No, not a dealer, a big guy. Like the leader of a drug cartel. Noah had," she stopped. She wouldn't tell these men that Noah had killed a man. He had only been following orders. "Noah was an undercover officer with the RCMP, the Criminal and Terrorist Project, or something like that. Anyway, he took down the drug cartel leader and now the son, Max, is after him."

Cortez frowned severely. Nguyen was no longer scanning the environment, his attention focussed on Ella. They resembled bodily question marks.

"After Max-Something-Guerra put a bomb in Noah's car to try and kill him, Noah went back to work to try and find him. He had taken a leave of absence from the RCMP to come and," she stopped again. *Find me and fall in love with me.* Those facts would slow the story for no purpose. "He was on a leave of absence. But Max must have found out. He sent some gang members to try and kill Noah in a helicopter. That's why Noah's blind. The helicopter crashed and they abandoned him in the bush. And then," Ella stopped once again. They didn't need to hear about orbital fractures and traumatic eye injuries, or even temporal bone fractures that caused vertigo. "Noah's boss, Mike Rainer, told everyone that Noah was severely injured in the crash or something. Anyway, we thought Max had stopped looking for him."

"Mike Rainer," Nguyen said. "I've heard of him. He was Team Commander on the case K and I worked together. Let me check." Nguyen moved away, pulling out his cell phone and making a call.

"Sergeant Cortez," she guessed he was also a sergeant. He didn't disagree, so she continued, "Please. What exactly happened here?"

"Your husband and the Roy boy were waiting on the curb." Cortez glanced at her face. "Waiting for you, I suppose. Based on witness accounts, two to five armed and masked men approached. One with a Spanish accent. They threatened them, assaulted and abducted them."

Tears flooded Ella's eyes. "He wouldn't have been able to protect himself. The cowards," Ella said fiercely. "What kind of wimp attacks a blind man and a little boy?"

"What kind, indeed?" Cortez' mouth quirked down at the corner. "All of the witnesses agreed that the man fought back, Mrs. Kristofer. He protected the boy. Your husband sounds like a brave man."

A single tear escaped Ella's eyes. "He is."

Nguyen returned, pocketing his cell phone. "Rainer's an hour away. He'll meet us at Kristofer's apartment. Do you have the key, ma'am?"

"Yes. We were going to move in until the house is fixed."

"What happened to your house?"

"A fire two nights ago."

"A bomb. A fire. Guns and helicopter crashes?" Cortez seemed to test each word.

"Macken Roy has come close to removing this kid several times through the years. What if Roy was here to grab the boy?" Nguyen asked.

"At the same time Guerra grabbed Kristofer?" Cortez asked.

"What if they are working together?" Ella asked.

Cortez snorted derisively and then paused. His eyes narrowed. "What if?"

"What?" Nguyen asked. "Common enemy?"

"There is nothing concrete against Macken Roy. That's why the RCMP was so keen to get the boy to talk. So they can finally put Roy away."

"That would explain the masks. He didn't want to be linked to the crime," Nguyen said.

"How would Guerra know to come here?" Cortez said.

"There was an article in the newspaper about the fire at our house," Ella said. "It doesn't matter who took them, though. Does it? Noah and Grady *were taken*. They're hurt. We have to find them."

"Do you have a way to contact them?" Nguyen said.

"I tried Noah's phone and Grady's. They both go to voicemail."

"Try again," Cortez said.

Ella did. She texted Grady first and then called. "It's Ella. Text me, please, Grady. I'm worried about you." She hung up and called Noah's. She frowned. "It rings and rings. That didn't happen last time I called."

"We can ping the phones," Nguyen suggested. "Find a location."

Cortez called in and gave instructions. Disconnecting, he asked, "Is the boy fitted with a tracking device of any sort?"

"No," Nguyen replied. "They tried that once when he was younger but Roy hacked in and found him. One officer and one civilian died."

"Wait," Ella said. Her body jittered with excitement. "Noah has GPS in his watch. I got this special watch at a conference I attended. It's designed for people with special needs." As she spoke, she punched the codes into her phone. "So that, if he got lost, I'd be able to find him. He was not pleased when I bought it for him but he always wears it." She gulped, emotion clogging her throat a moment. "Because I bought it for him."

A tiny map appeared on her phone screen. She turned it toward the men in triumph. "He's here. Moving away from the city."

"South. Get a map," Cortez instructed Nguyen who paced away to find a constable who brought him a map of British Columbia.

They moved back over to a black sedan which Ella assumed belonged to one of them and spread the map out on the hood. Looking back and forth between the tiny digital map and the paper one, Cortez and Nguyen searched the grids for commonality.

Cortez stabbed the map. "Here. This looks like it. South of the city. On highway 5. Wait. They're turning. West. Onto. 97?"

The light blinked off. "It's gone." Ella pulled her phone closer. "Where is it?"

Nguyen stilled her hands. "It doesn't matter. It's given us a direction, someplace to start."

"But they've been missing for," Ella checked the time on her phone, "Forty-five minutes. No. Longer. That's a long time to be alone with a killer."

"Don't lose hope, Mrs. Kristofer. If Macken Roy wants to stay out of prison, he needs to keep his hands clean. He's not going to kill the boy in front of witnesses."

Tears flooded Ella's eyes. "You can do a lot of bad things to people short of killing them." She knew that from experience.

"True," Cortez responded. He turned to Nguyen. "Send the coordinates to Rainer and have him meet us here." Cortez pointed to the intersection of the two highways. A large warehouse stood close by. "We need to know what's in that area. Where might they take them?"

Nguyen nodded and moved away again.

"Do you think they'll kill them?" Ella asked Cortez.

He met her gaze, his eyes dark and his expression full of meaning.

Hope faltered.

# CHAPTER 61

Noah came-to as the cargo van left the asphalt with a bump and continued on the crunching gravel of a back road. His head hurt and his wrist ached, like someone had wrenched it. His watch. It was missing. As was his sweater. And it was cold lying on the metal floor of the van. Little hands were fisted in his shirt, the weight of a body surprisingly light on his chest. The familiar scent of motel shampoo lingered on the head close to his face.

Noah heard feet shuffling against the van's floor, at least three different pairs, possibly four or more. He brought his arms around Grady. The boy responded by burrowing further into his body.

The van slowed and stopped. Doors opened.

"Haul 'em out!" Macken's voice was harsh and authoritative.

Grady shuddered and whimpered, his body torn from Noah's grip. Before he could react, beefy hands dragged Noah from the back of the cargo van.

"Grady." His voice croaked. *Grady.*

"There." Macken again, giving directions to the others.

Rough hands flung Noah to the frozen ground. Snow melted into his trousers. The air smelled dusty, laced with minerals. Outside somewhere, the area was bounded by walls that reflected sound unevenly.

Two slaps sounded in quick succession. Grady cried out. Noah heard his small body hit the packed earth.

"I'll take my belt to you before I kill you, you little pisser!" Macken's threat chilled Noah's heart. But Grady was silent. Still.

Noah listened for the shush of leather sliding through belt loops and launched himself in that direction. A right hook plowed into his jaw. Noah's head bounced off the ground. Rolling to his side, he struggled to his hands and knees. A boot connected with his ribs, sending him sprawling.

Max giggled. And the two men were distracted by the hilarious diversion of beating a blind man.

⚊⚊⚊ ▲ ⚊⚊⚊

Noah's strength was fading, his body hot with the humiliation of it all. His ears were filled with his own grunts and groans, and the laughter of his foes. His knuckles throbbed in time with the pounding of his heart, lending him some satisfaction. He'd gotten in a few good punches of his own, the air turning blue with the curses of his enemies.

The beating had gone on long enough that Noah memorized the pattern, head, back, legs, stomach, groin. He hoped Ella wasn't counting on having children, because he wasn't sure he ever wanted to use that organ again. The ache throbbed up through his body until it was all he felt.

Noah strained to hear the direction of the next punch. He widened his stance, tried to sense the heat and magnetism from the nearby bodies. A fist connected with his stomach. Another with his face.

White light burst for a moment behind Noah's eyes as he collapsed to his knees in the fine layer of snow. He almost wished Max N Mack would continue to beat on him. It was oddly exciting to see the light after so many months of darkness. The pain, however? He could do without.

A boot connected with his hip, knocking him headfirst toward the cold, hard ground. He caught himself on his right forearm, his left banding across his battered ribs. His skin flamed anew with humiliation. His body throbbed with pain. His ears rang with the laughter of his foes.

Finally, his strength gave out. Noah fell flat on his face. He didn't bother to move this time when a boot connected with his hip. Pain shot down his leg. Blood mixed with dirt to fill his nostrils with a cloying aroma.

"Enough?" Macken asked, his words loud enough to be heard over the pounding in Noah's head.

Booted footsteps approached then retreated as voices murmured. Noah shut out the noise, ignored the roaring in his own head, and reached out with his senses to try and locate Grady. He hadn't heard a peep from the boy since Macken had slapped him. Noah cursed the violence of the man. Grady had made so much progress in his time with him and Ella, playing games, carrying on conversations, and even voicing words from time to time. What would happen to the boy now? Would he ever use his voice again? Or would he retreat into a world where no one could touch him?

When he heard a soft clacking sound, Noah dragged his aching body toward it. "G," he said, keeping his voice soft so as not to draw attention.

The chattering quieted and then started up again. Something scuffed in the dirt. It made a sound softer than the boots of double M's team. Noah reached toward it and caught his hand around a tough rubber tread. Startled a moment, he almost pulled back. But if it belonged to the double M's, it would have landed in his ribs or his head. Noah wrapped his hand around the boot. It was small, smaller than Ella's.

"G," he whispered. "That you?"

The boot moved and Noah thought the boy might have attempted to nod with his foot.

Dragging his body closer, Noah traced his hand vertically up along a pair of cargo pants until he encountered an elbow and a knee. Grady's arms were banded around his knees and his face was tucked against his legs. He'd made himself as small as possible. He was rocking lightly and there were tears streaming down his face. Silent tears that cracked Noah's heart.

# CHAPTER 62

Thick arms hauled Noah upright. Two men dragged him forward. The man on his right smelled acrid, of cordite. He was most likely one of Macken's enforcers. The man on his left struggled more, given his laboured and uneven breathing. He smelled of weed, that sickly-sweet odour of stale urine and stupidity. Noah wouldn't trust this guy for much more than taking out the trash.

Apparently, that's what Noah was, Maximiano Guerra's trash.

In spite of today's events, Noah didn't regret sparing Maxi's young life that night a decade ago. The boy had been an innocent no different from the hundreds of children Chenche had sold into sexual slavery and addiction during his reign of terror. Noah wouldn't go back and remove Maxi's chance to make a new life, to chart a course different from his father's intent.

Neither would he surrender Grady to his uncle's dark intent. Grady had a right to life, he had a right to happiness. Noah intended to do everything in his power to keep the boy alive until help arrived. Help was coming, he was sure of it. Ella would not sit idly by while Noah suffered. She loved him. She trusted him to do his best to survive and to protect Grady.

Noah planted his feet, resisting the forward motion of the two men dragging him inexorably forward toward something cold and looming, a space he imagined as a gaping maw. The air was laced with the scents of mildew and ore.

"Grady!" Noah shouted the boy's name. His voice came out harsh and lacking full strength. But the effort made the two smelly men pause. "Grady!" Noah forced more authority into his voice while he dug his heels into the ground.

The enforcer's fists clenched and Noah had a moment to tighten his whimpering muscles before he was punched in the gut. The air whooshed out of lungs. His knees gave out. He was dragged forward before he could catch his breath.

Noah wheezed in a breath. "Grady, son."

Force impacted Noah from the back. The pothead on his left stumbled but the enforcer kept them moving inexorably forward. Little arms wrapped around Noah's waist from behind.

"Good job," Noah murmured.

"Too scared to be alone in the dark?" Macken sneered.

"Wait! *Un momento,*" Maxi intruded. He sounded almost panicked. "He's no dead yet."

"Copper mine will kill 'em," Macken said, ordering the men to continue inside. "Not our fault if they wandered away, fell in a mine shaft, and died." Macken's voice chilled with the tones of a sociopath enjoying the suffering of a child.

The air chilled, colder even than Grady's hands which clutched the fabric of his shirt, pulling and leaving gaps at the buttons. He was glad he'd worn a T-shirt beneath the flannel.

"Wait," Macken ordered and the men immediately obeyed, confirming Noah's suspicions that Macken had brought support while Maxi had blindly trusted the older man. All the muscle responded to Macken's orders and ignored Maxi's.

"What is?" Maxi asked. There was young confusion in his voice. He was a man by years but not by choice. Someone, some cruel person had fed this boy's heart with bile and hatred until he'd been forced to see Noah as his enemy. Perhaps Noah himself had done that when he had followed the order to terminate Chenche that night. If only he'd known the boy was there, he could have made a better plan to stop the father, a plan that would have helped the son.

"It's not too late, Maximiano," Noah said. "You don't have to live this way."

Footsteps. Booted feet. A resounding slap. Noah's head jerked back. Pothead jerked to the side to avoid getting a nose full of Noah's skull, but still held on.

Grady's arms tightened around Noah's waist, hurting him and making it hard to a draw full breath. But Noah wasn't doing anything to dislodge the boy. There was no way he was leaving this child to his uncle's nonexistent mercy.

"Shut up." Macken's voice was low, sinister. Vicious. His breath wafted into Noah's nostrils, rank with whiskey and a hint of oregano. "No salvation."

"What?" Noah asked, then ignored him. He felt the heat of Macken's face close to his. But he heard the indecision in Maxi's. That was the message to which he wanted to respond. "Leaving me to die won't bring your papa back. You have an opportunity to make a better life. You don't have to buy and sell your soul because Chenche did. Make a choice, Maxi. Make a better choice."

"Shut up!" Macken's fist shot out, the blows raining steadily down.

With his arms restrained by goons and his feet pinned to the ground by Grady's body weight, Noah had no choice but to absorb the punishment. He was barely conscious when he fell. But he knew that Grady was with him.

# CHAPTER 63

Noah fell. He dropped a few feet, straight down, landing on his side. The impact knocked the breath from his lungs. Grady's body was ripped from him. The angle changed and he slid, scrabbling for purchase. His fingers grasped, digging into dirt, scraping along rock, clutching at rotted wood, slivers piercing the skin of his palms.

The bottom disappeared. He fell. Impacted the earth. The world winked out.

When Noah woke, his trousers were damp. For a moment he thought he was back in the hospital and he'd wet his pants. But the ground beneath his prone body smelled of dirt and damp, not clean hospital sheets. His only pillow was the earth.

*Where am I?* Noah reached out with his senses. Cool humidity filled the air around him, soaking into his body to make him shiver. There was silence but for a repetitive clacking sound and the occasional drip-drip of water. His body ached. His head throbbed. The world was black. But that was nothing new.

Reaching out, he patted the chilled ground until his fingertips brushed fabric. "Grady?" he croaked. Swallowing a few times, he forced enough saliva into his mouth to try again. "Grady."

A breath of sound in reply while a small hand patted his head, little fingers tangling in his messy curls.

"Easy." Noah winced at the pull. He didn't need more pain added to the ache throbbing up his body.

Slowly, Noah rolled onto his side, pushing up to sit against the cold, stone wall, testing each new posture to gain information on the state of his body. It hurt. But nothing seemed broken.

"You okay, G?"

Chattering teeth were his only response. Noah followed the sound until he could pull Grady close. Grady resisted a moment and then collapsed into his embrace. His head connected with Noah's sore ribs but he hugged the little boy regardless. "It's okay, kid. We're alive. We'll be okay."

Aside from the chattering of his teeth, Grady made no sound. He clutched fistfuls of Noah's flannel shirt. Somewhere along the way, one of Macken's goons had stolen his sweater. Grady's shuddering increased and then gradually diminished until he was lying quietly against Noah's body. Grady's body had leeched the heat out of Noah's, leaving him chilled to the bone.

"They touch you, kid? After I passed out?"

Grady's head brushed against his chest in a negative response.

"Good. You know where we are?"

Grady shook his head again.

"You have your device?"

Grady gasped as though he meant to cry but instead he squeezed Noah's ribs tighter, making him grunt at the discomfort.

"It's okay, kid. You and me, we know how to communicate, don't we? We don't need a device." *We could use a phone, though.* They'd taken pleasure in searching Noah's pockets and removing everything, smashing his blind man's phone that contained the text from Ella, *"Can't wait to run my fingers through your hair and kiss you until you pass out from lack of oxygen."* Though it was unlikely there was cell coverage here, wherever *here* was.

Grady's face tilted up toward his as he relaxed his grip to a more comfortable level.

"We're going to be okay, G. Okay? You hear me?"

Grady finally nodded, his movements jerky.

"Okay. Cool. Did they leave my cane?"

Grady released one hand and Noah heard him patting around the ground. Grady returned, picking up one of Noah's hands and placing it on his head. Grady shook his head.

"No cane," Noah interpreted. "Okay. Can you see?"

Grady shook his head again.

"Dark. We must be inside somewhere. It doesn't feel like outside. The air is too stale. No animal sounds. The ground is hard-packed." Noah explored the area around him with his free hand, the ground and then up the wall at his back. "Stone walls, but unevenly cut. A tunnel, you suppose?"

"Mine," Grady replied. In his own voice.

Noah smiled in relief. If Grady was willing and able to use his voice, they stood a better chance of getting out of here.

"Mine," Grady repeated.

*Mine.* He'd already said that his device was gone. And he didn't have a cane to claim as *mine.*

"Did they take something that belongs to you besides your iPhone, dude?"

"Dig. Copper. Not police."

*Dig? Police? Copper. Je comprend.* "Okay. Cool. We're in a copper mine. There are tons of them around—Kamloops." *Home.* He'd almost called the place home. Boy had he ever changed his tune. "Disused one, I'd guess, or we'd be too easy to find. I don't think the two M's want us to get out of here."

"Say mine kill us." Grady's voice was rusty from disuse but his speech was clear.

"You and me?" Noah asked as though the idea was ludicrous. "Together we're getting out of here and going home. Just watch us."

"God with us. Lillian says."

"Lillian is one amazing lady, G. Thank you for reminding me. God is with us."

"She's dead," Grady said.

"That's true," Noah replied. What else could he say?

"Peter dead."

"Yes."

"No home."

Noah pulled Grady close. "You have a home, Grady. With Ella and me."

"How long?"

"As long as you want it."

"Forever?"

*"Absolument."*

"Okay."

This boy who spoke so few words knew just what to say to fill Noah's chest with warmth. He accepted the promise without question, and Noah wanted more than anything to fulfill it.

"We need to figure out which way to go. If this is a disused copper mine, there should be several paths that lead to the outside." *And several that lead nowhere.*

"Bomb."

"What do you mean? They exploded a bomb or something?"

"Hm."

*Hm* usually meant *yes.* "They probably collapsed the main entrance." Noah recalled a loud noise as he'd lost consciousness. Setting dynamite or a bomb at the entrance would make sense. It would seal them in. And Maxi did seem to like bombs, if the bomb that had destroyed his super-fine CR-Z was any indication. "They assumed we'd lie down and die. *Fou.* We are getting out of here. Help me up."

Noah let Grady pull him to his feet. He braced one hand on the wall behind him for support. As he came upright, his head pounded harder. His ribs ached as though they were definitely bruised but maybe not broken. His hands hurt and the ache in his groin was making him queasy. Even so, this was nothing compared to the pain he'd experienced in the bush. If he survived that to come home, he'd survive this. He had Grady to help him and Grady to save.

"Okay. Cool. We're on our feet. Now, we need to stay together. You wearing your webbed belt?"

"Hm."

"Take it off. We'll lengthen it and hook it through your belt loop and mine. That way we'll stay connected."

"Kay."

Noah remained still, waiting until Grady pressed the belt into his hands. He examined it with his fingers. Extended, it should provide a solid link, yet allow them to walk comfortably. Noah fastened and tested it. When he moved, Grady did, too. With that connection, they wouldn't need to hold hands and Noah would be able to use both his hands and his feet to map out the space.

"Okay. We need to explore this area and find all the openings. Okay?"

"Hm."

"Let's get started."

Noah and Grady slid their palms along the walls, Grady low and Noah high, to map out the cavern. The ledge they'd traveled down was slick and far too steep to climb. They weren't getting out the way they'd involuntarily entered. If Maxi had blown the entrance, it was futile to try. No, they needed to find an alternate route out.

The cavern in which they found themselves formed a lopsided oval with three openings. Noah led Grady to the first. "Stand here, bud. Put your hands out in front of you and stand still. Breathe slowly. What do you feel?"

Grady's breath shuddered in his chest. "C-cold."

Noah wrapped his arms around the boy's shoulders and pulled him into his body to offer warmth. "Yep. The air is cold. Is it moving?"

Grady slowed his breathing as he concentrated on the messages his body was sending him. "N-no."

"I agree. The air from this tunnel is still. Put your left hand on the wall and walk with me until we find the next one."

Noah shadowed Grady's movements, keeping their bodies close for warmth. He extended his right arm to test the space in front of them, in case anything had changed. Grady leaned into Noah's body when he decided they'd drifted too far apart.

Noah detected the slightly cooler air a moment before his left hand encountered an edge that indicated a tunnel opening. He positioned them in front of it. "Is the air moving? Is it warmer or colder?"

"C-c-cold." Grady moved a half-step forward causing the belt that connected them to tug on Noah. "Windy. Small wind."

"I feel it, too. There's a slight breeze coming toward us. Let's check the other one to be sure."

They slid their palms along the wall, keeping connected to each other as they moved slowly. The next tunnel opened almost directly across from what Noah thought of as Number Two, or, he hoped, The Exit in bright red letters with a flashing arrow pointing "this way out". They set their bodies in front of it like they'd done at the others.

"Windy. Behind us."

"Yes. This won't take us out of here. We go back to number two and walk along it. That wind moving toward us is coming from outside. If we follow the tunnel, we'll find our way out." *I hope.*

They made their way back, using their right hands on the rock this time. Before they entered the tunnel, Noah crouched awkwardly, positioning himself face to face with Grady. At least that was his intention. He rubbed his hands up and down the boy's arms to warm him. Grady responded by pressing his body against Noah's and gripping him tightly around the neck. Noah flinched at the pain it caused, repositioned the boy and hugged him.

"We're okay, G. Your uncle tried to kill you but he failed. We're going to get out of here and tell the police and he's going to prison."

"I…don't remember."

*Remember?* "When Macken killed your father?"

"Hm."

"Who cares? We know he did this today, don't we?"

"Hm."

"This is enough to put him away."

"Okay."

"Right. Now? I want to go home to Ella."

"Otto."

"Ella and Otto, here we come," Noah said. "We've got to watch for rubble that might trip us. And puddles. The water down here is very cold and some of the puddles might be deep, wide, and long. You see any light yet?"

"No."

"Tell me if you do, okay?"

Grady didn't respond but Noah was fairly certain he nodded because of the way his body moved. There was a sort of magnetic field around people. When you got close, you felt, or maybe sensed, a prickle of energy or heat or something. Anyway, it helped him interpret Grady's movements.

"We stay together. Keep moving toward the breeze. Get out of here and back to Ella and Otto."

"Pray?"

"We should pray?"

"Hm."

"You want to?"

"No. Too many words."

"Okay. Cool. You pray in your head and I'll pray out loud." Noah closed his eyes and bowed his head automatically. His mother would be pleased. "God, Grady and I need your help. Please get us out of here. Amen." Noah placed his hand on Grady's head after one miss. "My mother used to pray with me."

"Huh?"

"Did you think I didn't have a mother?"

Grady chuckled, a near-silent puff of air. It was good to hear him laugh. "Lillian."

"Lillian taught you to pray?"

"And Peter."

"They loved you very much."

"Mother?"

"*Pardon?*"

"Love you?"

"Yes. My mother loved me." *My father? Not so much.*

"Not me. Mother try to take me. Papa kill her. Take me back."

"I'm sorry, kid. You've survived a lot of wicked stuff. And you're a great kid in spite of it." Was that what Ella meant when she asked how he got to be so nice? So many lost their way when the nastiness of life touched them. But it was no excuse to spread the disease.

Grady squeezed him around the waist and then hooked his right hand in Noah's waistband. "Ready. Go."

"*Absolument.*"

# CHAPTER 64

Ella Kristofer was going out of her mind. Apparently, GPS was not as accurate as everyone said. The initial readings from the watch indicated that Noah, and hopefully, Grady, had traveled south then west. That was it, the sum total of information. Southwest of Kamloops, there were forests, lakes, copper mines and silver mines, both extinct and active. But where was Noah?

⅄

Grady Jones was in the dark. But he was not alone. Noah Kristofer walked beside him.

This was a darkness unlike any Grady had experienced. In the city, it seemed like there was always light somewhere. The nights had been darker at the campground, but there had been stars and, usually, the moon. Deep in the bowels of this copper mine, there were no stars, no streetlamps, nothing.

Was this what Noah saw all the time? If so, Grady didn't think he would like it. He'd be so scared all the time that he'd never be able to go to school or take Otto for walks. Noah was the bravest man that Grady knew. Except maybe for Jesus. He was God. He could have lived in heaven all the time and expected people to figure out the way to be saved. Instead, he became a human man and lived on the earth just like all the other human men and women. Then he let bad people hurt him and nail him to a cross.

All so everybody had a chance to be saved and go to heaven, too. Grady didn't have to talk out loud to get to heaven. Jesus loved him just the way he was. Grady believed that. He knew it in his head and in his belly. Jesus loved him, and because Grady believed in that, he had God with him all the time, and when he died, he would go to heaven.

But Grady didn't think it was time for him to die. Noah said they would be okay, that they would get back to Otto and Ella. Grady heard a quiet voice in his head that told him it would be okay, too. Grady knew that voice. It had warned him to run on the day the bad men killed Lillian and Peter. And it was a voice that whispered love when he was lonely and his chest hurt with sadness.

"Stop a minute," Noah said, interrupting Grady's thoughts. "I smell water."

Grady breathed deeply for a few breaths but he didn't smell anything except what he'd smelled ever since Uncle Macken and the other man, Max, had pushed them down the slopes to this tunnel. Dirt.

"Move slowly," Noah said.

Grady tapped his left foot in front of him. Nothing different. He pushed his other foot forward and the toe of his hiking boot splashed in a puddle. He froze, looking up at Noah. But even at that distance, he couldn't see his face. He couldn't see Noah's curly hair that flopped all over his head, or the scar across his left eye. That eye was all black. But his other eye was brown.

"You found it, kid. You're a genius," Noah said.

That made Grady feel good. Adults never said nice things about Grady. They all thought he was dumb, too stupid to understand, because he didn't talk. Except Peter and Lillian. And Noah and Ella. And Pastor Enoch. And maybe Ella's brother, Perry. He was funny. There was getting to be more and more people that thought that Grady was smart.

The belt attached to Grady's belt loop tugged—he thought that Noah must be kneeling down to examine the puddle—and so he dropped to his knees, too. What was to learn about a puddle?

"*Zut.* That water is cold." Noah paused. "And oily."

It was wet and cold. They knew that. They could walk through it. Grady didn't have rubber boots but so what? His hikers would get a little wet.

"I wish I had my cane," Noah murmured. Maybe Noah was scared of the water because he couldn't see. "You know how to swim, G?" Noah asked.

*Swim?* Did Noah think the puddle was a lake? Was it?

"G? Do you know how to swim?" Noah asked again. He reached out and touched Grady's face.

Grady flinched at the unexpected touch, but it reminded him that Noah didn't know what Grady was saying unless he talked out loud. That was hard. When he'd heard Uncle Macken's voice, all of his scared thoughts had come back and frozen his voice inside his head. But Noah was hurt. He had protected Grady, kept Uncle Macken from beating him with his belt. When Grady realized that he and Noah were alone down underground, and he remembered that Noah was unable to understand him unless he talked out loud, his speech kind of cracked open. And Grady could use his voice.

"Yes," he said now. *I can swim.*

Yet it was so dark. He knew how to swim but he couldn't swim here. Grady's muscles shook. He'd taken swimming lessons and liked it, liked the water and the freedom of moving through it. But he did not want to step into this water. What if something was in there? Like a shark or sea snakes or—

"G? What's wrong, kid?"

Grady's teeth chattered. His voice started to freeze up.

"Grady." Noah's voice was sharp.

"N-n-no." Grady pushed the word out through his clenched jaws.

"No what? No you can't swim?" Noah wrapped his arm around Grady's shoulders. "You're shaking."

Noah sighed and Grady knew he was disappointed in him. That made Grady feel like crying. "S-sorry," Grady said. His throat felt tight and his eyes filled with tears.

"Come here," Noah said. He drew Grady down to sit beside him. He hugged him tight. "G, it's okay. Don't be sorry. It's okay to be afraid."

347

"D-d-dark."

"Yeah. I bet it is. Sorry. I forgot about that. I guess I'm used to it."

Grady's body began to settle down. "Really?"

"Sure. It wouldn't do me much good to be able to see down here, anyway."

"Are you scared?"

Noah's chest moved like he laughed quietly. "Yeah. I'm scared. But I'm not going to die down here. And I'm not going to let you die, Grady."

"Scared. Dark water."

"I would say we can find another way out except I think this is the right way. I can feel the breeze moving toward us. The path is sloping upwards and the air gets fresher as we move along. We can do this together."

Grady realized that his body was still again. He was cold but not cold enough to make his teeth chatter. He was hungry. And so thirsty. "Drink?"

"We can't drink this water, G. It might make us sick, might even poison us. Sorry. We have to ignore the feeling," Noah said. "So do you think we can make it across this puddle or pond or whatever it is?"

*Can I do it? Am I brave enough?* "Otto." If Otto was on the other side, he would try.

"Yes. Otto is waiting for us to get out of here. Can we do it?"

"Yes."

"Okay. Cool."

Noah groaned as he shifted his body to sit a little differently. He was probably sore. Uncle Macken and Max had beaten him up for a long time. They had laughed. But Grady didn't think it was funny. Four against one was coward odds. Five against one if you counted the guy with the soul-patch who stayed with the van. That wasn't even a real beard. Now that Grady had seen Noah's beard covering his cheeks and chin and lips, he decided to grow one when his manhood changes got finished up.

"We have no way to know how deep the water is or how far it stretches. We need to strip down to our skivvies and T-shirts. I'll wrap everything in my shirt and sling it across my shoulders. It'll be like wearing a bathing suit."

Bathing suit. No chlorine so he wouldn't have to have a shower after. "Okay."

"*Bien.*"

Grady felt Noah shift his body. He copied his actions, unfastening his hiking boots, removing his socks and stuffing them inside.

"Trousers, too, buddy."

Grady unbuttoned his cargo pants then froze. "Belt."

"Right." Noah was quiet for a few minutes. "We can wrap it around our wrists. That will keep us connected."

"Okay. Cool."

Noah chuckled. "You're picking up my speech patterns, kid."

"Sorry."

"Don't apologize, G. It would make Ella smile."

He would like to make Ella smile. She was kind and fun. She liked to play games with him, even the stupid zombie game on her iPad.

Grady felt a tug on the belt. And then it was gone. The long, sharp claws of panic clutched at his chest. His lifeline slipped from his grip. If Noah got up and walked away Grady would be alone in the dark, dark mine.

Grady turned and clutched at Noah, burying one hand in his hair while his other clutched his shirt.

"Hey, kid. Stop. Settle down." Noah put his hands on Grady's arms. Grady pushed with his bare feet against the cold, damp ground, trying to get closer. But instead of pushing Grady away, Noah hugged him. "What's wrong, G? What happened?"

"D-don't...leave...m-me."

Noah squeezed him tighter. "I'm not leaving without you, Grady."

"D-d-don't leave m-m-me." Grady wrapped his arms around Noah's head.

"Grady." Noah said his name sharply. "Braeden!"

Grady pushed his face against Noah's to feel his beard against his cheeks. He'd never known another man with a bushy beard. It reminded him that this was Noah. It was dark and he couldn't see. But this was Noah here with him, Noah who had fed him and given him a safe place to sleep and movies to watch and taken care of Otto. Grady relaxed his hold a little.

Noah breathed in a long breath and coughed. "Yeesh, kid. What happened?"

He didn't know how to explain. He didn't even remember all the things that had come together in his life to make him feel so afraid at that moment. But he remembered that Noah had hugged him instead of hurting him.

"You okay to try this?" Noah asked.

Grady nodded, his cheek rubbing against Noah's beard.

"Okay. Cool. I need to take off my shirt. You can hold onto my undershirt. Okay? We'll stay together. I promise."

Grady nodded, releasing his hold enough so Noah could remove his flannel shirt. Grady thought back but he didn't remember what colour it was. Noah didn't make Grady move away. He simply shifted him enough to wrap their clothes in his shirt and then sling it across his chest like a satchel.

"You ready?" Noah asked.

Grady nodded again. His voice just wouldn't come.

The kid had shut down and Noah didn't understand why. Something about stripping down had freaked him out. He was compliant, doing what Noah asked without trying to climb him like a tree. But he wouldn't speak. Noah's heart cracked a little more for the boy.

Noah wrapped the belt a couple times around his own wrist and then Grady's. It was a risk and he'd much rather have had his hands free. Instead, he took Grady's hand and walked forward tentatively, testing every step. It was cold. So very cold. And the ground sloped down, the water rising to Noah's knees after the first few steps. Grady whimpered as the water hit his underpants, but he kept going. He was a brave kid. Noah would have told him so but he didn't want to let his attention stray for even a moment. The bottom of this puddle, which was seeming more and more like a pond, was slippery. Rubble made each step tricky. He couldn't afford to sprain an ankle, or worse to fall in and wet their clothes.

Noah shivered. Grady's teeth chattered, his hand gripping Noah's hard enough to hurt his bruised knuckles. Each wince reminded Noah that he'd gotten some payback. That a small portion of Grady's trauma had been avenged. At least it helped him to think that way. It kept him from feeling emasculated. But even at his best, he wasn't sure he'd been able to take on five men alone.

The water hit Noah's jockeys and he paused, taking a half step back. His foot slipped off a slimy stone and Noah released Grady's hand, waving his arms to recapture his balance. The belt loosened around his arm.

"Noah, Noah, Noah!" Grady cried aloud.

Noah's right hand splashed in the water. His feet pushed against the bottom of the lake. Grady grabbed a fistful of his T-shirt and Noah stood. Breathing hard, he remained in place.

"Thanks, Grady. I almost dropped us in the drink. I'm sorry. *Zut!* That was close."

Grady's entire arm was shaking, his little fist wound in the fabric of Noah's T-shirt. "N-N-Noah."

"This frigging water is cold. *Sacre bleu!*"

"So cold," Grady replied, his teeth chattering.

"You saved me, G. *Merci.*"

"I'm cold, N-Noah."

Noah kept his stance wide while he pulled Grady slowly in for a hug. He didn't want to risk falling again. He brushed his hand over the boy's head. "We're okay. We survived another hazard."

"Hazard?"

"Something dangerous like an obstruction or a lake of freezing cold water, a blown up tunnel, a pile of rubble."

Noah rewrapped the belt around his arm, took Grady's hand again and drew a deep breath. "Let's try this again."

"Yes. *Oui.*"

Noah chuckled. "*Oui.*"

# Chapter 65

By the time they reached the other side, Noah's legs were numb. Grady had gone quiet again but he kept moving, even when the water reached his chest. As soon as they stepped out of the underground pond, Grady collapsed to the hard-packed ground, nearly yanking Noah's arm out of its socket. Noah collapsed on the ground beside him.

Sleep. He wanted to sleep. Nothing seemed as important as sleep at that moment. Except possibly water. It was a unique form of torture to walk through a pond you couldn't drink. But when you were sleeping, thirst didn't matter. The cool breeze that pointed them toward the outside world merely chilled them further now. Sleep would eliminate that discomfort.

"Get up, Noah." Grady's hands pressed on Noah's chest and patted his face.

"Soon," Noah murmured.

"Get up, Noah," Grady insisted. "Otto."

"MacDog. Who named him?" Noah's voice lacked strength.

"Ella."

"Hm," Noah replied. Sleep tugged at him. Once he was asleep, his aching body would cease to torment him.

Noah's cheek stung. He must have lost consciousness a moment. The pain brought him back. "*Sacre bleu.*" Grady had slapped him.

"Ella." Grady's voice was firmer.

"Ella," Noah repeated the word. "Otto. She didn't name him. Couldn't have." His speech was lightly slurred. All he wanted to do was sleep. Quickly before the pain came back. He was cold. Numb. Tired.

"Ella. Ella. Ella." Grady took a firm hold on Noah's arm and yanked. "*Zut!* Kid. Ow!"

Noah realized that he was lying on the ground curled in a ball. Grady was pulling at him, slapping his chest, his shoulder, his leg. Each blow was accompanied by the words *Ella* and *Otto*.

"Ella. *Oui.* I want to get home to Ella. You, too. We need Ella and Otto."

Exploring the ground, Noah located the bundle that contained their clothes. He unwrapped it, wishing for the cheap, mock-wool hooded sweater Ella had bought him. He may have mocked the term "Sherpa-lined" by asking Ella if the store realized they claimed their clothing was made of mountain guides. But he'd pay a million for it now, to be warm again.

"Gotta get dressed. Get warm." Noah's voice was stronger now as he moved around.

He sensed Grady's movements as the boy got dressed. At least they hadn't stolen Grady's sweater.

Bracing his hands on his knees, Noah stood. "Belt. You find the belt, G?"

"Hm." Grady pressed the belt into Noah's hand. Noah hooked it through his belt loop. It took three tries to fasten the buckle, his fingers were so cold.

Waving his hand in the air, he connected with Grady's shoulder. He squeezed. "Your turn." Noah slid his hand down along Grady's arm to press the other end of the buckle into his hand. "Hook us up, G."

A shudder racked Noah's body. He rubbed his hands up and down his arms to warm them and then did the same for Grady. "We ready?"

"Ready."

Noah hugged the boy before setting him to the side. "Slow and careful. And G?"

"Yes?"

"You're the bravest kid I know."

Noah stepped forward. Grady halted his movement with a hard embrace, hard enough to hurt. "Thanks, kid," Noah said, swallowing a grunt of pain. "Let's get out of here."

He set the boy beside him once again and stepped forward, testing the ground with his feet and the air with his hands. He wanted to run forward, find an exit, and escape. Speed could kill them, however, and he wasn't ready to die. He wasn't willing to let Grady's young life come to an end.

They needed to keep going. So far, they'd crossed perhaps a hundred miles. Or two. He was pretty sure it was closer to one.

# CHAPTER 66

Noah trailed his right hand along the uneven surface of the stone wall, his left hand sweeping the air in front of him. His feet shuffled, scuffing along the rising slope of ground. One. Step. At. A. Time.

Grady frequently reached over to touch Noah's shirt or hook his fingers in Noah's waistband for a few steps. They spoke little, fatigued and thirsty. So thirsty.

The floor disappeared. Noah plunged forward, jarring to the ground on his hands and knees, dragging Grady down with him.

"*Idiot*," he muttered to himself. Being tired was no excuse for lack of vigilance. If that had been a hole rather than a ledge, they'd be dead. Their bodies would be smashed to pieces at the bottom of a shaft.

"Sssorry." Grady's quiet voice came out slightly slurred.

"Not your fault, bud," Noah croaked. "I'm the stupid one. Didn't pay close enough attention. I'm sorry."

"Thirsty."

Noah reached beside him to find Grady curled in a ball on the ground. He brushed the hair back from his face. "What colour is your hair, G?"

"Huh?"

Noah swallowed trying to get a little more spit into his mouth. "Hair. What colour?"

"Black. Like my mama. Brown skin like hers. Papa hated that."

"Ella says we're all brown."

"Same as Papa."

"Yep. If everybody is brown, what does it matter what shade?"

"Peter was brown with black curly hair."

"Cool." Noah shifted to sit on his heels. The position made him realize that he'd scraped his knees when he'd fallen. *Great. More pain.* "Brown, pink, or blue, none of it matters in here, does it?"

"No. So dark. Like nighttime but no stars."

"All the same to me," Noah murmured. "Lights out. Pfft." He snapped his fingers. Then paused.

Turning toward the wall of the tunnel, Noah snapped his fingers a few times. A high-pitched click. A quarter turn to the tunnel they'd just passed through, Noah snapped his fingers again, several times. Lower. The pitch of the click was lower. Noah rotated, testing the difference a few times.

"!-!-!" Grady mimicked the sound of Noah's fingers snapping by making clicks with his tongue against his palate, sort of like the sound adults made for children when playing horsey.

Noah made the same sound. He turned his face in the direction he remembered the wall to be, clicked, and then turned to the space behind them. He clicked. Excitement rushed through him. It was different. Different! When he clicked his tongue while facing a surface, the sound he heard was higher pitched than when he clicked toward an open space. Would these clicks help him navigate? Noah repeated the experiment once more. There was definitely an audible difference between space and surface.

Grady was quiet again, lying against the wall. Noah wanted to let him rest, but they were racing against thirst, hypothermia and exhaustion. They needed to get out of here.

"Are you scared of the dark?" Grady asked, his voice so quiet that Noah almost didn't hear him.

"I was at first." Best not to think about that right now.

The resonance in this space was different from the places they'd been. Noah called out, listening to the way the sound bounced around and returned. They must have stumbled into a cavern. Who would have thought that so much information could be obtained from making different noises?

"We need to map out this space. There might be piles of rock or holes or puddles. Let's explore and see if we can find a tunnel that leads out of here."

"Okay." Grady sighed long and loud. He sounded exhausted almost beyond endurance, but he didn't complain. He gamely crawled, patting the floor around him.

Noah tried out the new click-repeat process for mapping the space. With it, he located a large pile of rubble as well as two tunnels leading away from the cavern. The air in one tunnel was still, heavy. The breeze in the other wafted along his cheeks, speaking to him of flowers and fresh air. Two other piles of rubble he located with his toes, tripping over one and taking Grady down with him.

"Sorry, bud."

"!" Grady clicked in response and Noah couldn't resist chuckling.

"You're right. Maybe I should have clicked to test the space." He picked Grady up and dusted him off. "Let's find our tunnel and get out of here."

When Noah crouched, Grady did as well. His fingers were squished between Noah's waistband and his hip. But Grady didn't mind. Well, maybe he minded a little bit, but he didn't want to let go. Even though they were connected by Grady's belt, he still wanted the extra assurance that Noah wouldn't leave him by accident. Grady was sure Noah wouldn't leave him on purpose. But it was easy to get lost if adults weren't careful.

"Back the other way. We'll see if we can get around the puddle that way," Noah said. His voice was quiet; like he was thinking hard.

Grady shuffled to the left until his outstretched hand touched a cold, rock wall. "I touched the side," he said.

"Good job, Grady. I couldn't do this without you."

Pride swelled in Grady's chest. He drew in a deep breath. Coughed. "Thirsty. Throat hurts."

"Yeah. Me, too. My chest is burning something fierce."

"Water?" There was water right at their feet. Nice cold water to drink.

"No. We can't. No way to know what's in that puddle. Could make us sick." Noah hugged him. "What's your favourite candy?"

Grady shrugged. Thinking of eating made his stomach squeeze painfully.

"I like Certs," Noah said. "those kind that look translucent and have a kind of minty-menthol flavour. My grandmother used to carry them in her purse. She'd give them to me and my brothers to keep us quiet in church."

*Certs?* He'd never had that kind of candy, never had much candy at all in his life. Grady thought about the few times he'd had some. "I like candy canes."

"Okay. Cool. Think about a candy cane. Pretend you take a bite. Then roll it around on your tongue. What does it taste like?"

*Huh?* Grady wasn't so sure about this, but he would play the game. *Tastes like?* "Um, red and white candy?"

"And maybe peppermint?"

"Hm."

"Can you taste it?"

"No." His mouth tasted like dirt and blood.

"Pretend."

"Okay." Grady sounded disappointed even to his own ears. He didn't want to imagine a candy cane. He wanted a big, cold glass of water to drink.

But he tried. He remembered the first Christmas he'd spent with Lillian and Peter, just before he turned nine. He had refused to decorate the Christmas tree or to bake Santa cookies and since he didn't talk, he hadn't asked for any presents. Not that he'd ever asked anyone for presents, nor had anyone before Lillian and Peter ever wondered what he wanted.

On Christmas morning, Lillian had walked into Grady's bedroom very, very early and told him to come downstairs without asking him to get dressed first. She'd even taken his hand as if he was a baby and couldn't walk downstairs by himself. They'd walked into the living room, and the floor beneath the tree had been covered in colourfully wrapped presents. Peter had been standing beside it with his arms wide and a happy smile on his face. Lillian had hugged Grady and then hugged Peter. Peter had handed him a candy cane, opened one for himself and placed it in the corner of his mouth like a cigarette. Except Peter didn't smoke.

Lillian had led Grady to a spot on the couch and Otto jumped up beside him wearing a silly red Santa's coat. Peter prayed and then while Lillian picked a present from beneath the tree, Peter opened Grady's candy cane and put it against his lips. He wasn't a baby, had known how to open the package. He'd just never had a candy cane before. Grady pulled his face away. Peter broke off a small piece and tossed it to Otto. Otto had caught it and swished it around in his mouth before swallowing it. Then he'd smiled in that doggy way of his and yipped happily. Peter had offered the candy to Grady again and this time, Grady took it and licked it. It was sweet and good and made Grady's mouth water.

Grady's mouth watered now. And he swallowed, the trickle of saliva soothing his dry throat. "Better," he said to Noah.

"Yeah, me, too," Noah replied.

Noah put his hand on Grady's chest and pressed him back against the wall of the tunnel so they were walking sideways shoulder-to-shoulder. Or would have been if Grady was two feet taller. They inched along this way until Noah decided they were past the puddle. He stopped and clicked his tongue a few times—since he'd started the sound, Noah liked doing it. When he stopped clicking, Noah walked forward. Grady walked with him, side by side.

# Chapter 67

**Pretending she wasn't** going out of her mind with worry, Ella Kristofer stood at the head of a long conference table in the meeting room at the B.C. Forests District Office on Dalhousie Street in Kamloops. The table was constructed of laminate, made to look like grey marble. The two Sergeants, Nguyen and Cortez, along with three uniformed constables on the local force, were distributed around the table. They alternated between talking into their cell phones and badgering the representative of the local mining corporation and a city engineer. Laptop computers, maps and government reports were in abundance. With Otto sitting obediently beside her, Ella kept watch on them all.

Nguyen had finally stopped making jokes an hour ago, so Cortez was now driving everybody crazy by reciting the facts of the case aloud whenever a new clue was discovered.

"We've got a sighting of a dark blue cargo van on one of the Drive BC web cams. Heading south. Possible match to witness accounts."

All heads turned to the constable who'd spoken, Cordova, a veteran who'd apparently lived in the area all of his life.

"I've got satellite images of the Teck mines southwest of the city. Business as usual." All heads swung to the city engineer as he spoke, a man named, Seymour.

"What's this?" Cortez asked, pointing over Seymour's shoulder to a spot on the laptop screen.

Ella shifted position to see the brown amorphous shape he indicated.

Seymour zoomed in on the section then pushed away from the table in his wheeled chair. He came to rest across the room at another laptop running a program that caused the screen to flash green and brown. When he wheeled back across, Ella followed him.

The image on the screen, the amorphous blob, shifted to a map that grew, transitioned into trees and rocks, a satellite image, and then resolved into a dusty bowl with steppes carved into the curved sides. "Celestine Copper Mine," Seymour said. He zoomed in closer and traced his fingertips along the base of the bowl almost affectionately. "Tire tracks. I'd say one vehicle, large, with a long wheel base."

"Cargo van?" Cortez asked.

Nguyen lifted his head from the maps he was studying with Cordova to meet Seymour's gaze. Seymour focussed on the screen, zooming in and out and making calculations on a page. "Possible," he muttered.

"We've got nothing else at this point. That mine fits with the GPS information we got from Kristofer's watch," Cortez said as Nguyen walked around the table toward him. Their eyes met and held. "I'll take Seymour and a uniform. You stay here and keep looking."

"You confident about this?" Nguyen crossed his arms and tilted his head speculatively.

Cortez straightened. His eyes closed a moment as though he was calculating something, silently for a change, before he responded. "Yes."

"I'm coming."

Cortez frowned, his dark features arrowing down to reveal his skepticism. "Someone needs to look for alternatives."

"That boy is my responsibility. I'm coming."

Cortez pursed his lips as if in thought then tucked his emotions away. "Good."

"I'm coming, too," Ella insisted. "Noah and Grady have been missing for four hours now. I've been patient. I've waited for the experts. No more. I want to find my husband and my boy."

Nguyen tilted his head, his brows furrowing. "Grady—"

"Is mine to find." Ella stepped toward him. Otto stood, a low growl emanating from his throat. Ella's bottled urgency was escaping. "I don't care about witness protection or legal guardians or even criminal-type uncles. That boy is coming home with me." Picking up her pace, she strode over to poke Nguyen in the chest. "It's your job to make it legal."

Cortez lifted a brow, watching the interchange. Ella read neither support nor disagreement from him.

Abruptly, Nguyen broke into a smile. "Every kid should have such an advocate. I'll do what I can for you."

Emotion tightened Ella's voice but she forced the words out in spite of it. "Thank you."

"Let's go." Cortez mobilized the group, set up tasks for those remaining, and led the way out.

# CHAPTER 68

Ella kept Otto on his leash at the entrance to the Celestine Copper Mine. Even though what she wanted to do was release the dog and follow him to Grady. And then to Noah. Because she accepted that Grady was the single, most important person in the dog's life. Otto would brave darkness and death to find his young master. And without a doubt, Noah would keep the boy safe and try to bring him home. Ella was counting on that drive to keep her husband alive.

Mr. Smith—or Rainer, as the case may be—was supposedly on his way. He'd been due to arrive for hours but had been delayed, no one knew by what. Ella wasn't looking forward to seeing him. The two sergeants, Nguyen and Cortez seemed to be honest, straightforward police officers. But Ella didn't trust Mike Rainer.

There were fresh tire tracks near the entrance to the mine and several sets of footprints, five larger and one smaller. Grabbing a large flashlight, Nguyen headed in almost before Cortez's car stopped. Before Ella caught up, though, he returned.

"The entrance is blown." Nguyen huffed as he spoke, winded by the sprint. "Some kind of device, I'd say. Forensics can get more. No way through that I can see without equipment and a weeks' worth of time." He gestured over a uniformed constable, a tall African-American man named, Arnold Kogo. "When's the company's mining engineer due to arrive?"

Kogo shrugged, his broad shoulders lifting briefly. Two more patrol cars pulled into the area, lights flashing. Sirens blaring. Kogo followed Cortez to them, leaning his head inside one of the cars to ask, "You bring the map?"

He was talking about the map to the copper mine. The sergeants had argued about the geological survey completed in 2008. The survey had mapped the tunnels of all the played-out mines in the area as part of an initiative proposed by BC Tourism. The extinct mines were surveyed and shored-up so that a geo tour could be set up, sort of like the Big Nickel in Sudbury, Ontario. Their maps were well-detailed. Unfortunately, the Celestine was not one of the mines used in the tour.

Kogo handed the map to Cortez who spread it out on the hood of his car. Nguyen joined him. Ella walked Otto over and took up a position peering between the two men's shoulders as Cortez brushed his fingers over the lines and spaces denoting the explored areas of the Celestine. Slipping a pen out of his inner jacket pocket, he circled four.

"There are four exits," Cortez said, tapping each one.

"Adits," Kogo said. He swiped a hand over his shaved head, crossed his arms over his chest.

Cortez studied him a moment. "What's an adit?"

Kogo dropped his arms and hooked his thumbs in his gun belt. "Entrance to a copper mine."

"Right. Thanks," Nguyen replied, his manner friendly. Cortez didn't seem so sure.

Kogo reached across Nguyen to point to the horizontal passageways on the map. "Drift." He found a vertical passageway and traced it down. "Shaft." Kogo tapped the map in various places that looked like larger rooms or caverns. "Stopes. Basically the void created when the ore is removed."

Nguyen suppressed a smile, tilting his head to meet the man's gaze. "How do you know all this?"

"My mother is a geologist. My bedtime reading was rather odd as a child."

Nguyen chuckled. "I'll bet. My mother is a botanist. Same deal."

Kogo nodded as he crossed his arms.

"Where are Noah and Grady?" Ella asked, frustrated at the time it was taking to rescue her family. It had been over an hour since they'd discovered the tire tracks at the Celestine.

Otto yipped at the sound of Grady's name.

Nguyen glanced aside at her while Cortez ignored her.

"Sergeant Nguyen?"

Ella glanced up. Mike Rainer. She frowned her disapproval. Was he here to rescue Noah or cause more trouble for him? If Mike had left him alone, Noah would not have been blinded. If Mike had done his job and arrested Maximiano, Noah and Grady would be home and safe right now. She couldn't really blame Mike for Macken Roy's role in the abduction, but she'd be glad to try.

"Staff Sergeant." Nguyen extended a hand in greeting.

Mike's eyes scanned the area as he gripped Nguyen's hand and then Cortez's. Finally, his eyes found Ella. They dipped down to Otto who growled low in his throat, and rose again, settling on her. "Ms. Hanover."

"Kristofer. My name is Mrs. Kristofer."

"Hm," Mike mewed his interest.

"Why are you here?" Ella asked, angry and hopeful all at once.

"To find your husband, of course," Mike replied. He moved past Ella to stand shoulder-to-shoulder with Cortez and Nguyen, effectively blocking her out. She wanted to growl at him as Otto had.

Two more uniformed constables moved around at the main entrance, the adit.

"Sergeant Nguyen?" Ella asked, waiting until the man looked over his shoulder to meet her gaze. "What are those men doing?" She nodded toward the constables disappearing into the black maw of the mine.

"Collecting evidence to discover whether the boy and your husband are here. And who took them," Nguyen replied.

"We know who took them. Maximiano Guerra," she replied.

Why were they stalling? They needed to get to it. If the entrance to the mine was blocked, it meant Noah and Grady were alone in the bowels of the earth. She clung to the belief they were alive. But why bring them out to a remote area unless to dispose of their bodies?

"Keep their hands clean," Kogo said.

"Pardon?" Ella turned to face him.

"You asked why they would bring your guys out here," he replied.

Had she said that out loud?

"So they wouldn't be culpable for murder. They wore masks when they snatched them. Anonymous." He ticked off his points on his fingers. "Bring 'em to a deserted space. No witnesses. Blind man and a boy wander too far. Let the mine kill 'em. Anonymous."

Ella blanched.

"Sensitive, man," Cortez murmured in reprimand.

"My husband," Ella forced the words out, "is very hard to kill."

"That he is." Mike glanced over his shoulder at her before continuing. "Give me an update."

Cortez led them over the cordoned area near the adit. "They were alive when they arrived. Five sets of footprints in this area here. Possibly one set of smaller prints." Crouching, he gestured at the ground around them. "Prints over prints. Drag marks." He rose, pointing to the lines in the dirt. "Tire tracks arrive and then depart."

"Speculate," Mike said.

Cortez pursed his lips and tilted his head in a thoughtful gesture. "Snatched them at gunpoint. Drove them here. Dumped them down a shaft. Blew the entryway."

"There's blood," Kogo added.

Ella paled even more. Otto pressed his furry body against her leg, whining.

Nguyen placed a gentle hand on Ella's shoulder briefly. "The witnesses at the walk-in reported that the masked men beat on K."

Calling him "K" didn't lessen the punch of those words. Noah's inability to defend himself must have been humiliating.

"They likely couldn't resist the opportunity to continue the beating in private," Cortez replied. The harsh words were softened by his gentle tone.

"Blood leading back out," Kogo added.

Nguyen's face brightened. "K got in a few good licks."

"What?" Ella asked, confused.

"We know that Noah and Braeden, Grady, went into the mine but didn't come out. If there's blood leading out to the absent vehicle, it stands to reason that Noah made them bleed."

"I suppose that should make it better," Ella replied, tears leaking slowly down her cheeks. *And it does.* Ella distracted herself from more tears by bending to pet Otto.

"Cortez, take Kogo. Find Macken Roy and Maximiano Guerra. Nguyen, put out an all-points for both men. Armed and dangerous. I've contacted Vancouver. They're on the lookout. Constable," Mike snapped his fingers, gesturing Constable Cordova over. "Get that engineer out here now." There was no mistaking his seriousness.

The constable scampered away to do his bidding.

# Chapter 69

Grady was a zombie. His feet scraped along the ground. His arms stretched out in front of him. He wanted to groan and growl like they did on the silly game Ella played on her iPad. But he was too tired. And hungry. And so thirsty. His head hurt and he felt sick. There was nothing but rock beside him and a pile of rocks in front of him. They'd stepped around and over so many piles of rocks that Grady had lost count. They'd waded through two huge puddles. That was the worst, to hear and feel the water, so cold, but not be able to drink it.

Grady kept walking, every step taking him closer to the pile of rocks. The belt tugged on his waist. He looked up at Noah to see him frowning. He was doing that clicking thing again. When he pushed his right foot forward a little bit, it splashed in a small, black and rusty puddle.

"Is—" Grady couldn't get the words out past his dry throat. He thought about candy canes, swallowed the tiny bit of spit his mouth produced, then spoke. "It's little. Step over."

Noah's face turned abruptly toward him. "You can see it?" he asked. His eyes were wide, both the brown one and the black one.

Grady's heart sped up as he looked around. "Yes." Excitement fluttered in his chest.

"What do you see?" Noah's voice was excited. He reached out until he grabbed Grady's arm. He held it tight, but not too tight.

Grady turned his head from side to side, his eyes tracing everything in his line of vision. "Dark brown dirt under our feet. Reddish walls, like a tunnel. Up is too high to see. It's only black. Little puddle right there." He pointed then realized that Noah was unable to see. Grady took Noah's hand and pointed to the puddle on the ground. Then he pointed straight out in front of them. "There's a pile of rocks. Mostly on the same side as me. In front of us."

"Does it cover the whole way? Can we go around it?" Noah sounded more and more excited every time he spoke.

"Yes. Come." Grady put Noah's hand on his shoulder and moved forward. Noah clicked with his tongue every few steps. He looked excited as he twisted his head to-and-fro. In a few steps, they made it to the pile. By climbing, they were able to squeeze past.

"What do you see?" Noah asked, stopping Grady before he stepped down off the pile.

"I can't see the floor. But up high, not as tall as you, there is a bright, bright light. Sunshine white."

"Yellow, kid." Noah smiled at him. "Sunshine is yellow."

Grady shrugged. He didn't care what colour you called it.

Noah turned his face toward the light, tilting his head a little. "I can feel the air on my face. I can smell trees and flowers. We're almost out."

Grady stepped out with his foot but Noah pulled him back again. "Almost but not quite." Noah kept a firm grip on his arm. "Tell me what you see at our feet."

Grady looked down. But the floor was in the darkness created by the pile and the way they made a shadow from the light. "Down is only black. Can't see." He looked ahead. "I see a pile of rocks. The light is coming in between the rocks. But I can't see the floor."

Noah's face looked thoughtful for a long moment. He rubbed his free hand over his thick beard, scratching his chin. "Wish I had my cane," he said quietly. "Can't risk it."

His words didn't make sense to Grady.

"How far is it between here and the pile of rocks?" Noah asked.

"Three feet? Shorter than me."

Noah turned Grady so they were facing each other. "We need to find out what the ground is like between here and the opening. I'm going to unclip you and explore."

"No!" Grady shouted the word very fast, even before Noah finished what he was saying. "Stay together."

Noah knelt down. It must have hurt his knees to kneel on the rocks, but he did it. He pulled Grady close and hugged him. "I'm not going to leave you. But you are too important for me to risk dropping you down a hole or something."

Noah moved Grady so he was sitting on the pile of rocks. Grady shifted so they weren't poking his bottom. "You sit here," Noah said. "I'm going to check it out. Okay?"

"No."

"I won't leave you."

"No."

Noah sighed with a sharp burst of air. Grady automatically pulled his arms up to protect his face. That sort of sound usually meant a smack.

But when Noah spoke, his voice was calm. "What do you need from me, G?"

Slowly, Grady lowered his arms. "I don't know."

"I think you do know."

Grady thought about it. He was scared that Noah would leave him alone and that he would die in this dark tunnel. But Noah wouldn't leave him. He had held onto Grady when Uncle Macken tried to take him. He'd stood between him and Uncle Macken so his uncle forgot to beat him.

"Want to stay together."

"I won't leave you behind, G. I want to keep you safe. Damp air is rising from the floor and I'm afraid that there's a deep hole between here and outside. Does that make sense?"

"Y-yes," Grady responded cautiously. He was careful to think about all the words Noah said because he didn't want to accidentally agree to letting Noah leave him.

"Okay. Cool." Noah unclipped the belt from his belt loop and handed it, buckle first, to Grady. Noah got down on his hands and knees. He snapped his fingers, moving his hand around and listening. Grady couldn't see his hand because it was so dark below the line the shadow and light created. Noah clicked his tongue, turning his head toward the rock wall, the floor and the sides of the tunnel. It was a funny way to explore the floor, but Noah seemed to gain information from the sounds.

Noah shifted to the right, patting the ground there. After a few minutes, he sat back on his heels. "There's a ledge on the right-hand side, a few inches wide."

Grady stood. All of a sudden, he was moving. Noah stepped onto the ledge and kind of threw Grady at the pile of rubble with the light coming through. Grady gasped and grabbed at the rocks. His fingers slipped then held fast. He glanced back over his shoulder. Noah was balanced part on the ledge—though Grady couldn't see his leg below the knee—with one foot back where they'd come from. But his body was leaning forward and swaying. Grady grabbed tight on a rock, leaned back and grasped Noah's shirt sleeve. He tugged. "Come," he commanded.

Noah didn't hesitate. He stepped. Grady pulled until Noah grabbed the rocks. They were both breathing heavy and hard.

"Okay." Noah huffed a few breaths. "Cool." He huffed a few more. Then Noah kind of went still a moment. "I can feel the sunlight on my face." He tilted his head until it was covered in sunbeams. He smiled slowly. Both of his eyes looked so happy. "I wish I could see it."

"It just looks like light, Noah. Nothing special."

Noah laughed. "Right. Let's get out of here." Noah held on tight with his right hand and shifted rocks with his left. "Tell me what to move."

"Let's move them all," Grady said.

Soon they had a hole big enough for Grady. Noah lifted him through. He was on a hill with snow on top of grass and trees and flowers just like Noah had said.

Grady peeked back through. "Hold on. I'll kick the rocks." Noah shifted to the right, carefully balancing between the ledge and the rubble. Grady planted his butt on the ground and kicked with both feet. Rocks shifted until the hole was bigger.

Grady peeked back in. "Come." He extended his arm, snapping his fingers until Noah located it. Then he planted his feet on a big rock and pulled until Noah was through.

Noah collapsed on the ground beside him. Outside, on the snowy grass.

# Chapter 70

The mine engineer tapped his pencil on the large map he'd brought. He was a short man, not much taller than Ella, with narrow shoulders. His name was Miller, Miller Towne.

"These are the adits that are documented," Towne said. "Cave-ins could have created more."

"We should send small search parties to these areas," Nguyen suggested. "Search from the perimeter toward the mine."

"Sure," Towne agreed, though his tone didn't support the idea. "But if you're off by a couple hundred feet, you'd miss them."

"Dogs," Cortez suggested. "Are there any search and rescue dogs in the area?"

"I put Kamloops Search and Rescue on hold before we drove out here," Kogo said. "I'll call them in." He moved away to do so.

"Mrs. Kristofer," Cortez said. "Where do you think your husband will head if he gets out?"

"I have no idea. Was he conscious for the journey? Who knows? Even if he was alert, could he find his way back?"

"The dogs will need something to scent," Kogo called over.

"I have Noah's running shoes in the back of my Element. And one of Grady's shirts."

"That'll do." Kogo relayed the information through his radio.

Towne drew a semicircle on the map. "I would suggest a perimeter beginning here, working your way nearer."

# Chapter 71

"What now, Noah?" Grady asked him.

What now, indeed? Noah's body ached. He was cold and wet. His head pounded. Exhaustion sucked at him. And he needed a drink. The boy must be seriously thirsty as well. His small body had little reserve.

*Of course.* "Snow."

"Huh?"

"Snow. Look for clean snow that looks like it's never been touched. We can eat it." Noah forced himself to sit up. No more laying around, getting colder.

Grady shoved a handful of cold at him. Noah cupped his hands to receive it and placed a portion on his tongue. It was cold but so good. "Get some for yourself. Remember to eat the clean stuff."

Noah heard Grady moving around and then slurping. "Better, G?"

"Yes. I'm hungry."

"I know, bud." *I'd happily eat a mushroom and baloney pizza if I could get my hands on it.* "We need to get to somewhere safe. And then we can think about food."

Noah pushed to his feet, groaning as the movement pulled on his battered ribs and all the other muscles that had stiffened in the subterranean cold. He turned in a slow circle, stumbling on the uneven ground. "Grady? Can you see the sun?"

"Yes," Grady replied.

"Point me at it."

Grady took Noah's hand and tugged him forward a half-step and then turned him about forty-five degrees to the left. He stood in front of Noah and took his arm, raising it toward the sky.

Noah dug his heels into the ground and then instructed Grady to do the same. It was cold but not cold enough to freeze the ground. Noah took Grady's hand and formed it into a point. "Is that the sun?"

"Hm. Yes."

Noah drew the boy's hand vertically toward the ground. "What are we pointing at?"

"A tree. Dec...um, deciduous. Broad leaves. Except it's mostly bare."

"Right. Is there a stone or a sharp stick or anything around us?"

"Yes."

"Get it and make a mark on the tree, then put the stone or stick or whatever on the spot where our feet are."

"Okay."

"We'll rest a little while and look again. Once we know where the sun is headed, we'll have a sense of direction to head in. The sun rises in the east and moves west."

After a few minutes of rustling and movement, Grady patted Noah on the chest. "Done now."

Noah hugged the boy and ruffled his hair. "*Bien.*"

"I'm cold," Grady said.

"Yeah." He needed to get the boy warm before they got some rest. Otherwise, hypothermia would set in, and they might never wake. "You know how to do push-ups?"

Grady groaned. "Gym class." It was clear that was the boy's least favourite activity.

"Jumping jacks?"

"What are you talking about?"

"We need to get warm. Physical activity is the best way. Have you ever watched Bear Grylls?"

"Yeah. Peter watched him on television."

"What do you think Bear would tell us to do?"

"Um. Run on the spot?"

"Sure."

Noah heard Grady's movement and the change in his breathing which indicated that Bear Gryll's ideas were far better than Noah Kristofer's. That made Noah smile. Whatever got the job done.

"I'm warm now. Just hungry."

"Yeah. Me, too."

"Thirsty again."

"More snow. Clean snow, remember."

"Okay." The tenor of Grady's speech had changed. He was less afraid, more alert.

Suddenly, Grady's body went still. Noah was afraid he'd wandered out of ear shot.

"Grady?"

"Yes." The happiness had drained out of his voice.

"What's wrong?"

"Is Uncle Macken waiting for me?"

"We got away from him once, G. We'll manage it again." The boy needed something to keep his mind off his uncle. "You still got that sharp stone?"

"Yes."

"Why don't you carve your name into the tree? Then anyone who finds it will know you survived the copper mine."

"Okay." Grady moved swiftly, the happiness back in his tone.

When Grady was satisfied with his work, he returned to sit beside Noah on the ground. The light layer of snow was enough to melt into their clothes, chilling them.

"Has the sun shifted away from our tree?" Noah asked.

"Yes."

"Take us back to our spot and let's see which direction we need to go." Grady pulled Noah up and Noah let him. He groaned as he moved. Every time he stopped for more than a minute, his battered muscles stiffened.

"Point at the spot we marked on the tree."

Grady did.

Then Noah took the boy's hand and moved it directly up from there. "Move my arm to the sun now."

Grady moved their arms a few degrees to the left.

"Right." Noah pointed between the tree and the current position of the sun. "That is approximately north. I'm sure we traveled south out of Kamloops." *I've been north of the city, the day Ella had her accident on Highway 5. The roads were different, the quality of the highway was older, more potholes.* We head north," he said decisively. With no idea where they were, this was his best guess. They couldn't wait here until dark. They were both so dehydrated, wet and cold, they'd die of exposure if they were still out here after dark. There was no way to safely head back over the mine. Definitely weren't returning into the mine. North seemed the best option.

"Hook us up again, G. Let's get home to Ella and Otto."

# Chapter 72

"Zombie," Grady muttered.

Noah trudged two steps on before he processed what the boy said. "What?" His voice came out as a croak. It was only when the belt tugged on his waist that he realized he'd stopped. His body swayed. Grady stumbled back against him and collapsed at his feet.

A distant growl and yip dripped along the ether toward them. Noah nudged Grady with his foot. "You hear that?"

When Grady didn't respond, Noah crouched down, running his hands over the boy's body until he located his face. Grady was curled in a ball, his face tucked in his arms. But he was breathing. Shallowly but evenly.

The yips were joined by barks. They were coming closer, from behind them. Something had trailed them from the mine.

"G." Noah shook the boy gently and then with a little more energy. "Something's coming."

Grady didn't stir.

"I can't see, bud. What's coming?"

Noah had no choice. He could either curl up with Grady in the snow and wait for the animal to find them and eat them, or he could carry the boy. Sliding his arms beneath Grady's body, he lifted him. Every muscle strained. Every bruise wailed and sobbed.

Forcing his body into motion, Noah took one step and then another. He stumbled over the uneven ground, barely managing to avoid squashing the boy when he went down. Grady didn't even stir. *Can't stop. Must go. Need Ella.* Noah struggled to his feet again.

Dogs, because that's what it was. Dogs baying, growling, barking, chasing them. Hunters? Strays? Wild dogs? He had no idea. Only that he needed to keep moving. Like a zombie. Step. Step. Step. The howling curs got closer.

Noah's heart thumped in his chest. Grady stirred and panicked, whimpering and clinging to Noah. His little arms notched up Noah's pain. But Noah kept moving. Nothing else to do. Walk. Go. Blindly. No way to see. Nowhere within reach.

Noah walked until he couldn't. He dropped to his knees.

"Sergeant Kristofer! Noah!"

# Chapter 73

Ella walked. Through the stubby brown grass. Through the stands of spindly pine. Up one dusty hill and down another with Otto tugging at the leash, seeming to understand that this was business, not a grand adventure; that the other dog, a Border Collie mix named, Sasha, was leading her Search & Rescue handler, Marla, to Grady. Constable Kogo and Sergeant Cortez formed a wedge with Ella at the point. The air was filled with yips and barks, birds in the air and trees, the chatter from Kogo's walkie-talkie and the almost constant buzz of Cortez's phone. But no word on Noah or Grady.

They had been missing over eight hours and the sun had dropped. Ella's heart burned for them. Hungry, thirsty, alone in the black pit of the mine, if that's even where they were. She refused to believe they were dead. There was no point. Until she was presented with their stone-cold corpses, she was determined to look, to search, to find her family.

Sasha sounded, one short howl, then took off at a lope. Without a need to confer, Kogo, Cortez, Ella and Otto followed. Even though the young Collie had had a few false alarms, the dead rabbit and, later, the anonymous green toque, they ran, hope keeping pace with them. One of these times, Sasha or one of the other Search & Rescue dogs searching the adits to the Celestine Copper Mine would find something to lead them to Noah and Grady.

Cortez and Kogo reached the dog before her.

"Mrs. Kristofer," Cortez shouted as he ran back toward her. "Hold up."

"What?" Ella's heart sped as her throat closed until she wondered if she'd be able to keep breathing. "What is it? Did you find them?"

Otto barked and tugged, resenting the pause.

"There are bones," Cortez said, disappointment keen in his eyes.

"What?" Ella's hands flew to her mouth as tears filled her eyes. "They're dead?"

"No, no." Cortez grabbed her shoulders, shaking her lightly. "Bones. An animal. It's not them."

Ella's phone rang in her pocket and Cortez released her to answer it. "Hello?"

"El? Is that you?"

"Noah!" She gasped and tears welled up all over again. "Where are you? Are you okay? Where's Grady?"

Cortez snatched the phone from her. "Kristofer? This is Sergeant Cortez of the—"

Ella snatched it right back. "Noah. Where are you?"

"Who is that guy?" Noah replied.

"Where are you? Is Grady okay?"

"We're fine. A little battered."

Cortez's phone rang and he turned away to take the call.

"How can I get to where you are?" she asked. *He's alive! They're alive. Thank you, Lord.*

"They're sending a helicopter," Noah replied. His voice was harsh and unpleasant to listen to, and yet she'd never heard a more welcome sound. "They're taking Grady and me to the hospital and then coming to pick you up to meet us there."

"Is Grady okay?"

"Yes. He's the greatest."

"I'm so glad you're safe. I love you, Noah."

"I love you, too, *chérie*. See you soon."

"Mrs. Kristofer? Ella?" Cortez touched her arm.

Ella flung her arms around the startled sergeant.

"He's alive. They're alive!"

# CHAPTER 74

After years of waiting—forty-five minutes in actuality—Ella stepped through the door of the exam room in the emergency ward of the Royal Inland Hospital.

"El." He recognized knew her as soon as she entered the room.

Ella ran to him, throwing her arms around his neck. "I love you, Noah." She kissed his forehead then covered his face in kisses as she passed her hands over his head, his face. "Your hair. Is a mess. And you stink."

Noah chuckled, sweeping his hands from her hips to her bottom and then back up her spine to cup her head. "*Cher.*"

"Where's Grady?" she asked, her voice muffled against his skin.

"Here. Behind me."

Grady was huddled against Noah's back. One arm hooked around Noah's neck, Ella gathered Grady close. "Grady. Sweetheart. My boy. Are you okay?"

Unresponsive, Grady watched her from haunted eyes. Ella stroked his hair and kiss his face. "It's okay, now. You're safe."

Grady cried out and flung his arms around her. He burst into tears.

"El?" Noah said. "He okay?"

"It's okay, baby boy." Ella shifted so she could hold him and rock him but still keep her leg pressed against Noah for the contact.

Grady pressed his face into Ella's chest.

"Oh, Noah. What happened?"

"He's the bravest kid I've ever met; braver than many men I know."

Ella kissed Grady on the temple and then kissed Noah on the ear. She moved closer, pressing her cheek against Noah's shoulder and drawing Grady with her.

"Did you lose your device, Grady?" Ella asked.

He nodded against her.

Ella pulled back and retrieved her phone. "Here, you can use mine." She opened the Notes app on her phone. "Just type and turn the device so we can read it." She demonstrated, writing, "I love you."

Grady took the phone reverently, eyes wide, cheeks tear-stained. His thumbs typed. He turned the device. "Thank you. Where is Otto? I want to go home."

"Otto is safe. I'm not allowed to bring him into the hospital, so one of the police officers is watching him," Ella replied.

"Mounties?" Grady whispered.

Ella's eyes widened in shock. *He spoke.* She glanced up at Noah to check out his response and then remembered that he was unable to read the question in her eyes: *did you hear that?*

"These Mounties helped me find you, Grady. They called in Search and Rescue—"

"Who's involved?" Noah asked, his voice serious.

"A Sergeant Cortez from Calgary." Ella glanced at Grady. There was no point trying to ease the boy's suffering. He'd survived more than most adults. "He is investigating the crimes against Lillian and Peter."

Grady typed and Ella waited.

"El," Noah prompted her.

"Grady has something to say. Then I'll continue."

Noah waited. He put his arm around Grady and pulled him closer, jostling the boy a little. Grady didn't seem to mind if the warm sigh he emitted meant anything.

"Lillian and Peter were murdered?" Grady typed then turned the screen.

"Yes. I'm sorry. Sergeant Cortez is working to find whoever killed them."

"Uncle Macken," Grady typed.

"I don't think so," she said.

Grady frowned at her.

"I'm not saying that Macken Roy is not responsible. I'm saying they don't think it was his gang members that killed them."

"Guerra," Noah said. "Maximiano Guerra. That's why they were together. They were each doing the other's dirty work."

Grady nodded. "Yes," he said aloud.

Ella tried to stifle her surprise at his responsiveness.

"Uncle Macken don't want to go to prison."

"Makes sense," Noah said, speaking to Grady. "Maxi kills you. Macken kills me. No one would suspect it. Except that it didn't work. So they took us both."

"Let the mine kill us," Grady added in his own voice, looking up at Noah's face with admiration.

Noah grinned slowly. "They missed."

Grady smiled, huffing a near-silent laugh.

A knock sounded on the door. Grady's smile disappeared. He tucked the phone inside his shirt and slipped behind Noah again.

"Mrs. Kristofer?"

"That's Cortez," Ella explained. "I'll bet Nguyen is with him. Can I let them in?"

Noah nodded.

"Mike is here, too," she added.

Noah's brows flashed up.

Grady's head peeked around Noah's shoulder. "Otto," Grady whispered.

"Okay, honey," Ella replied. Grady and Noah had clearly breeched some sort of barrier in the copper mine. Grady was talking almost freely at times.

As Ella opened the door to admit the men she expected, Noah looked on, his eyes never lighting on the men. Why would they?

"Kristofer," Eric Nguyen said the name with true regard, paced over and thrust out his hand. Noah looked right through him. Nguyen's expression changed as he realized that Noah was indeed unable to see him. He reached down, grasped Noah's right hand and shook it. Noah flinched at first then gripped. "It's me, Eric Nguyen."

"Nguyen. Who'd a thought it? How have you been, man?" Noah asked, his bruised and battered face creasing for a moment into a smile.

Nguyen chuckled. "Better than you. What sort of mess have you gotten yourself into?"

Noah snorted. "This was none of my doing."

Nguyen tilted his head as he spied Grady tucked in a ball behind Noah. He softened his voice. "Hey, buddy."

Grady responded by curling his body tighter and hiding his eyes behind his raised knees.

"Braeden Roy?" Nguyen glanced at Noah's face for confirmation.

"Grady," Noah said, his voice firm. "He prefers to be called Grady Jones."

"Right," Nguyen said thoughtfully. "Grady."

Grady peeked at the man from beneath his filthy bangs.

Rafael Cortez crossed the room and introduced himself, "Cortez." He didn't offer his hand in greeting until Noah reached out first.

"Sergeant Cortez," Ella said. "Can you please text Constable Kogo and ask him to send a photo of my dog so Grady knows that he's okay?"

It took Cortez a moment to take his eyes from Grady before he agreed and complied. It was almost as if Grady was a missing piece the detective hadn't truly believed existed until he'd seen him with his very own eyes.

When the photo arrived, Grady wouldn't accept the phone Cortez offered him until Ella took it and showed him Otto. Then he held the phone reverently until Ella felt she needed to return it to Cortez. She asked him to email the photograph to her. The phone inside Grady's shirt pinged and he took it out. He held the phone and stared at the photo.

"So what happens now?" Noah asked. His intonation flattened out and his accent neutralized as soon as the officers entered the room.

The door opened and closed, admitting Mike Rainer. "The two of you need to be seen by a doctor. I've arranged a safe house after that."

"Mike," Noah said, displeasure on his tongue.

"Then we need to question you both."

"Grady doesn't speak," Ella said. *Just because he can manage a few sentences when he's alone with Noah and me does not mean he is ready to tell his story to strangers.* "And he's a minor. He's going to need an advocate. I think you'll find that Sergeant Nguyen has had me appointed as his guardian."

Nguyen looked a little unsure of himself—Mike had that effect on people—but he nodded slowly in support.

"Works for me," Mike replied, clearly amused. "We have several entwined cases to resolve. But the doctor won't let either of you out of here until you're checked."

"Doctor? Fine. I want to thank Search & Rescue, as well. They saved our lives," Noah said. "And then I need time alone with my family."

"After the debriefing," Mike began but Noah interrupted.

"Doctor, safe house, three hours alone. Then we'll answer your questions." Noah's voice was firm.

Grady peeked around Noah's arm, his gaze flitting between the Mounties.

"Two hours. I'll make the arrangements." Mike departed, already talking on his cell phone.

"Nicely done, K," Nguyen said. "I'll see you at the debriefing."

"It was a privilege to meet you, Sergeant Kristofer," Cortez said. He shifted to the right so he could see Grady. Grady huddled against Noah's back. "And you, Mr. Jones," Cortez added. Grady looked up through his bangs. Cortez met his gaze. Grady nodded once. Satisfied with that, Cortez left.

Noah kept a grip on Grady's knee as he slipped off the examining table. He inhaled deeply and moved unerringly toward Ella. Drawn by the greatest magnetism there is, she walked straight into his arms. She gripped him hard enough to make him grunt.

"I love you, Ella."

"I love you, too, Noah. So much."

She didn't even notice that someone had entered the room until the doctor cleared his throat.

"Let's see how everyone is doing, shall we?" He smiled as he said the words.

# CHAPTER 75

The safe house was an executive loft suite on the eleventh floor of the Residence and Conference Centre at Thompson Rivers University. There was a large bedroom with a queen-sized bed, a Jacuzzi tub in the bathroom, a kitchenette and furnished lounge with a pull-out sofa, rocker-recliner, table and chairs.

While Noah showered and Grady watched television with Otto beside him, Ella found the University Bookstore and purchased sweats, socks, T-shirts, and hoodies for both Grady and Noah, then picked up two coffees and a hot chocolate from the Common Grounds café adding three premium sandwich deals.

Returning to the suite, she called out to Grady who waved in reply. Otto didn't budge an inch. Setting her purchases on the kitchen counter, she discovered the steamy bathroom empty.

"Grady, sweetheart, bathtub is free. Come and wash the grubby mine off you."

The drone of the television ended and Grady jogged down the hall with Otto at his heels.

Ella pulled him into a hug. "I missed you, honey. I'm so glad you're safe."

Grady squeezed her around the waist. He drew in a big breath before he released her as if he was gathering courage to let go.

*I wish I knew what you were thinking, little boy.* Ella filled the tub, showing Grady how the jets activated. She poured in some of the hotel shampoo to create a few bubbles which delighted the boy. Otto, refusing to leave Grady's side, perched with his front paws on the edge of the tub, tongue lolling.

"I'll leave your new clothes on the toilet, sweetheart. Get dressed when you're ready. Call me if you need help," Ella said.

Grady nodded, sinking to his eyeballs in the foaming water.

Ella left the door open a crack and then moved to the bedroom to find Noah. This door, she closed.

"El." Noah turned toward her, gloriously nude, covered in bruises and scrapes.

"Oh, Noah." She touched him tentatively, brushing her fingers over what looked like a boot mark on his hip. His entire left side was a mottled patch of purple, black and blue. His right shoulder was scraped raw as were his knees. Pain, written all over his body.

"Come here," Noah murmured. He opened his arms and pulled her in. "There. That makes it all better."

"They told me you fought back, that you made them bleed," she whispered, her heart aching for her husband.

"*Oui.* I couldn't let them get away with it." He buried his face in her hair, water dripping from his freshly-washed curls onto her shoulder.

"I'm so proud of you, Huck. You're amazing."

He shrugged. "Needed you. Had to get out to get back to you. Had to protect Grady."

"He must have been so scared." *You must have been so scared.*

"He's a brave kid."

Ella kissed Noah on the chest. He tipped her chin up and kissed her mouth. She gripped his shoulders then released his right when her palm encountered the abraded skin there.

"Noah?" He kissed her jaw, her throat. "How did you navigate the mine? How did you get out of there?"

Noah lifted his head, tucking her close and resting his cheek on her head. "Touch. Smell. Sound. I realized something by accident. You know how if you yell at a mountain, the sound echoes back?"

"Mhm."

"Well, if you click your tongue, the sound bounces back. It sounds different when you click at a wall versus a space. High-pitched versus low-pitched. I'm not sure I ever would have noticed if not for the silent stillness down there. But Grady, he's the one who found the way out."

"After all the trauma he's experienced, I don't know how he has the reserves to go on. Being taken by his uncle, beaten, dropped down a mine shaft."

"He's strong. Resilient. He may never totally get beyond his past, but I'm going to make sure he has a good life."

Before Ella could talk about Grady's needs for counselling, about a plan for the future, Noah quieted her with his fingers on her lips.

"Wait one, G." Noah reached toward the bed, whispering. "Where are my pants?"

Ella handed them over and Noah sat on the bed to don them.

"Come in, Grady," Ella said as Noah pulled on the Thompson Rivers T-shirt she handed him.

Grady walked in with Otto at his side. He was wearing everything she'd bought him, the sweat pants, hoodie, and socks. The hem of the T-shirt hung below the hem of the hoodie.

"You hungry, buddy?" Noah asked. "I am."

"We have plenty of time to eat before the Mounties come to question us," Ella said. "I got sandwiches and hot drinks."

As much as Ella wanted to know everything, to relive every moment with Noah and Grady, she merely fed them and talked about senseless, mundane things while they ate. The four of them cuddled on the couch until it was time to meet Mike Rainer and the Mounties.

# CHAPTER 76

N oah was grateful that Mike had arranged to use a small conference room at the TRU residence for the debriefing. He was exhausted, too exhausted to navigate beyond a hallway and one floor in an elevator, and he realized that once he hit a horizontal surface, he was going to sleep for a week. He'd almost fallen asleep on the sofa in the suite after eating the turkey and Swiss Ella had bought. A fact that made him grudgingly agree that Mike was correct. They needed to tell their story now, because he and Grady would likely be unconscious for days once they crashed.

Mike had agreed to allow Ella to attend the debriefing as long as she sat in the corner and remained silent. Noah would have liked to see her expression when Mike delivered that dictate. Her verbal response had been calm and measured, but he was sure her features had clearly told Mike what she thought of him. Otto had flat-out growled at Mike—Noah was certain Ella was cheering the dog on—and so was allowed to remain with Grady.

Mike on one side of the conference table, Noah and Grady sat side by side on the other. Eric Nguyen entered soon after they settled, accompanied by a representative of the Criminal Justice Branch of the Ministry of Justice, Crown Counsel, Rhianna Wray. She had a firm handshake and deep voice for a woman. She was wearing heels and a dress or skirt if Noah had to guess given the click and rustle as she crossed the room to sit beside Mike.

Cortez arrived, greeted by Nguyen. Someone, likely Cortez, placed a glass of what he assumed was water near Noah's hand on the table. Cool air radiated to the backs of his fingers.

"Let's begin," Mike said, abruptly silencing the room.

Noah heard a click he assumed was the *record* button on a device of some sort.

Mike named the people in the room, informed everyone that the conversation was being recorded, and stated the purpose of the interview. "We are here because of allegations that Sergeant Noah Kristofer, RCMP officer-on-leave from the Terrorist and Criminal Extremist Project, and Braeden Roy, also known as Braeden Shaffer, Brent Hoffner, and Grady Jones, who will hereafter be referred to as Grady Jones, were abducted and assaulted by one Macken Roy of Vancouver, British Columbia, and one Maximiano Perez-Guerra of Mexico City, Mexico. Macken Roy is identified as the uncle of said Grady Jones. Maximiano Perez-Guerra is known to be the son of Chenche Hernandez-Guerra, former head of the Pandilla Cartel out of Mexico.

"Bringing us up to date, Canada Border Services has a report of a Mexican passport entering at the Peace Arch Border Crossing ten days ago. But there are reports of the same passport entering via other crossings thirty weeks ago, and sixteen weeks ago. The passport photo matches archived descriptions of the junior Guerra. Current location unknown. There is an All-Points-Bulletin out for him across British Columbia and Alberta. The FBI has been contacted and is watching all common border crossings.

"Macken Roy is a Canadian citizen known to be affiliated with the Dark Coast Warriors, a registered gang which primarily operates out of Vancouver."

Grady pressed his body into Noah's side. He was shaking. Noah moved his chair closer and put his arm around him.

Mike continued, "Previous surveillance on Roy revealed at least two face-to-face meetings with the junior Guerra over the past ten months."

"What?" Noah straightened. Fatigue fled. "You knew that Macken and Maxi were meeting and didn't warn me?"

"There was no indication of a threat at the time," Mike replied dispassionately.

"How could you?" A familiar, feminine voice filled the room with indignation.

"Mrs. Kristofer. You agreed to remain silent, did you not?" Mike demanded to know.

"Watch how you speak to my wife, Mike." Noah's tone was a low growl as he leaned forward, measuring the direction and distance from Mike's voice. Oddly enough, Grady began to settle at the shift in emotion in the room.

"Gentlemen. And lady." That must have been Crown Counsel Wray. "This gets us nowhere." She had more influence than Noah would have imagined because Mike murmured a terse apology.

"Mrs. Kristofer," Wray continued. "I understand this must be difficult for you and I thank you for your patience and assistance. Given how Grady looks to you and your husband for support, I can see your presence is very important to him. Why don't you move closer?"

"That's hardly protocol," Mike protested.

A tone of vindication in her voice, Ella replied, "Thank you."

Movement. Then Ella's scent teased Noah's senses. Before she sat on Grady's other side, a feather-light touch grazed Noah's shoulder, a momentary physical connection before she draped her arm across the back of Grady's chair.

A file opened. Papers shuffled, drawing Noah's attention back across the table.

"It is my understanding that Mrs. Kristofer has been appointed by the court as young Mr. Jones' guardian," Wray said. "Staff Sergeant Rainer, I'm not sure if you're aware of this. As a consequence, she is able act as his advocate."

*What? How did she manage that?*

"I understand," Ella replied.

"Fine," Mike responded tersely. "Let's begin. How can you prove it was Macken Roy who took you, K? His lieutenant, whose apprehension and questioning delayed me, claims Roy was in Vancouver at a club event." He shifted some papers around then added in a mutter, "as if he was a member of the Optimists."

"He used Grady's real name." Noah leaned forward in his chair. "He threatened him." Noah tapped his finger on the table to emphasize his point. "You can't let him get away with this."

"You never saw him," Mike said.

Noah flung his arms out, aiming high to avoid smacking either Grady or Ella. "Of course I never saw him. I'm blind. That doesn't mean I'm stupid. Find a recording of his voice. I'll identify him that way."

"It would be much easier if the boy testified," Wray commented.

"He doesn't speak," Noah insisted.

"Let me ask him," Nguyen said. He was sitting beside Mike, leaning back and looking toward Cortez who stood in the corner of the room, if Noah had to guess.

Frustrated, Noah said, "This eleven-year-old kid is one of the bravest people I know. He doesn't have to talk if he doesn't choose to."

"It won't fly, K," Mike said. "The Crown Attorney, as I'm certain Ms. Wray will tell you, is desperate to put Roy away and terrified of failing to get a conviction. He won't go after him if he can't succeed."

Wray murmured something that indicated agreement with Mike though in a more dignified manner.

"Let him use his device," Noah said.

"It may not hold up in court," Wray replied. "Decisions based on Augmentative and Alternative Communication devices are unpredictable. The judge could rule either way, to allow or disallow the evidence. The defence could claim bias or programmer error or something of the sort."

"What do you mean?" What right did the legal system have to ignore a voice simply because it was expressed through technology? "The device is his voice. It's how he talks."

"I can't guarantee that's how the court will see things," Wray insisted.

"Grady has to make that choice," Noah insisted. "It's his life on the—"

"I saw him." The words burst out of Grady. "Uncle Macken hurt Noah. He punched him. He kicked him. He slapped him. He said he let the mine kill us then he can't get caught." Grady gulped. He was breathing heavily as if he'd just run a race.

Ella released a quiet exclamation of pain and sorrow.

Noah tapped the table near where he suspected the cup of water was. He sensed Grady shift forward then heard him swallow several times. The boy sighed and wiped his sleeve across his mouth.

"He killed my papa," Grady said.

"Who, son?" Mike asked, his voice surprisingly gentle.

"Uncle Macken killed my papa. Cut him. So much blood." Grady shuddered and pressed his body against Noah's side. Noah wrapped his arm around his shoulders again. Ella's palm rubbed up and down Grady's back in a soothing gesture.

"He make Papa cry. Shoot him. Noise so loud." The vibrations in Grady's body increased in magnitude. The child was experiencing a full-body earthquake.

"That's good, G. You did great. You can stop now." Noah's heart beat with compassion for this little boy.

But Grady wasn't finished. "Uncle Macken say, 'shut up'." His voice grew strident. "Shut up or I kill you, too."

"He's not going to kill you, Grady," Noah assured him. "He's going to prison. Where he can never hurt you again."

Grady's head shifted against Noah's side and he imagined the boy tipping his face up. "He try to kill you."

"*Oui.* You and me. But we made it. We beat him together."

"You and me." Grady's body sank against Noah's again. "You. Me. Otto. And Ella."

"*Oui.*" "Yes." Ella and Noah replied as one.

"Okay." Grady relaxed against him.

"I think that will do," Wray replied.

# EPILOGUE

Macken Roy stretched out on the double bed in his secret apartment in Prince George, British Columbia. It was dingy but anonymous. No one would find him here, not his lieutenant, not his chief enforcer, not the cops, no one but the landlord, a faded beauty willing to loan him this space as well as her body when he demanded. The cloying scent of her cheap perfume still hung in the air. His nude body hummed with pleasure. Not from the release he'd forced from her reluctant body, but from the knowledge that he'd escaped.

He'd done it! Finally, Monroe's brat would breathe no more; he'd engineered his own closure.

Macken chuckled, a daytime television answer to the problems of the world. *Closure.* He loved to listen to those so-called experts as they bemoaned the fate of the disadvantaged, the poor children who fell into a life of crime through no fault of their own. Poor little babies whose daddies beat them. Poor wee mites whose mamas didn't love them. As if. Every man had a choice.

Macken's parents had loved him, had loved his brothers. His father never beat them. His mama loved him best of all. Father and mother had been passive, oblivious of the torment they delivered their eldest son to on Tuesdays, Thursdays, and every second Saturday, at the hands of a soccer coach. They had blithely ignored the signs, more concerned about their reputations and the symbols of success read in the sports trophies on their mantel, than in the true state of their children's health.

When Monroe's pain went unheeded, he spread the fury to his brothers.

That soccer coach was the first person Monroe killed. Recruiting Mason and Macken, Monroe dressed them all in black, donned ski masks, and invaded the man's home one dark and silent Saturday night. Trashing his house first, destroying everything precious, Monroe then slit the man from chin to 'nads.

They'd gotten away with it, too. No one had suspected the three Roy boys. Their father was on the parents' council. Their mother organized every high profile fundraiser in the community. Didn't she always look so nice?

Again, their parents ignored the base and inconvenient signs, the escalating behaviours, truancy, violence, drug use, and theft. Mason even spent six months in juvie for robbing a convenience store.

As the crimes grew, their parents looked harder away. They blamed the school, the community, the church. They excused and explained away. While under their roof, three killers blossomed. Monroe and Mason planned. Stole. Intimidated. Until the Dark Coast Warriors were born. Macken followed at his brothers' heels, earning his place in the gang by slitting his parents' throats. Passive even then, they'd watched in disbelief until the light faded from their eyes.

No more. Macken no longer followed his brothers. He charted his own path. Mason was in prison, serving life for murdering a guard. Monroe dead. His seed expunged. Leaving Macken the sole survivor of the clan. The chief.

Macken deserved a break, to lie low for a few weeks while the cops chased their tails. Then he'd be back in the game. With little Maxi's arrest—and Maxi would be arrested. Macken had arranged it. Payback for missing the boy, for contaminating Macken's hands with the filth of the copper mine—he'd need a new contact, a new source for Blow, Crank, anything he wanted. There were always those willing to make their fortune on the backs of addicts and scum.

With Alex Treherne serving time, his hold was weakened. Macken would take over the drugs trade on the entire west coast. He had a guy inside Kent prison who might even eliminate Treherne, clear the way.

Nothing could touch him. Macken was King of the World.

The noise of the lock brought Macken's imagination back to the duller truths of the moment. Rather than supper carried by a scantily clad woman smelling of sex and deprivation, the door opened to reveal an anonymous figure clad in black.

Macken reached for his gun, not concerned for his nudity.

"A gift from Treherne." As he spoke, the figure fired, filling the air with cordite. Two to the chest. One to the head.

"Hell."

⅄

Hands fisting, heart pounding, Maximiano Guerra paced the dingy third-floor room of the Mountain View Motor Inn in Vancouver, B.C. Macken Roy had betrayed him. He'd planted two kilos of Colombian coke in Maxi's suitcase. What a humiliating crime for the leader of *El Cartel Pandilla* to go down for, possession with intent to distribute. As if he would ever sell such inferior Blow.

If not for Alex Treherne, Maximiano would be on his way to *prisión*. Treherne had reached out from Kent to warn him; from within his cell at Kent Institution maximum security prison he had sent his man, Davidge, to stop Maximiano and bring him here. Davidge promised that the problem would be resolved, that Macken Roy would be eliminated for his crass stupidity in bringing the attention of the Mounties to the burgeoning drugs trade in British Columbia.

Maximiano Guerra now stood in the man's debt. *¡Que desastre!*

What good had avenging Chenche's death done him? The operative who had killed him was dead, buried in a copper mine. But Maximiano received no peace from that.

Chenche had been a cruel and capriciously violent father. He had lavished his only son with gifts while tainting his world with horror and violence. His idea of *amor paternal* had been severe, brutal punishments for anything he deemed an insult to his honour, lavish rewards for perverse behaviour.

Sander, as Chenche's lieutenant, had raised Maximiano as heir to the empire, sending him to the best schools, giving him an education and a future. But Maximiano's mother had filled his head and heart with the bile of revenge, revenge against the man who had eliminated her husband whom she'd bitterly hated. Then she had groomed her son as a weapon of death.

"It did not matter," Maximiano muttered. "It is not good for me. What is life if this is all I gain?"

⅄

Grady Jones was in limbo. It was warm in limbo, but a little confusing. Noah, Ella, and Otto were always with him. That was good. Along with the Mounties, two in the daytime and one at night. That was okay. They had to change houses every few days because no one had arrested Uncle Macken or Maxi yet. That was bad.

Grady had slept a lot in the first few days after the copper mine. So had Noah. Ella said that she and Otto went for lots of walks, read lots of books, and watched lots of television waiting for them to wake. She smiled when she said it so Grady was pretty sure she was happy about it. Or at least that she didn't mind.

Noah was grumpy with the Mounties once he woke up and stayed awake. Ella said it was because he felt like he had no control over his days. Grady had never had any control over his days or nights. So, whatever.

"Grady!" Noah's voice called him downstairs.

Grady's ears started to plug up so he couldn't hear because Noah sounded a little upset. When the world got too scary, Grady blocked things out. But Ella helped him see that listening wasn't so bad if there were people who loved you to share the scary stuff. Grady shook his head to clear it then hugged Otto.

"Grady, sweetheart, come down, please." That was Ella. She sounded calmer than Noah. Maybe she had convinced the Mountie on duty to get her banana muffins again, the ones with nuts in them. And she wanted to share. "Do you want me to come up and help?"

*No.* Grady could do this. He had a new iPhone that the Mounties had bought for him. Ella had bought and downloaded the app that Lillian had taught him to use. So he would go downstairs, and if the news was bad, he would hug Noah or Ella and tell them he was scared.

Grady jogged down the stairs with Otto at his heels. Otto was always with him these days. He was his first best friend.

When Grady reached the bottom of the stairs, Ella hugged him and held his hand to walk into the lounge of the oddly pink, one-and-a-half-storey, safe house cottage they were currently staying at in Douglas Lake, B.C. Noah was sitting on the wooden-backed futon, but he sat forward and reached toward Grady when he got close enough. Noah pulled Grady onto his lap like he was a little kid. Grady didn't mind, though, because Noah thought Grady was braver than most men. Noah knew he wasn't a little kid, he just wanted to give him a hug. Grady needed a hug right now.

Ella sat beside them and Otto jumped up to squeeze between.

"Hello, Mr. Jones. Do you remember who I am?"

*Of course.* This man was the one who asked most of the questions during the unbriefing, or whatever it was called, at Thompson Rivers University. That day was kind of fuzzy in Grady's mind because he'd been so tired. He remembered the bubble jets in the bathtub of the suite where they'd stayed. The pull-out sofa had been great for sleeping, though he'd often ended up in bed with Ella and Noah because of his nightmares. He didn't sleep with them anymore. The nightmares weren't so bad now and Otto always slept with him.

Grady nodded.

"I have some news to share with you. Your uncle, Macken Roy, is dead."

"Mike." Ella said the name like she was annoyed with Staff Sergeant Rainer.

"Go easy," Noah said. He also sounded a little annoyed.

But Grady wasn't annoyed, he was relieved. His whole entire chest was lighter. It was easier to breathe.

Leaning close to Noah's ear, Grady whispered, "Uncle Macken is dead?"

Noah hugged him. "Yes, bud. He can't ever come after you again."

"Did you kill him?" Grady whispered.

Noah flinched as if surprised at his question. "No, buddy. It wasn't me."

"Okay."

Ella was watching him, looking very concerned. But Grady didn't have the words to make her feel better. Some day, but not yet.

"What happened, Mike?" Ella asked softly, still keeping a close watch on Grady.

"Unclear. His body was discovered by the local police in a dumpster behind an apartment building in Prince George. Looks like an execution, two to the chest, one to the head."

Grady looked at Noah's face. He looked...thoughtful.

"Maximiano?" Noah asked.

"Nothing," Mike replied, pursing his lips.

"So, Grady is safe," Ella said.

"Seems to be," Mike replied.

Grady pulled his device out of his pants' pocket. He needed to say something to the Staff Sergeant but he couldn't use his voice with the man. He typed the words and then pressed the yellow speaker icon. "I want to stay with Ella and Noah."

Those words made Noah look worried.

"Have you thought anymore about my proposal?" Mike asked. He seemed to be talking to Noah. He was looking at both Noah and Grady, but Grady hadn't heard any proposal except the one where Noah asked Ella to marry him.

"What proposal?" Ella turned to look at Noah. Her eyebrows scrunched up like she was worried or confused.

Noah fumbled until he found Ella's hand, then he held it. "Mike has this idea." Noah stopped then started again. "That clicking thing that Grady and I figured out in the mine, well, I guess it's not exactly new. There's this technique called Flash Sonar that the blind can use to navigate spaces to gain more independence. Mike thinks I should go on the course and then teach the strategy to others with visual impairments."

"Not only civilians, K. This tool would be invaluable to undercover officers. There are plenty of advantages to being able to cope in the dim and dark, situations where an undercover officer's safety would be enhanced by this knowledge."

"I was also thinking," Noah started out speaking slowly and then sped up as he got excited, "that it might benefit Search & Rescue workers, particularly in situations underground."

"Like mine cave-ins or something?" Ella asked.

"*Oui*. That's what I was thinking."

"There are plenty of mines around here. We're already connected to the Search & Rescue community here," Ella said. A smile was growing in her eyes.

"You can't stay here," Mike said.

The smile dimmed from Ella's eyes. "What do you mean?"

"He's right, El," Noah said. His voice was soft as if he was sorry to tell her those words. "Grady deserves a shot at a real life. With his uncle no longer a threat, he can be free. But not if I bring danger home."

"What would we do? Where would we go?" Ella asked. Her eyes looked sad now.

The Staff Sergeant sat on the coffee table across from Ella and showed her the screen on a tablet computer. "Thunder Bay," he said. "In Ontario. We have a detachment there, can set up a training module for covert operations. I'd like to hire your husband to head this up." He shifted the tablet to show Grady a picture of snowy hills and rocky trails. "Thunder Bay is a hub for children's services in the North. There are sports clubs, swimming pools, skiing, skating, rock climbing, anything you can think of, it's available here." He moved the tablet so Ella could see again. "Mrs. Kristofer, there is a program called Integrated Services for Northern Children. They're looking for a psychologist."

Ella met the Staff Sergeant's eyes. "Mike?" She asked his name as a question then turned to Noah. "Did you know about this?"

"I, uh, Mike did mention something when he called this morning."

Was Noah in trouble? Why? Grady looped his arm around Noah's neck to give him a little extra hug.

"We can make the arrangements quickly," the Staff Sergeant, Mike, said. "It is the safest course of action. A new community far from here. New identities. A fresh start."

"Um, I don't know what to say," Ella said. She reached over to brush her fingers through Noah's curly hair. "What do you think?"

"It's a great opportunity for all of us," Noah replied. "But it's up to you."

"Me? What do you think, Grady? Mike is saying that we would move to Thunder Bay, that we would change our names."

Grady typed furiously into his device. "What about me and Otto?"

Ella smiled in a way that made Grady think he'd missed something important. But her voice was patient. "If you want to stay with us, Grady. We want that, too. We want to adopt you. And Otto, too, of course."

Grady's face exploded in a grin, his whole body light and happy. "Yes!" That was his own voice. He was so excited he didn't use the app. Just said the word himself. Because he couldn't keep it inside.

"Okay, then," Noah replied. He was smiling too. "That's easy to handle. When they create our new identities, they can make us your parents."

Grady squeezed both arms around Noah's neck. Noah chuckled and hugged him back. When he loosened his embrace, Grady leaned over and hugged Ella tightly.

"I love you, Grady," she said.

And Grady loved her, too. And Noah. And Peter and Lillian, even though they were dead now. And they all loved Grady. The world was getting to be a better and better place.

"We can keep our first names, if you like," Noah said. "Or have new names. What name do you want, kid? You can go back to Braeden, the name you were born to, or you can choose another."

Grady let go of Ella so he could respond with his device. "I am Grady. That is what Lillian called me."

Noah nodded once, accepting Grady's choice as the end of the discussion. "Now all we need is a surname."

Grady leaned his head against Noah's chest while he typed, "Clarke, like Lillian and Peter."

Noah tousled the boy's hair. "I'm sorry, G. We can't. Too many people know that you lived with the Clarkes."

Grady's expression sobered. But if Uncle Macken was dead? *Oh, yeah. Uncle Macken sent Max to get me. So Max must know about Clarke.*

"What about Peterson?" Ella suggested. "That way we'd all remember Grady's first real parents, the people who loved him before we found him."

Grady's eyes widened and he glanced up at Noah. "Can we do that?" he whispered, using his own voice because the question was so important to him.

"You bet, G. You'll be Grady Peterson, son of Noah and Ella Peterson."

Grady nodded. That was good. So good. He would have a mother and a father, a dog and a new home. But, "School?"

"Yes, buddy," Noah replied with a quiet chuckle. "You'll have to go to school. But we'll make sure we find the right one for you. We'll teach them how your device works. We'll do everything we can to make school better for you than it's been. We can even apply for a service dog to go to school with you."

"You've looked into this?" Ella asked, surprised.

"Looked? Perhaps not." Noah grinned in a funny way that made Ella smile. "But they talked about them during that rehab course I took in Vancouver. I made a few calls."

"You could get a Guide Dog," Ella suggested tentatively.

"It's possible. That's three dogs in one house. You sure you're ready for that?"

Ella smiled and chuckled. "I'm ready for anything this family needs. We'll need to have a baby so the humans outnumber the dogs."

Noah's face got really soft and serious. "You'd want that?"

Ella cupped her hand on Noah's neck and pulled him close. She kissed him and then wrapped her arms around Noah, and Grady, too. This was a whole family hug. Grady had never had one of those before. It was warm and so good.

Even though his uncle tried to kill him lots of times, Grady survived. He had Jesus in his heart, a dog to walk by his side, and a family who loved him.

"And to think," Ella said. "This all started with coffee."

Noah laughed, holding Ella in one arm and Grady in the other. "Then you dragged me all the way to Kamloops, that tiny burg in the middle of nowhere."

"Mine," Grady whispered.

"Yeah," Ella said, chuckling some more. "We belong to each other."

That wasn't what he'd meant, but it was okay. In fact, it was really good.

ISBN: 978-0-9937176-4-2 (sc)
ISBN: 978-0-9937176-5-9 (e)